Praise for the novels of

BARBARA DELINSKY

"There's no bigger name in women's fiction
than Barbara Delinsky."
—*Rocky Mountain News* (Denver)

"Delinsky is one of those authors who knows how to
introduce characters to her readers in such a way that
they become more like old friends than works of fiction."
—*Flint Journal*

"Barbara Delinsky knows the human heart
and its capacity to love and believe."
—*Observer-Reporter* (Washington, Pennsylvania)

"With brilliant precision and compassionate insight,
Ms. Delinsky explores the innermost depths of her
beautifully realized characters, creating a powerful,
ultimately uplifting novel of love and redemption."
—*Rave Reviews* on *More Than Friends*

"Ms. Delinsky is a master storyteller!
Her talent to create living characters is remarkable.
Her writing and plotting are first-rate."
—*Rendezvous*

"When you care enough to read the very best, the name
of Barbara Delinsky should come immediately to mind."
—*Rave Reviews* on *A Woman Betrayed*

"Definitely one of today's quintessential writers
of women's fiction, Barbara Delinsky
pulls out all the stops in this perceptive novel."
—*RT Book Reviews* on *The Passions of Chelsea Kane*

"Women's fiction at its finest."
—*RT Book Reviews*

BARBARA DELINSKY

Destiny

ISBN-13: 978-0-373-77714-3

DESTINY

Copyright © 2012 by Harlequin Books S.A.

PLEASE RECYCLE

Recycling programs for this product may not exist in your area.

The publisher acknowledges the copyright holder of the individual works as follows:

FULFILLMENT
Copyright © 1988 by Barbara Delinsky

THROUGH MY EYES
Copyright © 1989 by Barbara Delinsky

This edition published by arrangement with Harlequin Books S.A.

For questions and comments about the quality of this book, please contact us at CustomerService@Harlequin.com.

® and TM are trademarks of Harlequin Enterprises Limited or its corporate affiliates. Trademarks indicated with ® are registered in the United States Patent and Trademark Office, the Canadian Trade Marks Office and in other countries.

www.Harlequin.com

Printed in U.S.A.

CONTENTS

FULFILLMENT

CHAPTER ONE

WHEN DIANDRA CASEY'S plane was ninety minutes late landing, she feared it was an omen. When she swept through the door of Bartholomew York's spacious penthouse apartment to find Gregory York there, she knew it had been one.

Gregory York was her nemesis. Her first memory of him was when she'd been three and he eight, when he'd lured her into the boxwood labyrinth at his parents' Bar Harbor estate and abandoned her there. Just as she'd learned not to play with fire, she'd learned to be wary of Gregory, and if she'd been able to avoid him completely in the years subsequent to the labyrinth incident, she'd have done so.

It hadn't been possible. The link between their families was complex. Not only were their parents best of friends, but their grandparents—and great-grandparents—had been, as well. Ties dated back to the turn of the century, when Diandra's great-grandfather, Malcolm Casey, had teamed up with Greg's great-grandfather, Henry York, to open a small general store. That general store had grown into a small department store, which had grown into a larger department store, which had grown into two, then three, then more. CayCorp had evolved, and the posh chain known as Casey and York, with branches in the most select and sophisticated of cities, rivaled none.

Within CayCorp, though, there were rivals galore. Each of the seven stores was run by a Casey or a York, and while much good-natured competitive banter flew between them, all banter stopped with the appearance of the annual report. Bartholomew York, chairman of the board and patriarch of the families, read the report cover to cover. He noted how successful each branch was, and if one wasn't performing up to par, he wanted to know why.

No one argued with Old Bart. He'd been around too long and had proved his worth too many times for that. He was a shrewd businessman with an eye for character, which was why, once she'd completed her M.B.A. and an apprenticeship under her father, who ran the Chicago store, Diandra had been named a vice president of CayCorp and put in charge of the Washington, D.C., store. She'd been only twenty-seven at the time, but she'd shown the kind of drive that Bart liked. In the five years since then, she'd successfully rejuvenated that branch of Casey and York that had begun to stagnate.

Gregory had the trend-setting New York store. His job was to keep it in the forefront of high fashion, and for the past ten years he'd succeeded admirably—so much so that Diandra knew he had something up his sleeve. She also knew what it was.

He wanted San Francisco.

For two years, Old Bart had been making noises about opening a branch there. Those noises had consolidated into a single loud signal when, two months before, he'd sent an advance team to scout locations. He hadn't yet decided who would run the store, though, and that made for lively speculation when his back was turned.

Some said that Greg's eldest cousin, Brad, would be the one; he'd had the Beverly Hills branch for twenty years and knew the West Coast like the back of his hand. Some saw Diandra's Uncle Alex in the post; he'd done well with the Boston store, and San Francisco was like Boston in many respects, so they said. Some fingered Greg's mom, who had guided the Palm Beach branch for nine years and had the kind of quiet class San Francisco demanded.

Not many earmarked Greg for the slot. He was New York through and through, the epitome of the urban bachelor, so even apart from the problem of who would fill his shoes at the New York store if he went west, there was the matter of his seeming love affair with the Big Apple.

Only Diandra knew. She could see it in his eyes each time the subject of San Francisco arose. She could see his hunger. She recognized it because she felt it herself.

She wanted that store, too. She wanted a new challenge in a new city. She'd done what she'd set out to do in Washington, and though she loved the city, there was nothing—and no one—to keep her there.

Knowing that Greg wanted the assignment made her desire it all the more. For years she'd sailed first mate to his captain, earned magna cum laude to his summa, walked in his wake and swallowed water. She'd never again make the mistake of letting him lead her into a labyrinth, but neither had she paid him back for that stunt. She didn't like him. His presence in a room was enough to set her on edge. He'd caused her years of torment on the deepest levels, and if the San Francisco store was to be the great equalizer, she had no problem with that.

Her first thought when she'd received her summons from Old Bart the day before had been that he wanted to talk San Francisco. She'd flown to Palm Beach with her hopes high. But Gregory had been there. His presence had scotched the idea that Bart would hand her the store on a silver platter—either scotched it or boded ill.

Lest her frustration show, she concentrated on greeting Bart, for whom she felt a legitimate fondness. Though slightly short of breath from her dash from the limousine, she was the image of grace and control as she approached the old man with a smile.

Ever the gentleman, despite an eighty-four-year-old body that made physical movement a trial, he stood for her gentle hug.

"I'm sorry to keep you waiting, Bart. The plane was late."

"So Isaac said," Bart replied in the low, gravelly voice that could tear grown men to shreds. Isaac was the chauffeur; he was well-trained to report on delays. "But there wouldn't have been any problem if you'd come in last night, as I'd asked."

"Last night was the Cancer Society benefit at the art museum," she said, knowing that Bart couldn't turn his back on a benefit. "I wanted Casey and York to be represented properly."

"Where's Jordan?" Jordan was Diandra's cousin and, though, twelve years her senior, her second in command.

"With one of our buyers in Rome."

"You have other assistants."

"And they're just that—assistants. I felt I should be there myself. Besides, your invitation was for brunch today. I didn't see the conflict."

"Late planes," Bart grumped.

"I took the earliest flight I could get. I'm sorry." She took a breath that said Enough of that and asked quietly, "How are you, Bart?"

He scowled. "Not bad."

"You're looking well."

"Nah," he said, but his scowl softened. "Hair gets thinner every day, shoulders stoop more, feet shuffle."

"Still, you're looking well." And indeed he was. Inches shorter and pounds lighter than he'd been in his prime, he looked a little like an aging leprechaun—but a handsome one, nonetheless. She plucked at the burgundy handkerchief that peered from the pocket of his navy lounging jacket. "Pretty dapper for an eighty-four-year-old."

"Which isn't saying much, given the competition," Bart grumbled, but there was a hint of mischief in his eyes. "I have to keep up appearances, now, don't I?"

"Sure do," she said, then, in a test of will, forced her smile to remain in place when she turned to Greg. He, too, had risen with her entrance, but though Old Bart's gesture had been one of simple courtesy, Greg's was more complex. He stood to acknowledge her arrival with a show of manners. He also stood, she was convinced, for the sheer intimidation of it.

Gregory York was six foot three inches of well-honed masculinity. His hair, which was on the long side and suggested more than a hint of the rebel, was light brown, shot with gold. His eyes were dark gray and mysterious. The thick but trim beard that he'd worn for years added to that mystery. A shade darker than his hair, it was a barrier between the world and him. It set him apart and made the statement that he was his own man, that his thoughts were private, his emotions no one's affair.

To call the man handsome was to tell only half the story, because even beyond physical details was his manner. Like a lion in a three-piece suit, he exuded power. He was smooth and self-contained. A master of confidence, he knew where he wanted to go and how to get there. He was reasonable unless crossed, but when crossed, he was a terror. What Old Bart did with his voice, Gregory did with his eyes. One look could make strong men pause, weak men stutter, women of all strengths go still and stare.

Diandra had spent years steeling herself against that look, which wasn't to say that she was immune to it, just that she'd had more practice than most. She'd seen it often, not only in CayCorp boardrooms, but at banquets, family outings and on too many other occasions when she'd been haunted by Gregory's presence. He had the ability to stand at the side of a crowd, cross his arms over his chest and command attention without uttering a word. It never failed to infuriate her.

Intimidating was one word for him. *Seductive* was another. Subtle and deceptive, the combination was potent. His purr was as dangerous as his roar.

It was the purr she heard then, as quiet and confident as ever. "How have you been, Diandra?" Taking the hand he offered, he drew her close and kissed her cheek. He always greeted her that way—though he didn't kiss every woman he met. He wasn't the shallow kissy-huggy sort. He was picky. Not that she meant anything to him. He drew her close and kissed her because he knew it disturbed her.

Tamping down that disturbance for reasons of her own pride as well as Old Bart's presence, Diandra looked up to meet Greg's eyes. The firmness in her gaze contradicted the gentleness in her voice. "I've been just fine. And you?"

"Can't complain." He held her back and gave her a deliberate once-over. "You look great."

She returned the once-over. "So do you." He not only looked, but smelled fresh-from-the-shower clean. Ignoring the innate seductive quality in that, she forced herself to focus on his shirt. It was a fine-weave cotton, blue with the thinnest of white stripes at wide intervals—intervals made to look even wider by the breadth of his chest. "Nice shirt. Still shopping at Barney's?"

"Sure," Greg said with a small twist of his lips. It was an old joke. They both knew that the shirt was imported, expensive and sold exclusively in the States at Casey and York. A basic philosophy of the store was that if the people who ran it didn't think its goods either fashionable enough or of high enough quality to wear themselves, something was wrong—and if something was wrong, the blame was easily placed. Since neither Diandra nor Greg cared to take that blame, they took active roles in assuring that Casey and York carried the kinds of clothes they liked to wear. They were, in effect, walking advertisements for their merchandise, which was an extension of the basic philosophy that Old Bart preached.

Greg gave her a second, even more thorough, perusal. She was wearing a chic two-piece silk outfit that was as casual as it was elegant. When his eyes seemed to linger in the vicinity of first her breasts, then her hips, she wanted to scream. She hated men who ogled. She knew he was doing it only to test her patience with Bart looking on. He was baiting her. She was determined not to bite.

"That's next winter's, isn't it?" he asked innocently. The eyes he returned to hers weren't as innocent, nor were the hands that moved lightly on her shoulders.

She ignored both. "It was part of the Milan show two weeks ago." Greg had been in Milan, too, though they'd managed to avoid each other as much as possible. "Delgado's a pushover. Once the show is done, he gives me my pick of samples."

"He adores you."

"He also adores the little boys he has running errands," she said dryly.

"I trust you haven't given him the liberties they have."

She sent him a quelling look.

Undaunted, Greg made a third leisurely perusal of her slender form before dropping his hands. "You should have been a model, you know. You have the body for it."

"Not quite," she said curtly, then took a breath to ease the pique he caused. It helped that he was no longer touching her. His touch was nearly as powerful as his look. "So." She took another breath. "What have you been up to?"

"Not much. And you?"

She shrugged. "I didn't expect to see you here."

"Do tell," he drawled.

"Excuse me?"

His gaze was direct. "I assume you were hoping for a private meeting."

"I wasn't hoping for anything. I got the call that Bart wanted me to come, so I came."

"Without wondering why he'd called?"

"Of course I wondered. Didn't you?"

He didn't have to answer. His eyes said it all; they'd gone charcoal gray, a little faraway and a lot challenging. They had that San Francisco look to them.

And that look had an immediate effect. The competitive beast set butterflies loose in her stomach. "When did you arrive?"

"Last night."

"Things must be slower in New York than Washington."

"No. But I felt it important I be here."

The butterflies began to flutter their wings with greater strength. "Perhaps Bart told you something on the phone that he didn't tell me." She turned an innocent face to Bart, who'd been quietly observing the verbal exchange. "Did I misunderstand? Had you specifically planned something for last night?"

Bart glared at Greg. "No. And you didn't miss a thing. Greg didn't arrive until very late, then slept in this morning. The first time I saw him was twenty minutes ago. If your plane had been on time, he'd have been the one to keep us waiting on brunch." His glare left Greg and was little more than a disgruntled look when it hit Diandra. "I'm hungry." Holding his elbow out to her, he waited until she'd linked her arm through his, then, shuffling his Italian-leather-clad feet over first plush carpet, then polished wood floor, then marble tiles, led the way to the rooftop patio.

As Gregory York stood watching them, he thought of the ironies of life. He'd flown to Palm Beach so sure, *so sure* that Bart had made a decision on the San Francisco store. Of course, Bart had been sleeping when he'd arrived the night before, and he'd been exhausted himself. It had been a long, busy week—a long, busy month—a long, busy year. He vaguely remembered his travel alarm going off, vaguely remembered pushing the button that would set it off again ten minutes later. He must have pushed the wrong button. When he'd finally awoken, he'd bolted from bed and showered and dressed in record time—only to find that Bart was waiting for someone else.

Diandra. Lovely Diandra. Proud, prickly Diandra. Ambitious Diandra.

It was the last that bothered him most. He didn't mind seeing Diandra at corporate meetings or designers' shows or even at the family parties that Old Bart still insisted on throwing. He did mind the idea that she wanted San Francisco.

That store was his. He'd been quietly lobbying for it since before Old Bart had ever realized it was going to be. He'd spent the past ten years working his tail off in New York; he'd earned his stripes. He'd reached the time in his life when he needed a change, and the one he had in mind went beyond locations. He needed a total change of lifestyle. Regardless of Diandra's schemes, he intended to get it in San Francisco.

Thus determined, he went out onto the patio, where Diandra had just finished helping Bart to his seat. When she turned to her own chair, Greg was there to draw it out for her.

"Thank you," she said politely.

"You're welcome." He took the seat on her left, where the third place was set.

Bart picked up his linen napkin, shook it out and spread it over his lap. He looked from Diandra to Greg and back. "Everything okay?"

"Sure."

"Just fine."

Bart arched a brow and nodded toward the glasses of grapefruit juice that sat in beds of ice before Diandra and Greg. "Drink slowly and appreciate. The citrus crop was lousy this year."

Diandra took a sip. "Then you got the best of it. This is incredibly sweet. Gretchen's still squeezing it fresh?"

"Of course."

She glanced at the dish of prunes that sat at Bart's place in lieu of the juice and said nothing, but her gaze, happening on Greg's, found a ghost of humor there. In that instant, she was hard put not to grin. She didn't like Greg, but they did share a history, and that history included a youthful irreverence for their elders. More times than Diandra could remember, she and Greg—and whichever of their cousins happened to have been around—had snickered about Old Bart's prunes.

Greg cleared his throat and took a healthy drink of his juice.

Diandra busied herself eating the single plump strawberry that rested on the ice as a garnish.

"Just wait," Bart said. "You'll be old before you know it, and then you won't be so smug about what you eat."

"Did we say anything?" Greg asked innocently.

"Bah," Bart scolded. "I know what you were thinking. I'm not dumb or senile. It'd do you good to remember that."

"We do," Diandra said with feeling. "Believe me, we do."

Bart pursed his lips, nodded, then began to eat. Before he'd consumed little more than a third of his prunes, Diandra and Greg were done with their juice. Diandra looked at Greg, who was looking back at her. She glanced away, off toward the patio railing and beyond.

"I always liked the view here," she mused for the sake of harmless conversation, "and it improves with age. There's something hypnotic about the ocean."

"Good thing you don't have an office overlooking it," Greg said. He thought of the office he'd like to have overlooking San Francisco Bay. "You'd be too mesmerized to work."

"You look out on the Statue of Liberty," Diandra returned. "Does she distract you?"

He gave a negligent, one-shouldered shrug. "I don't have the luxury of being distracted. There's too much work to be done."

"That's why," she said in a confident tone, "Manhattan is perfect for you. It doesn't matter if you're surrounded by concrete. You wouldn't be able to take advantage of a view if you had one."

"Would you?"

"Sure." If it were the Golden Gate Bridge, she'd make a point to do it.

"You have that much free time?" he asked skeptically. "I wasn't under the impression we paid our executives to sit staring out windows all day."

"I haven't any more free time than you do."

"You should. Your store isn't as large as mine. If you were working up to capacity, you'd have time on your hands—unless, of course, your capacity is lower."

She sucked in a breath. "What a sexist statement."

"Did I mention sex?"

"You didn't have to."

"It's not a sexist statement," he said. His eyes bored into her. "It's a personal one. You may be doing just fine with the Washington store, but if you think you can handle—"

"Excuse me," Bart broke in, "but I'd like a little peace while I eat."

Greg fell silent. Diandra's eyes flashed him a warning that his own eyes proceeded to defy.

"How *is* everything in New York?" Bart asked him.

Greg stared at Diandra a minute longer before turning his attention to Bart. In the process he fully regained his composure. "I can't complain. The new ad campaign is going over well, if initial sales figures are anything to go by. I'm pleased with Wells-Wescott. The approach they've taken is fresh and aggressive."

Bart turned to Diandra. "What do you think?"

Diandra hadn't rebounded as fully as Greg, but the faint roughness that lingered in her voice passed as earnestness. "I think it's still too early to know anything conclusive. The campaign had to be modified for Washington."

"It was modified for all of our cities," Greg pointed out.

"I know that," she snapped, "but it was launched in New York, so you have a foot up on us with sales figures." She turned back to Bart and spoke more gently. "It'll be a while yet before we know something concrete."

"Any word-of-mouth feedback?" Bart asked.

"It's good."

Bart looked from one face to the other. "It had better be. There are times when I wake up in the middle of the night having dreamed that the obscene sum we're spending is going straight down the toilet."

"It'll be worth it," Diandra assured him.

"I hope so."

Greg was sure of it. "You have to spend money to make money. You taught us that."

"Oh, yes, but I was teaching you that in the days before inflation took over—and greed. The people at that advertising agency are thieves."

"They're professionals," Diandra said.

Greg added, "We've paid for their expertise. If things pan out the way we expect them to, our profit will pay their fee many times over."

Diandra arched an indulgent brow at Bart. "Does that make us the thieves?"

"Hell, no. People give us their money in exchange for something tangible. They look at whatever they buy, turn it over, wear it, taste it, smell it or whatever, and decide whether they've been gypped. The yardstick is more visible."

"But we're in this business for a profit, just like Wells-Wescott," Greg pointed out. "So in that sense, we are greedy."

"Speak for yourself," Diandra muttered.

Greg caught the words and refused to let them pass. "I speak for CayCorp. The bottom line is whether or not we make a profit, and if we don't do that, we might as well close shop."

"But there are different ways of making a profit. Nothing we do is underhand. We're not out to rob our customers."

"Of course not. I wasn't the one who mentioned thieves."

She shot a glance skyward. "I was kidding."

"Don't. If we'd been in a restaurant and someone from another table had overheard what you'd said, rumors would have been flying before we'd had dessert."

Diandra tipped up her chin. "I wouldn't know about that. You're the one who's had experience with restaurants and rumors."

During the long moment that Greg was silent, his only movement was the flexing of his jaw. His eyes drilled into hers, hard and sharp. "I assume," he said in a low, dark voice, "that you're referring to the incident last year with Monica Newman."

Working hard to counter the force of that penetrating gaze, Diandra shrugged.

"My lunch with her was solely for the sake of the celebrity telethon."

"That picture of the two of you was pretty condemning."

"That picture," he stated slowly, "was a piece of darkroom wizardry—"

"Which people believed, just the way we hope they'll believe our ad campaign. What kind of opinion do people form about CayCorp when they see one of its executive vice presidents carrying on with a woman who is not only half his age—"

"She isn't half my age. She's twenty."

"She was nineteen then, and married and—"

"Don't say it," he ordered in a deep, deep voice.

"Say what?"

"That she had a fifteen-month-old child whose paternity was in doubt, because that's no concern of mine. I had never met Monica Newman before that day, and I haven't seen her since."

"The papers said otherwise."

"But we know the truth."

"Do we?" she dared, irked by his patronizing tone. "Your reputation hasn't exactly been that of a monk—"

"Diandra," Bart growled. "Please."

But Greg held up a hand. Normally a master of self-control, he was livid. Diandra couldn't have chosen a more inappropriate time to raise something as petty.

"For the record," he said, measuring each word as he stared at her, "the Monica Newman incident was a nonincident. It was forgotten by the press nearly as quickly as it was forgotten by the public, which is what happens to empty stories. You're the only one who seems to remember it. Maybe there's a reason why. A psychological reason. Like jealousy? You love the attention of the press—and if you want to talk reputations, I seem to recall something about a recent issue of *Town Crier* that referred to Diandra Casey as quite the little number around Washington."

"*Town Crier* is always putting tags on people, very much tongue-in-cheek," she answered smoothly.

"Uh-huh."

"It's true-—"

"Oh, please," Bart growled. "Keep quiet. Both of you." A movement at the door caught his eye and he brightened. "Saved by the cook. I hope you have plenty of food there, Gretchen, because stuffing the mouths of these two may be the only way I'll get any peace."

Gretchen smiled. She'd been Bart's housekeeper and cook for better than twenty years and had survived where others had failed precisely because she did smile. A certain immunity to tension was a necessity in CayCorp environs.

"Diandra," she said with the faintest of brogues, "beautiful as ever."

Taking a deep, calming breath, Diandra smiled. She'd always liked Gretchen. "And you are a sight for sore eyes. What have you got there?"

Gretchen set the tray on the edge of the table and began to transfer plates. "I have scrambled eggs, Canadian bacon, apricot-filled croissants and date-nut muffins."

Diandra, minus her smile, looked at Greg. "Will that be enough to fill your mouth?"

Before he could answer, Gretchen was talking again. "I do not have the fried potatoes you like so much, Gregory. Mr. Bart wouldn't let me make them. He said they'd be too great a temptation for him. He's not supposed to eat them."

Greg was thinking that he wasn't, either, but he had no intention of opening that particular can of worms to either Bart's rumination or Diandra's pontification. "No harm." He patted his stomach. "We're all probably just as well without them." He lowered his voice and leaned closer to Gretchen. "Maybe another time you'll make up a batch and we'll pig out in the kitchen, just you and me. Deal?"

Gretchen's smile grew nearly as broad as her girth. "Deal." Having emptied her tray, she began to pour coffee while the three at the table helped themselves to the food she'd prepared. When she left, the only sound that remained was the soft click of utensils.

Conjuring up a blinder on her left side, Diandra did her best to ignore Gregory. It wasn't as difficult as it might have been, since Bart was the one who, at that moment, gave her pause. He seemed perfectly at ease and undisturbed, so much so that it was nerve-racking. Bart didn't do things without cause. He had summoned her to Palm Beach. She wanted to know why.

So did Greg. From the time he'd been five, when his grandfather had sat him down, given him a tiny spiral-bound notebook and taught him to keep a written tally of the money he had and the money he spent, he'd known Bart as a businessman. Business always came first. Even Bart's wife, Emma, had understood that. Bart never wasted time. He wasn't the kind of man who invited two of the corporation's vice presidents to brunch and then sat around discussing grapefruit.

Greg wondered if Bart's age was catching up to him. The physical slowdown was obvious and not new. Nor was the occasional lapse of memory with regard to a name or word. But otherwise Bart had remained sharp. Today, though, there seemed a softening to that sharpness. It made Greg uneasy.

Between his eggs and a muffin, Bart put down his fork. "Tell me," he said to Diandra. "How is young Marshall working out?"

Young Marshall was Diandra's cousin, twenty-two and fresh from school. Diandra exchanged an uncomfortable glance with Greg before answering. "I'm not sure. I sent him to St. Louis."

Bart blinked. "You did what?"

"Sent him to St. Louis. Thomas seemed the logical one to train him."

"Why wasn't I consulted?"

"Because it all happened last month, and you were in Hong Kong at the time."

"Why wasn't I notified when I got back?"

"Because it was settled," Diandra said quietly.

"But I wanted him in Washington."

"As I understood it," she corrected chidingly, "you wanted him in New York." She sliced a look to her left. "Greg foisted him on me."

Bart pursed his lips. "Greg's arguments were sound. The boy was lost in New York."

"Well, he wasn't lost in Washington. It was more the other way around. From the minute he arrived, he imagined himself the savior of every female page in the Senate. He was totally obnoxious." Catching herself, she tried to sound more professional. "Beyond that, there were problems at work."

"What kind of problems?" Bart demanded.

"He had," Greg joined the discussion to intone, "delusions of grandeur."

Diandra couldn't have put it better herself. "He thought himself above being a stock boy, but that's how we all began. Start at the bottom and know the business, you always said. We were working summers when we were in high school, so by the time we were in college we had already climbed some. Marshall didn't work summers when he was in high school."

"He said he didn't need the money," Greg interjected. "Neither did we, but still we worked. There was pride involved. He lacks it."

"He spent most of his college summers traveling," Diandra went on, "so suddenly he found himself with a college degree and no work experience. He expected to join the company as a junior-level executive, but he doesn't know the first thing about business. He argues that he's family and that he should be on par with the other cousins, but nearly all of us have graduate degrees." She paused for a breath. "I've worked hard to get where I am. He wants it for nothing."

"He's a nice kid, Bart, just a little spoiled."

"A *lot* spoiled," Diandra corrected.

Greg shot her an annoyed look before continuing. "He needs to have limits set. We sent him to St. Louis because Thomas runs a rigid bureaucracy. The kid isn't a total loss. He has potential."

"That's *your* opinion."

"Well, it's worth something," Greg argued. "I've seen lots of employees come and go, and the best have spunk. Marshall has that. It just needs to be channeled."

"But he hates the work!"

"So did I. I hated the stockroom, and I wasn't madly in love with selling shoes, either. There were times during those first few years when I seriously considered being an accountant."

"You should have been one."

"I was lousy with figures."

"Tell that to the teenyboppers," she muttered.

Greg glared. "What is that supposed to mean?"

"Stop!" Bart broke in gruffly. "What *is* it with you two?"

Both heads swung his way, both faces registering surprise, as though they'd momentarily forgotten he was there. Then they exchanged glances—a little annoyed, a little dismayed, even a little apprehensive. They jumped when Bart slapped both palms on the tabletop.

"I did not bring you here to discuss San Francisco."

Diandra's mouth felt suddenly dry. She didn't dare betray her guilt by looking at Greg, and she knew he wouldn't look at her. His expression would be smooth, confident. It wouldn't reveal a thing.

"I haven't made a decision on that," Bart went on, "and frankly, I'm not pleased with what I see here."

Diandra took a breath. "Gregory and I rub each other the wrong way—"

"But that has nothing to do with professional qualifications," Greg finished.

"But *why* do you rub each other the wrong way?" Bart asked.

"He's impossibly arrogant—"

"She's incredibly self-centered—"

Diandra gawked at Greg. "Self-centered? What have I ever done to you—"

"If I'm arrogant," Greg barked, "I've earned the right—"

"That's *enough,*" Bart said. He sat back in his chair and glared at them, his wrinkled brow all but meeting his eyes. Then he dropped his gaze to his lap. He pressed his lips together. Methodically he folded his napkin and put it beside his plate.

Diandra waited then, waited for that second shoe to fall. Bart had called them to Palm Beach for some reason, and he claimed it wasn't to talk about the San Francisco store. She held her breath in anticipation, as did Greg.

"I called the two of you here," Bart began in a voice that was low and oddly sad, "because I need your help." Slowly he raised his eyes and focused first on Greg, then Diandra. "I'm selling the Boston town house. Its contents have to be sorted through, cataloged and crated." His gaze linked them. "I want you to do it."

CHAPTER TWO

UNSURE THAT SHE'D heard right, Diandra stared at Bart. When she shifted a perplexed glance to Greg, she found him looking just as confused.

"You're selling the town house?" he asked in a strangely uncertain voice.

Bart nodded.

Diandra leaned forward. "But why?"

"Because I spend most of my time here, and when I'm not here, I'm at business meetings somewhere else. Since we moved our corporate headquarters to New York, I've had even less call to be in Boston. I only get there once or twice a year now. The town house is going to waste."

"But it's part of the family," Diandra argued, using the term "family" loosely but comfortably. As a Casey, she'd spent as much time in that Beacon Hill home as many a York had. "You've owned it for…how many years?"

"Sixty," Greg supplied. "He bought it when he and Emma were first married." He faced Bart. "That's a lot of history to cut off, just like that. There must be someone in the family who wants it."

"Do you?" Bart asked him.

Greg drew his head back at the sudden question. "Sure I do, but I live in New York. I wouldn't use it any more than you. Besides," he added with a wry twist of his lips, "I can't afford two homes. You don't pay me enough."

"Like hell I don't," Bart mumbled as his gaze swung to Diandra. "How about you?"

"I'd take it in a minute, but I'm in Washington. Even aside from the issue of money, I don't have the time to do the place justice." She gave a helpless frown. "There must be another one of us who would."

"Tell me who," Bart ordered. "I've been trying to find the right someone for months. My children either have their own homes or are dead. My grandchildren either have their own homes or don't deserve them. I've been through the list, including your side, Diandra, and the only one remotely in a position to take over the town house, since he has the Boston store, is your Uncle Alex, but, frankly, I'd rather sell it to Lassie."

Diandra knew enough to keep still. Uncle Alex was her late mother's twin brother, and despite the obvious sex difference, the physical resemblance between them had been marked. Unfortunately Bart hadn't thought well of Diandra's mother at the time of her death, and though he treated Alex with professional respect, there was no love lost between them. When Bart looked at Alex, he saw Abby, and when that happened, Bart was reminded that his favored son, Greg's father, was also dead. It was understandable that for purely emotional reasons Bart wouldn't want Alex taking over the town house.

"So," Bart went on, "there's no one. I've already had an offer on the place and if I accept it, it'll have to be emptied."

"You've had an offer?" Diandra echoed in dismay. "How long has it been on the market?"

"It hasn't officially been listed. But I've been talking with my broker for several weeks, and out of the blue she came up with an offer. The fellow who wants it is an executive who's being transferred to Boston. He's willing to pay top dollar, but he wants to get in soon. I'll be making a decision today."

"You sound as though you've already made it," Greg observed.

Bart didn't answer.

Leaning back in his chair, Greg buried his hands in the pockets of his slacks. He was surprised at how bothered he was by the idea of Bart's selling the town house. He'd never thought himself the sentimental sort, but he felt an affinity for the house. If only it were in San Francisco.

But it wasn't, and there was Bart's request to be considered. "Emptied. Okay. Exactly what does that entail?"

"Going through the place room by room. Listing the contents of each room. Disposing of everything in an appropriate fashion. Some things should be shipped to me, some sold, some donated to museums or charity, some tossed out."

"And you want us—" Diandra waggled a skeptical finger between herself and Greg "—to do that?"

Bart nodded.

Greg cleared his throat. He might have laughed— the proposal was that ludicrous—but one didn't laugh at Bartholomew York. One reasoned in a very quiet, very sane manner. "Do you have any idea how long a project like that would take?"

"As I see it—" Bart squinted one eye "—a week— two at the most." He opened both eyes. "If you go at it conscientiously, that is."

"You have to be kidding," Diandra said.

"I'm not."

She eyed him askance. "You're serious?"

"Very."

She raised both brows. "Two weeks?"

"One, if you're quick."

"But that's absurd!" she argued, momentarily throwing caution to the winds. "I don't know about Greg, but I can't take a week off from work. Forget two. That'd be a total pipe dream."

Outwardly calm, Greg came forward and linked his fingers at the top of his plate. Only someone who was aware of the smallest details would have noticed that his knuckles were white. "When had you intended to have this done?"

"Next week."

"Next week!" Diandra cried. "Bart, that's impossible!"

"Nothing's impossible."

"Easy for you to say. Have you any idea what's on my calendar for next week?"

Bart gave a small self-satisfied smile. "I know exactly what's on your calendar for next week. You have an assortment of management and sales meetings. You have a conference scheduled with Peter Walsh and his underlings to discuss a reorganization in gourmet foods. You have a meeting about the Christmas catalog. You have appointments with three potential replacements for Nancy Soo, who headed the personnel department for four years, has been on maternity leave for three months and now finds that she wants to play mother full-time. You have—" He paused, arched a sparse gray brow. "Shall I go on?"

She shook her head. "You've checked with my secretary. You know how fully booked next week is."

He flicked a gnarled hand at the insignificance of the problem. "There's nothing on your schedule that can't be either postponed or handled by someone else."

She stared. "Cleaning out the town house takes precedence over the running of a multimillion-dollar business?"

"In this case, yes."

"But *anyone* can clean out the town house."

His smile faded. "That's where you're wrong. It's not just a matter of cleaning. It's a matter of sorting through materials that have been collected over a period of more than half a century. For that I need someone who cares. I'd do it if I could, but I don't have the physical wherewithal. You have the strength. You also have the emotional involvement. And I trust you—both of you—which is more than I can say for most."

Both of you. Diandra looked at Greg. He held her gaze for a minute, then pushed back his chair, stood and crossed the patio to stand at the railing looking out to sea. She watched his tall form, saw the tension in his shoulders and knew he had to be thinking her thoughts.

She was right. He was thinking about the week that lay ahead of him in New York, thinking that the last thing he could afford to do was to cancel meetings, shift conferences, postpone interviews. Putting things off now would only jam-pack his schedule down the road, and the road ahead was busy enough. For just that reason, it had been years since he'd taken a bona fide vacation. Bart knew that.

Thrusting a hand through the thickness of his hair, he left that hand at the back of his head while he flexed the muscles of his shoulders. Tension settled there first; it always had. He swam to counter it, played tennis to expend even more nervous energy—for whatever good either activity did. When he chased the tension from his shoulders, it settled in his stomach. He really did need a break.

But at Bart's town house in Boston? With *Diandra*?

That was probably the worst part. It was bad enough that Bart was asking him to take a week off from work in New

York, but thinking of spending that week with Diandra was like watching a storm approach across a lake. He and she were misaligned gears; two minutes together, rubbing each other the wrong way, and sparks flew.

He could just see it. They'd be at each other's throat in no time. Didn't Bart know that?

His hand fell to the back of his neck and began to rub the tight muscles there as he listened to Diandra's voice at the table.

"But why this week?" she asked. "If we had some advance notice, we'd have an easier time making arrangements."

"This week because it may take you *two* weeks, and that will take us right up to the time when my buyer wants to take title."

"Put him off a little."

"There's no reason why I should."

She offered it. "An extra week or two would make things easier for Greg and me."

Bart ignored that. "None of us is using the house. He wants it cleared so that he can pass papers and get his decorators in there."

"He's asking a lot."

"He's paying a lot."

When she fell quiet, Greg allowed a wry smile. Apparently she didn't know the futility of arguing. Bart had his mind made up. That message came across in every sentence he spoke. He'd invited them to Palm Beach not to ask but to inform them that they'd be spending their next week in Boston, and the more she argued, the more he'd dig in his heels. But she was a rebellious creature. She refused to accept that someone else could control her. She was willful to the core—just as her mother had been. But he wasn't his father. He wasn't about to be brought down by Diandra Casey—any more than he was about to spend a week in close quarters with her.

He was about to offer to do the house himself when Diandra came up with her own suggestion. "Would it be possible," she began with cautious optimism, "for Greg and I to take shifts? I could work at the town house for several days, then return to Washington while he took over in Boston." She glanced up when Greg turned around, but quickly returned her attention to Bart. "After several more days, I'd relieve him, so he could go back to New York. That way neither of us would have such a solid stretch away from the office."

But Bart was shaking his head. "The most time-effective method is to have the two of you working together for as long as it takes."

Diandra wasn't giving up. "What if I brought an assistant with me from Washington? I'm sure Greg has someone he could bring. That way there'd always be two people working here."

"I don't want strangers in my house. I want you and Greg."

"I'd bring Jordan. Greg could bring Ben. They're not strangers, they're family."

Bart grunted. "If I didn't know better, Diandra, I'd think that you were frightened of spending a week with Greg."

Leaning back against the rail, Greg folded his arms over his chest and waited with interest for Diandra's response. It came very quickly and, to his satisfaction, with a crimson flush.

"Me? Frightened of him? That's absurd!"

"Then it must be that you're frightened of a little hard work, and if that's the case, I don't see how I can possibly consider you for San Francisco."

Diandra sucked in a sharp breath. Her gaze darted from

Bart to Greg and back, and even Greg could see the hurt there. "Low blow, Bart," she whispered. "I don't deserve that."

"Maybe not," Bart relented to a point, "but neither do I deserve this grief. If I had my druthers, I wouldn't be giving up the town house. If I had my druthers, I wouldn't be eighty-four years old." His expression softened, saddened. "But I don't have my druthers. I haven't many more years left, and I want the town house taken care of before I'm gone. It holds special memories for me. I'm entrusting you with their care."

Diandra was deeply touched, but before she could respond, he went on.

"I've paid my dues in life. I think it's time I called in a few IOUs." He paused. "I've been generous over the years, haven't I?"

His words brought an ache to her chest. She knew that he wasn't talking of money, or even of power, but of his feelings toward her mother. Another man might have taken those feelings out on Diandra. Bart hadn't.

"You've been more than generous," she conceded softly.

Pressing his thin lips together, Bart gave a half nod. "Then I'm asking for one week of your time in return. Will you give it?"

"Of course."

Bart swiveled his eyes toward Greg. "And you?"

Knowing that he had no other choice, given what Bart had just done to Diandra, Greg nodded. A storm might be coming across the lake, but he'd faced storms before and survived. He'd do it this time, too.

THE BRUNCH IN Palm Beach had been on Saturday. Later that day, Diandra flew back to Washington, Greg to New York, each with feelings of impending doom. Those feelings only intensified as the weekend passed, and by the time Monday morning arrived, both Greg's staff in New York and Diandra's in Washington were suffering the ill humor of their respective bosses.

Diandra had it worse than Greg. Thanks to the arrangements Bart had made even before her Palm Beach visit, she was to be picked up first. His private plane was to take off from Washington in midafternoon on Monday, go north to pick up Greg, then fly on to Boston. That gave her only part of Monday to reorganize a full week's worth of business—she couldn't even *think* what would happen if closing up the town house took longer than that. As it was, she'd called her secretary in to work on Sunday afternoon, had stayed at the office until past eleven that night, then met her there again at seven the next morning. By the time her staff arrived, she had lengthy lists of what was to be done in her absence and by whom. Unfortunately she ran a tight ship anyway, which meant that none of her top-level people sat twiddling their thumbs. Their schedules were nearly as busy as hers, a fact they reminded her of repeatedly as they ran in and out of her office that morning.

She was feeling totally besieged when the time came for her to leave for the airport. Grabbing the small bag that contained the few necessities she figured she'd need for the week, she dashed from her office with little more than a quick wave and collapsed wearily in the back of the limousine that waited outside. An hour later, she was in Bart's jet en route to New York.

GREG POPPED AN antacid into his mouth as his long strides ate up the stretch of tarmac between his limo and Bart's plane. He supposed he looked as composed as ever; that was part of the image. On the inside, though, he felt ragged. In essence, he had condensed five working days into one—

actually two since he'd spent most of Sunday in the office—and he was feeling the backlash.

When he'd been twenty-five, even thirty, he'd thrived on crises. Even when it seemed the world was going to hell in a bucket, he'd been able to come through calmly, coolly and constructively. He could still come through that way, but now he paid more of a price.

Somewhere it had to end, he knew. He had to find a compromise between his present hectic life and the more placid one his doctor recommended. He was pinning his hopes on San Francisco. If he got the assignment, he'd do things differently. He'd establish more regular hours, for one thing. For another, he'd delegate authority more. His shoulders were broad, but not broad enough to bear the weight they had. He was tired. It was as simple as that.

With a grimace, he took the last step and swung into the plane. He was greeted by the copilot, who immediately drew up the steps, closed the door and took his place in the cockpit with the pilot.

Tossing his duffel bag into the luggage bin, Greg turned toward the cabin. It was a single large compartment with a combination bar/kitchenette at one end and an assortment of upholstered furniture anchored at the other. Diandra was in one of the executive lounge chairs, her head against its back, her hands on each arm, her legs crossed gracefully at the knee. She wore a lightweight wool suit—pleated skirt, oversize blazer, silk blouse—and had clearly come straight from the office. The way she was staring at him suggested she was as disgusted with the situation as he was.

Lowering himself into a chair that matched hers, he buckled his seat belt, put his elbow on the arm of the chair and his jaw on his fist and stared right back at her.

Neither of them spoke as the plane taxied down the runway, waited a brief time for clearance, then took off.

Nor did they speak as they gained altitude and headed northeast.

Diandra didn't trust herself to say a thing. She was too annoyed to say anything nice, and saying something sarcastic would only invite retribution. She wasn't up for retribution. The past two days had been the pits. She was too tired to spar with Greg.

That put her at a disadvantage—and one more disadvantage she didn't need. As it was, the cabin seemed to have shrunk with Greg's arrival. He was a large man—lean but large—and the way his eyes pierced her made her heart thud. It was always that way. She could tell the moment he entered a room. Her skin would begin to prickle, her pulse to race. She'd long since stopped fighting it, had simply accepted that she was viscerally attuned to him.

He was her past, and he unsettled her. When she was unsettled, she tended to be less in control, and when she was less in control, she was less prudent. That was what had happened during brunch with Bart. She'd been trading barbs with Greg, which had unsettled her, so that even after he'd withdrawn from the fray, she'd run on at the mouth to Bart. While Greg had stood silently to the side—listening, letting her ask the questions he was, no doubt, wondering about himself—she'd nearly dug herself into a hole.

If only he'd spoken up. But he'd stood there, silent, while she'd argued. If he'd said no to Boston, she might have been able to do it, too. But he hadn't said no. He hadn't said a thing until Bart had softened her into saying yes—and once she'd done that, Greg had been locked in as well. He wasn't about to give her an edge on the San Francisco store, any more than she'd have given him one. She felt as though she were being held up for ransom and had no choice but to pay.

On the plus side, it looked as though she and Greg were the two remaining finalists for the post. Bart wasn't a manipulative man when it came to business; he was too blunt for that. If he were leaning toward someone else, he'd have said so instead of insisting that she and Greg handle the Beacon Hill town house because he "trusted" them.

Having come this far, she couldn't afford to antagonize Bart. Neither could Greg, which was why, she knew, he'd agreed to come. Unfortunately once they reached the town house they'd be on their own. Bart wouldn't be there to serve as a tempering force. She feared things were going to get hairy before the week was out.

Greg was thinking much the same thing but wondering at the same time how a woman who looked as harmless could be so lethal. She really was lovely; he had to grant her that. Her skin was an ivory hue, smooth and dewy. Her eyes were dark brown and large, her nose small and straight, her lips delicately defined. She wore makeup skillfully, if sparingly, using color to highlight rather than exaggerate. Her hair was raven black and lustrous, and she wore it straight, cut to just below the chin in a modern pageboy. The bangs that covered her forehead only added to the fragile look of her face—again a deception, he mused. She was a businesswoman through and through, about as fragile as a steel girder.

The plane reached its cruising altitude and leveled off, and still they regarded each other in silence. Diandra felt as if she were being dissected with a dull and rusty knife, though how much of that internal scraping was due to residual tension from the office, she didn't know. She did know, with each minute she held Greg's gaze, that she was exhausted. Making a small sound of disgust, she turned her head aside and closed her eyes.

"Something wrong?" Greg asked in a voice that was low and smooth.

The short question—and its underlying sarcasm—set her off. Without opening her eyes, she said, "Your hair's too long, do you know that? You look like a throwback to the sixties."

"Is that so?"

"Yes."

"I don't dress like one."

"You don't dare dress like one, or you'll be out of a job." She pictured the way he was dressed. Straight-from-the-office neat, he was wearing a dark three-piece suit. It was British, obviously hand cut and so conservative as to be mod—at least on him. He had the vest unbuttoned, which added to the rakish look of his hair and beard. Yes, rakish. Annoyingly so. "I'm surprised no one else has complained."

"About my hair? It hasn't hurt business."

"What kind of executive wears his hair long and shaggy?" It wasn't actually shaggy—he had it professionally styled—but still it brushed his collar at the back.

"The kind who thinks for himself," he answered without pause. "The successful kind."

She gave an unladylike snort but lapsed into silence. He always had a retort. She couldn't win, and if she couldn't win, there wasn't much point in playing the game.

Greg had other ideas. "And you're a fine one to mention my image, when you look like you're on your last leg." He felt as if he was on his, which, he supposed, was one reason that he was striking back. Normally he'd rise above the situation and remain still, but he was feeling testy. Even when he was at his best, Diandra could get to him where others couldn't, and he was far from his best just then.

"I'm tired," she said, opening her eyes to meet his. "I worked nearly round the clock to free things up so I could do this, and it's all your fault."

"*My* fault."

"You're a coward."

Greg didn't mind comments about his hair. He felt comfortable with his appearance, confident that he always looked clean and well-groomed. But attacks on his character were something else. Any smug, indulgent tone that had been in his voice vanished. "I think you ought to explain that."

"With pleasure. If you had spoken up in Palm Beach, neither of us would be here. It would have been two against one, us against Bart. We might have been able to convince him either not to sell the town house or to delay the sale for a while. What's his rush, anyway? He's owned the place for sixty years, what difference would a few more months make?"

"He has a buyer."

"So if that one fizzled, he'd get another. The town house is prime Beacon Hill property. He hadn't even officially listed the place, and it sold. Just think of what might have happened if he'd waited. *Five* people would have wanted it, there'd have been a bidding war, and Bart would have come away even richer."

"He doesn't need the money," Greg pointed out.

"Still, why the rush? It doesn't make sense."

Speaking very slowly and with disdain, Greg said, "Hasn't it occurred to you that he's feeling pain? He said that if he had his choice he wouldn't be selling. He may be afraid that if he waits, he'll chicken out. So he's looking to make a quick, clean break."

"But why us? I can name several others who could do the job."

"He trusts us."

"You and me—you *and* me? He knows we don't get along!"

"Oh? Now how does he know that?"

"He heard us bickering, for one thing."

"But that was on Saturday, after he'd made his plans. Has he ever seen us bickering before?"

Diandra thought about that and realized Greg was right. Bart had probably never seen them bicker before, and with good reason.

Greg spelled it out in a low, sure voice. "We see each other as little as possible. Family occasions, board meetings, conferences—maybe once or twice a month we're in the same room, but there are always other people around. One of us may express a view that conflicts with the other's, but there are usually a third and a fourth conflicting view, too. We've never had to work together, really work together. We've never tackled each other head-on. So how was Bart to know we're like fire and water?"

"Now who's underestimating him?" Diandra lashed back. "He knew, Greg. He had to know. There's no *way* we could get along, given what happened with my mother and your father."

Her words hung in the air, then left a resounding silence that not even the steady drone of the jet engines could break.

Greg didn't move an inch; every one of his muscles was taut. Diandra's remark had immediately focused his mind on the two gravestones that stood side by side in the old island cemetery off the coast of Maine. Sixteen years they'd been gone, and still it hurt. It would always hurt, because just as the bodies had never been found amid the airplane debris in the ocean, answers had never been found, either.

Nor would they be, it seemed. The two people who could explain why they'd done what they had were gone.

And Diandra's basic question remained. Why had Bart thrust her and Greg together?

The corner of Greg's mouth curled in a mirthless expression. "Maybe my grandfather has developed a warped sense of humor in his old age. He knows we both want San Francisco. He can't make the decision himself. So he's throwing us into the ring to slug it out. The one who emerges at the end of the week intact is the one who goes west."

"That's sick."

Greg shrugged. "Then again, maybe it's a simple test of loyalty. He wants to know how far we'll go for him. As people get older, they sometimes need that kind of reassurance—like the child who needs a special hug every so often."

"Ah, we're into psychology now."

Ignoring the barb, he stared her down. "My mother's going through something like that."

Diandra had always thought of Greg's mother as a totally together woman—no, she corrected herself, that had only been true in the last nine or ten years. Before that, Sophia had been a woman without a cause, and before that—before her husband had died—she'd been little more than a shadow.

Diandra wanted to ask more, but Greg's look didn't invite questions. He blamed her mother for his mother's woes, and she was her mother's daughter. Greg wasn't as generous as Bart.

The whole mess was painful for Diandra, too. So she closed her eyes and turned her head away again. In the minutes of silence that followed, the pain faded. A new pain arose when, out of nowhere, Greg asked, "Hot weekend?"

Her eyes popped back open. "What?"

"Who's keeping you awake at night these days?"

"Work is keeping me awake. I told you that."

Greg crossed his long legs. "Last I heard, you were dating a Senatorial aide from Wyoming, but that was more than a month ago. I assume it's over and you've moved on."

Diandra pressed her lips together and said nothing.

"Before that," Greg continued in a low, goading voice, "it was a lawyer from the Department of Justice. At least that's what the grapevine said."

"What grapevine?"

"The CayCorp one, comprising all sorts of aunts, uncles and cousins. Jealousy is rampant, Diandra. You've come a long way in a short time. The backstabbers are having a field day."

"And you're out there cheering them on?"

He shook his head. "Not my style. But I do hear what they say, and the word is that you're a siren."

You're a siren, Abby. Stay away from him.

Diandra lost some of her color. "Backstabbers are backstabbers. Their word isn't worth much."

"Still, they offer food for thought. So who's your latest catch? Someone with the Department of Defense? Or the Swedish embassy?"

"You're being unfair."

"I'm as curious as the next guy."

"My personal life is none of your business."

His features tightened. "Not so. We'll be together for the next week, you and me. I think I ought to know what's what." He made a slow perusal of her figure, and when his eyes returned to hers they were dark, oddly sensual. "Are there going to be late-night calls from a lover? Secret trysts in the park?"

That call you got late last night wasn't from your good

friend Donna, and you didn't go to her house to talk her out of a binge. You ran out to see him, *didn't you?*

Diandra felt a twinge of nausea. Slumping in the chair, she closed her eyes and took a deep breath.

"What's wrong, Diandra?" came Greg's quiet voice. "Have I hit a raw spot?"

"I don't believe you'd know a raw spot if it hit you in the face," she said in a weary voice. "You have to be one of the most insensitive men I've ever met." She opened her eyes. "But then, the apple doesn't fall far from the tree, does it?"

Greg stared at her hard. So she thought him insensitive? So she thought his *father* insensitive? That only proved how little she knew.

But of course she was Abby's daughter. What else could she say? She was Abby's daughter and a social butterfly just as her mother had been. Granted, Diandra had a demanding career, but that didn't mean she couldn't flit around during off hours.

Beautiful women were often that way, Greg had decided. Once they learned the power of their beauty, they played on it. Abby had done that. She'd enchanted men with the toss of her hair, the sway of her hips, the smallest of smiles. Some argued that she'd been bored with her life, but Greg couldn't buy that. She'd had a husband and a daughter, and if she'd wanted to work, she could have taken her pick of positions in the business. She'd turned all that down to spend her days plotting her nights, when she'd be in the arms of her husband's best friend.

Unbuckling his seat belt, Greg went to the bar, poured himself a shot of Scotch and tossed it back. Setting the glass down, he turned to lean against the bar.

Diandra hadn't moved. She was watching him, looking a little cornered, he thought. But beautiful, ah, yes, beautiful. Even exhausted, she had a certain aura, a promise of future fire. He could understand why men would flock to her. He bet she'd be dynamite in bed.

"We're starting our approach into Logan, Mr. York," the copilot appeared at the door of the cabin to say.

Returning to his chair, Greg buckled himself in.

He bet she'd be dynamite in bed.

He looked at Diandra. Her head was downcast, forehead resting on two fingertips. Her hair was a glossy black veil around her face, closing it from his view, but if she thought to tempt him with the pose, she had much to learn about his tastes. He liked his women open and honest.

He bet she'd be dynamite in bed.

She was tall, slender but shapely, with curves in all the right spots. She had the body of a California blonde, the temper of a redhead and the allure of a brunette, yet her hair was midnight black. A bundle of contradictions? No. Greg had her figured out. She was self-centered and aggressive, effective in business because she was bright and driven. On a personal level, she was trouble. Still...

He bet she'd be dynamite in bed.

The plane soared low over the harbor and touched down onto the runway with a small bump. The faint jarring was enough to bring Greg to his senses. Diandra might be dynamite in bed, but he'd never know for a fact, because he had no intention of joining her there.

She could lure other sailors to the rocks, but not him. He was deaf to her song.

FREDERICK, BART'S CHAUFFEUR, butler, spare cook and handyman, was waiting with the car near the executive hangar when the jet taxied up. He greeted Diandra and Greg with the formal nod that was his style, took their bags from the copilot and stowed them in the trunk of the large Mercedes.

"Will there be more?" he asked, eyeing the roomy trunk.

"That's it," Greg said.

Diandra was already heading for the car door. "No more."

Greg followed her into the back seat of the roomy sedan. "No more? That little bag couldn't hold much more than a blow dryer, a makeup case and a handful of sexy nighties. Of course, that may be all you'll need."

"All I'll need," she said, slicing him a sharp glance, "is my oldest shirts and jeans, and that's exactly what I brought."

Frederick started the car and pulled away from the hangar.

"No sexy nighties?" Greg asked in a suggestively deep voice.

"Not quite."

"What do you sleep in?"

She looked out the window. Dusk had fallen, blurring details of the terminals they passed. They might have been in any of a dozen airports in any of a dozen cities. She wished she were anywhere but here.

"Diandra?"

"Does it matter?"

"Yes, it matters. If it's going to be just you and me running around in the halls at night, I should know what to expect."

"Ask Frederick what he wears to bed."

"We won't be near Frederick. He has his own apartment in the basement. So what is it, Diandra? I'd have guessed sexy nighties or nothing, and since you've nixed sexy nighties, that leaves nothing."

"Suit yourself."

"I intend to."

Gritting her teeth, she concentrated on the scene beyond

the window. But there was nothing terribly exciting about rush-hour traffic, and when the Mercedes finally paid its toll and entered the tunnel, she felt as though the world had closed in. In sheer desperation—hearing Greg's voice was better than not hearing it and wondering what he was thinking—she blurted out, "What in the devil does that mean—you intend to suit yourself?"

"It means," he said in a menacingly low voice, "that I'm the senior member of this little operation, therefore I'm the one in command. If you want to play while you're here, you'll do it on your own time and somewhere else."

"I don't believe you," she murmured to the window. Traffic was stop and go in the tunnel. She looked at the tiles that lined the walls and wondered, as she had so many times before, what would happen if there were a leak and the harbor started pouring in. Just then, one part of her would have welcomed the diversion.

"Senior member," she muttered, then dropped her voice and mimicked, "I'm the one in command." The sputtering noise she made told her opinion of that, but it wasn't enough. "That's how trouble starts, when big men who think they know everything take command." She turned to him. His face had the eerie gray cast that came from the reflection of light in the tunnel, but his eyes were as dark and, yes, commanding as ever. Steeling herself against their force, she said, "I don't recall Bart saying anything about senior members. As far as I'm concerned, you can handle one room, I'll handle another. The less our paths cross the better."

"You're going to pack cartons, lift them, stack them?"

"I'm not a weakling."

"You're a woman."

"For *heaven's* sake."

"It's a biological fact. You have less muscle than I do."

"So I'll pack cartons, then leave them for you to lift and stack. Sound fair?"

"Sounds like I'm being used."

"Then you worry about your work, I'll worry about mine." She felt an invisible vise loosen as they left the tunnel and skirted the north end. Instinctively she turned her head for a look down Hanover Street. As always, people milled outside the shops and homes that lined the narrow street. There was a warmth to the Italian district that had always appealed to her. For the first time since she'd learned she was coming north, she felt a glimmer of affection for Boston.

Sitting back in her seat again, she watched the buildings of Government Center go by. Ahead was the climb up Beacon Hill, then the short descent to Bart's street. For a brief minute, she was comfortable, relaxing on the wave of a sense of homecoming. Then Greg's voice broke into her thoughts, and all comfort vanished.

"Pull over at the pharmacy, Frederick. I want to run in for something."

Diandra stared at his stony features. "The pharmacy," she stated slowly, "is only two blocks from the town house. The considerate thing to do would be to let us go to the town house first, then run to the drugstore yourself."

"I never claimed to be considerate," Greg said. He was out the door the minute the car reached the curb.

Diandra watched him go, saw him disappear into the store, then reappear moments later popping something into his mouth. He hadn't held them up for long, but she was in no mood to be indulgent.

"And you think I'm taking orders from you?" she burst out. "Think again, bud."

He swallowed whatever he'd chewed and said nothing. Frederick drove on.

She threw a hand in the air. "I don't know why I'm surprised. Your family specializes in taking command."

"It's the secret of our success," he said, staring straight ahead.

"Right. You thrive on controlling. Manipulating. Using."

He arched a brow. "Are you talking about me?"

"If the shoe fits…"

"It doesn't."

"Is that a fact?"

"Yes."

"Then I must be confusing you with another Gregory York."

Greg felt the antacid tablet he'd just chewed do an about-face in his gullet. He swallowed hard and said tightly, "My father's dead. Leave him be."

Diandra didn't respond. She was too busy trying to control her annoyance. Or was it panic? The town house had come into view, Frederick was slowing the car to make the turn into the drive, she felt as if she were trapped.

But the longer she remained silent, the more Greg needed to speak. She'd made specific accusations, and since his father wasn't there to defend himself, the job fell to Greg. "My father was neither a manipulator nor a user. His sole mistake was in falling for your mother. If anyone was the user in that relationship, she was."

Frederick guided the car down the brick-enclosed driveway and into the open courtyard.

"That's insane," Diandra muttered.

"I don't think so."

"How could my mother have possibly used your father? What did he have that she wanted—that her own husband couldn't give her?" The car had come to a halt. She tugged open the door and slid out, leaving the question rhetorical.

Greg wasn't satisfied with that. Following her out of the

car and toward the house, he said, "My dad had strength. He was an exciting man. Of him and John, he was by far the most vibrant."

"And arrogant. My father had more sensitivity in his baby finger than Greg Senior had in his entire body." Casting him a venomous look, she paused only for Frederick to unlock the door before storming into the house. "My mother knew that. No, she didn't use your father. It was the other way around. He was going through a midlife crisis and needed to know that women still found him attractive." Rounding the newel post, she began the climb from the basement to the first floor of the general living quarters. "What better way than to seduce his best friend's wife?"

"Seduce? Hah!" Greg was close on her heels. "And if she was so appreciative of her husband, why was she available? Hmm? How about an answer there?"

"He was a very attractive man, and she was human. Maybe she wasn't as strong as she might have been, but nothing would have happened if he'd left her alone." With the stairs behind her, Diandra strode angrily toward the living room. "She was old-fashioned. She wouldn't have dared initiate anything like that on her own."

"Dream on, little girl."

She whirled on him with her hands on her hips. "It's the truth."

"Says who?" Greg shot back. His hands, too, were on his hips, and his eyes were dark with fury. "You were fifteen at the time. You mean to tell me that your mother told you everything she was doing and feeling?"

"I was sixteen for at least part of that affair, and I know what I do because my father spent hours talking with me after she died."

"Do you honestly think he'd tell you that your mother

was a willing cheat? He couldn't admit that he'd failed her himself. So he blamed my dad."

"He *knew* your dad!" Diandra shouted. Turning on her heel, she went to the fireplace. "They were best friends for years and years. My mother a cheat?" She raised a hand to the mantel for support. "Oh, no, you've got it backward. Your dad was the cheat, and it wasn't only with my mother—" She broke off.

"Hold it. Hold it right there. You'd better think twice before you repeat that—"

His warning ended abruptly and was replaced by a thick silence. He went as still as Diandra, his gaze having joined hers, fixed on the ornate marble mantel, on a velvet box that sat there. It was slim, about six inches square and open. Nestled in its gentle velvet folds was a necklace so exquisite that it was a minute before either of them was able to speak.

CHAPTER THREE

"WHAT IS IT?" Diandra finally whispered.

Greg didn't know what to say. It was obviously a necklace, but that was where the obvious ended. He had never seen anything like it. On the bed of velvet lay one emerald teardrop after another, linked by diamond clusters and fine gold filigree to form a graceful circle. At the top was an intricate diamond-and-gold clasp. At the bottom, the throat, the emeralds paired up to descend in a plait that ended in twin fringes of diamond.

He guessed there to be twenty emeralds, each the size of one of Diandra's polished fingernails, and though far smaller, nearly sixty diamonds. Gemstone to gemstone, each was perfect, but the breathtaking thing was what they became together. Captured light shimmered between them. With the emeralds for strength, the diamonds for brilliance and the gold for delicacy, the necklace was a goddess of a gem. It fairly pulsed from its velvet bed.

It didn't take a connoisseur of fine jewels to know that the necklace was priceless.

Diandra reached out to touch it, but just short of their goal, her fingers hovered, then drew back. She curled them into a fist, pressed the fist to her chest. "Whose is it?" she whispered.

"I don't know," Greg answered on a mixed note of puzzlement and awe. "I've never seen it before."

She leaned closer to study the gold setting around one of

Fleetwood Diner

2211 S. Cedar Street
Lansing, MI. 48910
(517) 267-7606

TABLE # Table 9
CHECK# 614944

DATE/TIME: 4/17/2019 12:13:51 PM
SERVER: Dani
STATION: 01
PARTY SIZE: 1

Item Count: 2

1 SPRITE*	$2.69
1 #3 TWO EGGS*	$5.49
Over Medium	
Well Hash Browns	

Subtotal	$8.18
Tax1	$0.49
GRAND TOTAL	**$8.67**

Opened: 4/17/2019 12:13:51 PM

Thank you for visiting

the emeralds. "It looks old. Do you think it was Emma's?" Emma, Bart's first wife, had been dead for twenty-five years.

Greg shook his head. "If it had been Emma's, it would have been bequeathed either to my mother or my aunt, in which case I'd have seen it—and remembered seeing it—before. But I haven't."

"Not on Dotty or Pauline?" Dotty had been Bart's second wife, Pauline his third. Old Bart had outlived them both.

Again Greg shook his head. "Not even in pictures. And I would have remembered. It would take a certain kind of woman to wear a necklace like this. Neither Dotty nor Pauline could have pulled it off. They'd have been totally overshadowed." He paused. "Besides, Bart's a show-off. If any of his wives had owned a necklace like this, you can bet we'd all have known it."

Diandra ached to touch the necklace but didn't dare. "It's very beautiful. Almost...alive."

Greg was thinking the same thing. "What's it doing here?" he asked in the same quiet, almost reverent tone.

Shrugging, she peered around and behind the box. "There's no note."

"It's just sitting. Waiting."

"Where did it come from?"

It was Greg's turn to shrug.

"Maybe Frederick knows," she mused. The thing to do would be to ask him, she knew, but she didn't move from where she stood. She couldn't take her eyes off the necklace. It intrigued her.

Greg was similarly spellbound. "Whose *is* it?" he whispered.

"I don't know," she whispered back, "but it shouldn't

be lying around this way. Anyone could just walk in and take it. It must be worth an incredible amount."

"I hope Bart's insured."

"I hope he knows it's here."

"He has to know. This is his house. What's in it is his."

Diandra thought about that, then frowned. "Strange that he wouldn't have mentioned it. I mean, I'm sure the Waterford's valuable, and the Chippendale chairs and the Daumier prints, but this has to be even more so." She opened her palm on her chest, then moved her hand to the mantelpiece not far from the box. "So why's it sitting out here like this?"

"I don't know."

"It should be in a safe."

Greg moved closer to the necklace. That movement also brought him close enough to Diandra to catch gentle wisps of her perfume. He found both her scent and the closeness to be pleasant. "Bart has a safe in the den," he said. "I suppose we could put it there."

She bit her lip. "Seems a shame."

He knew. "Like burying something alive."

Just then, from beneath the living room arch, Frederick cleared his throat. "Excuse me." They whirled around, but he seemed oblivious to having intruded on anything out of the ordinary. "I've put your bag in the wicker room, Miss Diandra. Sir, yours is in the oak room."

Diandra gave him a puzzled look. Gregory frowned, got his bearings then asked, "Frederick, what's this doing here?"

Frederick stood stock still. "What's...what doing here?" he asked, as always enunciating his words with care.

"The necklace," Diandra said.

"What necklace?"

Diandra and Greg looked at each other before turning

back toward the mantel. Only then did Frederick look beyond them.

"Oh, my," he murmured and took a step forward.

"Whose is it?" Diandra asked.

He looked totally befuddled. "I have no idea."

"You didn't put it here?"

"No, I did not."

Gregory found that hard to believe. "But you're the only one living here."

"Living here, yes. Working here, no. There's Mrs. Potts, who comes in twice a week to clean, and Dominic, who works with the plants and the window boxes. Then, of course, there's young Miss Connolly from the office, who drops by every so often at Mr. Bartholomew's request to work with the books in his desk."

"So if you didn't put the necklace here," Diandra said, "one of them might have."

"I did not put the necklace there, miss."

"Have you ever seen it before?" Greg asked.

"No, sir."

"Then it had to have been put here while you were picking us up."

"Not necessarily," Frederick said. "I had no cause to be in this room today. The last time I was here was when I came in to polish the andirons yesterday morning."

"And the necklace wasn't here then?"

"It was not."

Diandra fell quiet. Her eyes were on the necklace, drawn there and held by something even beyond the beauty of the piece. Gregory, too, studied it in silence. He had to make an effort to recall the many questions that remained.

"So," he stated quietly, "one of those others had to have put it here. Which of them were in this room between the time you were here yesterday and now?"

Frederick tipped up his chin and stood very straight. Even then, the top of his head barely reached the level of Greg's chin, but what he lacked in height, he made up for in starch. "Mrs. Potts was here. And Miss Connolly." He paused, then murmured another "Oh, my."

"What is it?" Diandra asked.

Frederick looked distinctly uncomfortable, as though at that moment his own starch chafed. The tips of his ears turned pink, and he cleared his throat. "The gentlemen were here last evening."

"What gentlemen?"

He paused before answering. "Mr. Bartholomew's friends."

His uncharacteristic hesitancy puzzled Greg. "What friends?"

"Why, Mr. James, Mr. William, Mr. Louis and Mr. John."

That told Greg nothing. Old Bart had a large coterie of friends and acquaintances, with any number of men named James, William, Louis and John among them. Frederick would be able to fill in the last names, but for the moment another question seemed more pressing. "What were they doing here without Bart?"

Diandra, too, was looking at Frederick—with the same interest Greg felt. That interest piqued when Frederick seemed loath to answer. "What's going on, Frederick?" she asked.

Frederick craned his neck. "Nothing really, miss. Those friends of Mr. Bartholomew's meet here from time to time."

"Without Bart knowing?" Greg asked.

"Oh, Mr. Bartholomew knows."

"What do they do here?"

"They sit."

"Just sit?" Greg asked.

"They talk."

Diandra tipped her head. "Why here?" The butler didn't answer. "Frederick?"

Perhaps in search of a sympathetic male, Frederick chose to look at Greg, which was a mistake. Greg's expression was commanding. Frederick spoke. "The gentlemen in question are all retired and have wives who are…shall we say, repressive. Therefore the gentlemen come here once every few weeks."

"To do what?" Greg asked, though the question had been asked and answered before. He sensed Frederick had withheld a noteworthy piece of information—and he was right.

Looking slightly pinched, Frederick admitted, "They play poker."

Diandra tipped back her head and whispered, "Ahhhh."

Greg simply looked smug. "I take it," he said, "that they aren't playing for pennies?"

"Not quite," Frederick answered archly.

With that particular mystery solved, Greg and Diandra exchanged a glance. "One of them may have left the necklace," she suggested.

"As a stake?"

They looked at Frederick. He shook his head. "These gentlemen deal in stocks. Not jewelry. And I am sure that one of them would have reported having seen this necklace if it had been here then. Despite their…habit…they are honorable men."

Having always thought of Frederick as a man of high standards, Diandra was prepared to take his word for that. "But if they were here last night and made no mention to you of the necklace," she reasoned, "someone had to have put it here this morning. Were both Mrs. Potts and Miss Connolly here today?"

"Only Mrs. Potts," Frederick said, then raised his nose a fraction. "Of course, I have no way of knowing whether one of those others entered while I was either at the market this morning or at the airport this afternoon. They all possess keys."

The obvious course to take would be to call each of them. The even more obvious course to take would be to call Bart. Diandra knew it, just as Greg did, yet neither suggested either course. Instead, they let their eyes be drawn back to the necklace.

After several long moments of silence, Frederick asked, "Will there be anything else?"

Greg shook his head.

"Dinner will be served at seven. Perhaps you'd like to make yourselves comfortable until then?" Without awaiting an answer, he executed an efficient turn and left the room.

Both pairs of eyes remained on the necklace.

"It really is beautiful," Diandra whispered. Again she wanted to touch it, but something held her back. "Strange," she said, then caught her breath when the necklace seemed to sparkle in response.

Greg raised a hand. His long fingers came to rest on the edge of the case. He extended them, drew them back just shy of contact, let them lie lightly on the velvet.

"Greg?"

"It's okay."

"You were going to touch it, but you changed your mind."

"No." He hadn't actually changed his mind. He'd been about to touch it and…something…had stopped him. "It just seems so incredibly valuable."

"You've touched valuable things before."

"This is different. There's an aura to this thing."

Aura was a good word for it, she decided. The necklace

was mesmerizing. "Do you think," she whispered, trying to pass the eeriness of the situation off with humor, "that if you touch it a puff of smoke will rise up and spew out a genie?"

"Don't be dumb," he murmured back.

"Maybe you'll turn to stone."

"Not quite."

"Then touch it. I dare you."

They were standing so close that the slightest whisper could be heard by the other. Suddenly, though, Greg took a full breath, drew himself straighter and said in a normal voice, "This is ridiculous! It's just a necklace!"

Diandra jumped at the sound, then felt foolish. To compensate, she scowled up at him, which was a mistake. She was stunned to find him so close, so tall, large and imposing. Resentful of the fact that he made her feel small, she snapped, "What did you *think* it was?"

He scowled back. "I didn't know *what* to think, what with the way you were whispering, like it was some kind of sacred thing."

"It's just a necklace," she said, echoing his words, but she wondered who she was trying to convince. "Touch it. It won't bite."

"Why haven't *you* touched it?"

"Because I know the need you have." Her voice hardened. "You've always had it, Greg. Remember when we were kids and Bart's brother, your great-uncle Sam, bought a new horse for the farm in upstate New York? There were probably eight of us standing around, *dying* for a ride, but we stood back and waited because we knew that if you weren't the first one up, there'd be hell to pay. You always had to be the first to touch things. It never mattered that you walked away soon after, but you needed to put your mark there."

Greg felt his hackles rise. "Are you kidding? I was the only one with the *guts* to get on that horse."

"Guts, my foot. It was sheer machismo. You were a chauvinist from the time you were twelve!"

"And you were a pain in the butt!" he snapped. With a last scathing look at her, he lowered his gaze to the necklace. Instantly he felt calmer.

Diandra saw that change. Frowning, she, too, looked at the necklace, and the same calm she'd seen, she felt.

Without further ado, Greg touched it. He put a fingertip to one emerald, traced its teardrop shape, let two other fingertips join the first and move over the diamond-and-gold lacework.

"How does it feel?" Diandra whispered.

"Warm," he whispered back. "Why is it warm?"

She had no answer. April in Boston was that awkward time when it was too mild outside to turn up the heat but still too cool for air conditioning. The living room that early evening was on the chilly side. The gems should have transmitted that.

With great care, Greg slid his fingers under the stones and lifted the necklace from its box. It was surprisingly pliant, a credit to the skill of the goldsmith who had crafted the filigree links. The emeralds spread over his palm, their green seeming richer than rich, and the diamonds kept up a steady stream of sparkle.

Unable to resist, Diandra touched an emerald—very lightly and only for a minute, but one touch wasn't enough. Her hand came back, fingertips creeping over that emerald, and another, and a cluster of diamonds, as though they were braille and held a message for her. Their warmth was augmented by that of Greg's skin.

"What should we do with it?" she asked softly.

"We could leave it here until we make some calls."

"That seems risky."

"We could put it in the safe."

But she felt the same hesitancy she'd felt earlier, and when she gave the tiniest of headshakes, Greg agreed.

"You could wear it," he suggested.

"Oh, no. I couldn't do that."

"Sure you could."

"But it's not mine."

"You could wear it for safety's sake."

For safety's sake, she knew, they should lock it up in the den. It seemed so precious, not quite fragile, since the emeralds exuded too much strength for that, but certainly old and of great worth. The safe would be the way to go. But why did she get an odd feeling of suffocation when she thought of that?

Greg took one deep breath, then another. "We'll leave it here for now—at least until we call Bart."

Diandra was comfortable with that decision. "The outside doors are all locked, and Bart's alarm system is very effective." She gave the smallest, inadvertent emphasis to the "very," but it was enough to arouse Greg's curiosity.

He looked down past the smooth raven cap of her hair to her face. "You've had experience with it?"

She shot him a single sheepish glance. "Oh, yes."

He waited. When she didn't elaborate, he said, "I must have missed that story."

In another time and place, Diandra would have done her best to neatly change the subject. But just then she was feeling amiable. "Nothing to miss. Caroline, Susan and I were here with our folks. We were fourteen and feeling our oats. We wanted to see what Boston was like at night—like at one or two—so we snuck out."

"And the alarm went off."

"Not when we left. Our parents were all asleep, but

apparently Bart was still out—he was between wives at the time—so the alarm hadn't been activated for the night."

Greg knew what was coming. "While you were out, he came back, thought everyone was in, turned on the alarm and went to bed." His voice was that of experience. "You should have climbed the chestnut tree in the courtyard and crawled in the pantry window. None of the windows were wired back then. It was a pretty primitive system."

Diandra should have figured that he'd have been in a similar mess and found a way out—or in, in this case. Somehow, though, she wasn't annoyed. Her thoughts were on that long-ago night. "Primitive it may have been, but was it ever loud! There were the three of us, groping madly in the dark for the switch to turn the thing off, when Bart came down the stairs and switched on the light. Everyone in the house was awake. Half the *neighborhood* was awake. Our parents were furious." She paused for a breath, then added in a small voice, "And you never heard about it?"

Greg allowed a crooked smile. "Nope. I never heard."

As odd as Diandra thought that, because she'd imagined Greg to have a running list of every faux pas she'd made in life, she found his smile to be even more odd. It was gentle. She couldn't remember ever having received a gentle smile from him before, and she'd have remembered. It touched her somewhere deep inside.

The smile faded. Greg wasn't sure where it had come from—certainly not from the alarm incident, because it wasn't *that* funny. But what puzzled him was the look on Diandra's face. If he hadn't known better, he'd have said she needed that smile. But that was perfectly absurd, he knew. Diandra didn't need anything. She was independent and self-sufficient, and when she wanted a man, she had her pick of the Washington crop. She didn't need his smile.

She didn't need *him*. Which just went to show how wrongly certain looks could be interpreted.

Dropping his gaze to the necklace, which was a glowing thing winding across his palm and through his fingers, he felt instantly soothed. "Want a drink?" he asked quietly.

"I...uh-huh."

He reached for the velvet box, but rather than putting the necklace inside, he carried both with him from the living room and down the hall toward the back of the house, where Bart's den was tucked neatly behind the stairs.

Stopping at the desk, he set down the box and very carefully returned the necklace to it. Then he stood there for a minute, holding the hand that had held the necklace so it wouldn't feel so empty.

Diandra felt that emptiness. Confused by it, she pressed her own hands together and went to the bar. She was about to reach for the bottle of Scotch when Greg asked, "Any wine?"

Surprised, she looked up. Greg wasn't a heavy drinker. She couldn't remember ever having seen him high, much less drunk. But when he did drink, he drank Scotch. "Uh..." She ran an eye over the assortment of bottles, grabbed a tall one by its slender neck and separated it from the rest. "I don't know how long it's been here."

"It'll be fine." Shrugging out of his jacket, he let it drop over a corner of the sofa. He loosened his tie as he sat down, then, sinking even lower, stretched out his legs and crossed his ankles.

Unable to help herself, Diandra studied him. His hair wasn't all that bad. It was really quite attractive. *He* was really quite attractive...dashing looking...though he seemed half-asleep.

"You look the way I feel," she said. There was no sarcasm in her voice or in her manner as she handed him a glass of wine. Nor, as she stood over him, did she feel—or wish to feel—any superiority. At that moment, she identified with him. They were on the same side of an undesirable situation.

Taking the glass from her fingers, he lowered it to his lap, changed his mind, raised it and took a drink, then met her gaze. "It's been a lousy couple of days." And it seemed to be catching up with him. Relaxed was one word for what he felt, lethargic a second, drained a third. He concentrated on relaxed.

With her own glass of wine in hand, Diandra settled into the large side chair. It, too, was of aged leather, and though it didn't have quite the cushiony plushness that the sofa did, it had the wing back she loved. She'd always felt secure in it.

"Did you get everything taken care of?" she asked.

"No. There'll probably be a couple of frantic calls coming in while I'm here." He leaned his head against the sofa back to study her. "How about you?"

"The same. I spent most of Sunday in the office, for whatever good that did. Things were pretty hectic when I ran out of there this afternoon. This afternoon?" She rolled her eyes. "It seems longer than that since I left."

Greg was thinking the same thing. He glanced at the ship's clock on the wall and discovered that barely three hours had passed since he'd left New York. When he reviewed, act by act, what had taken place during each of those hours, the timing was right. Still, somehow, it seemed longer—almost as though someone had called "Cut!" in the middle and taken a lengthy break before resuming action.

Seeking out the necklace, which was propped regally on the desk, he took a deep breath, then a slow sip of wine. The pale liquid lingered on his tongue. Then he looked at

Diandra and asked in a perplexed tone, "How did we get ourselves into this?"

She nestled into a corner of the wing back and said quietly, "Bart set us up. I think he plotted it, right down to my late plane last Saturday. That rattled me, and *that* suited his purpose." She paused, thought. "He's a crafty old guy. The craftiest thing he did was getting us down to Palm Beach together. It wouldn't have worked if he hadn't done that. Confronted separately, we'd have come up with excuses."

"We did come up with excuses."

"But we didn't use them with any kind of force."

"I don't know," he mused in a moment's dry humor. "I thought you were using a little force there for a while."

She gave a soft snort. "I almost did myself in."

He grinned, which in turn made her bristle.

"I don't see anything funny in that," she told him. "I wasn't doing anything more than you wanted to do but were afraid to—"

"I was not afraid," he corrected, all humor vanishing.

"Sure looked it to me."

"I was being prudent."

"Well, the end result was the same. You left me standing there alone. I nearly took the fall for saying what you were feeling."

"Haven't we been through this before?"

"Apparently it's not settled."

"Fine," Greg said. "Let's settle it, then. What happened to you in Palm Beach was your own mouth, your own doing. You've always been too impulsive for your own good."

"That's called spontaneity, and it's gotten me where I am. Your dark, silent approach is limiting."

"It's worked for me."

"It may be fine for New York, where cold sophistication scores, but believe me, it's not right for San Francisco."

"And that's what this is all about, isn't it?" He came forward in his seat, eyes dark gray and direct. "There wouldn't be any problem if you'd just settle down in Washington. What in the devil do you want with a new store?"

He might as well have said, "Why don't you be a good girl and stay in the kitchen where you belong," for the effect his words had on Diandra. Furious, she set her wineglass down hard on the desk. In the process, though, the necklace caught her eye and she paused. Greg followed her line of sight. He, too, grew quiet. Their anger seemed to float upward and dissipate, as though it had been in a balloon that had popped.

Diandra felt a gradual easing in her body. Slipping her feet from her shoes, she curled her legs beneath her skirt. She took up her wineglass again and returned her head to the lush burgundy leather. Her gaze made a leisurely sweep of the room, making stops from time to time, pensive.

"I wish he weren't selling," she said in a soft voice. "I always liked this place." After a minute, she added an even quieter "Especially this room."

Greg agreed. He didn't have to look around to see the shelves filled to overflowing with books, the assorted memorabilia that covered every other free space, the blotter on the desk, the silver inkwell. In his mind, the den had always been a retreat. It was masculine but warm, as exemplified by the twin tall lamps covered with burgundy shades that stood on either side of the massive desk and cast a soft light about the room.

"What's your place like in Washington?" Greg heard himself ask. He wasn't sure where the question had come from, but it didn't seem out of place. Apparently Diandra didn't feel it was either, because she answered with little more than a wry smile.

"Not as nice as this." She raised a hand. "No, maybe that's wrong. It's just different from this. This town house is old and stately. It holds a world of memories. My place is in a building that was totally rehabbed four years ago. I'd been living in an apartment for the year before that, and I thought the condo would be heaven." She shot a glance at the ceiling in self-mockery. "Well, it isn't. It's modern and elegant, but somewhere in the rehab process it lost its character. When I had one of our decorators do it up for me, it lost even *more* character."

She frowned at her wine, trying to think of the words to explain to Greg what she felt about both that condo and Washington. Finally she raised her head. "My place is very pretty, but it has none of the personal feeling this place has, and I miss that."

Greg was silent for a long while, thinking that she'd voiced the major complaint he had about his own place. It was weird that she'd done that, weird that she felt the same thing. Then again, maybe her problem was simple unfamiliarity. Between the hours she put in at work and the time she no doubt spent elsewhere, her condominium was probably little more than a dress stop.

What puzzled him most, though, was not that she lacked an attachment to her place, but that it bothered her. He'd have thought that as long as the social whirl went on, she wouldn't mind.

"And you?" she asked. When he eyed her distractedly, she added, "Your place in New York."

"Oh. It's okay. High-rise condo. Chic. Every amenity."

"So enthusiastic," she mocked.

"It's fine. Really."

When he said nothing more, she yielded to the silence.

It was surprisingly comfortable, surprisingly free of the competitive edge that usually abraded the air between them. Her gaze wandered to the desktop, to the dark velvet box with its brilliant inhabitant, and she felt an odd kind of peace.

Greg, too, felt that peace, which was why only curiosity was in his voice when he asked, "Do you really want San Francisco?"

She rubbed the wineglass against her bottom lip and said over its rim, "Yes, I want it."

"Why?"

She lowered the glass and shrugged. "The change. The challenge. It must be the same with you."

The tiny movement of his head said it was. "Do you know many people out there?" He wondered if there were boyfriends waiting.

She shook her head. "I've met a few people over the years through business, but they're strictly acquaintances. I do have two friends, girls who were on my Europe trip when I graduated from high school. They were good to me," she said. What she didn't say was that Maren and Lyn had been understanding of the pain she was feeling that summer over her mother's death. "It's been a long time, but we've kept in touch. They're both living in the Bay area, both married, both mothers." She ran out of things to say, and her words seemed to hang in the air for a moment too long.

Greg wondered if she ever missed being a wife and mother. He was thinking of one or two pithy comments he could make about that when his eyes fell on the necklace. Those comments seemed suddenly wrong.

"It has a history," Diandra whispered. "I can feel it. The vibes are phenomenal."

Greg agreed. Every time he looked at the thing, he felt

something odd. The necklace made him stop, reconsider, grow mellow. Needing suddenly to understand what power it held, he came to his feet, turned the phone around on the desk and dialed Palm Beach.

Gretchen greeted him warmly, but when he asked to speak with Bart, she was unable to help. "Why, he's left."

Greg shot a glance at Diandra. "Left?" She was up in a minute, pressing her ear to the phone beside his.

"Set out this morning, they did, Mr. Nicholas Stuttingham and he," Gretchen went on. "At this minute, they are on Mr. Nicholas's boat heading for the Caribbean. As Mr. Bart told it to me, they will be out of touch for the next two weeks."

"Out of touch?" Greg echoed. "Bart's an old man, for goodness' sake. What if he needs a doctor?"

"I asked the same question, I did, and he did not appreciate my askin' it. He said that there was a full crew aboard Mr. Nicholas's boat, and that if there were to be any emergency, they would have adequate means of getting help."

Diandra drew back her head, only to exchange a glance with Greg and whisper, "He can send messages but not receive them. Doesn't that strike you as being convenient?"

"Very," he whispered back, then said into the phone, "Gretchen, do you know anything about a necklace?"

"A necklace?"

"A very old and beautiful one of emeralds and diamonds that has mysteriously shown up here at the town house."

"I don't know about any necklace."

Greg prodded her a bit, but it was clear she was speaking the truth. When he hung up the phone, he studied Diandra in silence. They were standing very close again, but it seemed appropriate. Bart had something up his sleeve, and they were allies.

"*Crafty* is one word for him," Greg mused, employing the word Diandra had used earlier.

"How can he be out of touch? Even aside from the necklace, doesn't he know that we'll have dozens of questions to ask him during the week?"

"He must have done it on purpose. He wants this place closed up, but he doesn't want any part of the closing."

Casting a look around the room, Diandra didn't blame him. Just thinking about dismantling this home made her lonely. She was glad Greg was standing close. The warmth of his body was something that would remain when all the rest had been crated and sealed.

Without moving away, she met his gaze and asked quietly, "What next? Do we call Mrs. Potts?"

At that moment, confronting her upturned face, Greg didn't want to make another call. An image had entered his mind and was crowding out most else. "We'll let Frederick do that," he said distractedly. "He knows how to be discreet."

"And the necklace?"

They looked at the object in question. As he'd done before, Greg carefully lifted it from its bed. After a long minute, he looked at Diandra. "Put it on."

She raised a hand to her throat. It was bare, save a single strand of pearls that fell loosely around the open collar of her silk blouse. She was about to repeat that she'd be uncomfortable wearing the necklace when she realized that wasn't so. Something in a corner of her mind was telling her that the jewels belonged around her neck.

Silently she removed the strand of pearls. But when Greg began to work at the necklace's clasp, an irregularity on the back caught her eye. She touched his hand, said, "Wait," and turned over the clasp to reveal a crest and an inscription delicately etched in the gold. "A. avec amour, C."

She'd been reading in a hushed voice. When she reached the end, she raised her eyes to Greg's and breathed, "Incredible."

"I know," he whispered. It looked as though the necklace hadn't belonged to a York at all; the initials were wrong.

"It has a real history. Look at that crest."

Greg looked. "Makes you wonder about the story behind it...."

"Who made it—"

"Who owned it—"

"Where it's been—"

"What it's lived through. Two hundred years worth of events—"

"And romance. Incredible."

The look in her eyes was so soft that Greg had to tear his gaze away. As quickly as he could, he finished releasing the clasp and moved behind Diandra to secure the necklace. Then he turned her around so that he could see.

Fortunately she remained quiet, because if she'd asked for a rational answer to a rational question at that moment, he'd have been unable to give it. The necklace, resting on her warm, ivory-hued skin, was exquisite. But what held him speechless was Diandra herself. *She* was exquisite. She was soft and beautiful, gentle and giving, but strong. She was, at that moment, everything a woman should be. And more. She was, at that moment, simultaneously the most innocent and sexy woman he'd ever seen. And at that moment, he wanted her.

CHAPTER FOUR

DIANDRA FELT SHAKY as she lay in bed that night. As though it had happened two minutes before, rather than several hours, she recalled the instant Greg had fastened the necklace around her neck, turned her around and looked at her. In that instant, like a bolt out of the blue, she'd felt an intense wave of desire.

It had passed. She'd made sure of that by withdrawing into herself and continually, if silently, repeating every reason why she *couldn't* want Gregory York—the most notable one being that she didn't *like* Gregory York.

Fortunately Greg hadn't been talkative himself. They'd eaten dinner largely in silence, and soon after, she'd excused herself and gone upstairs. She'd showered and put on the old football jersey that she used as a nightshirt, expecting to be out like a light when her head hit the pillow.

Tired as she was, though, she couldn't sleep. It didn't matter that she kept her mind diverted—her body had a will of its own. It seemed to be reverberating from that bolt out of the blue.

For two hours—she knew, because she looked at the bedside clock every ten minutes—she tossed and turned. Finally she climbed from bed and went to the window. But the night was dark, and there was little by way of entertainment on Chestnut Street late at night.

Chancing to glance back over her shoulder, she caught sight of the emerald necklace. It lay in a slender beam of moonlight, glittering more gently than before. Almost on whim, she took it from where it lay on the nightstand and fastened it around her neck. Then she sat in the wicker rocker, covered herself with the afghan that had been lying at the foot of the bed and rocked herself to sleep.

When she awoke in the morning, she felt vaguely stiff. She had moved from the rocker to the bed at four, but the damage had been done. On top of that, she was disoriented. The quaint wicker room in Bart's town house was a far cry from her bedroom in D.C. The decor was different, the light, the sounds. It took her a minute to remember where she was and why. On the tail of that awareness, she let out a groan.

She didn't want to be in Boston. She didn't want to be closing up the town house. She didn't want to be doing it with Greg.

Then she put her hand to her neck.

The necklace was there, warm to the touch. It didn't help her stiffness, but just touching it put her in a better frame of mind to face the day.

After taking a long, hot shower that soothed her aches some, she put on a shirt and jeans and went downstairs. Greg was in the kitchen, perched on a stool at the center island. He was dressed much as she was in an old shirt and jeans, but his seemed to positively stroke his large frame. His shirt was open at the collar and rolled at the sleeves, and the tails hung low over jeans that had worn soft and faded. He looked far more attractive than any man had a right to look so early in the morning and far more attractive than Gregory York had a right to look *any* time.

She could handle it, she told herself. She could handle the way he looked, because he'd always been gorgeous. And she knew that what she'd felt the night before hadn't been real. What she couldn't quite handle was the way he was looking her over. He wasn't leering; if he'd done that, she might have produced a little anger to use as a shield. But he was eyeing her with curiosity that verged on wariness.

"Something wrong?" she asked, doing her best to hold still beneath his scrutiny.

Slowly he shook his head, but his eyes continued their journey over her body. He was proving a point to himself—that what he'd felt the night before hadn't been desire but simple appreciation. Yes, he appreciated Diandra's looks. Who wouldn't? She could add elegance to a potato sack simply by the way she stood. Of course, she wasn't wearing a potato sack. She was wearing jeans that fitted her snugly and a shirt that was stylishly loose. And her face was totally devoid of makeup, which made him appreciate her natural beauty all the more.

So he appreciated her. Did he desire her?

"What are you *staring* at?" she asked with a sudden scowl.

"You." No, he didn't desire her. He couldn't desire a woman who was so quick to vex. Besides, he didn't *like* her, and in the eighties, a man didn't desire a woman he didn't like.

She glanced down at herself. "Do I have toothpaste on my shirt or torn jeans or mismatched sneakers?" When her eyes rose, his were focused on her breasts. She felt her skin prickle, and she was beginning to fear she was in trouble when he lifted his eyes to the necklace.

Instantly his expression softened. "Still have it on?"

Expelling a tiny sigh of relief, she put a hand to her throat. "I thought we agreed I should wear it. For safety's sake."

For the safety of the necklace, that was right, Greg knew. With Diandra wearing it, they always knew where it was. For his own safety, ah, that was something else. The necklace definitely did something—to her, to him, he wasn't sure. When he looked at that necklace he found it harder to remember that he disliked her.

Hard, but not impossible. Nothing was impossible, he told himself. "You didn't wear it in the shower, did you?"

"Of course not."

"Did you sleep with it on?"

She nodded. "It's a powerful narcotic."

"You needed one?"

Diandra didn't like his tone of voice. "No. I'd have fallen asleep without it, but I was in a strange bed and it helped." Anxious to change the subject—lest he probe more deeply into the cause of her unrest—she tucked her hands into the rear pockets of her jeans and eyed the cup of coffee he was nursing. "Who made it?" she asked cautiously.

He followed her gaze. "Me."

Instantly she headed for the cabinet. "Thank goodness. Frederick happens to make the worst coffee I've ever tasted."

"You haven't ever tasted mine," Gregory warned. Actually the coffee he'd made was probably fine full strength, but in deference to his stomach, he'd laced his own cup heavily with milk. He didn't particularly care for the taste of it that way, but he needed coffee in the morning, so weak it was.

Diandra wasn't being fussy, either. Figuring that she was going to have to be on her toes to survive a full day with Greg, she reached for a mug and filled it with the steaming dark brew. She was appalled to find that her hands shook, appalled to realize that Greg rattled her so. She was even more appalled to think that it wasn't just one day with him that she had to survive.

Cradling the mug between both palms, she leaned back

against the counter and set herself to thinking "confident and composed."

Greg waited. He watched her raise the mug to her lips, take a sip, then lower it. "Well?" he asked.

For a minute she drew a total blank. She couldn't remember his having asked a question. She tried to replay the conversation, but it was only when he dropped a pointed gaze to her mug that she realized what he wanted to know. "Oh. It's fine. Very good."

"Where were you just then?"

She wasn't about to tell him that she'd been in her private locker room giving herself a pep talk, so she shrugged and said, "It's taking me a few minutes to wake up," which wasn't a total lie.

"Are you always slow first thing in the morning?" he asked, wondering if he should note that for future reference. He never knew when a moment of slowness would come in handy where Diandra was concerned.

"Actually," she answered, surprised as she thought about it, "I'm usually pretty quick. The minute I wake up, my mind shifts into gear." She raised the mug to her lips, took a sip, then frowned. "I feel like I'm on hold. It's odd not going into the office."

"Pretend it's a weekend."

"Weekend or not, I work."

"*All* the time?" he asked skeptically.

"No, not all the time. But when I'm not working, my mind isn't far from it. I feel a little…lost right now." As soon as she said the words, she feared she'd been too revealing. It had always struck her as important to keep up a strong front before Greg. So she added hastily, "I guess that's because I've never done anything like packing up a house before." She wrinkled her nose. "Aren't there professionals who do this kind of thing? Shouldn't we have someone in to appraise things?"

Greg wished she wouldn't wrinkle her nose. When she did that, she looked innocent and adorable—which, surely, she knew, which, surely, was why she did it. All he had to do was to remind himself that the look was for show and he was safe.

Unfortunately the look had an effect before he could do the reminding. His voice came out a little more throaty than usual when he said, "Eventually we should," in response to her question. Then he took a deep breath and straightened his shoulders; that made him feel better, more his capable, formidable self. "For now we're on our own." He tossed a glance toward the large industrial stove that was polished to a high chrome sheen. "And I mean, *really* on our own. The cook's gone. I sent him out for cartons."

Diandra nodded. There seemed no point in getting ruffled that Greg had taken command. She'd obviously slept later than he had, and they did need cartons. So he'd sent Frederick after them. It made sense. The sooner they got to work, the sooner they'd finish and the sooner she could return to Washington.

Greg was watching the play of emotions on her face. "Any problem?" he asked when she'd been quiet a little too long.

"No, no."

"You do know how to make breakfast, don't you?"

"Of course."

"So what do you want?"

"Uh…I don't usually eat much. Maybe some toast."

He gave her a look as he rose from the stool and muttered, "I need more than that." Opening the refrigerator, he rummaged through its contents.

Diandra, meanwhile, moved to the far side of the room,

to the small window seat that overlooked the courtyard. In the instant when Greg had straightened from the stool, she'd felt a flare of awareness. She was sure it had to do with the fact that, for once, she wasn't wearing high heels, so he looked taller than usual. He also looked more casual. His clothes did that, and the way he wore them. The first two buttons of his shirt were undone, which left a taunting view of tawny chest hair. His exposed forearms were ropy. His hair fell rakishly over his brow.

While she couldn't quite flee the room in a paroxysm of primness, distancing herself from him wouldn't hurt.

Propping a knee on the window cushion, she sipped her coffee and looked out. The day was overcast and not terribly cheerful. A few flowers sprouted from a whiskey barrel that Bart's neighbor had set out in his backyard, no doubt to coax spring along, but spring wasn't to be hurried. The trees in the courtyard had only the bare beginnings of buds, unlike those in Washington, which were well into bloom. It was cherry blossom time there. Now *that* was cheerful.

Having let the refrigerator swing shut, Greg was watching her. In profile, her features were delicate and very sober. He couldn't help but wonder what she was thinking. "You look like your best friend just died."

She looked quickly around, let out a small laugh and shook her head. There was no smile to accompany the laugh though, and just as quickly as she'd turned her head, she faced the window again. "The courtyard is sad," she said. "It doesn't want Bart selling this place, either."

At her mention of selling, Greg felt a pang of regret. To counter that, he tossed off a nonchalant "It'll never know the difference."

"Sure, it will. It knows who takes care of it. Bart always made sure that the chestnut tree was fed and pruned. Emma used to sweep the cobblestones, even when there was help to do that. I took my turn painting the bench." She paused and looked over her shoulder at him. "Did you ever do it?"

Coming up behind her, Greg reached out to draw the curtain farther back. "Twice. Once when I was twelve, then again when I was fourteen."

His closeness comforted her, took away some of that empty feeling. "What colors?"

"Green the first time, brown the second." They were good, solid colors. He'd been proud of his work.

Diandra let a tiny smile escape then. "I did it in red."

"You were the one? That was *hideous*."

She shrugged. "Bart said to do it in whatever color I wanted. I wanted red."

"Why?" he asked, fascinated by the mischief in her expression.

"Because it was bright and cheerful. Painted red, that bench attracted attention."

"How old were you?"

"Fifteen."

Fifteen was the age when Diandra had come into her own. Greg remembered. After a slow start, she'd become a knockout really fast. Red had definitely been her color that year.

That year also marked the start of the affair between her mother and his father. He wondered if Diandra had known at the time what was happening. Interesting that she'd chosen red. Red had been Abby's color.

Turning his back on her, Greg returned to the refrigerator, took out all he needed to make a cheese omelet and toast, then went to work fixing it. He didn't look at Diandra until he'd finished, when he threw off a quick "Want some?"

She shook her head, so he piled everything he'd made

onto a single plate and, though it was truly more than he wanted, he forced himself to eat every bite—and that, purely as a matter of pride. Diandra had taken a refill of coffee and left the room before he'd finished.

A short time later, he found her in the first-floor parlor, sitting barefoot and cross-legged on the camelback settee. She had a yellow legal pad on her lap and was making notes.

"What are you doing?" he asked in a clipped tone. He stood at the door with one arm high on the jamb.

"Working." Which had always been and, she feared, would always be the antidote for her ills. The particular ill she was feeling at the moment had to do with Greg, with the moment of comfort he'd brought her in the kitchen and the abruptness with which he'd snatched it away. She could imagine why he'd done it; what she couldn't imagine was why it bothered her.

But she wasn't up for soul-searching, so she was setting to work. "I figured we should start from the bottom and work our way up. This room seemed as good a jumping-off point as any."

"What are you doing with the pad?" he demanded.

"Right now, holding it," she said, tossing his imperious tone right back at him. Then she sighed and looked around. "I guess the first thing to do is list everything that's here."

"And then?"

"I don't know—call the museum, call the appraiser, call the auction house…. Maybe call around and see if anyone else in the family wants what's here."

"Bart didn't suggest that."

"He said we should dispose of things in an appropriate fashion, but since he's opted out of the process, we'll have to use our own judgment as to what constitutes an appropriate fashion." She made a face that perfectly reflected her frustration. "He mentioned shipping some of this stuff to him, but how are we supposed to know what he wants and what he doesn't?"

Pushing away from the doorjamb, Greg sauntered across the room. "We both know that the secret to success is decisiveness." He lowered himself into a chair. "We also know that decisiveness isn't worth a damn if the person making the decision doesn't have a certain amount of basic information at his fingertips." He thrust out his bearded chin. "Well, we need more information. I'd suggest that we make your list—and make it in detail—then present it to Bart."

"He'll be gone for two weeks. We can't wait that long."

"We won't have to," Greg said succinctly.

Diandra considered that succinctness and the knowing look in his eye, and she realized he was right. Bart had never been one to cut himself off from his world for more than a few hours. He had ample means of communication from the boat. He just didn't want them to know about it.

"Okay," she conceded, "so we could reach him, but that might take time, too, and a waste of time is what we're trying to avoid. So what do we do meanwhile? He wanted things packed."

"We'll pack them, but we won't move them until Bart has gone over our lists."

"What about his buyer?"

"His buyer will wait. After all, if Bart is incommunicado for the next two weeks, his buyer won't be able to contact him, will he?" Eyeing her askance, he asked more cautiously, "You didn't catch the name of Bart's broker, did you?"

"He didn't mention it," she said. Then her eyes widened. "Do you think he was making it up?" Answering herself, she quickly shook her head. "He wouldn't have made that up, Greg. Bart isn't a liar."

"But he's crafty—to use your word. I have no doubt that he does have a buyer for this place. Whether the buyer needs to take title in two weeks, though, is the issue."

Diandra's frustration level took a jump. "But what purpose would Bart have for rushing us into this, when he knows we'd have been able to do it more comfortably at a later date?"

"He knows that given extra time we'd have come up with some scheme to get out of the job. Right?"

She let out a breath. "Right."

"But we are here, and all the speculating in the world about Bart's motives won't get the job done. Right?"

"Right."

"So." He glanced around the room. "You want to write?"

"Sure."

Starting at the archway and moving clockwise, Greg began to call off the various pieces of furniture in the parlor. There wasn't much on a large scale, since the parlor was half the size of the living room, though what there was was old and ornate. When he reached the china cabinets that were built into the wall, things grew more complex. Inside those cabinets and the drawers beneath, he found three china tea sets, numerous unmatched plates and platters, stacks of hand-stitched table linen, candles of assorted lengths and colors, and a sterling silver tea service. And that was before he began on the slew of small, original oil paintings that covered the walls.

"A woman could get writer's cramp with a job like this," Diandra remarked. She stretched her fingers.

"Too much for you?" Greg challenged.

She held up that same hand, writer's cramp ignored. "No, no. I can take it."

But Greg was wondering if *he* could. He glanced at his watch. It was only eleven. He felt as though he and Diandra had been working for hours—and they'd barely begun. There were still two other rooms on the first floor, and three full floors above them. And all they had to show for their morning was a three-page list. If he ever had a morning like that in New York, he'd hand in his resignation.

It wasn't that he was bored, just frustrated. Making lists wasn't efficient. It was what middle-level bureaucrats did to justify their positions. Making lists was a time filler, and in this case it was a poor excuse for Bart's not being there to point to this or that and say what he wanted done with it.

But more, there was the job itself. Greg didn't want to be dismantling Bart's town house. His heart wasn't in it.

He wondered what was happening at the office and why no one had called. Surely there'd been something they'd needed to ask him.

"It's so quiet here," Diandra murmured with an uncanny sense of timing. "I feel as though phones should be ringing or assistants barging in."

She had her feet on the sofa, her knees drawn up and the pad of paper propped against her thighs. It occurred to Greg that she looked perfectly comfortable that way, not at all like the executive she was. He wanted to think that she was being deliberately coy—except that she truly seemed indifferent to the pose.

"Do you kick off your shoes and tuck your legs up at work?" he asked. He tried to sound disdainful, but didn't quite make it, because more than anything just then, she looked refreshing.

"Not during the day. I don't dare then. I have an image to uphold." She gave him a sad smile. "That's the story of our lives, isn't it? Images to uphold." She looked around. "Take this room. It's a symbol, that's all. It's beautiful, the

stunning facsimile of a Victorian drawing room, just as
Emma intended, then Dotty, then Pauline. More than any
other room in the house, this one was the epitome of social
success. But we never used it much, did we?"

"It's too fussy."

"Fussy, formal, outdated… We used any other room
but this."

She was right, Greg knew. When the families gathered
in the town house—likewise, with the business gatherings
Bart had had there over the years—the crowd generally
flowed from the living room to the den, then up the stairs
to the dining room and the more casual family room. He
and Diandra hadn't been the only ones to find the parlor
too fussy for comfort. So why had Bart kept it as it was?

"Every Boston Brahman had to have a drawing room,"
he said in response to his own thoughts. "It was a sign of
social and financial arrival. Henry York built that first
store from nothing, and Bart lived through a part of that
early struggle. He needed this." A new thought popped into
Greg's mind, and it was on his tongue before he could hold
it back. "If the house were yours, what would you do here?"

"In this room?" Diandra asked. "Mmm, I'm not sure."
She thought for a minute as she looked around, thought
about what she—not a decorator—would do. Then she said
with a smile, "I'd get rid of those heavy velvet drapes, strip
the walls of purple flowers and auction off the furniture.
Then," she took a breath, as though she were suddenly
free, "I'd do up the room completely in white. White walls,
white woodwork, white area rug, white furniture—soft,
cushiony white furniture."

"With hands-off signs all over." Greg could picture it.
There had been a room like it in his parents' house when
he'd been growing up. He'd caught hell from his mother any

number of times when dirt from his pockets or his socks or the cuffs of his jeans had speckled the rug.

But Diandra was shaking her head. "Everything would be washable. It would be such a soft, inviting room that people would be naturally drawn to it."

"White is virginal and forbidding."

"It's pure and warm."

"Warm? White, as in snow?"

"White, as in sun-kissed, wind-swept sand."

"That's gritty."

She shook her head. "It's smooth and soothing. Misty. No rough edges. Everything calm and peaceful."

"Ahh," he mocked. "White, as in doves. Poetic."

In the echo of his sarcasm, Diandra was reminded of just why she disliked him. He made fun of her. Granted he'd gotten more subtle with age, but he still enjoyed putting her down. "Yes, white as in doves, and it is poetic *and* beautiful. I like peace. I want little patches of it in my life. It's not my problem if you don't have the appreciation for that. And by the way, don't ask my opinion if you're going to turn around and tear it to shreds." She rose from the settee and headed for the hall.

"You won't get peace in San Francisco," he called, scrambling from his seat.

"I can try," she replied without looking back.

"Where are you going?"

"To make lunch." She was running lightly up the stairs.

He followed, though not as lightly. "At this hour?"

"I'm hungry."

"You wouldn't be hungry if you'd had breakfast."

"I wasn't hungry then."

"You should have eaten, anyway. Breakfast is the most important meal of the day."

"I'll remember that when I get to be your age," she

said as she went through the kitchen door. Slapping the legal pad onto the nearest counter, she pulled open the refrigerator, from which she proceeded to take a head of lettuce, a ripe tomato, half a cucumber, a bag of shredded cheese and a plate of cold turkey.

Leaning against the doorjamb with his hands anchored in the pockets of his jeans, Greg watched her. "You're making a salad. I'm impressed."

"Why? I told you I could cook."

"Hold on. Making a salad isn't exactly cooking."

"Then why are you impressed?"

"Because it's something, and you're doing it yourself."

Not only was she doing it herself, but she was doing it deftly. With a single whack of the lettuce on the counter, she'd twisted out its core and put the head under the faucet. As soon as she set it down to drain, she took up a knife and began to do something very fast and skillful to first the cucumber, then the tomato.

For several minutes, Greg was mesmerized by the movement of her hands. Then he raised his eyes to her face, saw that her jaw was tight and guessed that nervous tension was behind much of the energy she was expending. He felt a tiny glimmer of satisfaction; it was reassuring to know that he still had the power to annoy her.

Then an emerald caught his eye. It disappeared, reappeared, disappeared, reappeared with the motion of her shirt as she worked, and it mesmerized him much as the movement of her hands had done. As he watched for it, the perverse satisfaction he'd felt was forgotten. In its place was something more gentle. Returning his eyes to Diandra's face, he felt as though he was seeing a new side, a softer side, a domestic side. It didn't replace the corporate image, but augmented it, gave it depth, made it richer.

To his chagrin, he felt his body tighten in desire.

Needing an immediate breather, he left the kitchen, trotted down two sets of stairs and went out into the courtyard. It was a damp April day, the kind that would be uncomfortably muggy if it were warmer. He was glad it wasn't warmer. He needed the slight chill to clear his head.

For a time, he ambled around the cobblestone drive. Then he propped himself against the old chestnut tree, crossed his arms over his chest and, for the first time in months, craved a cigarette.

But the craving would pass, he knew, as would that odd feeling in the pit of his stomach. He didn't desire Diandra. He couldn't. He didn't like her.

Having once more reminded himself of that fact, he took a final deep breath and went back inside. He didn't have to climb farther than the first floor; Diandra was in the living room. Again she was sitting Indian-style, this time on the chintz sofa, and she was holding one of the Oriental bowls that normally stood on a table nearby. She looked up when he appeared, carefully set the bowl aside and picked up her pad and pen.

Without a word, they went back to work. As he'd done in the parlor, Greg moved slowly around the room dictating to Diandra. He was fonder of the living room than the parlor. It had an eclectic air, created by the myriad of unusual pieces that Bart and his wives had collected over the years. He paused often to study one thing or another—a small African sculpture, an etched glass bottle, the set of French tapestry fragments that hung on the wall.

Diandra, too, found them interesting. They were also a diversion, because she was having a difficult time keeping her eyes off Greg. His legs fascinated her. They were long, lean but solid, and he moved them with an animal grace that was nearly erotic. Far more sensible, she knew, to admire a Baccarat vase.

She didn't know whether to be relieved or distressed when, far short of finishing the job, he dropped onto the far end of the sofa and scowled.

"What's wrong?" she asked.

He said nothing at first, simply sat in a slouch looking disgruntled. Not trusting his responses in the best of times, Diandra didn't push him to speak. She was almost surprised when he did.

"I don't want to be doing this," he muttered, running a hand through his hair in frustration. "It's a monumental waste of time. The house is practically a historical landmark. It shouldn't be sold." He turned cross eyes on Diandra. "Call Bart and tell him that."

"Call and tell him yourself."

"Are you enjoying this?"

"No."

"But we're locked in here." He pushed himself up and was across the floor in three long strides.

"Where are you going?" Diandra called, sitting straighter.

He disappeared, but his voice came back. "I'm hungry."

Tossing the pad aside, she jumped up and followed him. "After that breakfast you ate?"

He was taking the stairs two at a time. "That was early this morning."

"But it was huge."

"Well, I'm hungry again."

"You're just bored. The job has to be done, Greg. It won't go away."

"I know," he muttered from the top of the stairs. "I know." He continued on into the kitchen, only to pause in the middle of the floor with his hands on his hips and his head bowed. "Do you want a sandwich?"

"I just ate."

"I want a tongue sandwich."

Diandra tried not to grimace. "I don't think Frederick buys tongue. Where is he, by the way? Shouldn't he have been back by now?"

Greg's head was up, eyes focused on a slip of paper that was propped against the bowl of fruit on the counter. He crossed the floor, picked up the paper and read aloud, "'Sir, I have secured four dozen cartons, which should get you started. If you need more, please call the number attached.'"

"Four dozen?" Diandra cried in horror.

Greg silenced her with an upraised hand and read on. "'I spoke with Mrs. Potts. She knows nothing about a necklace. I have called no one else because I fear alerting too many people to the presence of something that valuable in this house.'"

"This house is *full* of valuable things," Diandra broke in to argue.

Greg dropped his gaze to the necklace, took in the creamy skin beneath it, the slenderness of the neck above it, the smoothness of Diandra's cheeks, her innocent eyes. "Not like that," he said a bit thickly, then cleared his throat and read on. "'As no one has come looking for it or reported it missing, I see no harm in keeping it here until Mr. Bartholomew can be reached. In the meantime, I must be off.'"

"Off?" Diandra asked with a frisson of alarm.

Greg silenced her with an impatient look and went on in the deep, resonant voice that in no way resembled Frederick's. "'I am on my way to Bermuda to see about lodging. I shall be retiring there when Mr. Bartholomew sells the town house.'"

Her eyes went wide. "On his way to Bermuda?"

"'Best of luck with your endeavor. Your faithful servant—'"

"*Faithful!* He calls running out and leaving us here alone faithful?"

Greg wasn't any more pleased with the turn of events than she was. It was one more ominous stroke on top of the others, and it was the one that snapped what little patience he'd had. Tossing the note on top of the fruit, he turned on his heel and, brushing past Diandra, left the room.

"Now where are you going?" she yelled. He was headed upstairs, rather than down.

"Out." He'd had it with closed rooms. He'd had it with stupid assignments. And he'd had it with the faint, elusive scent that was Diandra's—and that was driving him mad.

She ran up after him. "But what about the living room?"

"It'll wait," he answered from his room.

She planted herself at the door. "Greg, we have to get this done."

He had his duffel bag on the bed and was fishing around inside. "It'll *wait*," he growled. He pulled out a small piece of slinky navy stuff, followed by a pair of goggles.

Diandra couldn't believe it. "I have a whole office on hold while I'm doing Bart's bidding, and you're going swimming? Where are you going swimming?"

"The Y," he mumbled and disappeared into the bathroom.

"You can't go swimming," she cried, but he had reappeared with a bath towel in his hand. "We have a job to do." He proceeded to roll his swimsuit and goggles in the towel.

"There's no rush." With the towel tucked under his arm, he strode past her. "We have all week."

"Come on, Greg," she protested, heading downstairs fast on his heels. "This is unfair. I'm stuck here, too, and I want to do the work and be done. You're supposed to be doing it with me. You can't just walk out and leave me alone."

At the foot of the stairs he stopped and turned so abruptly that she would have barreled into him had he not caught her arms. "Sweetheart," he growled, "if I stay here alone with you, given the way I feel right now, you'll regret it."

But Diandra wasn't thinking of regrets. She was thinking that Frederick had betrayed her by flying to Bermuda, and now, when all she wanted was to do what she'd come for and leave, Greg was betraying her, too. But then, what had she expected? "Is this how you run things in New York—by going off for a swim when the going gets tough?"

"You know damned well it isn't."

"But Boston's different," she said with narrowed, knowing eyes. "You want *me* to do the work, don't you? You want me to do it while you're gone. And here Bart thought *I* was afraid of a little hard work. Hah! Look who's afraid."

"Keep still, Diandra."

She wasn't about to do that. Eyes ablaze, she raced on. "You're thinking that if you disappear, I'll be bored enough to keep on going. Or stupid enough. Well, let me clue you in on something, mister. You can walk out of this house, and I won't be bored. There are a dozen things I can do to keep myself busy, and none of them have anything to do with Bart's job. And as for stupid—"

He tightened his hands on her arms. "That's *enough*."

"I'm not stupid, Greg. I'm not about to do your work for you. And if you think you can scare me off with your moods, think again. Your moods don't scare me. I've been the butt of them for years."

"Not this one," he said in a quieter voice—not calmer, but quieter and more dangerous.

Diandra felt that danger. She even saw the dark gleam in his eye. But it only added to her agitation. "If it weren't for you, I wouldn't be here, but since I am, you're stuck, too. I'll be damned if I'm going to let you weasel out of your half of the work."

He tugged her closer. "You have a problem with your mouth, do you know that? It won't stay shut."

"If my mouth stayed shut, I'd be a total failure at my job. How do you think I turned that store around? By smiling sweetly at every Tom, Dick and——"

His mouth covered hers, cutting off Harry, and for a split second Diandra couldn't react. Then the second passed, and she began to push his chest, but he simply slipped an arm around her back, framed one hand to her face and held her still for his kiss.

It was as bold a kiss as she'd ever received. It molded her mouth with the force of a fine-tempered anger and refused to let the tiny sounds of protest escape from her throat. It plundered her softness, devouring the curve of her lips and the moisture within. It took her breath away and robbed her of the ability to move.

But it took Greg's breath away, too, and when he paused for air, she cried out in fury, "Gregory York! What do you think——"

He resealed her lips before she could say another word, because he didn't want to hear her anger. He'd heard enough of that to last a lifetime. What he wanted to hear were the sounds of a sweet, silky woman. That was what his mood called for, and he knew she had it in her. He also knew that she'd do her best not to respond to him that way. Which made for a very, very interesting challenge.

With that challenge foremost in his mind, his second

kiss was more persuasive. His mouth stroked rather than plundered. Rather than taking as much as it could get in as short a time, it explored the same terrain in a more leisurely fashion. This second kiss was as persistent as before, but it took its force from gentleness, and that had an effect.

Diandra stopped pushing his chest. Her fury was suspended, overshadowed by unexpected sensation. She didn't willingly open her mouth to return his kiss, but the rigidity in her body eased. Without conscious intent, she leaned into him for support. And when he paused a second time for air, her voice was softer, less shrill.

"Don't do this, Greg. There's no point—"

His third kiss was even more gentle, even more powerful. Somewhere along the line he'd forgotten about punishing her for the sharpness of her tongue. He'd even forgotten about the challenge of getting her to respond. All he could think of was how good she felt in his arms, how warm and soft and woman scented, and how sweet she tasted.

Keeping one arm firmly around her back, he slid his hand along the line of her neck, moved his fingers upward into her hair, then cupped the back of her head and controlled her that way. His mouth caressed hers, exploring its fine nuances, coaxing a response for the sheer need to feel his kiss returned.

It came slowly—first in the softening of her lips, then in their opening. Despite her intentions to the contrary, Diandra couldn't help herself. She'd been kissed, but never with such deliberate care. The movement of his mouth intrigued her, as did the brush of his beard and the sleekness of his tongue. And beyond that there was his body, long and firm, pressed close, taking her weight.

It didn't matter that she didn't like him. What he was doing to her senses was addictive. One stroke demanded another, one caress a second. Though she'd always prided herself on being in control, Greg awakened a stunning hunger.

Suddenly, though, he pulled back. Taking in slow, unsteady breaths, he looked down at the flush on her lips and the moistness he'd left there. He looked at the throbbing pulse at her neck and the desire in her eyes, and he felt the satisfaction he'd sought—and then some. That was the catch. Oh, yes, he'd aroused her. But she'd also done a damned good job of arousing *him*, and that hadn't been part of the scheme.

Lowering his gaze, he focused on the necklace and not for the first time wondered what power it held. That power frightened him.

What frightened him even more, though, was the possibility that the necklace didn't have any power at all.

CHAPTER FIVE

RELEASING HER, GREG crossed the second-floor landing and started down the next flight of stairs. The sound of his footsteps was muted by the runners that covered the oak treads, but in the silence that permeated the rest of the house, Diandra easily heard the front door open, then, seconds later, shut tight.

In the wake of his departure, she didn't move. Her heart beat loudly into the stillness, seeming to screech at her for what she'd just done. Slowly she raised a hand to her mouth and touched tentative fingertips to her lips, which were very soft, warm, moist. She dropped that hand to cover her heart in an attempt to ease its thunder, and when that didn't work, she touched the emerald necklace.

The stones were as warm as her lips had been, and though they couldn't possibly be as soft, they had that same strangely soothing effect they always had. It was as if they were telling her that everything was all right. Needing the reassurance, she remained still for another minute and let them speak.

Then, taking a single deep, if slightly unsteady breath, she went to the mahogany console that stood in the hall and stared at herself in the mirror. She was the same woman she'd always been—same hair, same skin, same eyes, nose and mouth—but something was different.

Something glowed.

It was the necklace, she reasoned. Moving her hand

aside, she looked at it, but it was half-hidden by her shirt. Slowly, almost nervously, she drew her collar open and studied the way the gems lay against her skin. They looked back at her, winking smugly.

But they didn't glow.

More nervously she raised her eyes to her face. Nothing had changed; she looked the same. She tilted her head a fraction and decided that, yes, perhaps her eyes were a bit wider and her cheeks a bit more flushed. Her lips were certainly different—they still felt Greg's, still tingled.

But did they glow?

Confused, she wandered into the kitchen, but it was too full of recent memories for comfort. So she continued on into the dining room, then the family room. Without direction, she soon found herself back at the mirror.

What she saw there then wasn't a totally unfamiliar sight. But she'd never seen it reflected in the mirrored walls of CayCorp's boardroom, or in shiny store windows on the city street, or in the rearview mirror of a cab. In those places she typically saw determination on her face, perhaps concentration, satisfaction, maybe fatigue, but always confidence.

The expression she wore now was different. She'd seen it from time to time in her mirror at home, mostly at night, sometimes early in the morning. She'd seen it at those times when she was most vulnerable, when she was feeling sad and alone.

Not wanting to feel that way, she mustered a spurt of energy and ran down the stairs for her sneakers. Then she went to the closet. Her hand sped past several overcoats, a trench coat and an old, baggy golf sweater before stopping at a leather jacket that looked sufficiently large and warm. Shrugging into it, she pulled up the collar and left the house.

She walked briskly—easy to do at midafternoon when there were fewer people on the sidewalks than there would be an hour or two later. Charles Street boasted several new shops that had opened since she'd been there last, but she barely noticed. She walked on to Beacon Street, went left onto Arlington, then began a long, rapid march around her favorite spot, the public garden. She figured that if anything could occupy her mind in a positive way, that would.

It did marginally, though she half-suspected that the physical exertion more than the scenery did the trick. She kept up a rapid pace, even extending her walk up and around the common before cutting back through the webwork of paths to the garden.

Gradually she began to feel calmer and more herself. She also began to feel tired, so she found a bench that overlooked the duck pond and lowered herself to its green planks. From that vantage point she could watch the workmen spruce up the swan boats for spring.

It was there, with a cool breeze blowing against her face, that she admitted that Gregory York turned her on. It wasn't right, because she didn't like him, and there was, therefore, no future to the relationship, but he did turn her on.

And why not, she asked herself? He had all the right goods, in all the right proportions, in all the right places. No, she corrected herself, that was wrong—he had more than that. His goods weren't just right, they were better than that. He had the looks, the stature, the style. He was a walking enticement for the joys of love. And she was both woman and human.

With a soft moan and a shift of position, she huddled more deeply inside the jacket and tried to push Greg from her mind. She focused on a trio of schoolgirls wearing uniforms of multilayered denim and wondered what frivolity made them laugh. When they passed through the Commonwealth Avenue gate, she switched her focus to a pair of elderly men who occupied the bench across the pond. Their faces were tired and expressionless. She wanted to see them smile, and when they didn't, she looked away, skimming the garden until her gaze fell on a young couple necking against a tree.

Diandra watched them without compunction, reasoning that if they chose to air their kisses in public, they deserved to be watched. They were teenagers, the girl petite, the boy taller, and their bodies were bonded together as though they intended to stay that way for a good long time. The boy, who occupied the sheltered spot against the tree, had his wrists crossed over the small of his girlfriend's back; hers were wrapped around his waist. Their heads moved slowly, while their mouths remained fused.

Feeling a wave of distaste, Diandra looked away. She recalled similar waves of distaste she'd felt in the past when men had kissed her and she'd turned away. Then again, perhaps it wasn't distaste as much as disappointment she'd felt. She wasn't a virgin. She knew what to do. But mechanics were one thing, true pleasure another. Not finding the latter with either of the two men, who, in fourteen years, she'd cared for enough to sleep with, she'd pretty much given up on the former.

Her reaction to Greg was something else. Pleasure had been the last thing she'd expected to feel from his kiss, but feel it she had. She'd fought it and *still* she'd felt it.

Was it the necklace? Or was it Greg? Or was it some invisible quality, some chemical reaction that occurred between Greg and her the same way it had between their parents? Greg had always had the power to move her, but never before in this particular way.

She wondered if her mother had felt that all pervasive melting sensation, that mindlessness, that hunger in Greg, Sr.'s arms. If so, she could understand why she'd been seduced.

But only to a point. No woman had a right to hurt her husband that way. No woman had a right to hurt her daughter that way. And Diandra had been hurt. She'd lost her mother just when she'd needed her most, and there had been times when she'd been furious about that. Attraction or not, Abby should have been able to control herself. She had responsibilities. She should have put her husband and daughter ahead of whatever wayward feelings she'd had. She should have—and easily could have—put distance between herself and the source of temptation.

That was exactly what Diandra knew she should do herself. She should leave Greg in Boston and go home. But she couldn't do that. She was in a bind. For one thing, she'd told Bart she'd help him out, and she wasn't one to go back on her word. For another thing, there was San Francisco. More than ever, she wanted that store. It would give her a new cause, keep her busy, fill that void in her life that she increasingly felt. In San Francisco there would be new sights, new people. And what greater distance could she ask than that between east coast and west?

She raised her eyes to the sky. It was leaden, more so, perhaps, than when she'd started out. She wondered if it was going to rain and, thinking as a clothier would, wondered if she should dash home for the sake of the leather jacket.

Drawing one hand from a pocket, she fingered the fabric. It was a high-quality leather, the type Casey and York always carried in its most chic sportswear departments. It was cut in the standard bomber style that had been around for years and years. Still it seemed too big to have fitted Bart, even in his prime. She wondered whose it was.

Greg knew. Walking slowly back through the public garden after his swim, he took one look at Diandra sitting on that bench wearing that jacket, and the irony of it all—coming on the heels of what had happened earlier that afternoon at the town house—was too much.

The jacket had belonged to his father.

Coming to a halt, Greg dropped his gaze to the ground. He'd swum seventy-two lengths and had not only worked off the worst of his distress but also built up a pleasant fatigue. He was feeling calmer than he had, far more in control, nicely relaxed. He wasn't sure if he wanted to see Diandra just then.

He could turn around and take another path, he knew. Or he could continue on straight to the town house. Her eyes were downcast. She seemed lost in her thoughts. She wouldn't even know he'd passed.

But he'd never been a coward. And, besides, he *was* feeling calmer and more in control. He could handle himself.

With deliberate slowness, he started walking. He crossed over the bridge and turned onto the path that led to Diandra's bench. At the far end from where she sat, he stopped.

Startled by the intrusion of a human form nearby, she looked quickly up. As quickly, she recognized Greg and her alarm faded. Her heart wasn't as accommodating; it continued to pound.

Above his trim beard, his cheeks were ruddy. The wind had tossed his hair some in the drying. He was dressed as he'd been when he'd left except for a sweatshirt he thrown on over his shirt. The sweatshirt was faded and had obviously shrunk with repeated washing so that it reached a point just below his waist, which left plenty of room for his shirttails to show.

Although he wasn't exactly a fashion plate by Casey and York standards, he looked handsome in a disreputable kind of way. In sheer self-defense, Diandra tore her eyes from his to look intently out over the pond.

Greg studied her for a minute. She seemed very alone just then, not the sophisticated career woman he'd always thought her, but more approachable. He suspected that had something to do with the way she was huddled into the jacket, as though she needed protection. Seeing her that way, he doubted he'd have been able to turn around and leave her alone.

"Mind if I sit?" he asked.

Eyes still on the pond, she shrugged.

Taking care to leave plenty of room between them, Greg lowered himself to the bench. He set his ball of damp towel beside him and stretched out his legs. Not in the mood for an argument and not sure what to say that wouldn't cause one, he sat quietly.

Diandra wasn't sure what to make of his presence. Reluctant to deliberately court danger, she didn't look at him. But, oddly, she was relieved that he was there. She didn't know why it should be so, but the day didn't seem quite as chilly as it had moments before.

"How was your swim?" she asked.

"Nice."

"The pool was okay?"

"Not bad."

Nodding, she dropped her gaze to a scrawny squirrel that ran past. It looked as though it had just barely survived the winter. The ducks that swam past on the pond were in better condition. Of course, they'd been south.

"I loved that story," Greg mused quietly.

"Me too."

Make Way for the Ducklings had been an institution in Bart's home. No child who spent more than a day within the walls of the town house escaped a reading. Most children asked for seconds and thirds. Greg had. So had Diandra.

The ducks flew off, and across the pond a running child tripped and fell on the rambling root of a huge oak and began to cry.

Diandra sucked in a breath. Within seconds the child's mother arrived to soothe the wounds. Diandra released that breath.

Out of the corner of his eye, Greg watched her. The wind was blowing her hair around, so that he couldn't always see her face, but he'd seen the child fall, had heard her sharp intake of breath, and he was surprised. He hadn't pegged her as a woman who'd feel maternal instincts. Her own mother hadn't. Then again, maybe he was reading too much into her small gasp.

"Where's the necklace?" he asked.

She darted him a second's glance before homing in on the bridge, where foot traffic was picking up. "I'm wearing it."

A silent alarm went off in Greg's head. "That makes you mugging material."

"No one can see it. You're the only one who knows it's there. I'm not carrying a purse, and I don't have any other jewelry on. A mugger wouldn't look twice at me."

"Are you kidding?" he asked, raising his voice against all good intentions. "You don't have to be wearing jewels to attract attention. *Any* man would look twice at you just the way you are."

Diandra's lips twisted. "Funny, but that doesn't sound like a compliment," she said dryly.

"It's not. You shouldn't be walking around like bait."

"I'm not. I'm sitting. Quietly and unobtrusively."

"You shouldn't be alone."

"I'm not. You're here."

"I wasn't until a minute ago."

She did look at him down the length of the bench then, and said in a facetious tone, "If I didn't know better, I'd think you cared."

"Not quite," he replied, but his eyes held hers, and their warmth ignited an answering spark, which bounced back and forth, gaining heat with each turn.

Diandra was thinking that he looked rugged, not at all like the polished urbanite she'd always thought him to be. She was thinking that he looked good in jeans and shrunken sweatshirts and that, with his beard, he could have been a mountain man. There was something mysterious about mountain men. Something very masculine. Something silently appealing.

Greg was thinking that it had been a long time since he'd held a woman who fitted him as well as Diandra did. He was thinking that she had just enough height, just enough weight and that, with her hair blown awry and her cheeks pink and her face nearly naked, she was ripe for kissing. For holding. For making very thorough love to.

When he spoke again, his voice was a bit husky, a bit curious, a bit unsure. "Have you ever stopped to wonder what would happen if we didn't dislike each other so?"

Diandra was feeling the effect of his gaze from the top of her head to her toes. Heat seemed to be gathering in her chest. She had to swallow before she could speak. "No." She cleared her throat. "No, there's no point in wondering. We've always disliked each other. We always will."

"But we're attracted to each other," Greg said. He figured that they'd best get the problem out in the open since they were going to be working so closely together. "Do you deny it?"

She knew it would have been foolish to do so. He'd felt the response she'd made to his kiss. "I don't deny it."

"So?"

"So...what?"

"Can you handle it?"

She gave a sigh that was meant to sound bored. Unfortunately the effect was spoiled when it came out a shaky. "If you're asking whether I'm going to pounce on you and ravish you the minute we get back to the house, the answer is no. I can handle it, Greg. You're safe from me."

Greg wasn't so sure. Just the thought of Diandra pouncing on him had a provocative effect on his body—and that was before he'd even contemplated the ravishing part.

"Besides," she went on, needing to say something to give her argument force, "it's the necklace."

"What is?"

"The attraction between us."

Greg wasn't all that sure. "You really think so?"

She nodded, then looked away. She knew the necklace had *some* effect. Whether it was wholly responsible for the physical attraction was an interesting question. She wasn't sure if she was ready for the answer. "I think we have to keep busy," she said. She sought his eyes in earnest. "I think we should go back and get to work."

Having no better suggestion, Greg rose from the bench. Side by side, he and Diandra walked back to Charles Street, then up the hill to Bart's town house. They didn't talk. At no point did they touch. But they seemed to gain speed as they went, and by the time they were inside, they were ready to return to work.

With commendable resolve, they finished listing the

contents of the living room. When they moved into the den, though, things got tougher. They both liked the den. The idea of dismantling it—and packing books was one of the few things they felt safe doing even before they'd contacted Bart—was distasteful.

Moreover, the room was small. Intimate. They were working side by side at the shelves, and it seemed that wherever one turned, the other was there. Very much there. And close.

Though the den held a wealth of memories for them, none of those was as vivid as the memory of that earlier kiss; Diandra and Greg were both thinking it. Each knew the *other* was thinking it. That knowledge made for awareness, awkwardness and tension.

Halfway through the second bookshelf, Diandra had had it. Dropping the pad of paper on the desk, she escaped to the wingback chair. Her skin felt warm, her limbs shaky. She was sure that Greg was purposely taunting her, purposely standing near, purposely stretching to reach books in a way that emphasized his height and strength. He was a beast, she decided. A large, lean, hairy beast. And she wanted to touch him.

Since she couldn't do that, she sat in the chair and glared at him.

He glared right back, but he didn't say a word. Instead, he moved behind the desk, picked up the phone and called New York.

Diandra knew he was trying the office. She knew because the very same thought had crossed her own mind not long before, when she'd been wanting a reminder of who she was and where she'd come from. But her timing, like Greg's, was off.

"No one's there," she informed him.

He turned his back on her and listened to the repeated

ring of the phone that his private secretary should have answered.

"Greg, it's nearly seven o'clock at night," Diandra said impatiently. "No one's there."

He slammed the receiver down. "*We're* working. Why aren't they?"

"Because they've been working since eight-thirty this morning, while we've been piddling around, going swimming, taking walks—" she tossed a disgusted glance at the pad of paper "—making stupid lists." She turned beseeching eyes on him. "This is a monumental waste of effort. If Bart were here, he could tell us what he wants and what he doesn't, and what he wants done with what he doesn't want to keep."

Greg thrust his fingers through his hair, then rubbed the back of his neck. "We've been through this before, Diandra. Bart doesn't want to be here. That's why he sent *us*." Already, Greg regretted having agreed to come, and it wasn't only because he didn't like Diandra. Over the past few hours, he'd been tormented by the curve of her hip, the swell of her breast, the gloss of her hair, the graceful way she moved. He'd been tormented by the memory of how her body had felt against his, and he resented that. He needed to get out.

"But *anyone* can make lists," she was arguing.

Angrily he came around the desk and made for the door. Just beyond her chair, though, he changed his mind, turned back and put his hands on his hips. "Right. Anyone can. But Bart told us to do it." He paused and arched a tawny brow. "You want San Francisco?"

"Yes!"

"Well, so do I!"

"Then we should both leave. That'd solve the problem."

Greg held a hand toward the door. "Ladies before gentlemen."

She mimicked the gesture. "Age before beauty."

He didn't budge. "You go first. I dare you."

"Are you kidding? And let you stay here making dumb little lists? I'm not giving you San Francisco *that* easily." She squeezed her eyes shut, put her fists to either side of her head and said forcefully through gritted teeth, "This is the last thing I want to be doing with my life. I need a break. I'm tired. I'm hungry." Her eyes flew open when Greg grabbed one of her wrists and hauled her from the chair. "What are you *doing?*"

He was acting purely on impulse, as he'd rarely done before. "We're going out."

"Us? Together?" She pulled back on her hand and shook her head. "I don't think that's such a hot idea."

With a single tug, he pulled her against him. "You'd rather we stayed here?" he asked in a deep, vibrant voice. Still holding her wrist, he doubled her arm to her back. Though his grip was gentle, he held her firmly to his long, hard frame. "If you're looking for hot ideas, that's one." His eyes were dark and sensual, expressing everything they'd both been feeling being cooped up together for the past few hours.

Diandra didn't have to focus in on the warm hum in her veins to realize that his warning was worth heeding. Staying in the den—or anywhere in the town house, for that matter—wasn't the best of ideas just then.

"Out," she breathed. "We'll go out."

But suddenly Greg was having other ideas. The feel of Diandra against him was like heaven. "Then again," he drawled softly, "maybe we shouldn't. Maybe we should stay right here and see what happens."

"You don't want that," she said, looking nervously up at him. "You don't like me."

"True. But that doesn't mean it wouldn't be good between us."

When she tried to twist away, Greg circled her waist with his free arm, effectively locking her in.

"Let me go," she ordered.

Lowering his head, he put his mouth by her ear. "Is that what you really want?"

She closed her eyes. "Yes."

"Is it really?" he asked more hoarsely. "Come on, Diandra. The truth. Do you really want me to let you go, or should we explore whatever it is that's going on here." At the "here," he exerted a slight pressure at the small of her back. She felt it echo in her womb.

"It's the necklace," she cried. "That's all it is. The necklace is causing this...this..."

"Attraction? Need? Lust?"

"Yes!"

He held her back then, but only so that he could look at the necklace. For a long minute he was silent. Then he said in a near whisper, "It really is beautiful."

"I'm going to take it off."

His eyes rose to hers, but his voice was the same hushed sound it had been when he'd looked at the necklace. "No. Don't do that."

"It's causing trouble."

He gave a short shake of his head. "It has a soothing effect. It kills the anger. It makes things better."

But Diandra couldn't see the necklace, so she wasn't experiencing a soothing. Nor, though, was she feeling anger. She was feeling...she was feeling Greg's broad chest against her breasts, his tapering torso and muscular thighs supporting her softer frame. She was also feeling his sex, firm and heavy, nestled snugly against hers.

Her body felt hot and alive.

In desperation, she took her free hand from his chest, where it had been holding him off, and touched the gems. Her fingers slid over emeralds, skittered over diamonds, traced gold. Filling her lungs with fresh air, she felt the soothing, and she understood what Greg had been trying to say. He'd been feeling anger, and the necklace had blunted it. She'd been feeling acute desire, and the necklace softened it.

Deepened it.

Enhanced it.

Aware of a trembling in her knees, she looked up at Greg, but he was engrossed in the necklace. Releasing her wrist, he brought his hand to her throat. He touched an emerald, then a cluster of diamonds. Then, using both hands, he gently eased open the collar of her shirt so that he could see the stones better.

Without his arms binding her, Diandra was free. She told herself to turn and run, but she couldn't. She could do nothing but hold her breath, because suddenly his fingers weren't touching the necklace. They were touching her skin. Very lightly. Very gently.

His eyes sought hers, capturing her in bounds of another sort and holding her while his fingertips skimmed her flesh. They brushed the tender skin beneath her jaw, slid down over her throat to a point just above the necklace, traced its outline. Then they skipped over the gems and continued the tracing, on the lower edge this time. That brought them under her shirt and around the back of her neck, then back over her shoulders and down, down to a point beneath the diamond fringe where her breasts formed a small cleavage.

With devastating slowness, he ran a single fingertip along first one gentle swell, then the other. And as if that weren't enough to set Diandra on fire, his coal-dark eyes smoldered with desire.

"Greg, stop," she whispered with mere remnants of breath.

"Let's make love," he whispered back. Wrapping one arm around her, he lowered his head and began to nuzzle her neck.

Diandra thought she'd faint. The feel of his beard against her skin was erotic in itself, but even beyond that, his mouth drove her wild. It moved moistly over the spot where her pulse beat a rapid tattoo.

Her legs felt like putty. Helplessly she shut her eyes and leaned into him for support, while her hands closed over fistfuls of his shirt. Driven by weak shreds of reason, she whimpered his name in protest.

Greg was more aroused than he'd been in months and months, but he wasn't so far gone that he didn't get her message. "Why not?" he asked in a voice that was muffled against her skin.

"Because…"

"That's not a good reason."

"Because…we're not…lovers."

"We could be," he coaxed. "Say the word and we could be. I want you, Diandra."

She could feel it. Lord, she could. He was richly aroused. "You'll regret it in the morning. *I*'ll regret it in the morning."

"But do you want me now?" When she didn't answer, he held her back. When she refused to meet his gaze, he caught her chin and tipped up her face. "Do you want me?" he asked again. More so even than the dictate of his voice, the command of his eyes evoked her response.

"Yes!" she cried, then whispered, "I want you. But I won't make love with you."

Feeling the brunt of frustration, Greg took an unsteady breath. "Just because you don't like me? Since when does that matter?"

She stiffened. "What does that mean?"

"Come on, Diandra. You're not an innocent."

"I'm not sure I know what you're getting at."

"Your other lovers—was liking them a prerequisite to sex?"

The implicit accusation, coming from any other man at any other time, would have set her off like a bomb. But having been so aroused short moments before, Diandra was feeling vulnerable.

"Don't," she said, shaking her head.

"Don't what?"

"Make generalizations based on what you want to believe. You don't know me."

"I know more than you think."

"No." She pulled away from him and, wrapping her arms around her middle, moved out of reach. "You made certain judgments about my mother, and you're assuming the same things hold for me. But you were wrong about her, and you're wrong about me. You *don't* know me, Greg, and that's as good a reason as any for our not making love."

The hurt in her eyes was as clear as the pallor of her skin. Greg noted both and surprised himself by feeling remorse. He wasn't about to believe that she was a saint, any more than he'd ever believe it about her mother, but he didn't like that look of hurt. It bothered him—particularly knowing he'd put it there himself.

Bowing his head, he took several slow breaths. When he looked back up, he felt in control once more. Holding his head high, he said, "I think we're back to square one.

I'm going out. Do you want to come, or would you rather stay here alone?"

As reluctant as Diandra was to go out with Greg, she was more reluctant to stay alone. She spent far too many nights alone as it was, and on this particular night, if her mind were idle it would have a field day. She needed to be occupied. She wanted a break. Since she wasn't about to go out on the town by herself, she guessed going with Greg was the lesser of the evils.

"I'll come."

Feeling an absurd sense of relief, he nodded and headed for the door, but Diandra wasn't moving so fast.

"Where to, Greg? I can't go anywhere fancy. I don't have the clothes."

He turned at the door and said, "Neither do I," which was ironic, given their occupations, but understandable, given the purpose of their trip. "I don't want fancy. I want casual and relaxed. Down to earth. Plebeian. I want to get something to eat. Walk around a little."

That all sounded comfortable to Diandra. And safe. "The Marketplace?"

He signaled his agreement with a small nod, then left to retrieve his sweatshirt. Soon after, he and Diandra were walking under the arches of the State House toward Faneuil Hall.

The Marketplace was perfect—just crowded enough, just loud enough, just busy enough. The atmosphere was positive and contagious. Diandra found herself relaxing. She didn't even mind when, guiding her one way or another, Greg put a light hand on her waist. The gesture was natural and nonthreatening.

For a time they went with the flow of the crowd, window-shopping, stopping to watch the street performers, ambling past one food booth after another. Unfortunately, when they decided to stop for dinner, it seemed that everyone else had the same idea. The restaurant lines were long. Greg, who'd been known to walk out of a restaurant when his reservation wasn't honored to the minute, wasn't in the mood to wait. So they did something neither of them had done in years and years. They returned to the food booths and picked up something here and something there, sharing most everything they bought, enjoying every last bite.

"Not the healthiest way to eat," Diandra remarked, using a paper napkin to wipe her hands of pizza grease. She'd already decided to avoid the bathroom scale the next morning.

Greg wasn't thinking about the scale as much as his doctor's warnings. He'd eaten several egg rolls, a chili dog, half of the taco that had been too hot for Diandra, and not one, not two, but three slices of pizza. "We'll live," he said in a droll tone, "and if we don't, at least we'll die happy." He steered her clear of a demon in a wheelchair and grinned. "There's something about eating junk food that boosts the spirits."

Diandra took his grin companionably. "I think it has to do with breaking the rules."

"Mmm. Our lives must be too structured. Too many formal dinners with rock cornish game hens—"

"And wild rice. Why always wild rice?"

"Beats me." As they ambled on, he looked down at her. "Are you tired?"

"No."

"Feel like going to Harvard Square?"

Her eyes lit up. "I haven't been there in ages."

"Me neither, but there's a bookstore that's open late— at least, it used to be open late. It could be we'd make the trip for nothing."

"Not that we have anything better to do," she reminded him.

"No," he said more quietly, then spread a hand on the back of the leather jacket and gently urged her out a side door of the arcade. "The Square is only ten minutes by T. If the bookstore's closed, something else will be open. We won't be bored."

The last thing on Diandra's mind was being bored. She felt extraordinarily relaxed and was having a good time. For the first time since she could remember, she didn't feel pressure either to look good or act properly executive or be witty or bright or intriguing. None of those things mattered. She knew people in Boston, but the chances were nil that those particular people would be walking these particular streets—let alone riding the T—at ten-thirty on a Tuesday night. And as for Greg, he didn't count. He didn't like her anyway, so it didn't matter what she said or did, or didn't say or do. As a result, she felt incredibly free.

Greg did, too, if the look of laid-back indulgence he wore was any indication. "I feel like I'm out on furlough," he said after they'd easily found seats on the half-empty train, which then began to rumble its way toward Cambridge. He grunted. "Strange that riding the subway should be a treat. That says something about one's life."

Diandra knew what he meant, but she wasn't in the mood to be philosophical. She was enjoying the rhythm of the train, the graffiti on the walls, the other passengers. "This place has character," she said with a grin.

Greg took in the grin. He took in the gentleness of her features, in such contrast to the "on" look she usually wore, and he wondered if she were truly enjoying herself, or simply too tired to be on. He'd never seen her quite that way, even at family gatherings. She always looked beautiful.

Now she looked pretty, and there was a difference. He wondered if pretty was what turned him on.

They were sitting close beside each other, so he barely had to breathe for his voice to carry. "Where's the necklace?"

She patted the leather jacket where it snapped at her throat.

He nodded.

Leaning closer, she whispered, "It doesn't really have power, does it, Greg?"

Greg's eyes were on his and Diandra's reflection in the pitch-black of the train window. They looked for all the world like a couple very much involved with each other. "I don't know."

"Can an inanimate object have power?"

"I don't know as I'd call that thing inanimate. Whenever I look at it, it seems alive."

She shivered. "You make me feel like I'm wearing a snake." Repulsed by that thought, she turned to more whimsical ones. "We know that the necklace is old. We know from the inscription that it was originally given in love. Maybe the stones do have some mystical quality."

Greg was ready to believe most anything. Here he was, sitting beside his long-time enemy in a slightly decrepit subway car, heading for a late-night bookstore at an hour when he was most often at home studying spreadsheets—and he was perfectly contented. Oh, yes, he was ready to believe something about those stones.

"We really should try Bart," Diandra said. She, too, saw the reflection in the glass, and though she knew she was probably sitting too close to Greg, she didn't move. She felt comfortable. Protected. Warm in all the right spots.

"There's more we can do by way of cataloging things before we need him."

She hesitated, then said, "About the necklace. Shouldn't we call him about the necklace?"

Greg mulled that over for a minute. "The way I see it," he decided, "Frederick was right. No one seems to be missing it, which means that Bart has to have been the one responsible for having it left on the mantel. Since he hasn't called to see if we've found it, why should we be concerned?"

There were any number of valid reasons why they should be concerned, Diandra knew, the major one being the sheer value of the piece. She also knew, though, that she didn't want to part with the necklace just yet. It did something; she knew it did. After all, she and Greg had been out together for several hours and neither of them had stormed off in a rage. Something had to be responsible for that.

Harvard Square was the same, yet not the same. The university spires were still there, as were the Coop and landmarks like the Out-of-Town News Agency and the Wursthaus, but redevelopers had been busy turning old brick buildings into chic minimalls. The stores and restaurants had definitely taken aim at yuppiedom.

The bookstore Greg had in mind was there, and open. They went in and browsed for better than an hour, moving from one rack to the next, one aisle to the next. Though they were often separated by books and people, if Diandra had been asked at any given moment where Greg was she'd have immediately been able to say.

And vice versa. In fact, Greg suspected he spent as much time looking between shelves at Diandra as he did thumbing through books.

When they finally left the store, they walked quietly back along Brattle Street. "Want some coffee?" he asked.

She smiled her thanks, but shook her head.

He looked down at her. "Tired?"

"Getting there."

"Should we take a cab back?"

She came to life then. "And spoil it all? No! I like being part of the masses." She wasn't ready to have the evening end. She wasn't ready to be confined in a small place with Greg. Just thinking of it was enough to stir sensitivities deep inside.

As it happened, though, the T ride back wasn't as carefree as the one out had been. The car was nearly empty, for one thing, which made for an intimacy of its own. For another thing, it was later at night than before, the time when sane folk were at home in bed, curled up in a lover's arms.

At least, that was what Greg was thinking. He'd always had an image of the way his life would be one day—coming home to an intimate dinner with his woman, spending quiet time with her, talking, laughing softly, going to bed together. If there was sex, great, if not, fine, because the important thing would be the closeness.

Thinking about that closeness now, he was confused, because he was feeling something like closeness to Diandra. And that couldn't be. He desired her. He didn't like her. She was too aggressive for his tastes, too contrary for comfort, too flighty where men were concerned. And sly… He knew that if he didn't watch out, she was more than capable of stealing San Francisco from under his nose.

Still, he felt that closeness. And desire.

It had to be the necklace.

Whatever its cause, he was thinking more and more about holding her as they emerged from the subway and walked back to the town house. She had her hands tucked safely in the pockets of the jacket, and her head was bowed, but the way she tossed him occasional glances, the way she pressed her lips together, then moistened them, the way she stayed close by his side suggested that she, too, felt the pull.

Opening the front door, Greg stood back and let her pass. She slipped out of the jacket and, when he took it from her hands to hang it up, murmured a soft thank-you. She didn't look at him, though, and by the time he was done she was halfway up the stairs.

"No good-night kiss?" he called in desperation.

She stopped on the stairs, bowed her head and said, "I don't think that'd be a good idea."

"Because you know it wouldn't stop there." He began the climb. "You know we'd end up in bed."

"We wouldn't. I wouldn't let us."

"Like you didn't let yourself respond to me before?"

When he came up behind her, she closed her eyes. She could feel his presence, feel it to her core. "Don't do this, Greg. It's been a nice night. Don't spoil it."

"I'm trying to make it even nicer."

She opened her eyes and turned to find him one step below her, which set them roughly at eye level with each other. While that didn't exactly give Diandra an advantage, it minimized Greg's. "No, you're not. You're trying to reduce the night to its lowest common denominator. Why can't you leave well enough alone?"

"Because I want you."

She shook her head. "Not good enough."

"You want me."

"Leave it, Greg."

"Just a kiss."

"No." She breathed out a sad sigh. "Kisses complicate things. I've got enough to handle without them." Turning, she continued on her way up the stairs, turned and climbed the second flight, then let herself into her room and shut the door.

If she'd yelled at him, called him a lecher, even told him he was a lousy kisser, Greg would have gone after her in a minute. But she'd been tired, sad and confused, and that had taken some of the punch out of the ache in his groin.

Actually the ache had moved to his stomach. He realized it when the last of desire faded, and he knew then that he was about to pay the piper for eating egg rolls, taco and pizza. He went to his room, took a healthy dose of antacid, then showered and went to bed knowing that if he was lucky the antacid would soothe the discomfort enough for him to sleep.

It wasn't his lucky night. He was still awake an hour later, and if the antacid had had any effect, he couldn't feel it. His punishment for disobedience was taking the form of real stomach pain—not intense enough to worry about, but strong enough to hurt.

He tossed and turned for a while, trying this position or that in search of a comfortable one. When he didn't find it, he got out of bed and tried walking around. When that didn't help, he went down to the kitchen, warmed a glass of milk, drank half of it as he wandered through the second-floor rooms, then returned to his bedroom and, propped up against the oak headboard, drank the rest.

It was there that Diandra found him a short time later. Used to the silence of living alone, she'd awoken when he'd first gone downstairs. She'd heard sounds coming from the kitchen, then silence, then the creak of the stairs, then silence again.

Something wasn't right. She felt odd. Holding a hand to the necklace, which in turn clung to her neck, she climbed from bed, crept to her door and, careful not to make a sound, opened it. Greg's room was around a corner, but even from her door she could see that his light was on. Walking softly, she went down the hall.

He was slouched against the headboard with two pillows bunched behind him, the sheet around his hips, one knee bent and an arm thrown over his eyes. All of him that showed above the sheet was bare, and she couldn't help but stare in appreciation.

His chest was beautiful. Large but not bulky, it was a canvas of tight muscle and lean flesh covered by swirls of tawny hair. His middle was a plane of sinewed ripples, his belly curved to accommodate his position. The tendons in his upper arm stood out in relief, as did the veins in his forearm. His fingers dangled limply.

She could have looked at him over and over again, but her gaze kept returning to those fingers. The Greg she knew was solid and strong, not limp. Something was wrong.

"Greg? Are you okay?"

His arm flew from his eyes. He held it in midair for a minute while he registered her sudden appearance. Then, knowing that he was in no shape to properly appreciate the fact that she was wearing nothing but an old football jersey and the emerald necklace, he returned his arm to his eyes.

"I'm okay."

But she'd seen otherwise when he'd uncovered his face. He was pale and tired, and that alarmed her. "Aren't you feeling well?"

"Something I ate didn't sit right."

"I ate everything you did and I'm fine," she said gently, "so it couldn't be food poisoning."

"It's not."

She noticed the glass on the nightstand, noticed the white film of the milk that he must have drunk, noticed the roll of antacid tablets nearby. She looked again at his face, but between his beard and his arm, little was left to see.

Then he made a small movement, the tiniest shift of his middle, and she realized that he was truly uncomfortable.

"Is there anything I can do?"

"No. Thanks."

"Are you sure?"

"Uh-huh."

"Will you call me if it gets worse?"

"It won't."

Diandra wasn't sure whether that was sheer determination speaking or the voice of experience. She did know that it bothered her that he was sick, and that she felt inordinately helpless. She wasn't a Florence Nightingale. She didn't know what to do, and even if she had, Greg wasn't inviting her help. There wasn't much she could do but go back to bed.

"Well…good night, then," she murmured. "I'll see you in the morning." She lingered at his door for another minute, but when he didn't respond, she quietly left.

Back in her own bed, as she stared at the door she'd left open in case he called, she realized a second heavy truth of the day. Not only did she desire Greg, but somewhere inside her there was the capacity for feeling gentle toward him.

Either the necklace was truly to blame, or she was in trouble.

CHAPTER SIX

DIANDRA WASN'T SURPRISED when she slept until ten the next morning. She'd lain in bed for a long time the night before listening for sounds of distress in Greg's room, and when she finally fell asleep she slept lightly. Sometime about dawn she'd awakened and crept down the hall. His light was out, but enough of a haze crept in through the window to show that he was sleeping soundly. Only then did she do the same.

She would probably have slept even later than ten had it not been for the repeated peal of the door chimes. It took her a minute to remember that Frederick was gone, and then she jumped out of bed, grabbed the shirt she'd worn the day before and drew it on over her jersey. Barefoot, she ran down the two sets of stairs and peered through the peephole of the front door, only to sag against the door, then straighten and steel herself before opening it.

"Uncle Alex," she said, clutching the neckline of the shirt and trying to look dignified in a totally undignified outfit. "What a surprise!"

"The surprise was mine when I learned you were here," Alex said a bit archly as he plopped a perfunctory kiss on her cheek. Without pause, he stepped into the hall and closed the door, then gave her an admonishing once-over. "Not exactly the cream of our lingerie department."

She didn't have to return the look to know that her uncle was impeccably dressed. He was a handsome man, made even more handsome by his good taste in clothes. Standing before him now in an old football jersey and a wrinkled shirt, with her hair a mess, her legs showing from midthigh down and her face totally bare, she felt outclassed.

"I'm off duty," she explained.

"That's not what I heard. I heard you were here to close up this place for Bart," he mumbled under his breath. "The old goat. He knew he'd have to sell it quickly or I'd make a bid, and he couldn't bear the thought of that."

Diandra wasn't sure if she was ready for cold warfare first thing in the morning, so she changed the subject by asking, "How's Aunt Ellen?"

Mercifully Alex went with her lead. His voice returned to normal. "Just fine. She sends her love. Wonders whether you'll come to the house for dinner one night while you're here."

Diandra could think of any number of things she'd rather do. "Uh, I don't know if I'll have time. I'd like to clear things up and get back to Washington as soon as possible. Thank her for asking, though."

"Well, keep it in mind. The invitation's open." The words were barely out of his mouth when he raised his eyes.

Diandra turned to see Greg leave the staircase. He wore nothing but a pair of low-slung jeans, and with his hair ruffled and his eyes only half-open there was no doubt as to where he'd been moments before.

"How are you, Alex?" he asked in a sleep-roughened voice. Coming to stand by Diandra's shoulder, he offered his hand. Although he didn't care for Alex personally, he always tried to maintain the amicable professional relationship Bart had established.

"Not bad," Alex said, but his voice had a new edge to it. He looked at Diandra, openly disapproving. "When I heard that the two of you were here together, I thought I'd better come over to make sure one of you hadn't killed the other. It looks like I was worried about the wrong thing."

Only then did Diandra realize the picture she and Greg made. She opened her mouth to protest, but Greg beat her to it. His voice was suddenly clearer, deeper, more dangerous.

"That's quite a conclusion you've reached."

"Do you blame me?" Alex asked. "It's ten o'clock on a Wednesday morning, and the two of you look like you've just rolled out of bed."

Greg moved closer to Diandra. "We have."

"Separate beds," Diandra stressed, but she held her position. "I don't believe you, Uncle Alex. You know how I feel about Greg—*and* how he feels about me. What were you thinking?"

Alex stared at her in silence.

She'd seen him stare that way before, not at her but at her mother. Abby had taken it in stride, simply tossing her head and turning away. Diandra was nowhere near as calm. "Bart sent the two of us here to go through this place," she said tightly, "and it'd be pretty stupid for one of us to stay in a hotel. But believe me, neither of us wants to be here—together or at all." Resentful at having to make explanations, she raised her chin. "And even if something *were* going on, it wouldn't matter. I'm an adult. I can do what I want."

"True," Alex said grimly. "I just hope that when you do what you want, you know what you're doing."

"Always," she asserted, then set her jaw and waited for him to make the next move.

It was Greg, standing so close and bare that she felt the warmth of his skin through two layers of shirts, who tired of the standoff first. He ran a hand over his face and said,

"It's too early in the morning for this. How about a rain check, Alex?"

Alex was standing stiffly. "No need. I just stopped by to say hello and to tell you that if there's anything you want while you're in town, you're to call."

"That's kind. Thank you."

Diandra remained silent.

With a final sharp look and a nod, Alex turned and left.

The instant the door was closed, she took off for the kitchen, where she angrily set to putting coffee on. By the time the beans had been ground and water was dripping through, she'd calmed down a bit. She turned to lean against the counter, then jumped when she saw Greg at the door.

The thought that he'd been watching her without her knowing it irked her. "Haven't you got anything better to do than to stand there gawking?"

"I'm not gawking."

"You're right. You're just standing there as calmly as you please." She pointed a finger toward the front door. "Didn't it bother you, what he said? He thought we were sleeping together!"

"So?"

"So we're not! But you know what's going to happen now, don't you? The grapevine will be humming."

"So?"

"So that's disgusting!"

Tucking his hands in the waistband of his jeans, Greg looked totally unconcerned. "Aren't you overreacting a little?"

"No! There's no *way* I'd sleep with you. You are arrogant, selfish, competitive to the point of being ruthless, scrupulous only when it suits you and when it doesn't you're as unscrupulous as the next. On top of all that, you're a playboy."

Yet he stirred her. She didn't understand why, since he'd been a thorn in her side for as long as she could remember, but he did stir her. Wearing nothing but jeans—all long, trim, hair-spattered body—he was more man than she'd run into in thirty-two years. And it was a waste, since they were destined to be rivals.

"What grapevine have *you* been listening to?" he asked, but his back was turned before he finished, and she soon found herself alone.

With only the sounds of brewing coffee to break the silence, his words echoed in the air for a long time. *"What grapevine...what grapevine...what grapevine..."*

Only after she had returned to her room, showered and dressed, then come back to the kitchen for a second cup of coffee did she admit that he was right. She had listened to grapevines, so many that she couldn't begin to remember where and who. It seemed she'd been picking up little tidbits about Greg forever—not that she was obsessed, simply guarding her own interests. After all, her reasoning went, if she was to protect herself from Greg, she had to know what he was about.

So she'd listened to gossip, though she knew how unreliable it could be—and when it came to Greg, she wasn't objective to begin with. She heard what she wanted to hear, believed what she wanted to believe. If the truth were told, she didn't know much about him at all.

And that, she realized, was something to remedy.

Pouring him a cup of coffee—and making it light, then lighter still when she thought about the night before—she carried it along with her own into the den. Having tossed on a sweatshirt since their last encounter, Greg was sitting on the floor holding a small book. He set it aside when she approached and eyed first her then the mug with caution.

She held it out as an olive branch. When, after what seemed an endless minute, he reached up and took it, she breathed a little more freely. Sinking into the chair, she laid her head back and said, "You were right. I overreacted when Alex was here. He gets to me sometimes."

"I'd have thought you and he would be close."

"Because he was my mother's twin?" She shook her head. "Except for looks, they were very different. She had more energy, more flair. She overshadowed him, and he resented that. So he took delight in putting her down—though I'm not sure he understood what he was doing and why. I'm not sure it was a conscious thing at all." She averted her eyes. "They say blood runs thicker than water, but even when things started falling apart, he wasn't supportive. I don't think he knew how much that hurt." She frowned and added in a grim voice, "Then again, maybe he did."

Greg suddenly wondered who had hurt more—Abby, or her sixteen-year-old daughter. If Diandra was telling the truth about Alex's criticism of Abby, Greg could understand why Diandra had reacted so strongly to his accusation. It had hit too close. She felt history was repeating itself.

Greg knew for a fact that the present accusation was unfounded. Not that he wouldn't change that. He still wanted Diandra. She was all the more appealing sitting in her chair looking a little bruised. Though he'd never seen himself as a healer, he could think of a number of enticing ways to soothe her.

That is, assuming she was legitimately bruised and not just acting the part. He wasn't sure how far to trust her. Old habits died hard.

Unaware of the dark turn of his thoughts, Diandra

was still thinking about Alex. "He didn't ask about the necklace."

Greg shifted his gaze from her face to the jewels and felt the incredible instant lightening that he was coming to expect. "He must not have seen it under your things."

She fingered an emerald. "But if he'd known about it—*anything* about it—he'd have asked. And he didn't. He didn't look guilty or suspicious or even curious."

They both sat quietly for a minute. Then Greg sighed. "It was Bart. It had to have been Bart."

"But what would he be doing with a necklace like this? Why would he have let someone leave it out on the mantel? I'm sure there are plenty of other jewels in his vault. Why isn't the necklace with them?"

Greg shrugged. "Maybe he thought he'd give us a thrill. It's a magnificent piece. Maybe he wanted us to see it for the sheer appreciation of it. Beneath all his bluff, Bart is a sentimental guy. Maybe he's a romantic, too."

She chuckled. "Anyone who makes *Make Way for the Ducklings* required reading for guests *has* to be a romantic." She focused in on the small book that Greg was picking up again. "What's that?"

He held it in his lap. "A book of poems. It's very old. He inscribed it to Emma, but from the notes in the margins it looks like he's been through it many times himself. I found it in the desk when I was looking for a pen."

"Poems?" She smiled and added on a note of surprise, "That's really sweet."

Greg had thought so, too, even though he knew more about Bart than most. "Most people think of him as a very organized, very shrewd, very efficient businessman. They'd never imagine that he was a packrat at home, but you wouldn't believe what he has hidden away behind these doors." He tossed his head toward the cabinets behind him.

Instantly curious, Diandra crossed to the cabinets, drew them open and dropped to her haunches to study their contents. Her eyes grew wider as she pulled out one bunch of papers, then another, then a pile of plastic bags filled with even more papers.

Lifting one of those plastic bags, she carefully reached in and withdrew the front pages of three separate newspapers, a handful of loose clippings and an assortment of handwritten letters. Selecting one at random, she read,

"Dear Bart, Just wanted to let you know how much we enjoyed ourselves at the party last Sunday. Juliet is a gem. It's hard to believe that she's just graduated from medical school. It must be even harder for you to believe that you have a granddaughter who is a doctor. You must be very proud. Enjoy her, and thanks again for including us in the festivities.

Most fondly,
Ethel and Brian Wright."

With growing amazement, Diandra quickly skimmed the newspapers, then the clippings. "These are the front pages of papers that were published on the day of Juliet's graduation."

Greg was looking through another plastic bag. "Same thing here, only this one's from the day of the christening of my cousin Tommy's first son, Bart's great-grandson. The invitation to the christening is here, several telegrams, the guest list."

Settling onto the floor, Diandra tugged out more bags. "He has them arranged chronologically, starting with recent events and working back." She flipped through. "Here's the big fund-raiser that was held in the Beverly Hills store eight years ago. And Joanna's wedding. And the grand opening in St. Louis." She looked up in time to see Greg take a shoe box from the bottom of the cabinet. "What's there?"

He removed the lid.

She caught a breath in delight. "Pictures? He saved pictures, too?" Shifting so that she was sitting flush to Greg's side, she looked on as he took out a handful of photos. They were old, black-and-white, faded to a misty brown. "These must have come from the original Kodak Brownie," she quipped, then asked, "Who is that?"

Greg studied the picture and turned it over, looking for identification on the back. There was none. "If I were to make a guess, I'd say the big guy is Bart's older brother, Henry Junior, and the little guy is Bart himself."

Entranced, Diandra pointed to a second picture. "And this one?"

"Bart's mother and aunt…or vice versa."

"Look at the clothes. Look at the car in the background. Look at the expressions! You'd think they were about to be shot."

"They were, euphemistically speaking."

Diandra laughed softly at that. "They look so sober." She urged his hand to the next picture. "I want to see more."

So did Greg. Studying one photo after another, he had a sense of history unraveling in his hand. Though there were many faces in the earliest pictures that they didn't recognize, Diandra was right—the clothes, the cars, the expressions were priceless.

Increasingly, as the time of the pictures advanced, they did recognize faces. Not only did they see aunts, uncles and cousins in younger days, but they saw their parents.

Two good-looking couples. A close foursome. Looking at the linked arms and smiling faces, they found it hard to believe that the future would hold what it did.

Less comfortable with those pictures than with the first, Greg slid a second shoe box from the cabinet. Balancing the box on his thigh, he let Diandra skim through. It didn't take her long to discover that they'd come upon the Thanksgiving pictures.

For as long as either of them could remember, it had been a tradition for the Caseys and the Yorks to celebrate Thanksgiving together. Diandra's grandfather had first started the custom soon after the store had begun to grow and the families had spread out; he'd wanted at least one reunion a year. When he'd died, Bart had faithfully carried on the practice.

At first, the gatherings had been held at one or another of the families' homes, and they'd been times of overall good cheer. After Diandra's mother and Greg's father had died, when there had been more tension between the clans, Bart had initiated the custom of gathering everyone on neutral ground for the long holiday weekend. They'd gone to Jamaica one year, Aruba another, St. Croix, St. Kitts, Guadaloupe and Martinique.... It had worked. Despite individual personality clashes, the vacation atmosphere had survived and the Thanksgiving tradition remained intact.

Diandra held up a picture taken on one of the more recent trips. "St. Bart's, three years ago." She smiled. "It was nice down there. Very French."

"Uh-huh."

Once she would have sent him a scathing look. Now she simply teased, "Don't sound so neutral. You spent the entire time on the beach, which just happened to be topless."

"I spent the entire time on the beach because I was exhausted and it was the only place I could get some rest. Your cousin had his six kids along. Once they discovered I could wiggle my ears, they wouldn't leave me alone. They drove me nuts."

"They're sweet kids—"

"When they're asleep." He pulled up another picture. "Santo Domingo."

"Ah, yes," she said wryly, "Santo Domingo. That was the year our reservations came through wrong and we ended up in a hole-in-the-wall where they had no idea what Thanksgiving was. Bart had to send home for turkey. It arrived the day after we left."

On impulse, she dug out a picture from the back of the box, took one look and gasped. "Look at us." There were at least twelve children in the shot, posed randomly on a cluster of rocks overlooking the sea. "I couldn't have been more than five." Her voice took on a humorous hush. "And you—without a beard."

"Without whiskers, period. Sorry to disappoint you," he drawled, "but I wasn't into puberty when I was ten."

At the sensuous note in his voice, her eyes flew to his. Only then did she realize how closely she was wrapped to his side. Subconsciously she'd gravitated to his warmth, and his body hadn't turned her away. She'd been comfortable, unaware of doing anything provocative or improper. Now, though, she started to straighten.

"Don't," he murmured, vaguely confused. He'd been enjoying the closeness. "It's okay."

Looking as confused as he, she gave a tiny shake of her head. It wasn't okay. It was too comfortable in ways that would lead to no good. She tried to remember whether her chin had touched his shoulder or her breast his arm, but the only recollection she had was of a general rightness.

Which puzzled her all the more.

With as little fanfare as possible, she slid to a safer spot against the open cabinet door, wrapped her arms around her bent knees and nodded toward the box.

Greg withdrew a new handful of pictures, thumbed

through the first few, held up the third for her to see. "Remember that?"

"Sure. That was at my Aunt Helene's in Westchester." She studied the picture. "I was twelve."

"I was seventeen." He hissed out a soft breath. "Lord I was young."

"Young and randy. You were after everything in skirts— the maids, Uncle Herman's private secretary, even your own cousin's fiancée."

"I wasn't 'after' them," he argued innocently. "I was just being friendly. I was a senior in high school and feeling pretty important. All guys go through stages like that."

"You were flirting."

"You *thought* I was flirting because that was what you chose to see. I was being friendly. Period." He paused, then set off on a different tack. "And why not? I'd had to leave my own bunch of friends behind for the weekend, and I was into a heavy social phase. The family friends I wanted to see had managed to fink out on me—John was on an exchange program in France and Brice had just had an appendectomy. The adults thought I was a kid; the kids annoyed me. So I talked to the women in between." When Diandra rolled her eyes, he added an indignant "I had to talk to *someone*. You wouldn't give me the time of day. You were as stuck-up as hell."

She frowned. "Stuck-up? I was never stuck-up."

"You sure were."

"You really thought that?"

He nodded. "You stayed off by yourself— No, you were with your cousin Betsy most of the time, and she was so obnoxious that I steered clear. But even when you were with her, you were above it all, and when you were alone, you were *totally* unapproachable."

Diandra was taken aback. She'd never thought herself

unapproachable. True, she'd been guarded whenever Greg was around, because she'd been burned once too often. But unapproachable? Or stuck-up?

"I wasn't stuck-up. I was shy."

He laughed. "That's a good one."

"I was," she insisted. She wanted him to know the truth. "When I was twelve, when that picture was taken—and for several years after—I was *painfully* shy. I felt as though I wasn't anywhere near as bright or attractive as every other girl." She paused. "Or woman." She paused again, then blurted out, "My mother was vivacious. She was poised, witty, the life of every party. And she was beautiful. I wasn't. I lived in her shadow."

Greg would have laughed at the absurdity of her claim had it not been for the earnestness of her expression. There was no doubt that she believed what she was saying. She might have been every bit as bright and attractive as every other girl, or as poised and witty as her mother, but she hadn't thought so. And that was what counted.

Uncomfortable with the compassion he felt, he tried to focus on a negative he did know about. Shuffling through several more pictures, he singled one out. "This was taken a year or two later. Look how you're standing, separate from the rest of us, looking angry. You were always snippy then. Perverse. You jumped at the slightest bait."

Diandra felt a dull ache as she studied the photograph. Oh, yes, she remembered. That dress. That vile dress. She'd had a huge argument with her mother over that dress. Abby had loved it. Diandra had hated it.

"If I ever have a daughter," Diandra vowed quietly, "I will be superattuned to her growing pains." Dropping her legs into a crossed position, she braced her hands on her thighs. "My fourteenth year was the pits. I wasn't smiling there—I never smiled—because I had braces and they looked ugly. Everyone else was getting theirs off, and I was getting mine on. That was because my teeth were two years behind my age—" she held up a hand "—but that wasn't surprising, since my *body* was two years behind, too. My friends had all developed, but I was totally flat. My mother said that my hair was adorable long and straight and pulled back with a ribbon, but I hated it. I wanted curls. And curves. I wanted to be pretty." She let out a breath. "I felt gauche. Out of it. I was constantly on the defensive."

Greg was surprised by her calm. "You were pretty then," he told her and meant it.

"I was not. I was backward."

"Was it so important that you look like your friends?"

She brushed her bangs from her brow with a forearm. "I've always been a competitor. I felt that I could do whatever I wanted—and be the best at it—if I tried hard enough." She frowned. "Puberty didn't respond to that kind of thinking. But the competitive angle tells only half the story. I didn't want to look like my friends, as much as I wanted to look like a woman. And yes, it was important. Identifying with a peer group is part of growing up. I was having trouble identifying with *any* group."

"Your parents couldn't help you over that rough stretch?"

She sputtered out a half-laugh. "My father thought I was just perfect the way I was. He adored me. He refused to hear that anything was wrong."

"And your mother?"

"My mother—" Her voice quavered, then steadied. "My mother was too busy to listen. If she wasn't having lunch with a friend, she was at a meeting of the hospital auxiliary or the garden club." Leaning forward, Diandra took the pictures from Greg's hand, flipped quickly through to a print she'd known would be there. Her hand shook slightly as she held it out. "I was fifteen when that was taken. Do you remember Thanksgiving of that year?"

Greg did. "We were at my aunt's place in Southampton." He stared at the picture. "One year made a big difference. You looked like a woman there."

"Uh-huh," Diandra said tightly. "I had popped out, all right. All of a sudden, I found myself with the body I'd been dying to have, and I didn't know what in the devil to do with it." She nodded toward the picture. "That Thanksgiving was probably the most miserable one of my life. I had gotten my period for the first time, the very first time. I had terrible cramps. I was terrified of going to the bathroom. And my mother was out somewhere with your father." Her voice fell to a whisper, as her anger dissolved into pain. "I needed her, and she wasn't there."

Feeling a desperate urge to move, she jumped up and crossed the room. She put her hand flat on a row of books, took a step back and looked down, then turned to lean back against the shelves with her arms wrapped around her middle.

"I'm sure it wasn't intentional on her part." She rushed the words out, trying to make up for sounding disloyal. "I'm sure she'd have been there if she'd known what I was feeling."

Greg wasn't so sure. He didn't credit Abby with having had anything in her character remotely related to self-sacrifice, which meant that if she was enjoying herself, she wouldn't have stopped for the world, let alone for her own daughter. He would have pointed that out to Diandra had she not been looking so upset.

Again he felt compassion for her, and again it unsettled him. To feel compassion was to be vulnerable. He feared that if Diandra suspected, she'd take advantage of him. So with little thought beyond shifting the focus of the discussion, he said, "You weren't the only one who suffered from that little affair. My mother was crushed. There hadn't ever been another man in her life. She adored my father. She lived to keep his home, raise his child, be the perfect hostess when he wanted to entertain, sit and hold his hand when he wanted quiet. The friends she had were his friends, and of those Abby was her *best* friend. Even at the end, when she learned what was going on, she blamed herself. Rather than yell and scream at my father or Abby, she withdrew into a corner and blamed herself."

He paused, remembering that time, feeling it again. "And I had to watch. I had to watch her in agony and know that nothing I could do or say would ease the pain. Not that I could have said or done much. I was crushed. My father had fallen from his pedestal. I was in my own kind of pain."

"But you were already a man," Diandra blurted out.

He didn't see the connection. "What's that got to do with anything?"

"You had graduated from college. You had just taken your own apartment."

"And I was supposed to be immune to it all?" Rising to his feet, he snorted as he went to the window behind the desk. Standing with his hands on his hips and his back to her, he said, "Sorry to disappoint you, sweetheart, but I was human."

She persisted. "You were a *man*. You'd already been through a dozen women and you hadn't settled down. Fidelity didn't mean much to you."

"A dozen women?" He turned to face her. "Sure, I'd dated a dozen women. I started dating when I was fifteen. Twelve different dates in seven years—not terribly decadent. But I never promised any of those women a thing, never swore undying love. And I didn't bed them all, you can be sure of that. Nor," he went on, nostrils flaring, "did my dad bed any other woman but my mom until Abby."

Diandra couldn't believe his naïveté. "Are you kidding? He fooled around for years."

"How do you know?"

"I know."

"How?"

"Everyone knew."

"Everyone but my mother and me?" Greg's eyes were as dark as pitch when he gave a slow, confident shake of his head. "My mother I could believe. She didn't have to look the other way because she was blinded by complete and utter trust. It never occurred to her to question that trust. I never had cause to suspect my father, either, but if there'd been cause I would have seen it before her. I'd seen parents of friends cheating on each other. I knew the signs. If my father had been fooling around before Abby, I'd have known it."

His gaze narrowed on her in challenge. "So how did 'everyone' know my father had fooled around for years? Was he ever caught?"

"No, but—"

"Did any woman ever claim to have had an affair with him?"

"No, but—"

"Was there every any *concrete proof* that he'd been unfaithful to my mother?"

"It's next to impossible to get proof like that." Nervously Diandra fingered an emerald.

The movement of her hand drew his eye to the necklace. As he stared at it, the momentum of his argument broke, leaving a residue of hurt. He quieted. "We got proof of his affair with your mother. They were found together in the boathouse at Bar Harbor."

Diandra raised her eyes to the ceiling. "By your father's cousin, Angie. Good Lord, why Angie? She was the biggest mouth east of the Mississippi. Anyone else, and things would have broken more gently. Half the family knew about it before my father finally did."

"Or my mother."

"How could they have been so indiscreet?" Diandra cried. "Couldn't they have controlled themselves at least enough to go to some no-name motel where they wouldn't have been seen?"

"That's a damn good question," Greg said sadly. "And we'll never know the answer, will we? We'll never know why they took off in the plane that day, where they were headed, what they intended. We'll never know why the plane went down. We'll never know why they had the affair to begin with."

He looked at Diandra across the short distance separating them. Her face was as beautiful as ever, but her eyes held a pain that shouldn't have been there, and the injustice of it hit him.

They were victims. Both of them. In that instant of realization, Greg saw that none of the hostility that had come before mattered. All that mattered was that they were the victims of a tragedy that should never have been, and that they both suffered.

His steps were slow but sure, the kind that happened and were done without notice. Taking Diandra in his arms, he drew her close. She came willingly. Sliding her arms around his waist, she put her cheek to his shoulder and took the comfort she needed. And she did need that comfort. She hadn't ever before verbalized the feelings as she just had. They'd been buried beneath years of diversion, but Greg's goading had dredged them up, and they hurt.

She'd dredged something up in him, too, though, and it

surprised her. It had never occurred to her to think of him as having been hurt by their parents' relationship. Angry, yes—at Abby, and her. But hurt? He'd been grown up, independent. She'd always assumed he was too arrogant to feel something as mundane as hurt. She'd never thought of him as feeling, period.

She'd been wrong. For all the comfort he was giving her now with the strength of his body and the warmth of his skin, he was taking a comfort of his own. She could feel it in the way his arms circled her and the way he bent his head to her neck. He held her as though she had something special to offer him—and as though he desperately needed that offering.

With a sigh, she tightened her arms. Holding him was like holding to a rock in a storm, but he was a rock that needed protection, too, and that made a difference in what she experienced. She was finding as much comfort in the giving of comfort as in the taking.

When he moved his mouth on her hair, she took a deep, satisfied breath. There was something very right about their holding each other, offering each other support for a pain they shared. She'd never thought Greg would be an ally in that particular respect.

Looking up, she found his eyes a clearer, softer gray than she'd ever seen them. They warmed his entire face and drew her to him all the more. Moving her arms higher on his back, she returned her head to his neck to find a spot just below his close beard that seemed made for her. She nestled there, feeling at home with the natural musk of his skin. And at peace. She was stunned by the incredible peace she felt, particularly coming as it did on the heels of inner turmoil.

Greg, too, felt the peace. He guessed that he could go on holding Diandra forever—she fitted in his arms that well.

But it wasn't only a physical thing. It was a communing of minds. Odd that he should be able to do that with Diandra, of all people. They'd been at opposite ends of the spectrum for as long as he could remember, yet the spectrum seemed to have suddenly shrunk. At that moment, they were close.

The minute stretched from one to two, then three, and still the sense of rightness went on. If anything, it intensified, gaining in strength as the seconds ticked away.

Without pausing to think of the consequences, Greg lowered his head and kissed her cheek. It was the most natural thing in the world for him to do, the most honest way to express the closeness he felt just then. Apparently Diandra thought so, too, because she turned her head the smallest amount until her lips touched his.

Her kiss wasn't seductive. It wasn't coy or contrived, but gentle and sincere. It said, "Thank you" and "I needed that" and "I need this, too" with such simplicity that Greg would have had to have been the insensitive clod she'd accused him of being to miss the message. But he wasn't that clod, and her silent voice rang through to his senses. He kissed her with the same thanks she offered, marveled at the newness of it, returned the same gentleness—then was promptly hit by a wave of greater need.

That, too, was mutual. When his mouth grew more hungry, Diandra's kept pace. Her lips fell slack when he began to nibble on the lower one, but by the time he was back to a full kiss, she was returning it in kind. Her arms were wrapped tightly around him, her body pressed close.

In the end, he was the one to draw back and look down into her flushed face. Her lips were moist and parted. Her eyes were dazed, but several seconds of his scrutiny gave them a confused look.

Greg needed that look as much as he'd needed the kiss.

If she was confused, it meant that her response to his kiss was unpremeditated. That mattered.

"What's wrong?" she whispered, disoriented.

In that instant, he felt true affection for her. "You don't know what you're doing," he murmured gently.

She shook her head to clear it and frowned. "I...no."

"We'd better stop."

Her eyes registered a faint protest. Disorientation notwithstanding, she knew that something felt very good and that she didn't want it to end.

His whisper was rough, yet gentle still, his breath warm on her face. "This is getting out of hand."

"We were only kissing. It was nice."

She said it so innocently that he couldn't find it in himself to be angry. "But I want more," he said quietly. Sliding a hand between their bodies, he ran his knuckles against the outer swell of her breast. "I want to touch you. Undress you." His eyes held hers while those knuckles passed with ghostly lightness over her nipple, which quickly hardened. "I want to see you naked," he added in a husky whisper.

Between his words, the brush of his hand, the dark sensuality of his eyes and the intimate pressure of his body, she was being assaulted on all sides. In an attempt to cut down on that sensory input, she closed her eyes, but that only enhanced her awareness of Greg. Or was it that he chose that moment to open his hand on her breast? Or that his arousal was becoming more pronounced against her belly?

A soft sound came from her throat, followed by a gruffer sound from Greg that brought her eyes open in a flash.

"You're no help," he muttered. "No help at all." Hands on her shoulders, he held her at arms' length. "Tell me you don't want to make love."

"I don't want to make love," Diandra echoed, knowing that despite the clamoring of her body it was the right thing to say.

"With conviction. Say it with conviction."

That took more doing, but she managed, if for no other reason than to prove to Greg that she wasn't the seducer. Given whose daughter she was, that was very important. "I don't want to make love," she said firmly.

Greg studied her face. He wasn't sure whether he was pleased or not that she'd done as he'd asked. He was still hard. There was only one antidote.

"Then let's get to work," he said. Releasing her, he turned away before he could change his mind.

CHAPTER SEVEN

DIANDRA AND GREG spent the rest of that day listing the books in the den, grouping them by category, packing them into well-marked cartons. It was an unpleasant task. With each shelf that was bared came a sense of loss. Working quickly helped. The more intense their participation, the less they could dwell on what had happened between them earlier. Neither wanted to analyze the kiss, the embrace, the words of need they'd exchanged. Analysis would invite criticism—of themselves and each other, if for no other reason than the force of habit—and those moments had been too special for that. It seemed best to leave well enough alone.

Unfortunately as the afternoon passed Diandra discovered that well enough wasn't satisfied with being left alone. The den was too small. Greg was too large. The task was too demanding of closeness to allow for breathing space. They seemed to be forever knocking arms or elbows, and she was aware of every touch. Her heartbeat echoed each. Her internal thermostat ran warmer than usual. It was as though, once turned on, the current of awareness defied detour.

More than once she put her hand to the emerald necklace in search of a balm, and she did get it, but not in quite the way she'd sought. The necklace calmed her. It made her feel as though, in the long run, things would be fine. It painted the world a little brighter.

But it did nothing to still the deep, throbbing reaction she had to Greg, and that reaction was triggered each time he came near. Her only hope against it was to work harder, which was what she did.

So did Greg. As he'd done the day before in the pool, he chipped away at sexual tension by pushing his body in another direction. Strangely he had an easier time of it precisely because Diandra was there. He was competitive; so was she. Though they divided the labor to maximize output, with one feeding books from the shelves to the other to pack, they kept each other working steadily. By the time late afternoon rolled around and the last of the books had been packed, they were understandably tired.

Standing into a stretch with her hands massaging the tired muscles of her lower back, Diandra looked around the room she'd once loved. It was no longer the same cozy haven, but had become something barren, not familiar at all.

"This is depressing," she announced.

Greg agreed. He'd tried not to notice the thrust of her breasts against her shirt when she'd stretched, but he'd noticed anyway, and his body—which was supposed to be worn out—had quickly tightened. Scowling for more reasons than one, he eyed a particularly high stack of cartons. "Bart better know what he wants done with these. I sure as hell don't."

"Me neither." She sank back against the desk, then, almost immediately rethought the move, pushed off and made for the door.

Moments later, Greg found her sitting on the bottom stair in the hall. One palm cupped her chin. The fingers of the other hand touched the necklace. Even in spite of the smooth grace of the emeralds, she was looking as upended as he felt. On impulse, he lowered himself to the stair beside her.

Diandra rolled her eyes.

"What's wrong?" he asked.

"I don't believe this. With an entire houseful of seats to choose from, you choose mine."

"I didn't see your name on this step."

"No, but my bottom's here."

He turned his head to slide a glance down her back to the item in question. "It's small enough. We fit."

She made the mistake of returning the glance. Thanks to the way he was sitting, leaning forward with his elbows propped on his knees, the ribbing of his sweatshirt didn't quite reach his jeans. In between was an inviting strip of firm flesh, slightly indented on either side as it approached the small of his back. Millimeters above his jeans was a thin white line that could only be his briefs.

"That's the problem," she murmured weakly.

Greg stared at his hands, then sent her a sidelong glance. "Getting to you, too, is it? Maybe if we move right on to another room and attack it the way we did the den, we'll wear ourselves out. If we work ourselves ragged, we won't have the strength, and that will be that."

Diandra wondered. She was beginning to think the attraction she felt for Greg was predestined. "The way I see it, it's either something we inherited from our parents… or it's coming from the necklace. There's no way you and I can want each other on our own."

"Because we hate each other."

"Right."

Focusing on the mahogany console across the hall, Greg idly gnawed on the inside of his cheek. He didn't hate Diandra. He always had—or thought he had—but he didn't feel it now. She could still annoy him, but there had been times in the past forty-eight hours when he'd thought her amusing, even sweet. What he'd once considered impulsiveness now seemed more like spontaneity—and he found that surprisingly refreshing.

Yes, there were moments when he liked her, and the small voice inside that told him to be wary was growing softer and softer. She seemed genuine, strangely genuine....

He shot her a glance. She was studying the floor, but at the movement from him she met his gaze.

"Ever been in love?" he asked with deliberate lightness.

She shook her head.

"Me neither."

"Ever missed it?" she asked back.

He shrugged. "How would I know what to miss if I've never felt it?"

"You'd know. You'd see it in other people. You'd look around at friends and see something you wish you had. You'd feel a void."

"Do you?"

Tearing her gaze from his, she moved her fingertips over a diamond cluster as though it were braille. Then she looked back at him and nodded. "Sometimes."

"You want a husband?"

"Sometimes."

"And kids?"

"Sometimes."

"Sometimes doesn't work when it comes to those things."

"Maybe that's why I don't have them. I've never been willing to make the commitment. I've been too busy building a career to allow the time for it."

"Has it been worth it?"

"I love my work."

"But has it been worth it?"

Diandra was frustrated. She wanted to give him an honest answer, but she wasn't sure she could. Dropping her hand, she dragged both palms along her thighs, back and forth, and said, "It's not fair. Modern society tells a woman to work. It doesn't recognize her as legitimate unless she brings home a paycheck, but if she does that, where is she supposed to find time for a husband and children?"

"Many women do it."

"Not ones who do what I do." She held up a hand. "I'm not complaining. Like I said, I love my work. And the fact is that I'd probably be as busy in any job I held, just because that's my nature. I like to do things well or not at all." She frowned then, and her voice shrank to a discouraged murmur. "I suppose that would apply to a husband and kids. I don't think I could do them justice if I tried to juggle them around CayCorp, and I'm not ready to give up CayCorp."

He studied her face. She seemed legitimately disturbed, but so was he. He was trying to figure her out, trying to somehow reconcile the different images he had of her. "So that's why you've never married?"

"I've never married because I've never been in love."

"Then love is the key? You'd give up CayCorp if you fell in love?"

"I didn't say that."

"But you would marry if you fell in love?"

"I don't *know*. I couldn't ever marry without being in love, but I could be in love without getting married. It would all depend on who and where and what the man I loved was."

"This is getting complicated."

"I know."

"But it shouldn't be. You've dated some illustrious people, had your choice of the best of the bunch, and nothing's clicked. Is CayCorp that tough a competitor? What is it you want from the business anyway? Are you aiming to be president one day? Chairman of the board?"

His tone wasn't harsh. It was conversational, curious. But his words touched a sensitive chord in Diandra. Stung by what smacked very much of the old Greg just when she was letting down her guard and opening up, she started to rise.

He grabbed her hand. "Whoa. I asked a simple question."

"You asked a bunch of questions, each one loaded." Her eyes were wide and confused. "How in the world should I know what I'm aiming to be? I'm too busy being what I *am* to aim further just now. That's the whole point of what I was saying, which you would have seen if you hadn't been trying to trip me up. I'm not ruthlessly ambitious. I'm not trying to steal either the presidency or the chairmanship of the board from you."

"You're trying to steal San Francisco," he said without thinking.

"Not steal, since you don't have it to begin with, but I'm convinced that I'm the best one for the job." She paused. "And just to set the record straight, I haven't dated any particularly illustrious men—nor do I care to. Illustrious men have illustrious egos. I don't have the time for men like that."

"So who do you date?"

"Not much of anyone." She glared at her wrist, what little of it she could see between his fingers. "Do you mind?"

"Yes." He gave a gentle tug. "Sit down again. I like it when your bottom's next to mine."

Pressing the heel of her free hand to her forehead, Diandra closed her eyes and sighed. "I wish you wouldn't say things like that."

"I won't say things like that if you'll sit down. Why do you always have to be so prickly?"

"Because you prod and prod until you pierce the skin and get underneath." Her eyes opened and went straight to his. "It hurts sometimes, Greg. Why can't you see that?"

He asked himself the same question as he studied her look of pain, and there seemed only one valid answer. "Maybe because I'm not used to seeing this side of you." His fingers gentled on her wrist, and he gave a lighter tug this time before releasing her entirely.

After a moment's pause—during which Diandra realized that she liked her bottom next to Greg's, too—she sank back to the step. Tucking her hands between her knees, she pressed them together.

"So," Greg said. "What next?"

"I don't know."

"Want to attack the dining room?"

"To eat or pack?"

"Pack."

"Not really."

"Eat?"

Without looking at him, she tipped her head and said in a musing tone, "I could use a little something."

"I could use a *lot* of something."

She did look at him then and found something terribly endearing on his face. With a will of its own, a small smile crept to her lips. "Spoken like a man who hasn't eaten in days."

He shook his head. "Spoken like a man who hasn't eaten since lunch and who's done hard physical labor ever since." His eyes narrowed. "I feel like a good, thick, juicy steak. Think Frederick has any good, thick, juicy steaks in the freezer?"

She turned up her nose. "You don't want frozen. You want fresh."

"I'd take anything right about now."

"Like tacos? Or pizza?"

"Uh…almost anything."

She'd been teasing him with her reminder of the trouble he'd had the night before, but with his qualification, her grin faded. "It's an ulcer, isn't it?" she asked softly.

Greg's eyes shot to hers, his guard instantly up. If she thought she'd use health as an argument against his getting San Francisco, she had another think coming. If need be, he would deny that he suffered anything more than indigestion.

But her voice was gentle, her eyes concerned, and the two combined to touch something deep inside him.

He gave a one-shouldered shrug. "A small one. Nothing that can't be controlled with sane eating."

"And we overdid it last night."

"*I* overdid it," he corrected, putting blame where blame was due. "I'm usually pretty careful. But it was fun last night."

She agreed with that, though she wondered, "Was the pain worth it?"

"Yes," he answered instantly. Even after he thought about it, he repeated, "Yes. My life is too controlled, everything orderly, structured, programmed. If the ulcer came from tension, I can't think of a better way to counter it than to relax and enjoy myself, and that's exactly what I did last night." He looked at her, almost defying her to say he'd been wrong.

"It's okay," she said quietly, then tacked on, "as long as you don't binge on fried foods every night. How will steak sit?"

He breathed more freely. "Great."

"Where can we get it?"

"The Chart House. It's on the waterfront."

Diandra dropped a despairing look at the shirt and jeans she wore, than at the sweatshirt and jeans on Greg. "Will they let us in?" she asked.

"Not like this." He glanced at his watch. "But we still have time."

Her face brightened. Then she broke into a smile. "Not a bad idea." Using his thigh as a prop, she pushed up from the stair. "Not a bad idea at all." Her smile grew impish. "We could do it dressy—full length, black tie and tails." When he wrinkled his nose at that suggestion, she asked, "How about city suave?"

"Maybe," he said, rising and starting up the stairs. "Or country club chic." He ran a palm across his chest. "I need a shower first. Feel really grubby."

"Hurry," she called after him. "The store closes at six."

Grubby or not, Greg was feeling incredibly buoyant. "We *are* the store," he declared. "It'll open for us whenever."

They arrived at Copley Place at five forty-five so Casey and York didn't have to open specially for them. To their mutual relief—which they joked about—Alex wasn't there to mark their less-than-noteworthy entrance. He had gone for the day, leaving a bevy of managers to supervise the store's closing.

For those fifteen minutes until closing time, Diandra and Greg wandered through the store with total anonymity. Though each had been there before, neither had been there at leisure. They wandered from department to department observing layout, admiring displays, noting the way the salespeople dealt with customers—and comparing all those things with their own respective stores.

In spite of whatever other faults either of them found in

Alex, they agreed that he was an effective administrator. The store was elegant, as befitted its location, and appeared to be well run. Although certain departments were played up or down in variance from their treatment in either New York or Washington, the merchandising was tailor-made for Boston.

Busman's holiday over, they identified themselves to floor managers and parted ways to choose clothes for the evening. Twenty minutes later, as prearranged, they met at the foot of the first floor escalator.

Diandra wore a silk jumpsuit with padded shoulders and a nipped-in waist. Buttons ran down the front, but she had them fastened high to conceal the emerald necklace. The corners of her collar crossed stylishly beneath her chin. A cardigan sweater-coat was draped over her shoulders. The coordinated mauve of both silk and knit played up the creamy hue of her skin and the raven blackness of her hair.

Greg wore a pair of gabardine pants, an open-neck silk shirt and a free-fitting tweed blazer. He looked very tall, very cosmopolitan, very dashing. The color of his shirt was nearly identical to that of Diandra's jumpsuit.

"Great minds think alike," she mused, noting that mauve made Greg look that much more tawny, even more striking than usual.

Greg didn't say a word at first. He couldn't take his eyes off her—off the gracefulness of her neck as her collar framed it, the swell of her breasts beneath silk, the lengthy look of her legs made even more so by slender high heels, and the soft flush on her cheeks. He wondered if dressing up had been such a good idea after all. He'd seen Diandra dressed up before. Never before had she done it for him, though, and that made a difference.

"I hope," he began, then cleared his throat and began again, "I hope we won't be taken for a couple of grapes."

She laughed at that, then said, "You look great." She stood with the Casey and York bag that held her old clothes dangling from her linked hands.

"So do you." He reached for her bag and tucked it into his own, which he then slung over his shoulder. "All set?"

She nodded.

"Hungry?"

She nodded more vigorously.

Without another word they left the store and hailed a cab for the waterfront.

The Chart House came through with two of the thickest, juiciest steaks they'd ever eaten, but the focus of the meal wasn't the food or the service or the harbor view. It was each other. Though they'd known each other since childhood, though their jobs overlapped and they saw each other often, they had never before sat down together at a restaurant, just the two of them for several hours of private conversation.

They discussed a wide range of neutral topics—mutual acquaintances, *Les Miserables*, the stock market. They exchanged tidbits of CayCorp gossip, then went on to discuss the advertising campaign that so worried Bart.

Diandra found that when he wasn't looking to zing her, Greg was the most interesting companion she'd had in years. He was intelligent and responsive, and though she'd always focused on their differences, she had to admit that they had a great deal in common.

The man who had been her nemesis seemed a world away. In his place was an eminently likable man. He asked questions without goading. He expressed his opinions without putting hers down. He seemed to have set aside enmity for the sake of the evening.

She wondered whether it was the wine they drank that sweetened his mood—and hers. She did feel sweeter. More relaxed, less guarded, less defensive. The mellowing hadn't been a deliberate thing, but had just happened, and it was self-perpetuating. Diandra hadn't enjoyed herself as much in a long, long time. She wanted to prolong that.

It helped that neither of them mentioned either San Francisco or their parents.

And it helped that she was wearing the necklace. Though hidden beneath her collar, it was a living presence against her skin. Like a talisman, it gave her confidence— both that she could hold her own with Greg and that being with him was right. It told her not to look to the past or future, but simply to enjoy the present, which was very much what she was doing.

By the time they reached dessert, they were constantly smiling. Between them, they had drained a full bottle of wine though Greg, for one, couldn't blame his light-headedness on that. He rarely got tipsy. Besides, he was feeling as lighthearted as he was light-headed, and he'd never had that particular reaction to wine. Not that he would have minded. Either light-headed or lighthearted was preferable to horny.

By mutual consent, when neither of them wanted dessert, they set off on foot for Beacon Hill. The exercise was welcome after the meal, and the chill in the air was just the thing to cure light-headedness—or so they reasoned.

That didn't prove to be the case. As they walked along at a jaunty pace with their elbows linked, they found one amusing tale after another to share. They laughed loudly and often, uncaring if passersby stared at their unbridled exuberance, which only gave them something else to laugh about once that particular passerby had passed by. They'd never in their adult lives been silly that way; they felt they were taking their due.

After cavorting their way through Government Center,

they passed a video rental store that catered to night owls. Greg promptly dragged her inside and insisted they rent a movie to play on Bart's VCR. From shelf to shelf they went, bickering good-naturedly about what choice to make. They studiously avoided those shelves with anything sexy, and when they finally checked out a newly released adventure film, they felt they'd made a safe choice.

So they returned to the town house, where they changed back into jeans for the sake of lounging more comfortably in front of the TV. The scene called for popcorn but they were too full to eat so they opened another bottle of wine. Then, sitting side by side on the floor with their backs against the sofa and every light in the room off, they proceeded to joke their way through the first half of a movie that, on any other occasion, would have been a thriller.

They didn't quite get involved in the plot. First Greg found that he could announce what was going to happen before it happened, then Diandra found that she could speak the dialogue before the characters did. They toasted themselves each time they were right, and they were right often enough to keep the wine flowing, which meant that they felt little pain when they were wrong.

In time, though, Diandra grew sleepy. Dropping her head to Greg's lap, she closed her eyes and was out within minutes. Too bleary-eyed to fully appreciate her position, Greg pulled pillows from the sofa, propped them under his head and was soon asleep himself. The movie ended with neither of them observing its climax. The set automatically shut itself off, filling the dark room with silence.

Greg was the first to stir. He'd been having an X-rated dream, and when he tried to shift position, he discovered the object of his dream in the flesh. Her head was no longer in his lap, since he'd stretched out earlier, but she was curled close to him with one arm across her chest and the other over his hip.

Eyes closed, he nuzzled her hair. Its scent and her warmth were extensions of his dream, so pleasant that he made no attempt to wake himself further. He brought a hand lightly through the silky mass, then bent his head lower and kissed her ear.

She moved. Just her head. Just enough to give his mouth better access. Still mostly asleep, she reacted instinctively to the gentleness of his lips and his warmth by gravitating toward both. It was her silent way of saying Mmm. I like that. It's nice.

As though he'd heard her, Greg drew a line of slow, moist kisses from her ear to her cheek. He liked the smoothness of her skin and its fresh smell, liked the idea that he didn't have to kiss his way through layers of makeup to reach the woman beneath. Diandra was pure in that sense. Though he couldn't see her in the dark, he knew the exact shade of that creamy skin. She was inviting, far more so than any woman he'd ever had or dreamed of having.

Needing to deepen the contact and prove it real, he slid his fingers into her hair to hold her while his lips covered hers. She tasted faintly of wine, faintly tart, faintly sweet. And he was suddenly more thirsty than he'd been seconds before. Caressing her lips apart, he slid his tongue into her mouth.

Diandra came awake with a muted gasp. Instinctively her hands rose, one to his chest, one to his shoulder. Her palms were against him, prepared to push him away. Her fingers were straight in surprise, but with the sensual stroking of his tongue, they closed around handfuls of his shirt and clung.

The kiss went on and on, deepening by increments until Diandra was as active and involved as Greg. All remnants of sleep had gone, but still there was something dreamlike about that mating of mouths. It was very new, very exciting. It was simultaneously the most satisfying and frustrating experience of her life.

Destiny. That was the one word that came to Diandra's mind as she slid her hands over Greg's shoulders and arched closer. She felt as though she'd arrived at a spot that had been preordained years before, and though that spot was hot with desire and far from peaceful, she felt she was home.

Greg, too, felt the homecoming, but on a far less cerebral level than Diandra. His body was tight, clamoring for a satisfaction only she could offer, and with each kiss, that need grew. Never before had he felt such a desperate need to be part of a woman. He'd always thought himself too self-contained, too self-controlled, too independent for that, but Diandra was proving him wrong. He felt less than whole; she was the only one who could complete him.

Sliding an arm around her, he brought her hard against his body. When even that pressure wasn't enough, he rolled over until he half-covered her and thrust against her heat.

The strength of his arousal was stunning. Diandra arched upward. While her hands found a hold in his hair, her hips began a slow undulation that harmonized with his, and the breath she was holding gradually found its escape through soft moans of desire.

To Greg, each moan was a promise. Each one painted a picture of their bodies, entwined as they were, but naked. The moan then was his, and no sooner was it out when he sat up on his knees, drew Diandra with him and settled her between his thighs.

He touched her everywhere. His hands made a statement of possession that was less than gentle at times, but always arousing. Her clothes didn't deter him. He greedily claimed her shoulders, her back, her breasts and belly, and as much as he touched her, she strained for more. Bombarded with sensation, she entered a state of overload where the only thing she felt was an incredible, searing heat. When he cupped her bottom and drew her to him hard, she bit her lip to keep from crying out. When his hand found its way beneath her to the greatest point of her need, she thought she'd die of want.

Trembling from the inside out, she made a small, strangled sound, but her thighs parted to accommodate him, leaving no doubt as to the meaning of the sound.

Of one mind as to their destination, they hurried. Between soft, shuddering breaths, they pulled at snaps and zippers, tugged at denim, kicked unwanted clothes aside. They barely had time to unbutton their shirts when the urgency of the moment took them. Diandra lay back on the carpet, Greg followed her and was inside with one, long thrust.

She cried out. As ready as she was for him, her body was tight. His sudden invasion, his sheer physical presence inside, startled her. She dug her nails into his arms to hold him still, but in less than a minute the strangeness was replaced by heat, and with that heat, passion burst into flame. It smoldered and sizzled between them, fed by Greg's long, fluid strokes. Diandra met the movement of his hips, picking up his rhythm until they were syncopated in the drive toward release.

That release came with a sudden flash of fire. It took Diandra, spun her around until she was dizzy with pleasure, then catapulted her into a moment's break with consciousness. She was barely aware of Greg's hoarse cry, of his stiffening, of the waves of pleasure that rolled over and through him, but deep inside, she felt the warmth of his release, and that brought her a second round of satisfaction.

For a time, the only sounds in the room were of ragged gasps for air. Coming down at length from what he was sure had been the high of his life, Greg rolled to her side, gathered her in his arms and held her close.

He knew the instant she realized what she'd done.

"Don't say it," he whispered, holding her tighter to counter the twinge of tension that winged through her. He raised his voice a bit, but it was hoarse. "Don't say it, because there's no point. What just happened happened because we wanted it. Sure, we could blame it on wine, or on sleep, or on that necklace you're wearing. But the fact is that we're both adults. We're both rational, thinking animals, and we wanted to make love. Period."

She didn't say anything at first, but he felt a subtle relaxation. Bringing one hand to her cheek, he lightly caressed it with his thumb.

"Thank you," she whispered at last.

The movement of his thumb stopped. "For what?"

"For not yelling at me…accusing me of…calling me…" She couldn't quite finish any one of the thoughts, though they were all very much the same. Her first thought when she'd regained her senses was that Greg would think her like her mother. After the beauty of what they'd just shared, the comparison would have hurt badly.

Greg could have returned the thanks, but he wasn't any more eager to think about, much less mention, their parents than she was. So he shifted her in his arms, keeping her very close, and sighed into her hair.

They lay that way for a time, though neither of them spoke. Greg was thinking that he couldn't remember ever being as satisfied—and how remarkable that was. As a lover, Diandra had been a surprise. He'd imagined her to be consummately skilled, but she wasn't. She was eager, but innocent. As hot as she was, she'd let him lead. She'd followed gladly and her touch had been wildly arousing, but not tutored. She'd been very tight. She hadn't made love in a while, and that gave him something to consider.

It gave Diandra something to consider, too, but her thoughts ran along slightly different lines. "Greg?" she whispered.

"Mmm?"

"You're not sterile, are you?"

He was about to burst out with a macho *Are you kidding?* when the oddness of the question hit him. Cautiously he said, "Not that I know of," then asked, "Why?"

"Because...I think..."

Concerned by the concern in her voice, he held her back and looked down into her face. Even then he was stymied; the room was too dark for him to see much. "What's wrong?"

"We could have a problem," she murmured softly, quickly, apologetically. "I didn't use anything. I don't use anything."

As her meaning hit, Greg sucked in a breath—not so much because he was worried, but because he wasn't. Incredibly a new surge of desire hit him. "Is it a risky time?"

"So-so," she said, trying to sound nonchalant, but her nervousness came through nonetheless.

"Do you get pregnant easily?"

"I don't know," she said, this time in a small wail.

Immediately he gathered her to him. "It's okay. Getting pregnant wouldn't be the end of the world."

"Fine for you to say. You're not the one who'd be affected."

"How do you figure that?"

"Come on, Greg—"

"No, I'm serious. Do you think I'd throw you to the wolves?"

"The wolves being our families, who would go positively nuts after…after…"

Greg pressed her face to his shoulder, muzzling her mouth with his skin. "Don't say it. Please. Not tonight. Tonight's ours, and if a baby comes from it, that's ours, too." His voice lowered. "We'd have a beautiful baby, Diandra."

She moaned against his skin.

"We would," he repeated, mistaking her moan for protest.

"I know," she whispered, not intending protest at all. She was finding the thought of carrying Greg's baby to be shockingly arousing. She was also realizing that she wasn't alone. Greg was obviously affected, too. She wanted to touch him. Lacking the courage to be so bold, she slid her hand to his chest, moved it lightly downward until it came to rest near his navel.

He went very still. "Di?"

She didn't answer, but her lips opened on his collarbone.

"What are you doing?" he asked.

"I don't know. Tell me to stop. This is crazy."

He didn't tell her to stop. Instead, he brought her up with him as he'd done before, only this time he removed her shirt and bra, then took off his own shirt. "I want to know everything this time," he whispered, and before she could remind him that they were increasing the risk each time they made love, he set about doing exactly that.

If the first time had been a hot sweep of passion, this second time was filled with details. Diandra was aware of everything—of the feel of his blunt-tipped fingers on her nipples, the slide of his palms in the hollows of her hips, the slow brush of his thumb over the aching bud between her legs. She was aware of his body, too, of the way she could bring his nipples to pebble hardness, the way his flanks tightened with his arousal, the way he sucked in his stomach when she slid her hand downward.

His fingers entered her first, opening her gently, testing her readiness, and when he looped her legs over his and brought her down on his full erection, he took her cry of delight into his mouth.

When sometime later he carried her to bed, her final thoughts before she drifted to sleep weren't of her parents or the possibility of pregnancy or of the emerald necklace that had pulsed with her climax but of the fact that Greg had claimed her. Greg had made love to her. He'd been the one inside her. That knowledge, more than anything else, filled her to overflowing.

CHAPTER EIGHT

DIANDRA AWOKE THE next morning feeling strangely shy.
Being in bed and naked with Gregory York was at the same
time very familiar and totally new. Although she'd known
him all her life, she'd never known him this way, and the
reality of that awareness hit her with the light of day.

Either he was incredibly understanding of her feelings
or he was feeling them himself, because he couldn't have
handled her better. Kissing her gently, he drew her up and
into the shower, then proceeded with normal things—
getting dressed, making the bed, fixing breakfast—as if
nothing out of the ordinary had happened the night before.
She might have been offended had it not been for the fact
that whenever she was near he touched her—a hand on her
arm or her back, a light kiss on her cheek, an arm around
her when he wanted to guide her this way or that. Once
or twice, when she looked up in surprise at the touch,
she caught a challenging look on his face, but she never
raised the protest he dared her to. Without analyzing it,
she enjoyed his closeness.

There was passion, but it came in sparks that were
tempered by the new gentleness that existed between them.
They were at peace with each other, satisfied with the
situation as it was for those few moments, hours, perhaps
days out of time—which was fortunate, because once
breakfast was done and they'd dallied long enough over

the morning paper, they had to face the task they'd been sent to do.

That they approached halfheartedly. They forced themselves to catalog the contents of the formal dining room, but when it was time to move on to the family room, which held many of the warm feelings the den had, Greg balked.

"Playtime," he announced, dragging her up from the floor where she'd been sitting with the pad of legal paper that had grown odious to them both.

She pulled back on her hand when he would have had pulled her through the door. "We have to get this done. It's already Thursday."

"I know."

She looked around in despair. "We're barely halfway through."

He pulled her against his shoulder. "I know."

She looked pleadingly up into his face. "I wanted to be back in the office on Monday."

"So did I. But I need a break." He ran his hand up and down her arm. "Come on, Diandra. I can't stand this job. I want to play tennis—and don't say you don't have the clothes for it, because we can get them at the health club. I know you play—at least you used to. You used to come pretty close to beating me."

The natural competitor in Diandra rose to the challenge. "I did, didn't I?"

"But you never quite made it. Want to try again?"

For what seemed an endless moment, she was lost in his eyes. He was her past, but he was much more now, and that much more sent warm currents of pleasure flowing through her. She liked his side pressed to hers, liked his mellow male scent. She wasn't thinking of the fact that they were rivals for the San Francisco store or that their parents had

had a tragic affair or that they'd been enemies for years. She was thinking that she felt protected, possessed and possessive. She liked knowing that for these moments out of time Greg was here. If the choice was between sending him off alone to swim or playing tennis with him, there was no choice at all.

Slowly she nodded. When he rewarded her with a kiss, she would have gladly reconsidered the form of activity he'd chosen, but when her eyes said as much, he sent her a chiding stare and led her off.

As with most everything he did in life, Greg played hard. But then so did Diandra. The only problem was that he was physically larger, heavier and stronger than she, hence he had a built-in advantage. Still, she played commendably. While she didn't win a set, she came close, forcing him beyond the six-game-win minimum in two of the three sets they played.

By the time they yielded the court to the next group of players, they were tired and sweaty. Showers in the locker room took care of the sweat; a leisurely lunch at the club's restaurant took care of the tiredness. When they returned to the town house, though, they were no more anxious to tackle the family room than they'd been before.

"Self-discipline is what's needed here," Greg said with a set jaw as he pulled an empty carton to the game cabinet and began to call out the names of the children's games that he packed.

Midway through the second carton, Diandra said, "Wait!" She jumped up from her chair, reached into the box and retrieved the game he'd just set inside. "I *love* Boggle. Let's play."

"I hate Boggle."

"That's because you're not as good at it as you are at

tennis. But fair is fair. I played tennis, knowing all along that I'd lose, and I was a good sport about it, wasn't I?"

"It was your own fault you lost. You were too busy looking at my legs to look at the ball."

"That's not true!"

"I saw you, Di. You like the way I look in shorts."

She certainly did, but she wasn't about to admit it. She'd played her hardest on the court. Okay, she'd been distracted once or twice, but mostly during breaks. "I was simply giving back what I got. You did your share of looking, Greg."

"And enjoyed every minute of it," he said with a lascivious grin. Diandra squeezed her eyes shut against its lure, only to open them quickly when he added, "Okay. I'll play Boggle. But on one condition."

Instantly wary, she asked, "What condition?"

He straightened his shoulders. "Whoever loses a round loses an item of clothing."

"*Strip* Boggle? Greg, that's indecent! I mean—" she lowered her voice to a facetious drawl "—poker is one thing. But...Boggle?"

"It sure would be fun."

She couldn't argue with that. At the mere suggestion, she'd begun to feel sexy tingles inside. Or maybe it was the way he was standing, so cocksure and manly. Or maybe it was the way he'd been touching her all day. Then again, maybe it had been his legs. They'd been long and lean, just muscular enough, just hairy enough. She'd wanted to touch them, but they'd been too far away.

"What do you say?" Greg asked.

Her eyes flew from his denim-encased thighs to his face, and her cheeks grew pink. A little disgusted with herself for her own lascivious thoughts, she sought to redeem herself. "I'll agree to Strip Boggle under one condition. Whoever loses has to answer a question."

It was Greg's turn to be wary. "What kind of question?"

"Any one the winner wants to ask."

"*Any* question?"

She nodded.

"Like really personal things?"

She shrugged a yes.

Greg wasn't sure he wanted to answer certain personal questions. On the other hand, he had a dozen personal questions he wanted to ask Diandra. He'd agree to her condition in a minute, if he had more faith in his ability to win.

"What's wrong, Greg?" she teased. "Hiding some mighty secrets? Or are you just worried you'll end up naked as a jaybird before I've even taken off my shirt?"

"You're not *that* much better than I am," he said, praying it was true, because he knew he'd play the game. He'd play because he wanted to ask Diandra those questions. The risk of exposing himself was worth it.

"Do we play?" she asked.

"We play."

Pushing the cartons aside, they cleared a space on the carpet, opened the Boggle box and each took a pad of paper and a pen. Diandra shook up the letter cubes, then set them down at the same time that Greg started the timer, and for the next three minutes, they worked in silence. When the timer ran out, Diandra read her list aloud, and they crossed off those words they'd both found. When they scored their remaining words, she was the winner.

Determined to be as good a sport at Boggle as she'd been at tennis, Greg kept his gaze steady. "What'll it be— clothes first, or question?"

Diandra feared that if the clothes went first—particularly

in the later stages of the game—she wouldn't be able to concentrate on the question. So she said, "Question," then made some quick calculations. Greg was wearing socks, a shirt, jeans and briefs. Four items. That was it. She had to make the most out of each one.

After a moment, she asked, "Where were you two weeks ago Saturday night at eleven-thirty?"

Greg wasn't sure what he'd expected, but it wasn't that. Brushing his beard with the pad of his thumb, he frowned. "Two weeks ago Saturday night at eleven-thirty? Am I really supposed to remember?"

"Yes."

He closed his eyes and concentrated.

"If you don't answer the question," she told him, "you forfeit another game, which means that you have to take off something else."

His eyes came open. "You're changing the rules."

"No, just making them more specific. Answer the question."

Without pause, he said, "Two weeks ago Saturday night at eleven-thirty, I was in bed."

"With whom?"

"That's another question," he pointed out, but gently. She was curious; that was good. It would also be good for her to hear his answer. "I was alone."

That wasn't what she'd been told. "Really?"

"Really."

"Why?"

"What do you mean, why?" he chided. "I was alone because I chose to be alone. I'd had a busy week, I'd had to go to a cocktail party on Long Island that night, and I was exhausted."

"Did you have a date for the party?"

"I'd gone with Caroline Mann," which was just what

Diandra had heard, "but it wasn't a date. We're good friends, that's all. Her lover was off visiting his family in Paris, and she didn't want to drive out alone. I benefited from the arrangement as much as she did. People thought we were together. That spared me some grief."

"You mean, from other women?"

"Life isn't always easy for a bachelor."

She was pleased enough by what he'd said about Caroline to tease, "Poor thing."

"I'm serious. There are some desperate women out there. They can be pests. I wasn't up for it that night." He put the cover on the cube tray and shook the letter cubes.

"Hold it," she cried. "You have to take something off."

Greg had legitimately forgotten. With a crooked smile doing naughty things to his mouth, he unstrapped his watch.

"Watches don't count," she protested.

"Sure they do. At least," he added in a sensual tone, "they always did in strip poker. And besides," he added as he set the watch on the carpet, "this way you'll have an extra question to ask."

The question Diandra wanted to ask just then was how often and with whom he played strip poker. But thoughts of his stripping made her insides hum, and she had to concentrate. He was shaking up the cubes again.

The letters fell into place. He removed the lid. She set the timer going, and they went to work. When Diandra won that round, too, Greg waited expectantly for her question.

"What went on between you and Jenny MacClain?"

He frowned. "Jenny MacClain is my secretary."

"Your personal secretary. I heard you had an affair with her."

"Who did you hear that from?"

"It doesn't matter. Is it true?"

Greg thought he'd been on top of the gossip. Apparently he'd missed something. "No, it's not true."

"She's a beautiful young woman."

"And a great secretary. She also happens to be married." His gaze grew sharper. "Despite what you may have heard or chosen to believe, I've never had an affair with a married woman. Even aside from the issue of morality, I'm fastidious when it comes to bedmates. The idea of sharing turns me off."

Diandra could almost see the curl of his lips before it blended with his mustache, and it was in keeping with the distaste in his eyes. Mixed in with that distaste was a warning. She waited for him to say something about what he expected of *her* as a bedmate, but as quickly as it had come, the sharpness faded.

"In Jenny's case," he said gently, "there's more. She has a six-year-old child who is severely handicapped. She has to work because she and her husband need the money to pay for special care for the child."

Diandra felt instantly contrite. "I didn't know," she whispered.

"Most people don't, and that's the way Jenny wants it. She's a proud woman. She isn't looking for pity."

"But the gossip—"

"I don't think it occurred to her any more than it occurred to me."

"But she's young and pretty. Didn't you ever wonder what she'd be like—"

"In bed? No. Contrary to popular belief, I don't look at every woman I meet as a potential lover. I've never looked at Jenny that way, and I never will." Having said it all, he tugged off a sock and tossed it aside.

Diandra looked at his foot, then at the one still covered.

When she saw that he wasn't moving, she raised her eyes to his. "Each sock separately?"

He nodded. "Gives you one more question. Remember that."

She did, and she assumed that was what distracted her, because she lost the next round.

Greg celebrated his victory with a cocky grin, which faded when he asked, "Who is McKinsey Post?"

She didn't flinch, but said softly, "You know who he is. He's the curator of the museum. I worked with him on a fund-raising effort in January."

"But who is he to you?"

"Someone very nice. Very sensitive. He's a friend."

"He's not married."

"No."

"Gay?"

"Not that I know of."

"Have you slept with him?"

She shook her head.

"Why not?"

"Because I don't want to."

"Why not?"

"Because he doesn't turn me on."

"Like I do?"

Her cheeks went pink as she stared at him. Then, with a shy smile tugging at the corners of her mouth, she said softly, "I suppose there's no point in denying it, is there?"

He shook his head. His eyes skimmed each of her features, slid down her neck, came to rest on the wink of green that showed through the collar of her shirt. He conjured an image of Diandra wearing nothing but that necklace, and his body was fast to respond.

He cleared his throat. "It's mutual." His eyes rose to hers. "Take something off."

Slightly shaky from his perusal, she pressed her lips together and swallowed. Greg had started with his watch, but she'd left hers in the bathroom upstairs. He'd gone on to take off a sock, but she wasn't wearing one, let alone two. Her hand went to the necklace, but she didn't want to—couldn't—take it off.

"This isn't fair," she complained. "You're wearing more than I am."

He shrugged smugly. "You knew that from the start."

Actually she hadn't. She'd counted how many things *he* had on to remove, but she hadn't thought about herself. Moreover, she hadn't counted on losing a game.

Again she pressed her lips together, this time moistening them first. She didn't have many options. Without raising a fuss, she shifted to her knees, unsnapped and unzipped her jeans, shifted back to her bottom and slid them off. Her shirttails covered her panties, but her legs were bare. She tucked them beneath her.

"Cold?" Greg asked in a voice that was anything but.

She shook her head and reached for the Boggle tray. When the cubes had been sufficiently jumbled, she put them down. Greg set the timer, and they were off.

There had been times during family vacations when Diandra had played Boggle for hours on end, hence she was far from a novice. She knew the kinds of words to look for and the directions. She could easily recognize a tough arrangement of cubes when it came.

This one wasn't. It had a comfortable assortment of consonants and vowels and should have yielded a healthy number of four-and five-letter words, as well as three-letter ones. Her hand seemed to be steadily working, writing down words, but when time ran out, her list wasn't as long as she'd expected.

Greg's was that much shorter.

Relieved, she put down her pen and asked quietly, "Are you seeing anyone special now?"

Beyond curious, she seemed unsure, almost as though she hadn't wanted to ask the question but needed to know the answer. That made Greg feel better. "No. No one special."

"Why not?"

"Special women are hard to come by."

"Who was the last one you had?"

"Had—as in sex, or relationship?"

Diandra hesitated for just a minute before saying, "Both."

"Corinne."

"It's been a while since Corinne," Diandra said, surprised that there hadn't been anyone more recently. "I liked Corinne."

"Me too."

"So what happened?"

"She began to crowd me."

It was a poor choice of words. Diandra reacted with quick sarcasm. "She threatened your freedom. She should have known better."

"It wasn't like that—not the way you make it sound. She began to press for marriage and a family, and I wasn't ready."

"Wasn't ready?"

"Didn't want it. Not with her. We weren't right that way."

"But you two were okay in bed."

Frustrated, he shot a glance out the window. "Why do you have to reduce everything to its lowest common denominator?" He looked back at her in a punishing sort of way. "Yes, we were okay in bed—better than okay—really good. And we got along well for the few nights a week that we were together. But I couldn't think of growing old with her, and that's what marriage means."

Diandra was left without a quick rejoinder. She was surprised that Greg thought about things like growing old. She was even more surprised that he thought about growing old with a woman. She'd have assumed he wouldn't mind little dalliances here and there. He'd been free for so many years that she'd have guessed he'd have trouble settling down.

She was still trying to think of something to say when, with a cavalier flourish, Greg peeled off his other sock, tossed it aside and eyed her expectantly.

"One sock at a time," she grumbled, shifting her bare legs, "is really cheap."

He grinned, shrugged, then reached for the tray of letter cubes.

Diandra won again. "Tell me about your bedroom," she said.

Greg had been wondering which bit of gossip she'd focus on next. He hadn't considered that she'd be curious about his bedroom. "It's a bedroom. What can I say?"

"Is it nice?"

"I suppose. It was professionally decorated, like yours. I haven't paid much attention to the details."

"Because you're otherwise occupied when you get there?"

"No," he said with careful enunciation, "because I'm usually exhausted when I get there, and when I wake up in the morning, I'm in a rush to leave."

"When do you go to bed?"

"After the news."

"On nights you're home. How about on nights you're out?"

"I'm not out that often."

"How often?"

"Once or twice a week. Mostly business things. How about you?"

"The same. Is your bedroom big?"

"Big enough to hold a bed, a couple of dressers and a chair."

"King-size bed?"

He nodded.

"What's the color scheme?"

"Navy and gray. It's just a room. Call it attractive or modern or chic or anything else, but it's just a room. A little cold, if you ask me."

Diandra wanted to ask whether he'd ever thought to warm it up, but just then she wanted to be warmed herself, and that would happen as soon as she stopped talking.

So she stopped talking. Looking directly into Greg's eyes, she waited.

One by one, he released the buttons of his shirt. He shrugged out of it. It fell to the rug.

She dropped her eyes to his chest. It was broad at the top and liberally sprinkled with tawny brown hair. Above it, his shoulders were straight and strong, skin stretched tightly over muscle that was firm and naturally earned. Below it, both body and hair tapered toward a slim waist and hips. His stomach rippled faintly thanks to the way he was sitting with one knee bent and the other leg folded beneath. That faint rippling provided an appealing softness. Every bit as appealing was the hint of a navel, cut off by the band of his jeans.

By the time she raised her eyes to his again, her breath was coming slightly faster.

"Okay?" he asked in a husky tone.

She nodded. Too late she realized that she wasn't. She lost the next round.

"Who was your first lover?" Greg asked. He'd been wondering about that. It occurred to him that he'd been wondering about it for years.

"You don't really want to know," Diandra murmured a bit uncomfortably.

"I do."

She hesitated. "It's really not important."

"But it's my question."

"It's not relevant to anything."

"None of this is. But I won the round. Answer the question."

She looked at him for a minute, then looked away and said, "Tommy Nolan."

"Pardon me?"

Looking back, she said more clearly, "Tommy Nolan."

Greg was surprised. He was also a little hurt, though he had no right to be. Tommy Nolan had been one of his best friends for a time. They'd gone to prep school together, and though they'd parted ways when they'd gone off to college, they'd still seen each other from time to time. Apparently, during one of those times, Tommy had seen Diandra, too.

"Tommy Nolan," he repeated softly, a bit dryly. "Good old Tommy."

Feeling awkward, Diandra shrugged.

"How old were you?" he asked.

"Twenty-three."

Greg's eyes widened. "That old? You mean, you went through college a virgin?"

Her chin rose. "Something wrong with that?"

"No, no. I'm surprised, that's all." He'd fully expected that she'd been deflowered at seventeen. Twenty-three was remarkable. "Why Tommy?"

"I really liked Tommy."

"So did I, but I didn't go to bed with him."

"I'm relieved to hear that."

"I can't believe you did."

"Why not?"

He shrugged. "Tommy was my friend."

"Should I have disliked him because I disliked you?"

"No, maybe it was the reverse. Maybe you went with him to spite me."

Diandra snorted. "That's ridiculous. You two weren't all that close at the time. There was no reason you'd have known what happened between him and me, so if I'd wanted to spite you, it wouldn't have worked."

Greg regarded her sadly. "Tommy Nolan. I'd never have guessed."

It was the sadness that got to her. "You're making too much of this, Greg," she told him. "I felt comfortable with Tommy. He was like family in some ways. He was tall and handsome, ambitious, interesting. He reminded me a lot of you."

"Was that why you did it?" Greg asked on impulse.

She was struck speechless as the question echoed in her mind. The thought that she'd been attracted to Tommy specifically because he reminded her of Greg had never occurred to her. It didn't make sense; she'd disliked Greg so.

Then again, it would never have occurred to her that she'd be with Greg now, and when she tried to think of all those things she disliked about him, she felt confused. Too many things were happening too fast. She needed time to think.

Bowing her head, she pressed two fingers to her temple and closed her eyes.

"Diandra?"

She looked up.

His gaze fell with deliberate intent to her shirt.

The game. She remembered the game, and a wave of awareness swept through her. With hands that trembled slightly, she unbuttoned her shirt and let it slip from her shoulders.

Greg was the one to tremble then. Diandra was beautiful, so beautiful. Sitting opposite him with her legs tucked beneath her, wearing nothing but lace panties, a matching bra and the emerald necklace, she was a sight to behold. Her skin was smooth and cream colored, her limbs graceful. The slenderness of her torso was relieved by the most feminine of curves. She couldn't have looked more sexy if she'd been stark naked.

He cleared his throat. "Okay?"

She nodded.

With an effort, he redirected his eyes toward the cube tray. He shook it with more force than was absolutely necessary, then set the timer himself. The arrangement of letters was awkward this time. He managed to compose a few words, then twisted his head to view the letters from a different angle. By the time the timer ran out, he was sure he'd listed a record low number of words. Diandra hadn't done much better, but still she won.

"What do you dream about?" she asked quietly.

"Middle-of-the-night kind of dream?"

"No. Daydream. Wish. Hope for."

In Greg's opinion, it was the most personal question she'd asked yet. She had her sights on his thoughts, and when it came to those, he was vulnerable. But she looked vulnerable, too, sitting there in her bra and panties, awaiting his answer. The emerald necklace glimmered its encouragement, giving him the final impetus to speak.

"I dream about success," he began. "I want to do well within the company."

"I already know that. Tell me something else."

"I want success beyond the company."

A tiny frown ghosted over her brow. "In what way?"

"For nearly fifteen years, the company has been my life. That's not healthy. I want to change it."

"How?"

He hesitated. He could take his clothes off in a minute, bare his body to her eyes. Baring his thoughts was harder. For a split second, he wondered if he had the courage. Then he realized that if he didn't, he was truly a loser in the game.

"I want a family," he said. "I want to be able to come home at night to the woman I love. I want the children we'll have, and I want to be there when they grow up." He paused, pursed his lips contemplatively, looked down. "I dream about lying in a meadow on a warm, sunny day. My woman is in my arms, and we're watching our children play." Without looking up, he shrugged. "I dream about sitting before a warm fire in the cold of winter. Same thing—woman in my arms, kids playing."

He raised his eyes. "I want a home that's a haven from the world, and I want to know that no one and nothing can take that away."

The flow of his words ended as quickly as it had begun, leaving Diandra with a tight knot in her throat. She didn't doubt for a minute that he meant what he said; the heart-rending look in his eyes vouched for it. What she couldn't understand was why she'd never known that he had this side, why she'd never guessed it. She supposed she'd been too busy bickering with him to wonder why he did what he did. She'd been too busy looking for the bad to see the good.

Aware of a slow gathering of tears in her eyes, she averted them. But Greg saw. He felt those tears as shards of pain deep inside. "Diandra?"

She held up a hand, needing that minute to compose herself.

Coming forward on his knees, he reached over and touched her cheek. "What's wrong?"

She shook her head, took a deep breath, then raised her eyes. "I'm okay."

"You felt something."

She nodded and said in a very soft voice, "Your dreams aren't far off from mine. Ironic, isn't it—that we're both in such enviable professional positions, but still we want more? Where does it end, do you think? If we find a haven, will we want something else?"

"I can't imagine anything I'd want beyond that."

"Me either." She took a shaky breath. "There are times, though, when it feels like an impossible dream. Do you think we'll ever get there?"

Greg didn't know the answer to that, and something odd had just struck him. When he'd been describing the dream to Diandra, she'd been the woman in it. She fitted his dream. Looking down at her, he suddenly wanted her on a myriad of different levels.

Unable to fully understand what that meant, he picked the one of those levels that was clearest. Lowering his head, he put a light kiss on her lips, then sat back and reached for the snap of his jeans.

Diandra caught her breath. Holding it, she watched him open the snap and lower the zipper. He stood and pushed the denim to his thighs, then off one foot, then the other. Then he returned to his perch on the rug, but not before she'd learned two things. The first was that he looked wonderful in nothing but hip-hugging white briefs. The second was that he was aroused.

Her eyes flew to his.

"You can't be surprised," he chided.

She nodded, then as quickly shook her head.

"You could always get more of a rise out of me than any other woman I know," he said, which was exactly the kind of suggestive statement that, in the past, would have brought an angry response from Diandra.

She remained quiet, though. It occurred to her that she wanted to get more of a rise from him—both emotionally and physically. The meaning of that left her unsettled, which, she assumed, was why she lost the next round of Boggle.

"Tell me a fantasy," Greg ordered in a throbbingly low voice.

She swallowed. "Fantasy?"

"Sexual fantasy."

"I don't have any."

"Sure you do. Don't be shy. I'll tell you mine if you tell me yours."

"I don't have any."

"Everyone has sexual fantasies."

She shook her head. "Not me."

"Come on, Di. You're like fire in my arms. You're a very passionate woman."

"I've never thought of myself that way." At his dubious look, she said, "I'm not all that experienced. Couldn't you tell?"

Thinking back, he could. Her responses to him had been innocent. She'd followed his lead, gained courage as she'd gone along. Still, she was a very passionate woman. "Surely you've imagined sexy things."

She shook her head. "I figured that if I imagined them, I'd want them, and if I couldn't get them, I'd be frustrated."

She was making a statement about her past, and Greg would have been deaf not to hear. He'd put money on the fact that she could realize any fantasy she wanted in his arms.

"I still think you're shy," he teased, but didn't push the issue because his mind was already zipping ahead. Diandra had lost a round. Another item of clothing had to go. "The bra," he breathed, dropping his gaze to that piece of lace. "Take off the bra."

For a minute, Diandra didn't move. Then her hands met at the front catch of her bra. She twisted it, released it, peeled the lace cups from her breasts and the straps from her shoulders. The air felt cool on her newly exposed skin, but she was so warm inside that she barely noticed.

Greg was the one with goose bumps. He wasn't sure how much more he could take of watching Diandra undress piece by piece. If he'd thought her sexy in her bra and panties, he had to redefine the word to describe what she looked like now. She was sitting demurely, her legs folded gracefully to one side. Her chin had the slightest downward tilt, causing her hair to brush her cheeks, and her bangs had an unintended part. Her shoulders were straight, made positively regal by the emerald necklace that lay pulsing around her neck, and beneath it were her breasts. Firm and nicely rounded, they were alabaster in the soft light of late day that filtered in through the window.

He was aware that while he was feeling shaky most everywhere else, that part between his legs was solid as a rock. If he hadn't been a man of self-control, he'd have lunged at her then and there. But the game wasn't through.

"Still okay?" he whispered, half-wishing she'd shake her head so he could take her in his arms.

She nodded. The game was nearly over. One more round, and one of them would be naked. Dragging her eyes from his, she focused on the letter cubes for the last time.

Neither of them was sharp. But then, neither of them

was concentrating on the game. When Diandra managed to score ten points more than Greg, the victory seemed anticlimactic.

"Last chance," he warned softly as he waited for her question.

"*Your* fantasy," she said in a breathy tone. "I want to know yours."

"I have more than one."

Her voice fell to a whisper. "Tell me the most erotic one."

Her whisper seared him. He was already painfully aroused, and she wanted a retelling of his most erotic fantasy. He would have laughed, except that there was nothing funny about the fantasy. Nor was there anything funny about his revealing it to Diandra. He'd never shared his most intimate thoughts with a woman before. That he was about to share them with Diandra was telling.

"I fantasize," he said quietly, "that I've been imprisoned in a room with a woman I don't know. I can't see her, because it's night and the room is pitch-black. Our lives are in danger. We need each other to survive, which means sharing a very basic trust, but the only way we can build that trust is by making love." His view grew lower, more hoarse. "So we do. We make love to each other first in traditional ways, then in more unusual ways, then even more sensual ways, then risqué ways. Still I can't see her, but my hands and mouth know her. My body knows her. She is warm and gentle, a little adventurous, very beautiful in my mind's eye." He paused, then said softly, "I trust her with my life."

"Do you love her?" Diandra heard herself ask.

"It's just a fantasy."

"But do you love her?"

"I trust her. I suppose I'd love her if I had a chance, but the fantasy always ends too soon."

"Sad," Diandra whispered.

But Greg was no longer thinking of the fantasy. He was thinking that his body was aching for Diandra, and that just then he needed her desperately. Too aroused to let pride stand in the way, he eased his briefs over his hardness and tossed them aside. Then, sitting back on his heels with the blood pounding from his heart to his groin and back, he waited for her to make her move.

Diandra couldn't take her eyes from him. She'd never seen a man as glorious, and she knew she never would. He was maleness at its best. He was Gregory York, and he wanted her, wanted her in a very beautiful way.

With the explosion of wild emotions inside, she came up on her knees and crossed the short distance to where he knelt. She put her fingertips to his mouth, slid them gently inside, drew them out only when her lips covered his. Her damp fingers found their way down his body to that part of him that was swollen with need. They closed on him and gently began to stroke.

"I need you, Greg," she whispered into his mouth. "Make love to me like you made love to her. Trust me that way."

Wanting her more than he'd wanted anything before, Greg slid his hands up her sides. He tried to temper his need by holding her lightly, but the brush of her nipples against his chest was his undoing. When his mouth took hers, there was no holding back. While his passion became hers, trust was the fuel that sent them higher and higher through the night.

CHAPTER NINE

GIVEN THE LENGTH and intensity of their lovemaking, Diandra should have slept until noon the next day. But she was awake at dawn, lying silently beside Greg, wondering how she was going to handle the fact that she was in love.

On the one hand, it made such sense. Their families' fates were intricately entwined.

Then again, it made no sense at all. Diandra had spent years detesting first Greg, then his father, too. True, she saw Greg in a different light now. But she didn't think she'd ever forgive his father; that was bound to be a bone of contention between them.

And then there was the issue of work. She and Greg were vice presidents of the same corporation, but they were rivals for the San Francisco store, which was still very much up for grabs.

And all that was before she considered Greg's feelings for her. She loved him, but did he love her? He'd never once said the words, despite all they'd done to each other the night before—and they'd done a lot. Diandra hadn't imagined that two people could do what they'd done. Even now, thinking back on it, she blushed.

But did he love her?

Carefully she turned her head to look at him. He was sprawled on his back, sleeping soundly, his hair mussed, his features relaxed. In the past hours, those features had become nearly as familiar to her as her own, and more dear.

There was a vague sense of unreality to it. They'd been cooped up together for four days, partners in a task neither of them wanted to do. Their normal lives were a world away. They were in a limbo of sorts, and therefore vulnerable when they might not normally have been so.

Her hand went to the emerald necklace. For what had to be the hundredth time since Monday, she wondered at its power. It hadn't made her love Greg; she'd done that on her own. But the necklace had created the force field in which she'd acted. Would the force field disintegrate once the necklace was removed? Would her feelings for Greg fizzle?

She didn't know the answers to those questions, or to the others that chipped away at the peace she'd found in Greg's arms. The future held such promise—yet no promise at all. She felt as though she were once more back in that boxwood labyrinth, lost and confused, not knowing which way to turn.

What she needed, she realized, was to return to familiar ground. She needed not only to think, but to think under circumstances that were normal. She needed to view what had happened from the world she knew in the hope that she could make some sense of it.

That meant leaving. The very thought of it created a void inside her, but it seemed the only way. She couldn't think straight as long as Greg was around, and while there was something beautiful about that, it was also frightening. He held a power over her, always had, always would. She had to know exactly how vulnerable she was.

With a final, heart-wrenching look at him, she crept silently from his bed and returned to her room, where she put on the business clothes she'd worn Monday and packed the few other things she'd brought. Then she stole down the stairs to the living room. Pausing before the marble mantel, she bowed her head and closed her eyes in a silent prayer that she was doing the right thing. Hands trembling, she removed the emerald necklace. She held it to her cheek for a lingering moment before returning it to its box. Then, hurrying lest she change her mind, she let herself out into the early morning air.

"WHAT IN THE hell did you do that for?" Greg bellowed over the line late that day. "I thought we'd established something last night. How do you think it felt to wake up and find out you'd gone?" He snorted. "So much for trust. And what about respect? You didn't even bother to leave a note. Did you think I wouldn't worry? I assumed you'd go straight to the office, but no, not you. And you didn't go home, either; I've been trying this number for hours. Where in the hell have you *been*?" Before she could answer, he raced on, "I thought we'd straightened a few things out, but I was wrong. You must still think I'm an insensitive clod if you thought I'd let you go without a word. I was *worried*, Diandra." He gave a harsh guffaw. "But I suppose that wouldn't mean anything to you. You're just as selfish as ever. Or maybe it's that you're a coward. You ran out of here because you couldn't face what was happening. Maybe you thought I'd start making demands on your precious time. Is the idea of fidelity that odious to you? Or is it San Francisco that's got you in a snit? Or," he went on in an icy voice, "was it your warped idea of revenge? You'd string me along until I was hooked, then leave me in the lurch? Did it feel good walking out on me like that? Huh? *Answer me*, Diandra."

But she couldn't. Her eyes were filled with tears, and there was a huge lump in her throat that wouldn't allow for any sound at all.

Greg didn't have that problem. "Well, let me tell you

something, sweetheart. Two can play the game. You may have given me the best time I've had in bed in months, but you're not the only woman in town. Not by a long shot." The connection was severed with an abrupt click.

Diandra held the phone to her ear for another minute, then let it slowly fall past her cheek and neck to her breast. Ducking her head low, she began to cry. She pressed the phone to the ache in her chest, and when that didn't help she began to sway back and forth. The ache persisted, and the tears kept coming.

There had been more times in her life than she cared to count when Diandra had felt alone. The earliest times had been when she'd wanted her mother, but her mother hadn't been around. There had been times during college when she'd wanted nothing more than to be tied to a man who was tied to her, but the right man had never come along. So she'd graduated, earned an advanced degree and immersed herself in CayCorp. Even then, after long days at the office, she'd too often come home feeling as empty as her apartment.

But she'd never felt more alone than she did just then.

How long she stood holding the dead receiver in her hand she didn't know. Gradually she stopped crying, and still she stood, not knowing where to go or what to do. At length, when she realized that she was cold, she replaced the receiver, went into the bedroom and climbed under the covers. There, huddled beneath satin sheets and a handmade comforter, she cried herself to sleep.

FIRST THING SATURDAY morning, after deciding that life must go on, Diandra went to work. Her office was as it had been when she'd left it the Monday before, except for the pile of papers on the desk. Distractedly she flipped through them, pulled out several for closer study, then set them aside and spent the next hour looking out the window. She was grateful that her secretary wasn't there to witness her idleness; she'd have thought her sick.

Heartsick was the correct term, though Diandra tried not to dwell on it. When she couldn't muster interest in the papers on her desk, she went shopping—not at Casey and York, but in the small boutiques of Georgetown.

The Saturday crowds were moderate, comforting in ways, since they assured her anonymity, disturbing in others, since they were largely made up of people in pairs or larger groups that, by comparison, made her feel all the more single. Still, she weathered them as the lesser of the evils. She didn't relish the idea of returning to her apartment alone.

Three times she passed public phones. Three times she bit her lip and silently debated making calls.

The first time, she thought of the party that was being given by a friend in Virginia. She'd been invited but had refused the invitation well before she'd gone to Boston, simply because she was tired of parties. Her feelings hadn't changed.

The second time, she thought of Anthony Adams. He was nothing more than a friend, and she needed a friend. But he'd ask questions she wouldn't want to answer. And besides, friend or not, she felt disloyal running to Anthony.

The third time, she thought of Greg. That time she turned away, knowing that her call wouldn't be welcome. He wasn't thinking highly of her. She'd only be asking for grief.

Time and again as she walked her hand went to her throat. Once the saleswoman in a lingerie boutique even eyed her in alarm, as though expecting her to keel over choking, and Diandra assumed she'd been looking as pained as she felt. It was absurd, she knew, but she felt raw. The emerald necklace had become part of her. Its removal had left an open wound.

In the end, for sheer lack of energy, she did go home, where she spent an unheard-of night in front of the television. She fell asleep there; she awoke there. Angry at herself, at Greg, at the world, she took jeans from the bag she'd never unpacked, threw on a sweater and sneakers and went out to walk through Washington like a tourist.

She was so lonely. It amazed her, because she'd only been with Greg for four days, but she kept remembering the things they'd done together, and her loneliness increased. Her only hope was that when she got back to work on Monday, when her office was full of the people who seemed to stream in and out on a regular basis, she'd feel more like herself. At least then she'd be able to deal with the loneliness. She always had in the past. She supposed she could do it again.

When she got back to work on Monday, her office was indeed full of the people who seemed to stream in and out on a regular basis, but they offered no relief from her pain. Though she dealt with each in a competent manner, competence was all they got. Her heart was elsewhere.

By the end of the day, she was beginning to wonder whether things would ever be the same again. The world seemed monochromatic. She couldn't garner enthusiasm for much at all.

It was almost a relief when an irate Bart called to demand her presence in Palm Beach the next morning. He gave no details, barely allowed her a word. He made it clear that she was to be there with no questions asked.

She went. She flew down by commercial airline, thinking that though she'd made the same trip a mere ten days before, it seemed more like a year. With that earlier trip on her mind, she half-expected to find Greg in Bart's penthouse. When she didn't, she felt simultaneously relieved and disappointed.

Both of those sentiments were premature. She'd simply arrived before him. Half an hour later and only minutes after a scowling Bart joined her on the patio, Greg came through the door looking like thunder.

"This had better be good, Bart," he growled, too consumed by his own anger to note Bart's. "You're pushing it."

Bart's voice rang as loudly as his age and style would allow. "I'll push it as far as I want, mister. I want some answers, and I want them now." His eyes flashed from Greg to Diandra and back. "What happened?"

Diandra was suffering too much to answer. Seeing Greg was bad enough; feeling the force of his angry gaze was like having a knife twisting in the wound.

"What happened," Greg seethed, "is that you sent us to do your dirty work. You didn't want to wade through all that stuff—"

"Not the town house," Bart interrupted with the sharp wave of a gnarled hand. "I don't give a hoot about that. What happened to the necklace?"

Greg shifted his glare to Greg before returning it to Bart. "Nothing happened to the necklace. We left it on the mantel right where we found it."

"But it was supposed to work!" Bart claimed indignantly. "It was supposed to work like a charm!" He looked at Diandra. "Yet you ran out of there early Friday morning—" his eyes flew to Greg "—and you left that afternoon, and neither of you spoke to the other all weekend, and you were zombies in the office yesterday."

Diandra was beginning to come around. Something was strange about what Bart was saying, strange enough to temporarily blunt her pain. "What are you talking about?" she asked cautiously.

"The *necklace!*" he shouted, then began to cough.

She shot a worried look at Greg. Sliding from her chair to the next, she put a hand on Bart's. "Relax. Please. Whatever it is isn't worth choking over."

Bart took one breath, coughed again, took another breath, then a third. He seemed to be calming himself by sheer force of will, and indeed, when he spoke again, his voice was more even. "That necklace is part of a set they call the Montclair Emeralds."

Diandra looked questioningly at Greg, who looked questioningly back.

Bart explained. "Charles de Montclair was a renegade Frenchman. As the legend goes, he lost his heart to a beautiful woman, stole her from the powerful duke to whom she'd been betrothed and brought her to live with him on his secluded estate. As a token of his undying love, he presented her with the emeralds. They were passed from generation to generation until the time of the French Revolution, when the couple's great-great-granddaughter fled to America. There, for the sake of survival, she was forced to sell the jewels one by one."

His tale ended. The echo of waves rolling onto the shore filled the background, but Diandra didn't hear. Her heart was thudding too loudly.

"How did you get the necklace?" she asked.

"I bought it from a friend, a collector. He said it was like Cupid's arrow. He assured me it would work."

She swallowed. "Work how? What was it supposed to do?"

Bart's furrowed brow grew all the more so. "Bring you two together!" He was clearly annoyed that they'd missed the point. "You're perfect for each other! Even a blind man could see it. You're a match physically and intellectually. You share a professional interest. You've never married, either of you, because there's no one else who can give you a run for your money. You're the best these families has come up with in years. You belong together. But you're so *damned bullheaded* that you can't see it for yourselves."

"So you decided to give us a push," Diandra murmured in dismay.

Greg was appalled. "You sent us up there on that cock-and-bull mission just to throw us in with that necklace?"

"It wasn't a cock-and-bull mission," Bart argued. "The town house had to be closed up sometime."

"But you don't have a buyer, do you?" Diandra asked. She was feeling the beginnings of the same slow burn that she'd heard in Greg's voice.

"I have buyers all the time. I just turn them down."

"But you told us you had one and that you needed the town house closed quickly. You used us, Bart. How could you have done that?"

"I did what I thought was right."

"Well, it wasn't," Greg told him. "Diandra and I are adults. We have a right to know what we're doing and why, and we have a right to decide for ourselves who to love."

"You can't force something like that on people," Diandra added, but Bart had a ready answer.

"I didn't force a thing. The necklace was supposed to do it without your even knowing."

"The necklace," Greg muttered. "Without us even knowing—fat chance! That necklace may be a magnificent piece of jewelry, but subtle it isn't. We felt its force from the start."

Bart old face brightened. "You did? That's a good sign. Maybe you just left too early. You didn't give it long enough to work."

"Oh, Bart, you aren't *listening*," Diandra cried. "That necklace—*no* necklace—is magical. It can't perform miracles. It can't do something that isn't supposed to be."

"But you *are* supposed to be," Bart insisted. His hopeful expression made him look every bit the leprechaun. "You and Greg should have been together years ago."

Greg shook his head with force. "Impossible."

Diandra agreed. "Greg and I have rubbed each other the wrong way since we were kids, and that was even before the business with..." She didn't want to say it.

Bart did, and with surprising composure. "With your parents? That business with your parents happened at a vulnerable time for both of you. If it hadn't been for that, I'm *sure* you'd have been together. It was destined that one day a Casey and a York would fall in love." He glanced off toward the sea, looking sober, and said in a sad voice, "It happened once, but too late. If only the timing had been better."

Greg was furious. "That whole *thing* sucked. There wasn't any love involved."

Diandra agreed. "It was pure lust."

"She seduced him—"

"He seduced her—"

"Keep still, both of you," Bart growled. "This is hard enough for me without your degenerating into juveniles spatting." Then he admitted on a note of defeat what he'd been too proud, after the stance he'd originally taken, to confess to any other family members. "There was no seducing done. They fell in love." He raised a hand as though to say, That's all, then dropped it back to his lap.

For a minute neither Greg nor Diandra spoke. They were too surprised to utter a word.

Greg was the first to recover. His tone was harsh and skeptical. "She didn't seduce him?"

Bart shook his head.

Diandra was as disbelieving as Greg. "Love?"

Bart nodded.

Greg waited for an explanation. When it didn't come, he burst out with, "Do you know what you're saying? You're saying that your son willingly betrayed both his wife and his best friend to have an affair with Abby. Willingly, Bart. That's some indictment. And it's a far different story from the one you've always told."

"I was hurt. Angry, at first. Disillusioned."

Straightening in her seat, Diandra took her own shot. "You blamed my mother for what happened. You looked at her like she was something dirty, something cheap. Every time her name came up, you turned your back."

"I was wrong," he said quietly. Slowly he added, "I didn't know then what I know now."

For the second time in as many minutes, a silence hung over his words. It was a very cautious Diandra who broke it this time.

"Do you know something that we don't?"

Looking uncomfortable, he said, "I found letters, letters from Abby to Greg. They were in my den. Greg must have stashed them there at some point. Maybe he wanted them found—I don't know—but I came across them by accident and I read every one."

Diandra was sitting on the edge of her seat, her hands tightly clasped in her lap. "What did they say?"

Bart sniffed in a breath in prelude to a reluctant confession. "She loved him. She was torn apart by that love. She felt guilty, because she knew that John and Sophia were being hurt. She kept asking what to do."

"And we'll never know what he said, will we?" Greg snapped. He was standing with his back rigid and his features tense, looking as dark as Diandra had ever seen him look.

"Not in his own hand," Bart conceded. In the wake of Greg's resistance, his confession became more forceful. "But some of it came through in Abby's letters. She wrote things like, 'You told me you feel the guilt,' or 'You love us both, Sophia and me,' or 'I'm glad last weekend meant as much to you as it did to me.' It was clear that they shared something special. It was also clear from the letters that they tried to control themselves."

Greg snorted.

Bart stared him down, gaining even greater strength as he spoke on. "At one point in her letters, Abby talked about years. That may have been how long their feelings for each other were simmering, and if so they have to be admired for fighting it as long as they did. It's possible that much of Abby's flitting was an attempt to escape her feelings for Greg. They were lovers who met at the wrong time, but what they felt was so strong that they couldn't stop it."

"Lust," Greg muttered. "Maybe mutual, but pure lust."

But Bart was shaking his head. "*No.* It was more than that. Apparently I knew my son better than you knew your father. He was a man who loved—he loved your mother, he loved you, and in the final years of his life he loved Abby. His mistake—*their* mistake, perhaps—was that they never made a choice. Abby couldn't cut off what she felt for John and Diandra anymore than Greg could cut off what he felt for your mother and you."

Switching his gaze to Diandra, he held up a hand. "I'm not saying that Abby was the best of mothers to begin with, any more than Greg was the best of fathers. They were who they were, but they tried. They tried to do it all and did none of it justice. In the end, they were probably as unhappy, if not more so, than the rest of us."

Greg swore softly. "Are you suggesting that they committed suicide in that plane?"

"No," Bart said gruffly. "I don't believe that. I can't believe it. And in any case, we'll never know. But the point is that if what happened between your parents is what's keeping you and Diandra apart, it shouldn't. You belong together. Abby and Greg came so close; you two could clinch it. It would be a damn shame if the love your parents shared is the one thing that prevents you from sharing your own." He paused for an instant, then went on with an air of belligerence. "These families were meant to be united. I want a Casey to marry a York, and I want to see it before I die."

"Dammit," Greg barked, "you can't program love! You can't just order it up!"

But that wasn't what Bart wanted to hear. Scowling at the patio tiles, suddenly looking and sounding every bit his eighty-four-years of age, he muttered, "The necklace was supposed to do it. Miller promised me it would work. I paid a pretty penny, and what do I have to show for it? Two disgruntled children and a messy town house."

"The town house," Diandra echoed in a high voice. "I don't believe you're worried about the town house."

"Frederick can get a crew to pack up in a day," Greg said angrily, "and as for two disgruntled children, we wouldn't be disgruntled at all if you hadn't butted in. Dammit, Bart," he went on in an ominous voice, "I don't like being manipulated. It's an insult to my intelligence."

Undaunted, Bart said, "So I maneuvered you up to Boston. I needed the work done, and you're family. I had a right to ask."

Diandra was feeling as angry as Greg. "You didn't ask. You ordered. Even when we suggested alternatives, you insisted that we do it your way. But the *worst* of it was that you held us hostage. You dangled something in front of us that you knew we both wanted."

Bart stared at her hard. "I never once tied San Francisco to that job."

"Maybe not verbally," Greg argued, "but it was right there, the perfect lure. You knew we both wanted it, and you knew that neither of us would give the other the edge by begging off the Boston job. Well, let me tell you something—" he began, only to be interrupted by Diandra.

"I don't *want* San Francisco," she declared in as sure a voice as she'd ever used. "You can do what you want with it, but—"

"The appeal is gone. That goes for me, too," Greg said with force. "I've got New York. I'll stay on there."

For the first time, Bart seemed rattled. "But—but you wanted San Francisco from the start."

"I wanted it from *before* the start, but that doesn't matter. If there's one thing I've learned from this mess it's that a store is a store. That's all. Believe it or not, there is more to life than Casey and York." He paused for a split second with a look of utter distaste on his face, then said in a voice that vibrated with anger, "I think you know what you can do with your San Francisco store." Turning on his heel, he stalked from the room.

Diandra would have applauded had she not been as livid. In the minute she took to compose herself, Bart spoke.

"He's angry. When he calms down, he'll realize that he didn't mean what he said."

"He meant it," she said with conviction. "And he's right. A store is a store. Not much of a basis for extortion."

Bart bristled. "Just a minute, young lady. I have never in my life stooped to extortion."

"There are subtle forms of it. But subtle or not, in this case it won't work. I don't want San Francisco."

"Then you're a fool. It's yours for the asking, now that Greg's turned away."

"A fool I may be, but I don't want it. Funny," she said without a hint of a smile, "I can't even remember why I wanted it to begin with." Standing, she slipped the slim strap of her purse over her shoulder.

Bart's frail body stiffened. "You can't leave me in the lurch this way."

"No one's left in the lurch. I can think of a dozen people who want San Francisco and who'd do a great job. You'll have your store."

"But I want that marriage!" he cried.

With the height of emotion passed, the anger that had kept Diandra going began to slip. Beneath it was a soul-deep sadness. "We can't always have what we want," she said. "I'm sorry." She started for the door.

His voice followed her, pleading now. "Try it again, Diandra. That necklace has power, I know it does."

She knew it, too. But the power of a gem was only as good as the strength of its wearer. And at that moment she wasn't feeling strong at all. Fearful that she'd break down in tears, she sent Bart a final tremulous look and quickly left.

GREG FLEW DIRECTLY back to New York, but by the time he arrived his anger had gone. In its place was a sense of loss that was more pervasive than he'd have imagined possible.

Acting out of the force of sheer habit, he distractedly climbed into a cab and gave his address. Then he slumped low on the torn leather seat and grappled with that loss.

It had nothing to do with San Francisco. He wasn't at all sorry about his decision. He knew New York. The New York branch of Casey and York was the largest, the most prestigious, the most challenging. Heading the San Francisco branch would be a novelty, but novelties wore off, and then where would he be? He'd be on the West Coast trying to deal with the same problems he'd had to deal with on the East Coast. So what was it worth?

Diandra. It all came back to Diandra. During the four days they'd spent together in Boston, she'd come to mean the world to him. He didn't know how it had happened, certainly didn't believe that the Montclair jewels had created something where it hadn't existed, but he'd come to see things in a new light.

Like Boggle. A new angle, new words. In Boston, he'd seen Diandra in a different context. Apart from CayCorp. Apart from family. She'd been a different woman from the one he'd expected. Then again, he supposed he'd been a different man. More relaxed. More open. More honest.

Wily old Bart.

Greg didn't have to wonder where he'd gone wrong. It had been the phone call he'd made to Diandra in Washington. He'd been such a fool. He'd been overwhelmed by a dozen strange emotions. Unable to deal with them, he'd lashed out in anger. If there had been any chance for them, he'd killed it then.

She hadn't tried calling him back, hadn't tried calling him since. She'd barely said two words to him at Palm Beach, and she'd looked nearly as miserable as he'd felt.

Which was interesting.

Would she have looked so miserable if she didn't care for him?

Would she have declared that she didn't want San Francisco even before he'd said *he* didn't want it—if she weren't sincere in her claim?

Would she have been so innocent in her sexual responses if she'd lived the wild life he'd always assumed?

Would she have given him her soul and then some in

bed that last night if she hadn't harbored the same deep and abiding feeling he did?

Coming up in his seat, he instructed the cabbie to head back to the airport. He needed some answers, and there was only one person who had them.

His destination was Washington. But first, he wanted another look at that necklace.

CHAPTER TEN

DIANDRA STARED AT the emerald teardrops and vowed not to cry. She'd done enough crying in the past few days to last her a lifetime, and it hadn't accomplished a thing.

What was called for was action. Action and honesty.

Oh, she'd been plenty honest with Bart. She'd meant what she'd said about San Francisco. She didn't want the assignment, wasn't sure why she ever had. But she hadn't been honest about her feelings for Greg, and that was what needed changing.

Standing before the necklace with her fingers curled over the edge of the marble mantel, she enumerated her mistakes.

First, she never should have left Greg that Friday morning—at least, not in the way she had. She should have told him her plans, should have explained that she was overwhelmed by what had happened. She should have woken him up or left a note or called him later that day. But she hadn't. He'd had a right to be angry.

Second, she should have said something when he'd finally called her. True, she would have had to squeeze the words out between the lump in her throat and his anger, but she should have done it somehow.

Third, she should have called him afterward. She'd had Saturday and Sunday. She should have tried to contact him, tried to tell him how she felt.

Fourth and finally, in Palm Beach, she could have,

should have spoken up. With all that talk about a love that was destined to be, she'd had more than one opportunity to bare her heart. But there'd been Bart and his scheming, which had angered her, then the revelations about her mother and Greg's father, which had shocked her. And there'd been Greg. He hadn't said a thing about love, hadn't said much about her at all.

But would he have been so short with Bart, right from the start, if he hadn't been deeply disturbed?

Would he have thrown San Francisco in the old man's face if something momentous hadn't changed inside him?

Would there have been as much hurt as anger in his voice when he'd called her if he hadn't felt something?

Would he have raised the issue of fidelity without good cause?

She swayed, and the emeralds winked. Indeed, the necklace was a charm. It had power. Without it, she and Greg would have bickered their way through those four days. They'd never have stopped long enough to give each other a chance. But the necklace could only do so much. It could no more force deeper emotions than it could control stubborn pride.

Eyes on the gems, she took one deep breath, then another. She wasn't about to put the necklace on—she had to stand on her own this time. But she felt calmer. She knew what had to be done, and she was determined to do it.

Then she heard the sound of a lower door closing. Head whipping around, she stared at the living room archway. Frederick had been on his way out when she'd arrived and had said he'd be gone for the evening. It had been her impression that Mrs. Potts had ceased her cleaning sessions, since Bart was supposedly selling the town house—at least, she hadn't shown up the week before.

Nor had any of those other who had keys, not that they would be coming this late in the day.

There was another person who had a key. Just as she did. She held her breath, listening to the rapidly rising patter of muted steps on the stair runners.

Then he appeared. His momentum would have taken him straight into the room had he not caught sight of her first. He came to a stunned halt just inside the archway and stared.

Totally immobile but for the thudding of her heart, Diandra stared right back. *Action and honesty.* The words blinked their subliminal message in her mind, but she was unable to move or speak. To do either would have been to expose her heart's feelings, and she'd spent so many years protecting herself from Greg that she supposed it was a conditioned reflex.

Suddenly it struck her, though, that what had worked during her childhood was now simply a childish response. The woman she was demanded better. The man Greg was deserved more.

But before she could act, Greg did. With slow, sure steps that were in contradiction to the vulnerable look on his face, he crossed the floor to stand before her. His eyes searched hers, asking all the questions he'd wondered about, and in the asking were the answers she wanted. When he raised a hand to her cheek, she tipped her head to his palm.

So little action, so much honesty.

With a low moan, Greg wrapped his arms around her and clasped her so tightly to him that for a minute her toes actually left the ground. She might well have floated. She felt suddenly light-headed and lighthearted, relieved of an awesome weight. Her arms were coiled high around his neck, trembling with the strength of her emotions.

His lips moved against her hair, but his whispered words were sporadic and broken. "Ah…Di…when I thought…of never being close to you again…."

Sinking her hands into his hair, she tugged until his head came up. "Were you in agony?" she whispered soberly.

"Yes."

"So was I."

"Why do we do this to each other?"

"Habit, I think."

"We're fools."

She nodded and put a hand on his beard, wanting to touch, to verify that he was there. "I think we've been fools for a long time."

"How long?"

"Years."

"I think that's how long we've been drawn to each other. We fought because of the attraction. It was there even back then, but we couldn't accept it."

She touched her thumb to the corner of his mouth. "That was dumb of us."

"Stubborn."

"Defensive."

"Shortsighted."

"Self-defeating. Bart was wrong," she decided. "The reason neither of us has settled down is because no one else would *have* us."

Greg's arms rose on her back until his fingertips braced her head. "Will you have me?"

She nodded, then arched both brows to return the question.

"What do you think?" he growled and gave her another bone-crushing hug.

Diandra thought she had to be the happiest woman alive. And the luckiest. To have Greg was to have far more than money could ever buy. He was unique. He was magnificent. He was priceless.

Unique, magnificent, priceless. With her cheek pressed snugly to his collar, she opened her eyes to the emerald necklace. It sat in its box on the mantel, smugly, she thought. At the slight movement of Greg's head, she looked up to find that he, too, was studying it. When he looked back at her, his gaze was dark and intense. It fell to her lips.

Lowering his head, he met her in a deep, heart-throbbing, tongue-tangling, open-mouthed kiss. And by the time either of them spoke again, they were lying spoon fashion on the bed in the Oak Room. They'd made spectacular love. Their bodies were sated, but their minds were coming to life.

"I love you," Greg whispered against the warm curve of her ear.

Diandra hugged his arm, which lay between her breasts and whispered back, "I love you, too." The words echoed in the silence like a beautiful song. For an encore, she turned her head and instigated another kiss. Then she asked, "When did you know?"

"Know, or admit?"

"Either. Both."

"Know—the last night we spent together. I'd never done those things with another woman. They require trust and devotion and a hunger so intense that it rises above the physical. Admit—when I got back to New York today. I realized that I'd used my anger as a shield. When it slipped, the road ahead looked mighty bleak." He rose on an elbow, caught her chin with his fingers and turned up her face. "I won't have to live through that kind of hell, will I?"

"No."

"You'll marry me?"

"Yes."

He kissed her soundly, then passionately, but passion became gentleness when he felt an overpowering need to talk. Settling her back against him again, he said, "You bring out sides of me that no other woman has. I've never felt tender or possessive or protective before, but I feel those things with you." He sighed deeply. "Besides, you're a tough opponent. I like it better when we're on the same side."

"You could always win."

"I want *us* to win."

The fullness of love welled within Diandra. It was several minutes before she spoke again. "I want *us* to win, too. How will we manage it with work?"

"Are you tied to Washington?"

"No, but you've got New York neatly taken care of. There'd be nothing for me to do there."

"That's good, because I'm tired of New York. I was thinking of—"

"Boston, why don't we try Boston?" she asked, squirming onto her back and looking up into his face. "Let Alex take San Francisco. He's done a super job with the store here; he'd be great there. He'd consider it a personal victory if Bart gave it to him. We could convince Bart to do it."

"In a minute. He owes us."

The flicker of a frown crossed her brow. "Or do we owe him?"

"I think it's a little of both, but don't tell him that. He deserves to feel guilty."

"He'll get pleasure out of our marriage."

"And if we sell our places in New York and Washington and buy the town house from him…what do you think?"

She didn't have to spend long at it. "He'd love it. *I'd*

love it. But only if I can do the parlor over in white. I want warm and welcoming."

"You'll get virginal and forbidding."

"Trust me. It'll be warm and welcoming."

"It'll be filthy in a week."

"Only if you stomp through it wearing muddy boots."

"I won't. But what about the kids?"

She sucked in an audible breath and whispered, "The kids. That's an exciting thought. They can get the rug dirty. I don't care. You were right when you said they'll be beautiful. They will be."

He slid a hand to her tummy. "They may be right now. At least, the first of them."

She covered his hand to keep it there. "If we're sharing the Boston store, you can cover for me while I'm home with the kids. That way I could keep a hand in the till while they're little, but still have a career when they're grown."

"When they're grown, I want us to travel. Even before they're grown, I want us to do that." He urged her onto her side to face him, smoothed wisps of raven hair from her cheeks and left the backs of his fingers lightly caressing her skin. "I don't like the pace I've kept. I don't like the person I've been, working that way. Let's do things differently. Let's be more laid-back. We've each had our own store; we know the ropes. We should be able to do it with one eye closed by now. So we'll hire and train people to be the other eye. That way we'll have a real life."

Diandra liked that idea. She showed him so by smiling and turning her head just enough to kiss his fingers. She was feeling very relaxed, very laid-back indeed, which was why she was surprised when Greg said, "Let's get married tomorrow."

"Tomorrow?" So quickly! "I don't think we can. There's a waiting period—"

"Let's fly someplace where there isn't a waiting period. I want to be married, and I want it soon."

"But I want a big wedding. I've always wanted a big wedding."

"Then we'll have two. A secret one now and an unsecret one later."

"You're worried I'm pregnant."

"Not worried, because I'd be thrilled if you were, but it's something we should consider." His gray eyes were warm, yet they held an urgency. "There's been so much controversy between our families. I don't want anyone thinking, much less suggesting, that we had to get married. Because that's not true. You know it as well as I do. If we didn't feel what we do for each other, you'd never agree to the marriage, baby or no baby. And anyway, the possibility of a baby is only one reason to get married now. The other is that I don't want to risk losing you."

"You couldn't lose me."

"I almost did last weekend. I almost did this morning."

"But that was before we knew what we know. I love you, Greg. I'm not leaving."

He wasn't completely convinced. "We'll fight. We always have, always will. We're both capable of doing rash things in anger."

"Then we'll have to work on that. But I want a big wedding, and I want it in June. I'll elope with you tomorrow only if you'll let me have that."

"You've always dreamed of a big June wedding?"

"No. But I want the world to know who I'm marrying, and a big June wedding sounds like fun."

Greg realized that her argument worked both ways. He wanted the world to know who he was marrying, too. And besides, he was in a compromising mood. "Okay. We'll have two weddings. But if we go for the big shindig in

June, we'll go for a big honeymoon afterward. What say you to a cruise to France, then a trip to the chateau of this renegade Frenchman, Charles de Montclair?"

She draped an arm over his shoulder. "I say that's very romantic."

"Could be less than luxurious if the chateau turns out to be a barn."

Diandra squeezed her eyes shut and wailed, "Don't ruin the image."

"But it could be so."

"So?"

"So the accommodations could be lousy."

"So?"

"So honeymoons are supposed to be posh."

She shook her head. "Honeymoons are supposed to be a time when husband and wife are together. We will be. I don't care where."

Splaying a large hand over her bottom, he pressed her close. "As long as there's a bed," he murmured and, dipping his head, sucked her lower lip into his mouth.

She didn't get it back for a while, and it was a while after that before she could gather enough breath to speak. Her head was on his chest, her leg fallen limply between his. "Greg?" she asked in a whisper.

He was lying on his back with one arm thrown to the side and the other resting along her spine. "Mmm?"

"Am I as good as Corinne?"

"Better. Much better." He paused. "Tommy Nolan?"

"No comparison."

"Him, or me?"

"You. He didn't know what he was doing. Or maybe it was me who didn't know what I was doing. It wasn't a particularly satisfying experience."

"I'm glad." Again he paused. "Diandra?"

"Mmm?"

"About our parents…"

"Hard to accept," she said in a small voice. "I know."

"I've thought one way for such a long time."

"Me, too."

"It may take a while to change."

"Mmm."

"Will you be patient?"

"If you will."

"I will."

They lay in silence for a time. Greg drew the blanket over them and shifted her more comfortably in his arms. Her face was nestled beneath his chin, in the spot she loved just below his beard.

"Greg?" she murmured against his skin. "Who do you think left the necklace on the mantel?"

"One of Bart's elves."

"Seriously."

"Seriously. He's a little bit of magic, that old man."

"And the necklace? Do you think it's magic?"

"I think it's suggestive. Maybe even seductive."

"I was worried that without it what we felt would fizzle, but last weekend in Washington, what I felt grew even stronger and the necklace was here."

Greg suddenly tossed the covers back, rolled to the side of the bed and was up.

"Where are you going?" she cried in alarm.

"To get it. It's still downstairs."

She put a hand to her throat, surprised to find it bare. She was still grappling with that discovery when Greg returned. Putting one knee on the mattress, he pulled her up, propped her against his thigh and fastened the emeralds around her neck. He traced the circle of gems with his hand, trailing his fingers slowly down her throat and over the last diamond fringe. When his eyes met hers, they were gray velvet and deep.

"You are," he breathed on a note of awe, "the one woman in the world who can wear this necklace with style. Legend may have it that it was made for another woman, but as far as I'm concerned it was made for you."

Diandra was feeling all warm and tingly inside. Lean muscles, long limbs and more than six feet of hair-spattered skin could do it to her every time. Actually, she realized, Greg did it whether he was naked or not. All he had to do was to look at her with those hungry gray eyes, and she was lost.

"What about Bart?" she asked distractedly.

Greg followed her down to the bed. "What about him?"

"Should we tell him the necklace did it?" she whispered.

Dipping his head, Greg drew a line with his tongue up her throat from the necklace to her chin. "That'd give him a thrill."

She rubbed his thighs with hers. "He's such a romantic."

"So are you." While his mouth did erotic things to her ear, his hand cupped her breast, thumb dabbing her taut nipple. "Did the necklace do it?"

"I don't…know…ah, Greg…" She slid her open palm down his front. "What do you…think?"

"No…yes…maybe…harder, Di, oh, yes…"

There was no more talk then, and the issue of the emerald necklace and its power remained unresolved, but somehow that didn't matter. What mattered was their love and the fact that it made them complete. A Casey would marry a York, just as Bart had hoped, just as fate had decreed. The legend lived on.

* * * * *

YOUR PARTICIPATION IS REQUESTED!

Dear Reader,

Since you are a lover of romance fiction –
we would like to get to know you!

Inside you will find a short Reader's Survey.
Sharing your answers with us will help our
editorial staff understand who you are and
what activities you enjoy.

To thank you for your participation, we
would like to send you 2 books and 2 gifts –
ABSOLUTELY FREE!

Enjoy your gifts with our appreciation,

Pam Powers

**SEE INSIDE
FOR READER'S
SURVEY**

CHAPTER ONE

BAD VIBES. From the start, I had bad vibes about the plan. But I ignored them, because Cooper was in trouble and given all Cooper had done and been for me in the past six years, I reasoned that a small sacrifice on my part was the least I could do in return. So I swallowed my pride and called home. Cooper needed counsel, and who was more qualified to give me the name of the best criminal lawyer money could buy than my mother, the judge?

Peter Hathaway, she'd said.

I didn't recognize the name, but Mother assured me that he was the best in the business. She hadn't actually seen him in action, since she sat in Philadelphia and he practiced in New York, but she'd heard plenty about him. She sounded delighted to have an excuse to call him. That made me uneasy.

Then Dad checked him out with his friends the Humphreys who, after making their millions in pharmaceuticals, had hired Peter Hathaway to defend them against charges of falsifying research data. Lovely reference source, the Humphreys. They'd been found guilty and been heavily fined. Still, they'd praised Peter Hathaway to the hilt. That made me even more uneasy.

It didn't help matters when suddenly the whole family was involved in my affairs. I shouldn't have been surprised. It had always been that way. But I'd been removed from it for a while, so I was jolted when my brother Ian felt called upon to phone and inform me, in his own inimitably arrogant manner, that Peter Hathaway was serious legal business. Then Ian's wife, Helaine, always the vamp, added—a little too suggestively, I thought—that the lawyer was a lady-killer. My sister Samantha went so far as to say that if she divorced David, which she was seriously considering doing because he hadn't yet begun to recover the hundreds of thousands of dollars he'd lost in the stock market crash of '87, she'd go after Peter Hathaway herself. He had the Midas touch, she said.

I wondered how she knew, but I wasn't about to ask.

In any case, the endorsement was unanimous. It was the first time I could remember my family agreeing on anything—with the exception, of course, of their disapproval of my life-style—and that made me the most uneasy of all.

Peter Hathaway. He was big city, big name, big bucks—everything I'd rejected. And Cooper knew it, which was one of the reasons he was angry. He argued that Adam would never have called in reinforcements from home. Cooper may have been right. But Adam had been dead for six years. And Adam had never been charged with smuggling stolen goods.

It had been nearly a decade since I'd left what my parents considered to be civilization, but that didn't mean I was out of touch. I read the papers. I knew what Cooper would face if he was convicted. So, bad vibes or not, I hired Peter Hathaway sight unseen.

That was on Tuesday. On Friday, I steeled myself for his visit. I prepared myself for a man who was whistle smooth and arrogant, who was direct to the point of curtness and who would very likely cross-examine me even before he got to Cooper. If he *ever* got to Cooper. I hadn't yet convinced Cooper to agree to be represented.

I hadn't told Peter Hathaway that, of course. I doubt he'd have agreed to come all the way to Maine if the fact of a client had been in doubt. Then again, I'd offered him his own private, shore-front hotel for the weekend, and if that wasn't lure enough, I'd promised that a retainer would be waiting when he got here. I assumed that was adequate incentive. Still, I was going to have some explaining to do—to Peter and Cooper both.

A simple life. That was all I'd ever wanted. How things had suddenly gotten so complex, I didn't know. But then, there were lots of things I didn't know.

Like why Adam had abandoned me.

Like how Elizabeth Taylor could love my work.

Like who put a cache of stolen diamonds on Cooper's boat.

I did know how I got the headache that was building behind my eyes. I got headaches when I agonized over those things I didn't know. Adam's remedy had been a gentle forehead massage, accompanied by soothing songs sung in his soft tenor. Cooper's remedy was a dark, silent room, a comfortable bed, a warm cloth on my eyes.

Given that neither Adam nor Cooper was around, I settled for three aspirin and a cup of strong, hot tea, which I carried to the window. My front yard was looking wild and windblown, understandable since the small stone house in which I lived stood high on a bluff overlooking the ocean. I'd always found the view beyond the poor, misshapen pine to be hypnotic. Wave after wave swelled from the horizon, rolling toward the shore and imminent destruction against the rocks. I couldn't see the crash from where I stood, but its thunder was second nature to me, as was the high spray of sea foam that rose by my bluff.

I loved the ocean. Bleak as it was, particularly now that Columbus Day had come and gone, I was drawn to it. I felt at home here. I could be me. I could pull my hair into a ponytail and wear jeans and a sweater whether I was throwing clay, visiting with friends at Sam's Saloon, or waiting for a hotshot lawyer from Manhattan to arrive.

I would have glanced at my watch if I'd had one, but it had been years since I'd cared whether it was one or two or three. So I concentrated on drinking my tea with a mind toward relaxation.

All too soon the cup held little more than bits of leaves that had escaped the tea bag. They weren't much more than shadows against the porcelain; still, I studied them. I turned the cup, swirled the leaves in the few drops of tea that lingered. I imagined I saw weird configurations, shapes with no patterns, and wondered what a tea reader would say. Better still, I wondered what a psychiatrist would say. Not that it mattered. I was comfortable with myself and my life.

Tipping my head back, I swallowed the lingering drops of tea and with them any configurations of leaves, weird or otherwise. Lowering the cup, I was turning toward the kitchen when a movement at the side window caught my eye. A black car rolled to a halt on the pebbled drive. I hadn't heard a sound; the whip of the wind would have drowned it out even if it had managed to penetrate the thick, double-paned windows of the house. But then, a Jaguar would purr so softly that there would be little to hear.

Uh-huh. A Jaguar. Peter Hathaway—legal eagle, lady-killer, man with the Midas touch—would be the Jaguar type.

For a split second, every one of those bad vibes I'd experienced in the past few days belted my insides, and in that split second I felt utterly insecure. Then I caught myself, took a deep breath, looked around. This was my house, my world. I had no cause to be insecure.

Life was what you made of it. Adam and I had always believed that, and for the most part I still did. Cooper needed help; I was going to see that he got it. To do that, I had to approach this interview with confidence.

Drawing myself to my full five-foot-four even as I held the empty tea cup to my chest, I leveled a glance out the window. The first thing I noticed was that the car wasn't a Jaguar, but a more sedate-looking Saab. It was an incidental point, likely insignificant, since the car was probably a rental, but it occupied my mind for those few brief moments until its driver stepped out.

He wasn't what I'd expected at all. I'd expected a three-piece suit, not a sweater and slacks. I'd expected silver hair, not dark brown. I'd expected a slick veneer, not a rakish one.

The vibes came again, stronger than ever, setting off tremors in my stomach while the rest of me stood stock still.

I'd expected European handsome, not American handsome, but American handsome was defying the wind to stand straight and tall by his car, making a slow study of his surroundings. He looked out toward the sea; his shoulders broadened with the deep breath he took, and I could have sworn I saw a fleeting smile. More straight-faced, perhaps assessingly, he took in the front yard, its small, sad pine, the clumps of scrub grass that valiantly battled the elements. Then he looked at the house, at the roof, the fieldstone siding, the window.

Suddenly his gaze penetrated the glass and caught mine. I didn't move. It wasn't that his eyes pinned me to the spot, because if I'd wanted to leave it I could have. But I didn't want to look skittish. I didn't want to look nervous or uncertain. It seemed important that he know I wasn't afraid. It seemed important that *I* know it.

So I held his gaze until he turned and strode confidently toward the house. By the time he passed the front window, I was on my way to meet him. Confidence demanded confidence; so I'd been taught as a child, and though I'd spurned others of those childhood teachings, this one survived. Peter Hathaway barely had time to cross the small, sheltered porch and lift a hand to knock when I opened the old oak door.

Very slowly that hand lowered, but I was already looking beyond it to his face. I had to look up; he stood at least six foot two. His broad shoulders and lean hips suggested man at his best. Nothing I saw in his features dispelled that notion.

His hair wasn't just brown, it was a rich mahogany and unfairly thick. Its texture appealed to the artist in me, though it didn't take an artist to realize that the tossing the wind had given it simply improved on the work of a skilled stylist.

He wasn't tanned. I wasn't sure if I'd expected him to be, and in any case, it didn't matter because his skin had a healthy glow. It, too, was textured—rougher where he shaved, creased where he squinted, laughed or frowned— and there was a small scar on his cheekbone that gave him a mysterious air.

But it was his eyes that grabbed me. They were pale green, almost to the point of luminescence. I'd never seen any like them. On the one hand they were eerie, on the other enticing. They probed with an intensity that frightened me, then soothed in the next blink. I tried to look away, but couldn't. Nor could I control the sudden, wild beating of my heart.

"Jill Moncrieff?"

His deep voice cut through the thunder of the sea and the echo of the wind to say my name, and I've never been more grateful for anything in my life. For, God help me, in those few short moments when I'd been bound by his gaze, I'd forgotten who I was.

A single, hard swallow brought me back. "Yes," I said with all the composure I could muster in a matter of seconds. I extended my hand. "You must be Peter Hathaway."

His hand was large and warm, enveloping mine with the same confidence that surrounded the rest of him, but I didn't have long to dwell on it when he did something that drove all other thoughts from my mind.

He smiled.

Actually it was more of a half smile, a lopsided curve of his mouth. It held surprise, smug pleasure and utter maleness, reflecting the thoughts I assumed to be swirling through his head. It was a dangerous smile if ever there was one, but for the life of me I couldn't look away.

"So you're Judge Madigan's daughter," he announced in a soft, self-satisfied tone of voice. Still holding my hand, he made a slow sweep of my body, and while his gaze was more curious than insolent, I had to work not to squirm. He was a man with far greater experience than I possessed, and I felt vulnerable.

Reacting against that, I retrieved my hand, steadied my chin in a self-assured manner and said quietly, "That's right."

"You don't look the way I expected you would." His eyes caught mine again, this time in mild challenge.

"What had you expected?"

"A dog."

I couldn't believe he'd said that. "Excuse me?"

"I figured that being a Madigan heiress, there'd have to

be something desperately wrong with your looks for you to be stashed away up here."

"There's nothing wrong with my looks."

The lazy half smile came again, along with an appreciative, "So I see." Then the smile faded. "I'd also expected someone a little older. I met your brother at a party not long ago. It turned out he went to Penn with a high school buddy of mine. You must be fifteen years younger than us."

Slowly I shook my head. "If that was meant as a compliment, you missed. I wouldn't want to be twenty-five again for the world."

"Why not?"

"When I was twenty-five, my husband died. My career was in limbo. I went through a rough time." In a chilly reminder of those dark days, the wind chose that moment to gust through the door. "That was six years ago, Mr. Hathaway," I said, holding back the hair that wanted to blow into my eyes. "I've come a long way since then. I'm quite happy with my life now, except for this little problem with Cooper." I stood back. "It's chilly. Why don't you come in and let me close the door?"

I wasn't sure whether I'd shocked him with my blunt revelation about Adam. I hoped so. It bothered me that he should think me an innocent, when I wasn't. While I wouldn't call my life in Maine as sophisticated as the one I'd once known, I'd probably seen more hardship and pain—and more joy—in the past ten years than any of *my* classmates at Penn.

Keeping his feelings well to himself now, much as I would have expected from a smooth city boy, Peter Hathaway stepped over my threshold and into the living room. Instantly the room seemed smaller than usual, which was absurd, I told myself. Cooper was every bit as tall as

Peter Hathaway, perhaps even broader. When a little voice inside me whispered something about an aura of virility surrounding Peter, I tuned it out.

"Have a seat," I suggested, hoping that if his body were folded I wouldn't feel as threatened.

But he started to wander around the room, pausing before a table here, a shelf there, to study my work. "Your mother said you were a potter." He examined a pair of candlesticks that were irrevocably entwined. "She said that your things are shown in some of the best galleries in New York, but that you choose to work here for the sake of concentration."

"Mother would say that," I remarked, though not unkindly. I'd mellowed enough over the years to allow my family its excuses for what they considered to be my bizarre behavior.

"Is it untrue?" he asked. His back was to me, but I could see him touch a small vase that looked all the more delicate in contrast to his long, blunt-tipped fingers.

"To some extent. Life here is simpler than it is in the city, and in that sense it's easier to concentrate. Then again, there are many artists who work in city garrets and do just fine. Where one lives is a matter of personal choice. I've chosen to live here for reasons that have nothing to do with concentration."

He did turn then, and I half wished he hadn't. Facing him head-on, I suffered that same inner jolt that I'd felt earlier. Something about the way he looked at me made my heart catch.

"If I asked what those reasons are," he said, "would you tell me?"

I forced myself to breathe normally. "No."

"Why not?"

"Because you're not here to talk about me. You're here to talk about Cooper."

"Then why isn't Cooper here?" he asked, with a blunt and simple logic that put me quickly on the spot—which was where, when I thought of it, I'd felt from the moment Peter Hathaway had appeared at my door.

"Cooper isn't here," I said slowly, wishing all the while that Peter Hathaway was short, fat and balding, "because I wanted to talk with you first. There are certain things you should understand before you meet Cooper."

Peter slipped both hands into the pockets of his slacks, drawing the fine gray fabric more snugly across his hips. I don't know why, but my eyes fell, then bobbed back up on a silent command, and I prayed that my face didn't look as warm as it felt.

Gesturing beseechfully toward a chair, I again urged him to sit. "Please." When he seemed determined to simply stand there, so tall and straight and beautifully masculine, looking at me, I tried a different diversion. "Did they serve you anything on the plane? Have you had lunch?"

"I didn't fly. I drove up."

That surprised me. "All the way from New York?"

"I got an early start," he explained. "I enjoy driving. I don't get to do it enough." He paused for an instant before adding, "Besides, the alternative was flying into Boston and switching to a small commuter plane. They can be harrowing. I avoid them at all costs."

Big city, big name, big bucks, afraid of flying? I had trouble believing that. If his reputation was indicative of his practice, he flew all the time. I wasn't quite sure whether he was trying to charm me into forgetting the danger of his smile by presenting me with a flaw, but if so, I wasn't buying.

"It would have been faster to fly," I told him. "I'm

prepared to spend whatever it takes to clear Cooper's name. Still, the well isn't bottomless. If I'm paying you for travel time—"

"You're not," he cut in, looking around again. "If I choose to take the longer route, I cover myself. Besides, I'm not on retainer yet. I haven't agreed to take this case."

"Oh." Thanks for nothing, Mom. "I'm sorry. I was misinformed." And for that I'd offered my house for the weekend? Thanks for *nothing*, Mom.

Peter Hathaway didn't look at all disturbed. "No problem," he said and crossed to the small table that Adam and I had picked up so long ago in Nanny Walker's attic. Like most of the furniture in the room, it was a local relic. Like most, it had been stripped, sanded and restained. I loved doing things like that, loved thinking of the artisan who had originally made a piece, loved caressing the curves he or she had so painstakingly carved. After all, I was an artist, too, a partner in obsession.

This particular table was a round mahogany piece that stood on an intricately crafted pedestal and had delicate fluting around its rim. On its surface was a small, gently swirling candy dish of my own making and two photographs, each mounted in strikingly unusual metal frames made by my friend, Hans, who lived in Bangor.

Peter raised the larger of the two. It was a picture of Adam and his crew in front of the *Free Reign*. "Who's who?" he asked.

Knowing that the sooner he started learning names, the better, I crossed to where he stood and moved a light finger over the glass. "Adam…Cooper… Jack…Tonof…Benjie."

"Was that the pecking order?"

"Pretty much so. Cooper was second in command to Adam. Jack and Tonof were experienced men who worked hard but had no stake in the endeavor other than what money they earned. Benjie is Cooper's brother."

"He's just a kid."

"He was fourteen when this was taken. He's twenty now."

Peter studied the picture a little longer, then set it back on the table and lifted the smaller one. It was of Adam and me, taken during the first year of our marriage. Adam hugged me from behind in the waist-up shot. We were windblown, two blond beach bums, scantily clad, looking tanned, carefree, immortal.

"He was a handsome man," Peter commented.

"Yes."

"How did he die?"

It occurred to me to remind him a second time that he was there to discuss Cooper, not me, when I realized that, as with the identity of the crew, my answer would provide necessary background information. Besides, I had nothing to hide. Adam's death had been reported in the papers. It was matter of public record. In fact, I was surprised my mother hadn't already told him.

"There was a fishing accident. A piece of equipment went berserk. Adam was swept overboard and underwater before his crew could see, much less help."

Peter slid his gaze to me, stunning me again with its force. This time it penetrated the protective skin I'd grown following Adam's death, and for an instant, the pain was exposed, raw once more. He touched it. I would have gasped if he hadn't suddenly looked back at the photograph.

His features gave nothing away as he stood there, silently studying the picture. Only when he returned it to its place and looked at me did I realize how close we were standing. Tearing my eyes from his, I glanced down at the cold cup in my hand. "I'd like some fresh tea," I murmured and started off toward the kitchen. I thought I'd made my escape and was taking a deep, shaky breath when Peter's voice came from several paces behind.

"Any coffee?"

I swallowed the tail end of the breath and, without turning, said, "Sure."

"I'd love some, if it wouldn't be too much trouble."

"No trouble." I would have given anything to have him back in the living room, but it was too late. He was well into the kitchen. I could feel his presence through the fine hairs at the back of my neck.

Putting a hand there, I used my free hand to put the kettle on to boil, then reached for the coffee cannister.

"Neck problems?"

"No, no." Dropping my hand, I quickly measured coffee beans into the mill.

"This is charming," Peter said. I turned to find him within arm's length, looking around much as he'd done in the other room. "It has character."

Following his gaze, I took in the dovetailing of wood and tile that gave the kitchen its pecan color and its warmth. "I thought so."

"I'll bet it wasn't like this when you bought it."

Remembering that day so long ago when I'd first seen the house, I couldn't help but smile. "You bet right. It was old and ugly, the worst room in the place. We tore everything out, then put new things in piece by piece. Not that it's state of the art," I added quickly, lest he think I'd left luxury to create luxury. The kitchen wasn't luxurious, just comfortable and efficient and aesthetically pleasing. "What you see here are the basic amenities, but they're more than adequate. I can put together as elegant a meal as any situation warrants."

"Can you manage a tuna sandwich?"

That wasn't quite the kind of elegant meal I'd been picturing. "Excuse me?"

"I drove straight through," he said, immobilizing me with those luminescent green eyes of his. "I haven't eaten since breakfast, and that was before seven this morning. If you have a can of tuna and a little mayo in the house, I'd love a sandwich. If you give me the workings, I'll make it myself. In fact," he swallowed, "give me a fork and I'll eat the tuna from the can."

I stared up at him. "You're that hungry?"

"That hungry."

"Why didn't you say so before?"

"It seemed rude. I'd just arrived."

"And the difference now?"

"This kitchen. It's very inviting."

So was he. Uncomfortably so. Looking up into those eyes, aware of the tousle of his hair, the shadow of a beard on his cheeks, the faint scent of something clean and male that clung to his skin, I felt attracted to him in ways that were strange and unbidden. After all, I loved Adam. He'd been all I'd needed when he was alive, and his memory was all I needed now.

Peter Hathaway was in my house for one reason and one reason alone—to defend Cooper. And the sooner he set about doing that, the better I'd feel.

"If you'll give me a little room," I cleared my throat and turned back to the counter, "I'll put together some lunch."

Out of the silence, I heard Peter step back, then pull a stool from beneath the adjacent counter. The stool creaked when he sat. If I'd been on the ball, I'd have taken the stool for myself, leaving him to sit a little farther off at the table. I'd have preferred that. This way, not only could he watch everything I did, but I was aware of his doing it.

I'd missed my chance, though. Determined to ignore the large, dark form in my periphery, I focused in on my work.

"Tell me about Cooper," Peter said.

I waited until the noise of the coffee mill died, then said, "Where should I begin?"

"How long have you known him?"

"Nine years. He was one of the first people we met when we moved here."

"Why did you move here?"

"Because I wanted to pot and Adam wanted to fish."

"Was Adam's family as wealthy as yours?"

I dumped the ground coffee beans into a filter. "I thought you wanted to know about Cooper."

"I do. I'm getting there."

"A little roundabout, wouldn't you say?"

"Not really. You feel strongly enough about Cooper to bankroll his defense. If I'm to represent him well, I have to know about the people around him."

The relevance of Adam's roots to Cooper's defense was arguable; I made no attempt to hide my skepticism. But I had trouble sustaining it, trouble keeping my mind on track. Peter looked so comfortable sitting on the stool not far from my elbow that I also had trouble thinking of him as a big-shot lawyer. Big-shot lawyers didn't make themselves at home in country kitchens miles and miles from the nearest city. If it hadn't been for my mother's recommendation, I might have wondered how "big-shot" he really was.

I wondered, then, whether he read the doubt on my face, because he did turn his attention to Cooper.

"You said that he was second in command to your husband. Was he hired specifically for that purpose?"

"Yes. Adam had the boat and the desire, but he wasn't an experienced fisherman. Cooper was. It was a comfortable arrangement all around." Having poured water into the coffee maker and flipped the brew switch, I wiped my hands on the flowered towel that hung on the wall.

"Did Cooper have his own boat?"

I shook my head. "He'd always worked for other people."

"Because he couldn't afford a boat?"

"Actually," I said, moving to take a can of tuna from a side cabinet, "he could afford one. Cooper isn't a poor man. He lives modestly by choice."

The teapot began to whistle. Setting down the tuna, I turned off the gas and reached into a second cannister. Purely by chance, because there was an assortment inside, I came up with camomile tea. Camomile was calming, so they said. I needed calming, particularly when the silence lingered, for without words, Peter's presence was all the stronger. It unsettled me. Determined not to let him know, I very deliberately put the tea bag in my cup, added water from the kettle, then dipped the bag up and down, up and down, up and down. I nearly cried out in relief when his voice came again.

"So Cooper chose to work for you. I take it you liked him."

"We both did. He was quiet, but smart and hard working."

"Where was he when Adam died?"

My eyes shot to Peter's. Maybe I was being oversensitive, but his question hit me the wrong way. The look on my face must have told him so. Almost instantly he held up a hand.

"Sorry. That sounded accusatory, but I didn't mean it that way. I'm just trying to get my bearings." He paused, then, when I didn't argue, went on. "Was Cooper on the boat when Adam died?"

Setting a mixing bowl on the counter, I said with feeling, "Yes, and he was nearly as sick as I was about the accident.

There was no way he could have prevented it, still he blamed himself." I went to the refrigerator. "He and Adam were close. Cooper may not be the most demonstrative of men, but he loved Adam like a brother."

"What was his relationship to you?"

Holding the refrigerator door ajar, I thought for a minute, trying to put a word to nine years of mutual respect and genuine affection. "Brotherly," I said at last.

"Is it still that?" he asked. In the echo of his deep voice, there was no doubt as to his thoughts.

Closing the refrigerator door, I looked him in the eye. It mattered to me that Peter Hathaway know the truth, because I saw it as an important point in Cooper's favor. "If you're asking whether Cooper and I are sexually involved, the answer is no. I adore Cooper. He's been my backbone for the past six years, but there has never been anything remotely sexual about our relationship."

"Why not?"

I frowned at his directness. "Because."

"Not good enough. If that picture I saw was a fair representation of the two men, Cooper is even better looking than your husband. Is he already married?"

"No."

"Gay?"

"No!"

"How do you know?"

"Because he has women to satisfy the urge when he gets it."

"How do you know?"

Because Swansy told me, though how Swansy knew was a mystery, but Swansy was never wrong. "I know. Trust me. I know."

"And he's never made a pass at you."

I stared at him for a minute, making no attempt to hide my annoyance. "Why does sex have to be involved?"

"Because you're no slouch."

"What does *that* have to do with anything?"

His voice was low. "Two attractive, unattached people in a secluded place, a place where winters are made for sharing the heat of a lover?" His eyes seemed suddenly darker. "If I were in Cooper's shoes, I'd have made a pass at you."

I felt that little heart-catch again and ignored it, just as I refused to acknowledge his claim. "But why does it matter?" I asked more quickly than I might have if I'd been perfectly calm. "What does it have to do with Cooper's case?"

Peter was watching me closely. "I'm just trying to figure out what you two mean to each other."

"We're the best of friends. The very best. But that's all."

He eyed me cautiously. "Are you sure?"

"Very."

For a minute longer, he studied me. Though his eyes never left my face, they seemed to take in far more than mere features. They delved into me, touching things that were deep and private and had to do with Adam and me, more so than with Cooper. They asked questions, probed territory that had been untouched for years.

I didn't understand it. I'd met many people, made many friends in the past six years, yet none had ever gotten to me this way. It frightened me that Peter Hathaway should. He was a total stranger. But powerful, so powerful. Beneath his gaze, I felt bared.

Pulling the refrigerator door open, I ducked inside. When I emerged, my arms were filled with a jar of mayonnaise, a head of lettuce and a loaf of bread. It wasn't that I believed they could shield me from his gaze, but I had to try something.

As it happened, by the time I straightened, Peter was looking out the window. I followed his gaze, thinking maybe Cooper was coming. He'd promised me that he would, though I'd had to work hard for that promise.

I could have used his help right about then. But there was no sign of him on the walk.

"Where does he live?" Peter asked.

I set to work mixing the tuna. "In town. It's five minutes by car, fifteen by foot."

"Does he live alone?"

"No. Benjie lives with him."

"Any other relatives?"

"There used to be," I told him, keeping my eyes on my work. "Cooper's lived here all his life. His father died when he was seven or eight. He had a sister, but she left when their mother remarried." I took a breath. "Benjie is actually Cooper's half brother, the son of his mother and her second husband."

"Where are they?"

"His mother and stepfather? Dead."

"Both of them?"

"Yes. There was a fire one night. Neither of them made it out of the house."

"When was this?"

"About a year before Adam and I moved here."

"Where was Cooper at the time?"

My fork snagged in the tuna. Slowly I looked up. "Cooper was working on a boat two days north of here. It took the Coast Guard that long to reach him. No, he didn't have anything to do with that fire. Arthur managed it all by himself."

Rather than trying to catch Cooper in something, Peter seemed totally engrossed in the tale. "Arthur?"

"Cooper's stepfather. He was an alcoholic. When he wasn't drinking, he was abusing Cooper's mother. He'd done both on the night of the fire. According to the medical examiner, MayJean was unconscious when the fire started."

"How did it start?"

"He was smoking. Fell asleep. He couldn't get himself out any more than he could get her out."

"And Benjie?"

"Thank God, Cooper had sent him to stay with a friend. He often did that when he had to be away for more than a day or two. Arthur had been known to take his ugliness out on Benjie, too."

Peter frowned. "How could Cooper stand by and let that happen?"

I was taken aback by his criticism, which was rash and unfounded. "What could he do?" I asked angrily. "He argued with his mother until he was blue in the face, trying to get her to bring charges against Arthur, but she wouldn't. And she wouldn't leave him. So there wasn't much of a case. The best Cooper could do was to try to keep Benjie out of the line of fire." I went back to mixing the tuna with greater force. "Cooper's life hasn't been easy. I've always admired his fortitude in the face of that."

Peter was quiet. I dared a glance at him. He looked pensive as he stared out the window, but I didn't have time to wonder why before he grew alert and met my gaze. "I take it Cooper took over the fishing business when Adam died."

Satisfied that I'd successfully defended Cooper on the matter of his family, I felt comfortable moving on. "That's right."

"Do you still own the boat?"

"No. I deeded it to Cooper three years ago. It took me that long to get him to take it."

"Strange."

"Not if you know Cooper. He's as loyal a person as I've ever met. Running the boat for me meant as much to him as running it for himself. He simply didn't aspire to more." I reached for the loaf of bread. "Which is what makes these charges against him so absurd. Cooper Drake doesn't want or need money, so there's no motive. Aside from a speeding ticket or two, he hasn't broken a law in his life. He picks and chooses his friends with care, and he doesn't mix with thugs. There is no way he had anything to do with the smuggling of those diamonds."

"They were found on his boat. In his cabin. In a laundry bag with his name stenciled on it."

My heart beat faster. "You've talked with someone."

He nodded. "Assistant U.S. Attorney Hummel. We have a mutual friend in New York. When I told him I'd been asked to take the case, he filled me in on what's happened so far."

And that, I supposed, was why I was willing to overlook the bad vibes I'd had. A lawyer with clout could get things done. It was as simple as that.

"How is the State's case?" I asked cautiously.

Peter shrugged with his mouth. "Not great. At least, based on what he told me, it's not."

"But Cooper was caught with the diamonds. Isn't possession nine-tenths of a conviction?"

"All it takes is one-tenth to establish reasonable doubt, and with reasonable doubt comes an acquittal."

"Do you think you can get one?"

"If I can establish reasonable doubt."

"Do you think you can?"

"I won't know until I've spoken with Cooper."

"But you will take the case."

"Again, I won't know until I've spoken with Cooper."

All roads led to Cooper. I was beginning to feel uneasy. "Why is that?"

"Because I have to get a feel for the man. I can't represent him unless I believe in him. And if it turns out that he and I don't see eye to eye on what has to be done—" He made a "pfft" sound and tossed his head.

With deliberate care, I took two slices of bread from the package, put them on a plate, covered one with tuna, then lettuce, then set the other on top. I made a neat diagonal cut in the finished product and set the plate before Peter. Instantly he began to eat, which was just what I'd hoped he'd do. Hungry and mean was fine for the trial; for now, I needed full and indulgent.

Crossing my hands on the counter, I said, "By definition, a criminal lawyer defends criminals—"

He interrupted me with a raised finger, held it there until he'd swallowed, then said, "Alleged criminals."

"Alleged criminals. Some of whom are totally innocent. They must be angry at having been accused. You must bear the brunt of their anger sometimes."

"Sometimes."

I thought for a minute, choosing my words with care. "There must be times when a client sees you as part of the system and resents you for that."

Having taken another mouthful, he gave a slow, silent nod.

"And times," I went on, "when a client doesn't want help from anyone, least of all you."

Peter stopped eating and gave the smallest tilt to his head. "Are you trying to tell me something, Jill?"

"Tell you something?" I asked. My voice was a little higher than usual. I wasn't sure whether it was because he saw too much too fast, or whether it was simply the way he said my name. In either case, I was in trouble.

"Is Cooper angry?"

I debated lying, but it seemed pointless. "Yes."

"Is he resisting help?"

"Would you like milk with this, or just coffee?"

"Jill?"

I felt a flicker of annoyance. "Yes, he's resisting."

"Does he know I'm here?"

"Of course, he knows you're here. I wouldn't have dragged you all the way from New York without mentioning it to him."

Looking thoughtful, Peter popped the last of the sandwich half into his mouth. When it was gone, he speared me with an accusatory gaze. "You mentioned that I was coming, but he hasn't agreed to cooperate."

"He's upset. He doesn't understand the difference a good lawyer can make."

"Did he agree to talk with me?"

"Yes."

"Is he coming over here?"

"Yes."

"When?"

"Sometime this afternoon. I couldn't pin him down to a time. But he promised he'd be here."

Without another word, Peter started eating again. When he'd finished his first sandwich, he reached over, removed another two slices of bread from the loaf, forked up some of the tuna left in the bowl and made a second sandwich. Swiveling in the other direction, he pulled the refrigerator open. He had to leave the stool to get at the milk, and before I had time to prepare myself, he was standing beside me, looking for a glass.

Again I felt that tiny catch in my chest. It was hard to

ignore this time because it made my hand shake when I opened the cabinet. I made a vague gesture that he should help himself and quickly lowered my hand to the solidity of the counter. He took the glass, but didn't move away. Nor did he say a word.

Barely a hair's breadth separated us. My shoulder was an inhalation away from his chest, my arm his middle, my hip his groin. He was close enough for me to feel the soft movement of his breath in my hair and smell the wonderfully male scent that had taunted me earlier. But it was the heat of his body that affected me most; it penetrated both his clothing and mine to tempt me with the kind of solace that I'd been without for six long years.

Move, I told myself, but I couldn't budge. The message of my mind couldn't reach my legs because of the swelling of all kinds of sensations in between. So I stood there helplessly, feeling the lure, the attraction, the desire. My breath came shallowly, working around my hammering heart as I stared at the tiled countertop and waited for him to speak. When I felt my body begin to list that smallest, smallest bit into his heat, I knew I could wait no longer. I had to break the spell, because that was what it was, I was sure of it. Peter Hathaway had put me under a spell. I wasn't normally affected by men this way. I just wasn't.

"Peter?" I said in a voice that was barely more than a whisper.

"Hmm?"

It wasn't a mischievous "hmm" or a mocking one or even a seductive one. It was a very quiet "hmm" that was so innocent, so thoughtful that it was indeed sexy.

Distracted by the idea of sexy, I started again. "Peter?"

"Yes?"

There was something I wanted to tell him but the words weren't coming. "I, uh…" It had to do with Cooper. I struggled, dug deep for the thoughts. "There are several things you should understand...before he gets here."

For another minute, Peter didn't move. Then, slowly, he stepped away from me. Without caring how it would look, I hung my head and took in the deep breath my lungs craved. When I raised my head and glanced over at him, his back was to me. He was pouring milk into the glass that had brought him so close to me in the first place.

At first glance he looked perfectly calm, totally unaffected by what had just shaken me to the bone. Then I noted that his shoulders were very straight, and his head remained bowed well after he'd finished pouring the milk.

Something had touched him, too. I wasn't sure what it was, wasn't sure whether he found it as unwelcome as I did, but knowing that I wasn't the only one with a problem made me feel better.

Taking advantage of his momentary distraction, which gave me the only edge I might have in a while, I addressed what I told myself were the first of my priorities. "There are several things you have to understand about this case," I said quietly. "The first is that your bills are to be sent to me. I don't want any mention of money in front of Cooper. The second is that I want the best defense possible. If you can get the case dropped before it goes to trial, so much the better, but in any case, I want Cooper exonerated. And the third," I said, "is that I don't care how reluctant Cooper is, I want you as his lawyer."

Peter looked past his shoulder at me. "Are you sure?" he asked cautiously, and I knew he was thinking of what had just happened.

So was I. But I was also thinking that I was in control. I couldn't deny that Peter Hathaway turned me on, but I sure as hell could overcome it. After all, I had the strength of Adam's love on my side.

"I'm sure," I said. "I think you're just the man to defend Cooper."

"Why?"

I supposed I could say that he seemed bright and articulate, honest and dedicated, and all of that was true, but the thing that stuck out most in my mind was the picture he and Cooper would make in the courtroom. Between them, they'd knock the socks off any females who happened to sit on the jury.

Not wanting to tell Peter that, I said, "Because my mother says you're the toughest and the best. I trust her judgment."

After a long, expectant silence, Peter said, "I accept that."

Something in his tone made my eyes widen. "You'll take the case?"

"I'll take the case."

I hadn't expected the turnaround. "But you haven't met Cooper. You said it would depend on—"

"I know what I said, but I've changed my mind."

"Why?"

"Because you intrigue me."

My mouth fell open. "That's a *lousy* reason for accepting a case."

"Not really." His eyes held mine as he came closer. "Between you and your mom and Hummel, I've learned enough about the case to know that it'll be a challenge. If Cooper and you are best friends, he can't be all that bad. I need a break from the city. This is perfect. You've offered me your hospitality. And you're here." He paused, then said in a husky tone, "This case is just what I need."

I didn't like the tone any more than I liked the look in his eyes. It was hungry—hungry in the way of a man who

knew how to satisfy a woman and satisfy her well, hungry
for the kinds of things I'd sworn I'd never give again.

Hunger alone I could resist, but there was a gentleness
there, too, that posed a far greater threat. I was a sucker
for gentle men. Adam had been one. So, in his dark way,
was Cooper—who, praise be, chose that moment to walk
through the kitchen door.

Looking disgruntled, he stared first at me, then at Peter.
In the silence that ensued, I had the uncanny notion that
it was my future, not Cooper's, that hung in the balance.

Without leaving my side, Peter extended his hand.
Cooper eyed it, eyed me, eyed Peter. I held my breath,
unsettled as I'd never been, because though Peter would
be the best thing for Cooper, he might well be the worst
thing for me.

Then Cooper's hand slowly went out, and I was trapped.

CHAPTER TWO

FROM MY PERCH on the stool, I silently watched the two men at the table. Though they'd asked me to join them, I'd declined. It seemed important that they establish a relationship without my interference. At least, that was the excuse I gave myself, though if I'd truly wanted to give them privacy, I'd have left the room.

I didn't do that for two reasons. First, I wanted to make sure Cooper cooperated. And second, I wanted to see how Peter Hathaway worked.

Sitting on the stool by the counter gave me spectator status. It also removed me just a bit from Peter, which meant that I could relax some. Cooper's presence helped; he was my ally, loyal, devoted, steadfast. He was also in a lousy mood. Yes, he'd come, but he was looking tired and taut. He participated in the meeting only to the extent of answering the questions Peter asked. He didn't volunteer a thing.

I had to hand it to Peter. Undaunted by Cooper's reluctance, he posed question after question, each in the low, even tone that reminded me of what Ian had said. "Serious legal business," he'd attributed to Peter, and I could see it. There were no grins, no editorial comments, no questions that didn't have direct relevance to the case. He read Cooper well. Perhaps he'd had experience with dozens of Coopers, but he understood that this one needed a low-keyed, meat-and-potatoes approach. That was one of the reasons I assumed he made notes by hand on a yellow legal pad, rather than using the small recorder I'd seen in the briefcase he'd brought in from the car.

Since I was familiar with the facts of the case, I listened to the discussion with only half an ear. I already knew that the *Free Reign* had been on a two-week trip fishing off the shores of Newfoundland, that she'd stopped at Grand Bank for supplies midway through, that she'd returned to Maine right on schedule. There had been nothing new about the itinerary; Cooper had followed it dozens of times before. This time, though, U.S. Customs agents had been waiting to welcome him home.

Without making a big deal of it, Peter asked, "Did you know anything about those diamonds?"

"No," Cooper answered.

"You had no idea they were on the boat?"

"None."

"They were found in your cabin. If you don't know how they got there, maybe one of your crew does. Any suggestions?"

"No. My men are all honest and hardworking."

"Are any of them financially strapped?"

"They all are. If they weren't, they wouldn't be in this line of work. It's hard."

"Forget strapped. Talk panicked. Are any of them in the midst of serious financial crises?"

"All the time," Cooper said with a cynical twist to his lips.

I wanted to shake him. He knew what Peter was getting at, but he was being difficult. At that moment, I admired Peter his patience. Though he spoke a little slower than normal when he rephrased the question, he made it sound more pensive than tempering.

"Has any of your crew suffered any recent out-of-the-ordinary financial crisis?"

"Not that I know of."

"Would you know?"

"Probably."

Peter made several notes on his pad. I couldn't read them from where I sat, but I could watch the movement of his head. He held the pen oddly, as though awkward with it, and though he wrote quickly enough, I wondered what kind of student he'd been in school.

Brilliant, no doubt. I wondered why I'd wondered in the first place.

Drawing several broad lines across the page, he began to ask Cooper questions about individual members of the crew. While my half-an-ear continued to listen, the rest of me strayed.

I'd guessed right; Peter and Cooper were a handsome team. Both were tall, each imposing in his way. Cooper, wearing T-shirt, flannel shirt and jeans, clearly was the rougher-edged of the two. His hair was darker, the stubble on his cheeks darker, his eyes darker. I wanted to blame the grimness of his expression on the situation, but the fact was that Cooper had a shadowed side not even I had touched in nine years of trying. I'd long since learned that parts of Cooper were off-limits; but then, parts of me were, too. Cooper and I accepted that about each other, which was one of the things that made our relationship work.

Peter, on the other hand, wasn't so much dark as new and, therefore, an enigma. Whereas I could guess that Cooper was feeling frustrated and constrained and angry as hell at the situation and all those related to it, Peter's feelings escaped me. I supposed it was to be expected. I didn't know the man. His features were controlled. Little slipped past his professional facade.

Oh, I could guess things. I could guess that he found me attractive. I intrigued him, he said. And I wasn't so ignorant as to think he was fascinated by my mind. He was male through and through. I was willing to wager that his sexual prowess rivaled his legal skill. Whether wandering through my living room, standing by my counter or sitting in one of the ladder-back chairs at my table, his lines flowed. He was comfortable with his body; he handled it well.

I supposed others had handled it well, too, over the years.

But I wasn't entirely sure. Helaine had called him a lady-killer, but what did Helaine know? Rumor had a way of feeding upon itself, particularly where sex was involved. Perhaps rumor was wrong. Perhaps Peter Hathaway was the monogamous type. Perhaps he'd been married and divorced, or engaged and burned. Perhaps he had a long-time steady lover in Manhattan. Or he'd sworn off women completely. Or he was hung up on his mother.

His love life was one big, fat question mark. Even the half smile he'd given me, the one that had set my equilibrium back so, had been mysterious in its way, as though it held a secret that I ought to know but didn't.

"Hutter Johns wouldn't have done anything like that," Cooper barked, intruding on my thoughts, retraining them on the discussion at hand. "Yes, he's the newest member of my crew, but he's one of the most open."

"Sometimes the open ones are the most deceptive," Peter returned. "They toss out red herrings left and right."

"Not Hutter," Cooper vowed. "Not to me." He clamped his mouth shut.

Reaching quickly for the coffeepot, I skirted the table and went to his side. When I put a tentative hand on his shoulder, his gaze flew to mine in surprise—as though he'd momentarily forgotten I was in the room—and then softened in the subtle way that was characteristically Cooper. I refilled his mug, then moved around and did the same for Peter. Once I'd replaced the glass carafe on its warmer, I returned to Cooper's side.

Peter looked up from his mug. If he thought anything of my change of position, he didn't let on, and it certainly didn't deter him from his purpose. He'd apparently reached the point where he felt a little pushing was in order. Though his voice was quiet, his eyes were clear and sharp. "If neither you nor your crew had anything to do with the smuggling of those diamonds, how did they get onto the boat and into your cabin?"

Stone-voiced, Cooper said, "I don't know."

"You must have a theory."

"I assume they were put on the boat while we were docked at Grand Bank."

"By whom?"

"If I knew that, I wouldn't be sitting here now."

"Where would you be?"

"Fishing."

More softly than Cooper, I told Peter, "The boat's been impounded, and the crew is filing for unemployment. It isn't a great situation."

Peter's gaze caught mine, and I imagined I saw a germ of compassion there before he turned back to Cooper. "Why would someone have picked the *Free Reign*?"

"Because," Cooper said without pause, "we're predictable. And reliable. We leave here on schedule, we come back on schedule. And we're above reproach."

"Until now."

Cooper didn't respond. Since I stood slightly behind his shoulder, I couldn't see his face, still I knew without a doubt that it was granite hard. I could feel his anger, a tangible thing very much in control of his being, and I had the uncomfortable notion that he was getting ready to bolt. That was the last thing I wanted. So I spoke up in his defense.

"Cooper is innocent. In the nine years I've known him, he's never done anything even remotely questionable. He keeps detailed records of where he's fished and what he's caught. The fishing authorities trust him. I trust him. He's innocent. So is the *Free Reign*. They've been used, that's all. We have to find out by whom."

"How do you propose we do that?" Peter asked.

"I was going to ask you the same question."

He took a slow swallow of his coffee, set the mug down and leaned back in his seat. "I could talk with the police, but obviously they feel they already have their man. I will plant some doubt. That won't hurt, and I can do it easily enough, but a little doubt won't spark an active investigation." He looked from Cooper's face to mine, then back. "We could conduct one ourselves. We could hire an investigator. But it'll cost."

"No," Cooper said. "No investigator."

Tightening my hand on his shoulder, I said to Peter, "We'll think about it. In the meantime, what can we do?"

His answer was on the tip of his tongue. "Talk with people, anyone and everyone around here who has anything to do with Cooper or the boat. The crew comes first. I want to talk with each of them."

Feeling the tension coil tighter in Cooper's shoulder, I leaned forward. "It has to be," I told him in a private voice, "if for no other reason than to line up witnesses who'll speak on your behalf."

Staring at me, he spoke nearly as quietly as I had, albeit rigidly. "I didn't want this."

"What was the alternative?"

"McHenry."

"McHenry couldn't have done it." I sighed. "Cooper, we've been through this before. McHenry got you out on bail in twice the time it should have taken. He would defend you, and you're right, he wouldn't ask any questions or make any waves, but neither would he get you an acquittal and that's what you need. The alternative, Cooper, is jail."

"I know that," he growled, but I wasn't done. Once started, I had trouble stopping.

"You've worked too hard. You've worked too hard to make a life for yourself. And for Benjie—if you go to prison, where will that leave him? Where will it leave *me*?" I looked at Peter. "Reasonable doubt. That's all we have to show. Reasonable doubt." The phone rang. Ignoring it, I told Cooper, "Peter can do it, but it won't be easy. You have to cooperate. We'll all have to cooperate."

"I'm missing out on good fishing."

"I'm missing out on good potting, but this is more important than either of those things. It's your *life*, Cooper."

"What's it worth?" he muttered.

The phone rang again.

"A whole lot, damn it," I cried in an angry whisper, "at least, that's what you told me after Adam died, when I didn't care what happened to me. Or was it a line? Were you lying?" I'd reached him. He was looking at me with the kind of dark awareness I knew so well. "Peter knows what he's doing. All we have to do is to cooperate with him. I'm asking you, *begging* you to do that."

"He's expensive, Jill."

The phone rang again.

"It's my money. What else am I going to do with it?"

"Buy a condo in the city."

"What?"

"You heard."

I was sorry I had. "I don't want a condo, and I don't want the city!"

"Not now. Maybe in a year or two."

"Never."

"It's getting time, Jill."

"Never!" The phone rang again. Swearing, I crossed the room and snatched it up. "Hello!"

"Jill?"

Hanging my head, I took a minute to compose myself. Then I said brightly, "Hi, Samantha."

"Is he there?"

"Who?" I asked, as if I didn't know.

"Peter."

"Oh." I looked at the floor. "Uh-huh."

"Is he gorgeous?" she asked. I could just see her eyes. They'd be wide and as eager as her grin.

I turned my back on the two in the room. "How's David?"

Samantha ignored my pointed question, which was nothing new. She was my older sister by seven years and had always seen me more as a nuisance than a friend. Of course that didn't mean she couldn't seek me out when it suited her purpose. Now was one of those times.

"I've never met Peter," she said in a breezy tone that was a little too intent to be casual. "It's only in the past five years that he's made a name for himself. Supposedly he went to law school late, and what he did before that is a big mystery. Is he as handsome as he looks in the papers?"

I heard the murmur of voices behind me. "I can't talk now, Samantha."

"He sitting right there? Oh, Lord. And Mom says you have him for the weekend. You are one lucky woman. Then again, you probably don't realize it. Or you're a nervous wreck. You haven't dated since Adam died, have you?"

Stretching the cord, I moved into the hall, put a shoulder to the wall and my back to the kitchen and spoke into the receiver, which was practically touching my lips, "I don't know what you're talking about. This is a business meeting."

"It may start out as one, but it doesn't have to end that way." Her voice dropped with conspiratorial urgency. "Listen to me, Jill. Peter Hathaway is a catch. He'd be good for you and good for us. We need new blood in this family, and I can't think of better blood than his. He's successful, he's loaded and he's available. You have him for the weekend. *Go* for it."

I didn't want to be listening to that, when far more important things were being said in the kitchen. "I can't talk now. *Really*, Samantha."

I'd tried to keep the words as soft as possible, but my impatience must have shown. Samantha's corresponding pique came through loud and clear.

"You don't want to talk. You *never* want to talk, because you think you know it all. Well, you don't, Jill. You don't know anything about men. You dated Adam from day one at Penn. You married him. You went off to live in the wilds. Then he died on you, and you've lived the life of a nun ever since. Is that what you want for the rest of your life?"

"For God's sake!" I cried, then, remembering the men not far away, lowered my voice to a rough whisper. "What's with you?" Back to the wall, I slid down until my bottom hit the floor. "You're trying to make something out of absolutely nothing!" Turning away from the kitchen, I tucked myself up to prevent my voice from carrying far. "My best friend is in need of legal assistance. I'm seeing that he gets it. This is business. That's all. Business. Period."

In the silence that followed, I turned my head and tried

to tune in to what was being said behind me, but the words were low and indistinct. Then Samantha's voice came more stridently, and I gave up trying.

"Business, period? What about broadening yourself? Hmm? I thought you were interested in doing that. You moved to the boondocks to be closer to nature. You said you wanted to broaden yourself artistically. Well, what about socially? Or romantically? This is your chance, Jill. Don't blow it!"

Against my will, my temper rose. "My chance for what? To have a wild and sexy weekend? If that's your definition of exciting, or broadening, fine. But don't impose it on me. I have better ways to spend my time."

"Sure you do—playing the martyr. You've been doing it so long, you don't know anything else."

"Shut up, Sam."

"You're such a pill. Either that or you're totally ignorant. If I didn't have other plans, I'd fly up there and show you how it's done. Obviously you have no idea how to seduce a man."

It had hurt when she'd called me a martyr, but I could rationalize that when it came to my feelings for Adam, she didn't know what she was talking about. When it came to sex, though, she did, so her insult stung. I'd grown up being put down, feeling inadequate in comparison to Samantha, but I was no longer a child. I didn't have to stand for her abuse.

Angrily sitting straighter, I said, "If that's what you think, Samantha, then you're the one who's ignorant. I haven't led as sheltered a life as you'd like to believe. There are some stunning men up here, and I mean stunning. They don't have designer clothes and cars and condos to fall back on, so they have to produce the appeal all by themselves, and they do it well. They have what's called unfettered virility. They're sexy as hell. I could seduce a man like that in a minute."

"But have you?" Samantha hummed smugly.

"Wouldn't you like to know?" I hummed back just as smugly.

She paused for the space of a breath before offering an arch, "Excu-se me. I thought I might be of some help. Obviously you don't need it. Have a good weekend."

Seconds later I found myself holding a dead receiver. Pressing the end of it to my mouth, I felt an old, familiar sadness steal through me. I'd accepted the fact that Samantha and I would never be close, and it wasn't just her fault. I was, in many ways, nearly as headstrong as she, so I shared the blame. But I was sorry. There had been times over the years when I could have used a sister.

Taking a deep breath, I swiveled on my bottom in a prelude to standing, only to come face to face with a long pair of legs. I cried out in alarm. My gaze shot upward, over narrow hips, a lean middle, then wider shoulders to Peter's complacent face.

"My Lord, you scared me," I breathed, pressing a hand—with its telephone receiver—to my pounding heart. "I'm so used to being alone. I'd forgotten anyone was here." But remembrance came fast. I glanced past him and grew uneasy. "Where's Cooper?"

"He left."

"Oh no," I wailed softly.

"No sweat. We're meeting again tomorrow afternoon."

I sank back against the wall in relief. For an instant, I'd imagined that Cooper had taken advantage of my absence to storm off. If he'd done that, I'd have been furious with him, and with Samantha for having distracted me, and with myself for having been distracted.

And I had definitely been distracted. I'd completely

forgotten about the men nearby. Looking off in the opposite direction from where Peter stood, I tried to think of what I'd said at the end of my conversation with Samantha that he might have overheard. One possibility was as bad as the next.

And Peter simply gazed down at me, not letting on what he'd heard, leaving me to wonder.

I raised my eyes to his, then dropped them back to the floor. Along the way, I had a second viewing of his length. It was impressive. He was a large man, long and lean. Beneath him, I felt small.

Delicate.

Feminine.

Get up, I told myself, but I couldn't budge. My legs felt like rubber, and no wonder. The blood that was normally there had been rerouted to my chest. At least, it felt that way, my heart was thudding so loudly.

Nearly frantic to fill the silence between us with some sort of diversion, I looked up at Peter and said, "So. What do you think of Cooper?"

He didn't answer at first. He had a shoulder propped against the wall and looked as if he could stay that way for a while. I was glad one of us was comfortable.

"I'm not sure," he answered at last. "He's tense. And angry."

"I told you he would be. But do you think you can work with him?"

Again he didn't immediately answer, and this time I wondered if the pause was for my benefit. With each minute that passed, I grew more aware of the way he dominated the narrow hall. "Mastery" was the word that came to mind. Peter Hathaway was definitely in control.

"I can work with him," he said.

I was grateful for small favors. "Good."

"Not that it'll be easy. He doesn't trust me."

"Only because you're new. But distrust is the least of Cooper's worries." With the directing of my thoughts to something constructive, I found the strength to stand. Not to move away, though. I figured I'd take it step by step. "It's the whole situation," I said, trying to explain. I leaned against the wall, hugging the telephone to my chest. "He's furious with it. If he had his way, good old Chad McHenry would wave his hands and say a few words to the judge and the whole thing would be over and forgotten. But that won't happen and, deep inside, Cooper knows it. Deep inside, he knows you're his best hope. But it's like exercising, you know? No pain, no gain. Trouble is he's already in pain. He doesn't relish the thought of more."

"Why will it be so painful for him if I talk with people in town?" His voice seemed softer, more intimate now that my face was closer.

I took a shallow breath. "Because he's a private—and prideful—man. He doesn't like the idea of other people talking about him, and I can't blame him for that. It's a disconcerting feeling."

"You've had personal experience?"

"Oh, yeah." I thought of all the family gatherings I'd absented myself from where the topic of conversation had no doubt been my self-imposed exile. And then there was Adam's death. "For months after the accident, I'd walk down a street and wonder who was watching from which window feeling sorry for me. I didn't want pity. Neither does Cooper."

"I'm not looking for pity. I'm looking for information. I want to know what people around here think about what's happened and why."

"They're apt to be wary, just like Cooper was," I warned. "You're a stranger."

"But you'll be with me," he said calmly.

I blinked. "I will?"

"You're my entrée."

I hadn't counted on that. I'd assumed that Peter would talk with Cooper, then go about his business on his own. I was paying the bills and throwing in room and board. I hadn't expected to be an assistant to the attorney, as well.

"This weekend?" I asked in a thin voice.

Peter nodded.

"Uh, I don't know if I can handle that." In more ways than one. "I've pretty much booked up my time."

"With something wild and sexy?"

My pulse tripped. He'd heard what I'd said. Then again, maybe he hadn't. Maybe he was just trying to be cute. "Actually I have work to do. I have a show coming up in a month. My sales representative wants to have a dozen new pieces by then. I've only got four done."

Peter gave that some thought, but when I expected him to come up with something as cute as "wild and sexy," he asked instead, "Where is the show?"

"New York."

"Ah. Then you'll be coming to the city."

"I haven't decided yet." There was no harm in telling the truth. "I don't really love going to those things. Moni— that's the woman who handles my work—says I have to be there, but I missed the last one and it didn't hurt sales."

"Why don't you like shows?"

"I don't know." I looked down at the phone which I held more loosely now against my chest. "Maybe I've gotten un-used to big crowds and wearing high heels and nursing drinks that I didn't want in the first place."

His voice came lower, closer. "Art shows are notorious for stunning men."

Once I could chalk up to coincidence. Not twice. He'd

definitely heard what I'd said to Samantha. Looking up, I found his eyes no more than a foot away from mine. I searched them, looking for the taunting I was sure I'd heard, and indeed, hidden in their luminescent green depths was a flicker of amusement, but just a flicker. There was also a whole lot of curiosity.

It was the curiosity that started the quivers inside me this time, because it was honest and genuine and very serious. There were things about me that had Peter Hathaway guessing.

There were parts of me that liked it that way.

I made light of his remark. "Stunning men are a dime a dozen in New York. If they want to be seen, it's either there or L.A."

"Or here."

It struck me then that he wanted to discuss what he'd overheard. I knew I could put him off, but I wasn't sure it was worth the effort. "Okay. You heard what I said to Samantha."

He didn't try to deny it. "You're right. City men often do depend on material things to enhance their virility. Maybe they feel that's the only way they'll be noticed among the hordes. Everywhere they turn, they face competition. They lead congested lives. Sometimes the raw basics are forgotten."

"They? Don't you consider yourself one of them?"

He gave a slow, almost somnolent shake of his head, and though his eyes were half-lidded, there was nothing lazy about their look. It was intense in a way that threatened to melt my thighs. The threat increased when he said in a deep, rough-edged voice, "I don't need designer clothes or cars or condos. I never have. That's not where I come from." Even deeper. "It's not where I want to be."

I was having trouble catching my breath. A hard

swallow didn't help much. *It's not where I want to be.* My voice was thready, still I couldn't keep from asking, "Where do you want to be?"

His gaze smoldered. "Right here, on this floor, naked, with you."

A bubble of air tripped down my windpipes the wrong way. I gasped, then coughed and once again pressed a hand to my heart. In so doing, I realized that I still held the phone. Returning it to the kitchen was as good an excuse as any for leaving the hall, which had suddenly shrunk to suffocating proportions. I started to move—only to find that the cord went behind Peter's back.

Keeping myself as far from him as I could while maintaining a measure of dignity, I tugged at the cord. "Excuse me. I'd better hang this up. If someone should be trying to call—"

I didn't finish what I was saying, because Peter had hooked his elbow around my neck, grasped the spot where my ponytail was anchored to the crown of my head and gently pulled. With the tipping back of my head, I had no choice but to look at him.

"You're frightened."

"Of course, I'm frightened. A strange man walks into my house, which happens to sit high on an isolated bluff that would do most gothic novels proud, and informs me that right then he'd like to be on the floor, naked with me. What woman wouldn't be frightened?"

"A woman who is honest about her sexuality."

"No, a woman who is nuts. Where have you been? The days of sexual promiscuity are gone. Women don't just sprawl on the floor and make love with men they don't know."

He was moving my ponytail in a light, caressive, undulating way. "You know me."

"I do not," I argued. Rays of warmth were spreading over my scalp. I fought their seduction with a spurt of anger. "Up until two hours ago, I'd never laid eyes on you."

"But you know me," he insisted in that same deep, confident, exquisitely male tone of voice. "You know that I don't jump into things with my eyes closed. I know what I want and I know how to get it. I'd never force you to do something you didn't want to do. I'd never hurt you. I wouldn't make you pregnant, unless that was what we wanted." He paused for a single, chiding moment. "And I don't have AIDS."

He'd covered everything, yet he hadn't allayed my fears one bit. He was right; I knew that he wouldn't force me, or hurt me, or give me something I didn't want to have. Instinct told me he was more responsible than most. But I didn't want to become involved with him. I didn't want to become involved with any man. After all Adam had done for me, I owed him my loyalty.

For the first time, that loyalty was being threatened. *That* was what frightened me, and the more frightened I became, the more my insides trembled as I looked up into Peter's handsome face. And the more I trembled, the more I wanted to lean into his body, to take refuge in his arms from the danger that lurked.

Which was bizarre, given that he was the danger.

Uncaring that my voice shook, I said weakly, "I have to hang up the phone. Please?"

I squeezed my eyes shut, but I could feel the heat of his gaze on my face for another minute before he finally uncoupled his fingers from my hair and stepped aside. After returning the receiver to its wall cradle, I quickly scooped up the mugs from the table and set to washing them in the sink.

Peter propped a lean hip against the counter and crossed

his ankles. "Cooper said that your sister wouldn't be bothering you on the phone if it weren't for me. Is it true?"

I continued to wash the mugs, soaping and rinsing a second, then a third time.

"They're clean," he said.

I ignored him.

"Is it true?" he asked. "What does your sister have against me?"

"Nothing," I blurted out. "She thinks you're the cat's meow."

He frowned. "Have I ever met her?"

"You'd have remembered if you had." Hands dripping into the sink, I drilled him with a sharp look. "Samantha is gorgeous. So is my sister-in-law, who also thinks you're terrific. You see, their definition of terrific is wealthy and good-looking. Be grateful it's not mine. If it were, you'd be fighting me off."

"That wouldn't be so bad," he said, just about the time I realized I'd asked for it. The next thing I realized was that honesty couldn't hurt. Peter should know exactly where he stood.

"Samantha told me that I should go after you. She said that I'd be passing up a golden opportunity if I didn't seduce you, since I have you here in my clutches for the weekend. And she wasn't going to stop with the weekend. She had it all planned that I'd have you hooked by the time Monday rolled around. She thinks we need new blood in the family." I snorted. "You'd think we were vampires."

Peter didn't look particularly perturbed. "Is she a matchmaker?"

"No, she's a golddigger. She has her eye on your wallet. I'm not sure who's worse—she or Helaine."

"Helaine?"

"My sister-in-law. She has her eye on your crotch."

Peter cracked a crooked grin. "You Madigan women certainly know what you want."

"And what we don't. I don't want your wallet, and I don't want—" I darted a quick look at his fly. "All I want from you is the best possible legal defense for Cooper Drake. Do you think you can give me that?" I demanded in as imperious a tone as I could muster.

"I wouldn't be here if I couldn't."

"Can you give it to me without all the other—" the word momentarily eluded me "—garbage?"

He shrugged. "Sure."

"Say it with conviction."

"Sure," he said in a more forceful voice.

I wasn't sure I believed him, but the fact was that I couldn't stand there wondering. If I was to guarantee my safety with Peter Hathaway under my roof for the night, I was going to have to wear him out somehow before then.

The day was waning. I had to get to it.

CHAPTER THREE

IN THEORY, IT was a great idea. Peter wanted me to show him around, so I'd show him around—starting with an extra-long, brisk hike through the late-afternoon wind, the salt-laden air and the bracken. That would take the starch out of his pretty city shirt collar, I calculated. I felt smug in anticipation.

In practice, something went wrong. As soon as I suggested we walk into town, Peter retrieved his suitcase from the car and disappeared into the second of the two upstairs bedrooms, the spare one, the one I'd pointed him to when he'd said something about changing his shoes. When he trotted back down the stairs less than five minutes later, he'd removed the shirt I'd hoped to take the starch from. In fact, I was the one who felt unstarched. Not only had he removed the shirt, sweater, slacks and loafers that had given him a semblance of urbanity, but he'd replaced them with clothes that might well have come from Down East Army and Navy ten years before.

His sneakers had been run long and hard. Above them were a pair of basic Levi's that had been blue many washings ago but were faded now, and the fading was real. It was uneven, more so in spots that saw the most friction— the knees, the thighs and, oh Lord, the fly. Above the jeans was a faded maroon sweatshirt, beneath the sweatshirt a gray turtleneck jersey. Hooked on a finger over his shoulder was a venerable sherpa-lined jacket.

It wouldn't have been so bad if he'd looked dirty, but he didn't. He just looked comfortable. He looked as much at ease in my kind of clothes as he did in his. I wasn't sure how it could be, given the number of hours he surely had to devote to his career to be as successful as he was, but he looked as though he spent a good part of his life in those jeans. They fit him like a well-worn glove, conforming snugly to his rangy frame, yet allowing for the movement that was uniquely his.

The worst of it was that dressed this way, he was more devastating than ever. While he still didn't look as rough as Cooper, the jeans and sweatshirt brought him close. They broadcast the fact of a hard male body beneath, and that fact did nothing at all to still my racing pulse.

I should have guessed he'd be the athletic type. A man didn't wear running shoes, a sweatshirt and jeans simply to be a paper pusher. And sure enough, when I set a hardy pace away from the house, winding over the bluffs, then across and through the scrubby pines on the long way to town, he didn't say a word. After a while, my own breathing came a little faster—frustration, I told myself—but his was as even as ever.

That was when I knew I needed Swansy. I'd intended to stop in anyway to introduce her to Peter, though I'd originally planned to do it on the way home. Swansy was a calming force for me, and I knew I was going to need something before being shut in with Peter Hathaway for the night.

I needed calming now, though. I needed to see a familiar face, hear a familiar voice, share the problem of Peter Hathaway with someone who would understand and care. Swansy was just the one.

She lived in a small, wood-frame house near the end of Main Street, which was not only the town's main street, but it's only one. I'd led Peter on the roundabout route, so we approached from the opposite direction and had to walk through town. On the one hand, that worked out just fine; I talked as we walked and was able to give him a feel for the layout of the town. The down side was that the self-consciousness I'd felt after Adam had died was nothing compared to the way I felt walking along with Peter.

Klieg lights couldn't have been worse.

But this was my town, these were my people, and I'd come a long, long way in six years. So I told myself, as I held my chin high and walked along. We passed a dozen simple frame houses on the south end of town, passed the grocery store, the hardware store, the post office and Sam's Saloon, passed the lane that led to the docks, then a few shops and a dozen more houses on the north end of town.

When we reached Swansy's, I led Peter up the gravel drive to the side door and pushed it open. "Hi, Swansy," I called in a voice loud enough to carry through the bottom floor of the house. The scent that greeted me was wonderful, the atmosphere in the small kitchen warm and homey. Though I'd been well dressed for the trek from my house and hadn't been physically chilled, being with Peter was unbalancing. Already, stepping into Swansy's house, knowing that the safe and familiar was just down the hall, I felt better.

Tossing my jacket to a chair, I lifted the cover off a pot on the stove and stirred the stew inside. By the time I'd replaced the cover, a cool nose was nudging my hip.

"Hi, sweetheart," I crooned to the gentle German shepherd who'd come to greet me. Scratching her ears, I bent over to offer my cheek for a lick. "Her name's Rebecca," I told Peter as I straightened. Peter went down on his haunches to greet the dog at eye level. He looked so serious about it that I nearly laughed. Not wanting to offend him that way, I went on into the parlor.

Swansy was there, looking like a septuagenarian doll ensconced in the bentwood rocker I'd given her one Mother's Day. Little more than five feet tall, she was as slim as she was small. Though she was wrinkled enough to attest to her age, her skin maintained a softness that I'd always attributed to her complexion. Peaches and cream it was, with spots of high color on her cheeks that were as natural as the pure white hair on her head. Her smile was every bit as natural as that, and always ready.

But she wasn't smiling now. She was scowling in the direction of the television, which was tuned loud and clear to the last of the Friday afternoon soap operas. I had no sooner approached her chair when she started in.

"They do it to me every time," she complained in her sweet, birdlike warble. "Leave me hangin' right up in the air for the weekend. This time it's Babette bein' drunk and walkin' out in front of that car. We hear the squeal of brakes, and then they switch the scene. Well, I don't *want* to know that Mark is gettin' fired from his job, 'cause he'll have another one come Monday, and he doesn't even need one, 'cause he's rich as a shiek. I want to know about Babette. She's goin' to be hurt bad, and—" her warble lowered to a conspiratorial whisper "—y'know who was drivin' that car? Gordon was drivin' it. I'm tellin' you, there's goin' to be trouble, and now I have to wait until Monday to find out how much."

I smiled. "That's okay. The wondering will keep you busy." I leaned low to brush her cheek with a kiss, at the same time pressing the remote control in her lap to turn off the set. "The stew looks divine. It *smells* divine. Bettina's been up?" Bettina Gregorian lived on the outskirts of town, south to my north. She had five children under the age of nine and was not only a supermom but a supercook. She was also a superfriend. At least one morning a week, she showed up at Swansy's with the makings for something that would cook without tending and last for days. While we all looked after Swansy in this way and others, Bettina's stew took first prize.

"Stopped up first thing," Swansy confirmed. A tiny frown drew on her wrinkles. "The littlest boys have chicken pox."

"Daniel and Port? Oh, dear."

"Three weeks to the day after Mim and Sally. She's hopin' the baby stays well. It's no fun gettin' that at six months."

"For baby or for mother. I'll stop by tomorrow and see how they're doing."

"Have you had 'em?"

I smiled. "When I was two, I'm told, though I don't remember, myself. I caught it from Samantha, who caught it from Ian. The maid caught it somewhere in between, and the nanny didn't know how to cook, so my mother was fit to be tied."

"Didn't your daddy help out?"

I felt my smile turn crooked. "His way of helping was to hire a temporary girl, who proceeded to scorch his best shirts. To this day, my family talks of that time as a dark one."

Swansy knew enough about me and my family to understand the mockery in my voice. She raised a hand to my cheek, moved it lightly, open-palmed. The gesture was as comforting to me as it was informative to Swansy. "It's gettin' colder. Winter'll be on us soon. You've been walkin' over the hill?"

She could smell it, I knew. There was a special scent, a

combination of salt air and pine mist that clung to my hair and my coat. It was a dead giveaway every time.

"And your lawyer is here." Her hand returned to mine and held it tightly. "Please," she whispered. "Introduce me to him."

A quick glance over my shoulder told me that, indeed, Peter had joined us. Ironic that Swansy should know before me, blind as she was. But her hearing was incredible. She must have heard his step.

I continued to hold her hand as I stood by the side of her chair and watched Peter as he studied her. He knew. He'd seen it right off. Whether it was Rebecca's docility that had alerted him, or the harness lying close by the rocker, or the opaqueness of Swansy's blue eyes, I didn't know, but he took it in stride.

"Swansy, this is Peter Hathaway. Peter, Swansy Tabb."

Coming forward Peter put his hand in the one Swansy offered. "How do you do?" he said with gentle formality.

"I'm doin' just fine," Swansy answered brightly. Freeing her other hand from mine, she closed it over his. "It's a pleasure to meet you."

"The pleasure is mine." He left his hand where it was, even when Swansy's top hand began to move. I wondered whether he knew how much she could tell from a hand. Either he didn't, or he had nothing to hide.

I watched her closely, anxious to know her reaction to Peter. But she wasn't letting on. Leisurely she finished exploring the back of his hand and tracking the length of his fingers. Then she wagged his hand toward a chair. "Sit by me, please."

Peter sent me a lopsided grin. In return I shot a pointed look at the cushioned armchair that sat not far from the bentwood. As Swansy released his fingers, he backed into it. I stayed close by her chair.

"Is this your first trip north?" she asked.

"No, ma'am. I've been many a time to Camden, though not in a long, long time."

"Camden." She was silent for a minute. "What was your business in Camden?"

I knew what he'd say. Camden was a summer playground for the big bucks crowd. My family and I had visited friends there many a time. Funny, we'd never heard about him then.

"When I was in my teens," he said, "I waited tables at the big old hotel that used to be there."

Which was why we'd never heard about him then. The Madigans and their friends didn't mix with the hired help. If either Samantha or I had dared to flirt with an attractive young waiter, Dad would have cut off our allowances for a month. We'd never have risked that.

Besides, the years would have been wrong. Peter was forty. When he'd been in his teens, I'd have been too young to flirt. Not that I ever really got the knack of it.

So Peter had worked. I remembered Samantha saying something—what was it?—about his having made it big only in the past five years? That opened up dozens of questions, none of which I had the nerve to ask.

Swansy did. She started with, "Where are you from?"

"Originally? Columbus, Ohio."

She mulled that over. "It's a long way from Ohio to Maine."

"Uh-huh."

Swansy pulled a Swansy, then. I'd seen her do it to others, and heaven only knew how many times she'd done it to me, but I was surprised that it worked on Peter. He seemed too sharp, shrewd enough to hold the cards to his chest in the face of a bluff. But when Swansy sat there, training her opaque blue eyes his way and smiling with such sweet anticipation, he fell prey and, without another word from her, began to talk.

"I'd been a troublesome kid. My mother died when I was ten, my older brother had long since left, and I was stuck with my dad, who was as rigid a man as you'd ever want to meet. I ran away whenever I could. Those summers, I hitched my way to the coast. I was fourteen the first time, but I was a big kid. I had no trouble finding a job. In the summers after that, my dad was pleased to see me go."

He tossed me a glance. Only then did I realize that I'd been holding my breath. I let it out slowly, but I couldn't take my eyes from him. "What did your dad do for a living?" I asked softly.

"He worked in a factory. Punched in every morning, punched out every night. I couldn't bear the thought of growing up to do that. Prison was preferable in my mind— at least, that was what I told myself when I did some of the things I did. I came really close to finding out."

"What did you do?"

He shrugged. "Petty stuff. Nothing felonious."

"Like what?"

He looked bemused. "You really want to know."

It was halfway between a question and a statement, and either way, I couldn't deny it. I wanted to know, not because it had anything to do with what he could or could not do for Cooper, but because I was curious.

"I stole cars."

I didn't say anything for a minute. Then I couldn't help myself. "That's petty? Do you know what havoc you wreak when you steal someone's car? I had a car stolen when I was twenty. It was my mother's, but I'd been the one driving, so I felt the burden. There was the hassle of being without it, the hassle of waiting for the police to call and report it found, the hassle of having it repaired, not to mention the expense, and then the feeling of driving a car that's been diddled with by some faceless creep."

Peter looked amused. "'Diddled with'?"

I'd used the phrase in all innocence, but the way Peter said it, and the look in his eye when he did, suggested something X-rated. "You know what I mean," I muttered and looked away.

Quietly Peter said, "I never damaged any of the cars I stole. I just rode them around. It was an ego trip. I stepped on the gas, really stepped on it, and watched the speedometer needle pass sixty, seventy, eighty, ninety...." His breath caught, then broke free. "It was a wild feeling of power."

My gaze had returned to his as he'd been talking, lured by the excitement that, even then, crept into his voice. It was in his eyes, too, that excitement, and as I looked it seemed at the same time dangerous and sexy. Unable to accept either, I snorted. "It was a miracle you didn't crash."

"I did," he said, and the excitement was gone. "Two weeks after my eighteenth birthday, I got drunk, went for a spin and rammed headlong into a bridge abutment. I was driving my dad's old shebang that time, so I didn't get into trouble with the law. My dad gave me up for dead, literally and figuratively. I was in a coma for a month and woke up to find that I'd broken most every bone in my body."

I exhaled. "What happened then?"

"Not much. At least, not quickly. I was in the hospital for months. There was a first round of operations, then a second round. I had surgery to correct things that hadn't healed properly, then I had to lie there and let them reheal. When that was done, I started in on the endless physical therapy it took to get my body working again."

My gaze dropped to his legs. Lovingly encased in

denim, they were long, strong and straight. "It's hard to believe."

"I could show you scars," he said in a very soft voice, one that conjured up tummy-tingling images.

"I'm sure," I said quickly. "Still, it's hard to believe."

"Why so?"

"You move so well. So fluidly. You don't have any sign of a limp. You kept up with me all the way from my house." I felt a stab of guilt. "It wasn't the easiest walk. I'd never have suggested it if I'd known what you'd been through."

"What I've been through is over and done. I'm fine. I swim regularly. I play tennis twice a week. I ran a marathon last month. I'm probably in better shape than I'd have been if I'd never crashed that car." He paused before adding, "I know I am mentally."

That got me wondering some more. "How did you do it?"

"Do what?"

"Get from that hospital bed to the courtrooms of America."

"It wasn't easy."

I could have guessed that, but I wanted to know the details. I raised both brows in as tempting a silent invitation as I could muster, pulling a Swansy of my own. Then it struck me that, for all intents and purposes, I'd forgotten Swansy was there.

I quickly looked to her face. She was sitting quietly in the rocker, wearing an innocent smile, as unobtrusive—and intent—as a fly on the wall. I had the distinct impression that she was pleased with the way the conversation was going.

I leaned low and murmured, "Can I get you anything?"

She shook her head, but reached for my hand. Still the focus of her attention was Peter. "How?" she asked him.

Before he spoke, he looked at me, pointed silently to the chair on which he sat, asking me with his hands whether I wanted to sit. It was a courtly gesture, but I shook my head. I felt safer standing by Swansy's shoulder, holding her hand. She grounded me.

Peter stretched out his legs and loosely folded his hands over the buckle of his belt. "I had lots of time to think when I was laid up—lots of time with nothing to do and no one to see. I felt pretty low. At some point I decided that there had to be more to life than the kind of cheap thrills I'd been looking for. So I buckled down. I took correspondence courses during my recovery and graduated from high school. I was still in intensive physical therapy, so I couldn't do much for another year. I read a lot, thought a lot. Little by little I was able to go to work. I had stacks of hospital bills to pay, and when I'd done that, I worked for another two years to stash money away for college. By the time I entered the state university, I was twenty-four. I did well, transferred to Penn, went from there to NYU Law, and the rest is history."

He summed the struggle up so quickly that it took me a minute to ingest it. When I did, I couldn't help but let out a breath. "That's a wonderful story." It was just the kind that had always appealed to me. "You fought the odds and came through on top. There must be any number of people who are sitting back, shell-shocked to think that the drunken kid who went head-on into that bridge abutment is as successful as you are."

"I didn't have much choice. It was curl up and die or do something with my life."

"You could have done less. You could have gotten yourself back on your feet only enough to hold down the barest excuse for a job. You could have been satisfied with punching in and out like your father did, then going to the corner bar and drinking your way through Monday night football."

"If that's the kind of life that works for a man, there's nothing wrong with it," he said in a voice that wasn't quite as gentle.

"It's a waste," I argued. "That kind of existence goes nowhere."

"For some people, it's all that's possible."

I was shaking my head even before he'd finished. "There's always more. Small things. Subtle things. There's always something to work for."

"Try telling that to the guy who can't get a better job because he can't read, and he can't read because he dropped out of school to work so his family could eat. I had friends like that. They're still back in the same neighborhood, living in the same houses, only those houses are now older and more rundown."

There were people right here in town who fit his description. "So they keep them clean. That's something. And they work so their children don't have to drop out of school to earn money to eat. So their children move ahead in ways they can't. That's something. Upward mobility is relative. You took it by leaps and bounds, and you're right, some people can't do that, but neither do they have to give up and stagnate. There's always room for *some* movement."

The movement I felt just then was the subtle squeeze of Swansy's hand. Peter looked ready to argue more, but Swansy was right. It was time to move on.

"Is your dad still alive?" I asked.

He shook his head.

"Have you kept in touch with your brother?"

Again, he shook his head.

All of which seemed very sad to me. Peter had made

it, but there was no member of his family to see and share the pleasure.

Then it struck me that I wasn't much different. I had family, and plenty of it, yet I chose to keep them at arm's length. Not that they could appreciate my success. In their minds, I was a dabbler. I worked with clay for the artsy image it portrayed and sold a piece here or there. Not even the shows in New York had alerted them to the fact that I'd come into my own. But then, I told them as little as possible about myself and my success. Was I still afraid of their criticism?

Again, Swansy squeezed my hand. "It's all right," she said softly as she tipped her face up toward mine. "Some things are special, whether they're shared or not." Then she turned to Peter. "Do you think you can help our Cooper?"

"I think so. I'll know more after the weekend, after I've had a chance to look around and talk with people."

"Cooper is special."

"So I gather." He spared me a dry look, then glanced at Rebecca, who'd risen from where she'd been lying between his chair and the rocker and was nuzzling his hand.

"Would you take her out?" Swansy asked. "She likes you. She's always been a sucker for tall, good-looking men."

How she'd known Peter was tall was no mystery; she formed impressions based on how far a person's voice was above her head, or with a sitting figure, how far from the chair a pair of shoes shifted on the floor. In Peter's case, there'd also been the size of his hand and the length of his fingers. There was only one way, though, that she could have known he was good-looking, and that was from me.

That was one of the things I felt self-conscious about. The other was that Rebecca didn't need an escort. Swansy knew it, I knew it, and Peter had to know it, too. That was the only thing that could account for the cross between suspicion and amusement in his look.

I focused on Rebecca so that I wouldn't have to suffer that look.

"Does she have a favorite spot?" he asked as he stood.

"She'll lead you to it," Swansy answered sweetly. As soon as Peter and Rebecca had left the room, she tugged at my hand. I settled on the edge of the chair Peter had just left.

"What do you think?" I asked softly.

She answered as softly. "He'll understand Cooper. With a history like his, he'll be better 'n some. I think you did well."

"I can't take the credit. He was Mom's idea."

"And you're still regretting it. You're tense, girl. I'd have to be deaf and dumb not to see it. What worries you?"

"I don't know. I…don't know."

"Do you question his skill?"

"It's not that."

"Then it's something personal. He's younger than you thought he'd be."

"Yes."

"And more attractive. Are you drawn to him?"

"I'm not drawn to any man. You know that, Swansy."

"You haven't been. That doesn't mean you can't be."

"I can't be."

"Hogwash. You're a woman. You have womanly instincts."

"I can't be attracted to another man." Swansy stared at me quietly, sweetly. Inevitably, I began to talk. "I loved Adam. He was everything to me. We were like two peas in a pod, two halfs of a whole. We had something special. We shared a dream. We were going to build a life for ourselves that was pure and simple, and we were going to do it well.

Just because he's gone doesn't mean I have to give up the dream."

"No one's askin' you to."

"But if there was another man—"

"It wouldn't make any difference. You'd still have your dream."

"But not with Adam."

"You're not gonna have it with Adam anyway, girl. Adam's dead."

I felt the sting of her words and wasn't sure whether I was more upset by the words themselves or the way she'd said them. I could have sworn I heard impatience in her voice. I'd never heard that from Swansy before.

Sensing my distress in the silence, she reached out and slid a withered hand to my knee. "It's the truth, Jillie. You know it as well as I do. You just won't accept it."

"I accept it," I argued. "I've *had* to accept it. I'm the one who's missed him for six years. I'm the one who's made dinner for one and then spent my evenings with no one to share the news of the day. I'm the one who's gone to bed alone and woken up alone. Adam's dead. Gone. More than anyone, I know that."

"But you haven't moved on. Think of what you were saying not so long ago to your Peter—"

"He's not my Peter."

"Well, he's more yours than mine, since you were the one who brought him up here, and don't try to distract me from the point I'm wantin' to make, which is that you've got to do something more with your life."

"More? More! Swansy, I've built an entire career since Adam died. Up to then, I hadn't done much more than sell the occasional piece in a gallery somewhere. I'm having showings in New York now, and my things are selling as soon as they're seen. Doesn't that count for doing something with my life?"

"Yes, ma'am," Swansy said with feeling. "It sure does. But what about the woman in you? You're a woman of feeling. There was more than a little of the romantic in you when you and Adam moved up here, and don't tell me there wasn't."

"I won't."

"So where's it gone? What've you done with it?"

"I've put it into my work."

Swansy acknowledged that with a pause, then a nod, then a softly warbled, "Yes, you have. It's one of the things that makes your work special and different and beautiful. You put your feelings into that clay." Her voice grew even softer. "But what about the rest, Jillie? What about the rest of the dream?"

I swallowed. I knew just what she was thinking. She and I had discussed it often in the months before and after Adam died. We hadn't discussed it in a long, long time.

Looking down at my hands, I said, "It's not that important. I've been lucky with my career. It's more than I could have asked for. It'd be selfish of me to think that I can have everything. No one has everything."

"You wanted children."

"I can live without them."

"Why should you have to?"

"Because Adam's dead. I wanted Adam's children."

"And if you'd fallen in love with another man before Adam, you'd have wanted that man's children. You are a nurturer. I see it here. You nurture every one of us in your own special way, but it's not the same as having children of your own."

"I have all of you, and I have my career. I'm perfectly satisfied with that."

"Are you?"

"Yes!"

"Then what is it about your lawyer that makes you nervous? If you're perfectly satisfied with your life, how can he pose a threat?"

"It's no big *thing*. The man makes me nervous, that's all."

"Because you're attracted to him, just the way you should be, and you're feelin' guilty, 'cause you're still married to Adam, only Adam's dead, so's you have every right to be attracted to Peter, only you're shaky like a young girl, and you don't like that."

"Damn right, I don't." Mostly I didn't like being analyzed so well. Blind as she was, Swansy saw right through me, and I didn't like what she saw. "First Samantha, now you. What is it with you people? Do I tell you how to live your lives?"

"Yes, you do. You told me that I should have a dog. You said that if I had one, I'd be more independent. Think of it, independent, at my age. But you were right. I listened to you, and you were right."

"Listen to me, hah. I had to make all the arrangements behind your back, then tell you that Rebecca had nowhere to go but here because she was allergic to smog."

"And it worked. So what about you? Should I tell you that Peter Hathaway has an ulcer and needs a cure by the seaside?"

"An ulcer?" came a deep voice from the door. "That's an interesting thought. Actually, I'd forego the ulcer and just take the cure by the seaside. It's great out there, all woolly and wild."

Attesting to that was his thoroughly tossed hair, his ruddy cheeks and his eyes, which held added life as they homed in on me. The collar of his jacket stood up against the back of his neck. He looked healthier than a man of forty had a right to look. And more virile.

I couldn't think of a thing to say.

But Peter wasn't done. He said to Swansy, "Why would you want to tell Jill that I had an ulcer?"

In the flash of an instant, I imagined what Swansy's answer would be. I decided to beat her at her game. "So I'd take pity on you and take you in," I said in a brassy tone. I rose from my chair and started toward him. "She thinks there's something missing in my life. Not only should I take you in, she thinks, but she thinks that I should let you father my children." I made a small sound of disgust. "Can you believe that? She hasn't known you for more than twenty minutes and she's got you and me having kids."

I slipped past him, raising my voice as I returned to the kitchen. "You're being a *busybody*, Swansy, and it's not right. I know what I want and what I need, and I don't need a husband any more than I need children. My life is full." I grabbed my coat from the chair. "Very full." I shoved my arms into the sleeves. "If I wanted kids, there are a dozen guys up here who would volunteer their services," I started back toward the parlor, "and if I wanted a husband, I'd find my own. But I don't want either. I'm doing fine. Just fine."

Stalking past Peter, I went to Swansy's rocker, put a hand on either arm and leaned low to kiss her cheek. "I do love you, though," I whispered. "You'll be okay?"

Swansy touched my cheek and nodded.

"Should I put dinner on the table?"

"I can do that myself," she warbled, but didactically. "I can do it because I've accepted my weaknesses and moved on. I'm learning to do things I didn't think I'd be able to do. I've grown."

Her message couldn't have been more blunt if she'd framed it in neon and stuck it in front of my nose. But

I couldn't get angry; I'd used up my allotment for the day. And this was Swansy. I loved her like—sometimes more than—my mother. She was there when I needed her, comforting me when I was blue, laughing with me when I was high.

So she'd spoken out of turn this time. She'd earned the right.

"I'll stop by tomorrow," I said, then straightened and passed Peter again on my way to the back door. I had no desire to wait while he said goodbye to Swansy. I didn't want to hear any words that might be exchanged between them. I'd about had it with being the brunt of other people's good intentions. I was very definitely on the offensive.

DUSK WAS APPROACHING when I led Peter back down Main Street, then down the lane that led to the dock. "The *Free Reign*," I said, gesturing toward the sturdy trawler that bobbed by the rotting wood pier. She was secured both bow and stern by heavy ropes that I could only think of as manacles, and the way she tugged at them, while maintaining her pride and presence, reminded me of Cooper.

His house was next on our list of stops. It was conveniently situated at a midway point on the lane. Though smaller than the frame houses that corded Main Street, it was clearly well tended, in fine repair. I wanted Peter to see that.

With a single rap of the brass knocker, I opened the front door, which put me right into the small living room. Cooper was there, straddling a bench before the fire, creating a work of art with a piece of wood and a small knife. He was surrounded by shavings. I guessed that he'd been furiously working off his frustration since he'd left my house, but the boat he was carving didn't seem to be suffering any from the frustration. It was still in its early stages, still nearly as much a log as a model boat, but there was a gracefulness to the part he'd carved that promised good things ahead.

I wanted Peter to see that, too.

Quietly I crossed to the fire. "Are you okay?"

Cooper's dark eyes slid past me to Peter, then returned to mine. With a brief nod, he returned to his work.

"I was worried."

"No need." He chipped off a sliver of wood, chipped off a second, chipped off a third.

"I'm trying to give Peter a feel for the town. We've been to Swansy's. I thought we'd stop off at Sam's for dinner. Will you join us?" I wanted that more than anything. Having dinner alone with Peter came second only to spending the night alone in my house with him on a list of things I was dreading.

But Cooper wasn't cooperating. "Not tonight, Jill. I'm not much in the mood."

"Maybe it would help cheer you up," I suggested, but even as I said it, I knew it wouldn't. Cooper's look made that clear. His sharing a table with the big-time lawyer from New York would be broadcasting his dilemma to the world. It didn't matter that this world already knew his dilemma; the broadcasting would dig at him much as he dug at his log, chip after chip after chip.

"Is Benjie around?" I asked. Not only did I like the idea of his being with Cooper, but I wanted to introduce him to Peter.

But Cooper said, "He's not back yet."

I frowned. "Wasn't he due back yesterday?"

"He called to say he was staying till tomorrow."

Benjie Drake and New York City weren't the best twosome in the world. Benjie had always been a little on the wild side, and though Cooper rode him hard, there was only so much he could do. It wasn't as though Benjie was a kid anymore. He was an adult. He earned a living working on the boat. Or used to.

"There's not much for him to do here," Cooper said in echo of my thoughts. "I don't much like his being there, but if I raise a stink, he may just decide to stay." He chipped off one sliver of wood, then another. "I can be patient."

"Do you do much of this?" Peter asked. He was standing before the stone mantel with his hands in his pockets, pinning his jacket open. His eyes were on the boat that sat there. It was a finished model—or as finished as Cooper ever made them. Upward from midpoint in the hull, it was an intricately carved schooner; downward from that point, it was rough-hewn, blending into the log from which it had been carved and which now served as its stand.

"It's a hobby," Cooper said in a flat tone.

Taking one of his hands from his pockets, Peter touched the boat with much the same care that he'd touched my pieces earlier that day. "I wish I could do this," he said quietly and with utter sincerity. "I don't have any artistic ability at all. My handwriting's so bad that in my office, decoding is a major secretarial prerequisite."

I watched the way his thumb smoothed wistfully over the wood. "Your strength is with words," I said. "And legal strategies."

"Maybe, but I've always admired people who could make things like this. Art is way up there, on a plane by itself. It's a beautiful outlet for a whole world of emotions."

"Swansy and I were just saying that," I said on impulse and regretted it seconds later when Peter looked suddenly curious. "You said it much better than we did, though. You do have a way with words." I turned quickly to Cooper, who had paused in his whittling to witness my exchange with Peter. "You'll be coming over tomorrow afternoon?"

Cooper hesitated for several seconds, during which his

eyes once again told me that he didn't want to be working with Peter. I held mine steady. No way was I yielding. Peter Hathaway was going to clear Cooper of the charges against him, and that was that.

"I'll be there," Cooper said, and there was a tiny movement at the corner of his mouth that, magnified, would have denoted wryness. "If I'm not, I'll never hear the end of it."

"You're right."

"You're tough."

Cooper was the one person beside Swansy who knew how untough I really was. "Oh, yeah." I turned to Peter. "All set?" I wasn't sure whether he had any questions for Cooper or whether he was satisfied to wait until the next day to really get started.

His touch lingered on Cooper's boat for a final minute before he returned his hand to his pocket and cocked his head toward the door. With a wave to Cooper, I led Peter on.

We stopped next at the grocery store, where I picked up additional food for the weekend—additional, because though I'd already stocked up on the basics, I knew they weren't going to be enough. Part of it had to do with the way Peter had downed two thick tuna sandwiches without blinking. The other part had to do with his size. He was lean but solid. His shoulders alone, I figured, would warrant extra bacon and eggs and milk.

When I turned toward Sam's Saloon after leaving the grocery store, Peter paused. "Shouldn't we have saved the shopping for last," he peered into the bag he held, "so nothing spoils?"

"It would have been too late. Claude's closing."

"But it'll be another hour or two until we get back to your place."

"No problem. Sam has a huge refrigerator. He'll put the bag there while we eat." He did it all the time for me. It was, I supposed, one of the perks of living in a close-knit community. I couldn't imagine any of the pricey restaurants that my family frequented in Phillie offering such a service. But it was a nice touch, like Claude's keeping my charges on account, payable at my convenience, or Greta's special-ordering me the latest paperback bestsellers from her distributor, who stopped by the drugstore monthly to refill the single small rack with books.

Everyone knew everyone else here, which meant that when I entered Sam's Saloon with Peter, we created something of a stir. It was a small one; the people who lived here were private, even shy, certainly laconic in the way that was typically Maine. But we had their attention, almost to a man.

With Peter in tow, I headed for the kitchen. I responded personally to those who called out as I passed—a smile for Tom Kaskins, a wave to Joan Tunney, a wink at Stu Schultz. These people were my friends. I enjoyed seeing them. By virtue of their presence, I didn't feel quite so alone with Peter.

Sam Thorn, owner and chef of the Saloon, was in the kitchen. One look at me and he burst into a grin wide enough to rival his girth. "I knew there was a special reason I made lasagna tonight," he teased.

I adored his lasagna. Though I'd had lasagna in little Italys around the world, Irish-born Sam's was the best. Of course, he had the edge on ambiance. The Saloon was a thoroughly relaxing place to be.

And I did relax. After stowing my groceries in Sam's fridge, I settled across from Peter in a booth and let Sam treat us not only to his lasagna, but to Caesar salad and garlic bread. Sam, himself, kept us company for a bit, then others stopped by to say hello.

They were curious about Peter, I knew. They were also timid, unsure of what to say to him. As mild as he was, as smiling and patient, they were awkward. It didn't matter that he looked very much like them in his dress, in the wind-muss of his hair and the late-day shadow on his cheeks. In their eyes, he represented glitz, and glitz was foreign to them.

It wasn't foreign to me, still I knew what they felt. In his own subtle way, Peter was larger than life. He'd seen more, done more than we had, and he ran in circles that I'd given up on fitting into long ago. Had he and I been alone, I'd definitely have felt awkward—though how much of that would have been due to his looks alone, I wasn't about to wager. Fortunately we weren't alone for long.

Steven Willow, whose family had run the hardware store for three generations, stopped by to quietly ask what I thought about his buying a computer. "To keep watch on inventory," he told me. "Paulie says we should."

"Paul is a student at the Community College," I told Peter. "He's taking business courses." To Steve, I said, "It's worth looking into. Computers cost less now than they used to. Would you want to use one?" I knew that the major force against modernization in a town like this was habit. Steve's answer supported that.

"Not me. But Paulie. He'll be takin' over one day."

I thought about that for a minute before repeating, "Look into it with Paulie. There are probably uses you'd have for a computer besides the one you'd be buying it for. It might be well worth the money."

With a two-fingered salute of thanks, he moved on, only to be replaced several moments later by Noreen McNard.

She was one of the town's newest residents, having married Buck McNard, Jr., only two years before.

"My parents are coming to visit," she told me after shyly greeting Peter.

Noreen came from northern Vermont. Since the drive was a long one, with precious few superhighways on the way, she didn't see her parents often. She'd been particularly lonely of late. I was pleased for her now. "That's exciting! When?"

"Next Friday." Her eyes sparkled. "A week from today. They'll stay the weekend." She was slightly breathless. "We'll give them our room. We can sleep in the attic." Her eyes widened, her voice lowered. "But I don't know what to cook."

"No problem. I have dozens of good recipes."

"I'm a terrible cook."

I squeezed her arm. "You are not. I tasted your potato salad at the fair last month, and it was great."

"But that was *her* recipe," Noreen whispered. "I can't serve her everything she taught me to make. She has those things all the time. But I ruin every new recipe I try."

"You won't ruin mine. You can't. I have nine years' worth of fool-proof recipes. None of them has more than five ingredients. It's impossible to spoil them." I saw glimmers of hope and relief in Noreen's eyes. "Want to come by on Monday and we'll go through my file?"

"That would be great," she said with a grateful smile. Still smiling, she lowered her eyes and darted a self-conscious look at Peter. "Pleasure meeting you," she murmured and scurried off.

Peter watched her leave, then arched a brow my way. "You're a regular consultant. Is it always this way when you hit town?"

I shook my head. As though to contradict me, Noel

Bunker chose that moment to walk up. I dragged in a breath, feeling vaguely sheepish. "How's it going, Noel?"

"Okay."

I introduced him to Peter as the owner of the local gas station and a good friend of Cooper's. Peter took that in, as he had all the other information I'd given him on people we'd seen or talked with, but he didn't ask questions. I assumed he'd taken to heart my warning about the townspeople being wary, but in any case, it was a wise move on his part. He was giving us time to get used to having him around, which implied that he was going to be around for a while.

I didn't like the idea of having him around for long.

I didn't want to *think* about having him around for long.

So I looked up at Noel and asked, "How's Lisa?"

"'bout the same," Noel answered. Kneading the pocket of his checkered wool jacket, he added, "We got to do something."

In a quiet voice, I explained to Peter, "Lisa is Noel's daughter. She's seven. She broke her leg this summer. The cast has been off for four weeks now, but she's still not walking right. The doctors say that the pain will go away, but the leg just doesn't look right."

"Has it been X-rayed?" Peter asked.

"Oh yes. They say the broken bones have knit, but I wonder how well." Feeling Noel's worry as my own, I looked up at him. "Can I get the name of that specialist?" I'd been offering to do it for two weeks, but Noel and his wife had resisted. Until now.

Noel nodded. He continued to knead his pocket, as though the wool were worry beads.

"First thing tomorrow," I assured him gently. "Boston's a little closer. Should we try there?"

"Guess so."

I knew he was feeling low and tried to convey encouragment in a smile. "Done. I'll get a good man, Noel. Lisa will be fine."

He nodded at me, nodded at Peter, then moved on.

"They love you," Peter said, picking up where he'd left off before Noel had arrived.

"It's mutual. These people are real people. They may not say much, but when they do speak, you can bet it's the truth, and I love them for that."

"But they *love* you. You're their guru."

That embarrassed me. "I am not. I've just had more experience than they have in the world beyond this town, so they come to me with their questions. I like being involved in their lives. They sense that, I suppose, and that encourages them to come back. If I weren't here, they'd find the answers all by themselves—" I paused "—but I don't usually tell myself that. These people make me feel needed. Illusion or not, I don't care. I like the feeling."

Indeed, I did. I was in my element here. Among these simple and unpretentious people, I felt as fulfilled as I ever did—except when I was home, in my attic studio, pouring my heart and soul into slabs of clay. They were two different kinds of fulfillment. The first gave me satisfaction as a human being, the second as an artist. But there was a third kind of fulfillment, one that I became acutely aware of several hours later as I prepared for bed.

Wearing my long white nightgown with lace at the hem, wrists and high collar, I sat on the end of my bed and listened to the sounds of Peter preparing for the night in the room beside mine. My cheeks grew pink, my palms damp. Against my wishes, my body tingled in places where tingling wasn't allowed.

I wondered then about the kind of fulfillment that a woman can only get in the arms of a man, and I prayed that the urges I felt were passing ones. Because I wasn't about to experience that kind of fulfillment again—particularly not with Peter, who was the kind of man Adam might have been, had I not led him off to the sea.

CHAPTER FOUR

"Wake me at nine."

They were the last words Peter said to me before closing the door to his room, and they echoed in my brain for most of the night. When I finally fell asleep—after trying in vain to read, then trying in vain to do a crossword puzzle, even creeping upstairs and trying in vain to sketch out the glaze pattern for the fruit bowl I'd thrown earlier that week—it was nearly one in the morning. I awoke again at two-thirty, four fifty-five and six-ten, and each time the same thing happened. I turned over and came slowly to consciousness, then opened my eyes with a start when I remembered that Peter was there. With that recollection came a simultaneous jumping in my stomach that was a long time in settling. When I finally gave up the fight at seven-fifteen and climbed out of bed, I wasn't at my best.

Wake me at nine.

The hands of the small stove clock crept. It wasn't that I was eager for Peter to be up and with me, because I certainly wasn't. I had nothing to say to him. He was here for one reason and one reason alone—to defend Cooper. I assumed that he planned to spend the morning in town chatting with whomever he could find who'd be willing to open up on the subject. That was fine with me. If he thought he'd just sit around the kitchen, dawdling over breakfast for several hours, or hang around the living room—or worse, my studio—that wasn't so fine. I wasn't sure I could take it. He might just as well sleep later.

It appeared that that was just what he was going to end up doing. At nine on the dot, I went upstairs and knocked on his door. When there was no answer, I knocked again. After a minute, I accompanied a third knock with his name, but even that failed to elicit a response. So, slowly and cautiously, I turned the knob and eased the door open.

Peter was sprawled facedown on the too-small bed. One bare arm was hooked over its edge and hung nearly to the floor, the other was curved under the pillow. The covers cut diagonally across his body, starting beneath his right arm and ending at his left hip, and beneath the covers, his legs were widespread. I even detected his feet conforming to the vertical end of the mattress.

My stomach was at it again, jumping in the way that had become familiar during the night.

I looked toward the ceiling, but that didn't do much good. In the minute that I'd studied what was on the bed, certain things had etched themselves indelibly on my mind. Such as the hard muscles of Peter's shoulder. The dark tuft of hair beneath his arm. The firm flesh at that spot on his hip that would normally be covered by briefs.

Helplessly my gaze fell back to the bed. "Peter?" I called softly, then wondered why I wasted the effort. If my knocks hadn't woken him, a soft call wouldn't. Something stronger was needed.

"Peter!" I called more sharply, then, in annoyance as much as anything else, "*Peter.*"

He stirred. He moved his legs, then his hips, but when he went still again, it was clear that he'd simply made himself more comfortable.

"*Peter!*" I shouted. I was beginning to feel mildly panicked. If he didn't wake to my voice, I was going to

have to shake him, which meant putting my hand on his
skin. I wasn't sure I could do that.

"Hmmm."

I breathed a sigh of relief. It hadn't been much of a
sound, but it had been something. "It's nine o'clock, Peter.
You said to wake you at nine."

He turned his head on the pillow so that I could see his
face. His eyes were still closed. "Mmmm."

"It's nine." When he didn't respond to that, I said,
"Peter?"

"I hear," he grumbled groggily and turned his head the
other way.

I had the distinct impression that he was going right
back to sleep. "Are you getting up?"

"Ten," he mumbled. "Wake me at ten." The words were
slurred.

Eager for any excuse to leave the room, I said, "Fine,"
and backed out, closing the door behind me.

That left me with the dilemma of what to do with my
time. What I'd planned to do, before Peter had popped his
little surprise about wanting me for his girl Friday, was to
work. But an hour wasn't much time. No sooner would I
have everything set up than it would be ten, and at ten I
was supposed to wake him again, and that meant breakfast
soon after, and Lord knew when he'd be finished. By that
time whatever I'd been working on would have dried out.

So I ruled out working. I'd already showered, dressed,
made my bed, dusted my room, as well as dusted and
dry-mopped the entire downstairs, which was really quite
funny, since I'd done it all just the day before. But there
was something to be said for expending nervous energy,
and I was filled with that.

Baking seemed like a good idea.

I wasn't normally any more compulsive a baker than I

was a cleaner. Though my family occasionally mentioned my having gone north to commune with the sea and bake my own bread, I'd never gotten into that routine. Oh, I'd tried. It was truly a romantic thought, and there was nothing more divine than the smell of fresh-baked bread. But I never seemed to do it quite right. My bread came out looking deformed, and all too often the smell that filled the kitchen was of something burning. Far easier, I decided, to buy my bread at the store.

Muffins, on the other hand, were my pals. Mix everything in a bowl, pour into paper-lined muffin tins, bake. Very easy.

Over the years, I'd made the standard blueberry muffins, corn muffins and bran muffins. With the taste of success, I'd grown bolder. Among my repertoire were apple-nut, zucchini and wheat germ, cottage cheese and chive, even ones heavily laced with dried fruit and rum.

Today I decided on cranberry-pumpkin. I had a bag of fresh cranberries in the fridge and several cans of pumpkin on the shelf. The other ingredients were all staples. So I went to work.

Two dozen muffins were in the oven baking when ten o'clock rolled around.

Wiping my hands on the dishtowel, I went upstairs. I tried knocking first. After all, Peter was a new acquaintance. I couldn't just barge into his room, assuming familiarity simply because he'd been in a dead sleep earlier.

I discovered to my chagrin, after repeating the ritual of knocking, then calling his name, then timidly opening the door, that he was still in a dead sleep, sprawled much as he'd been at nine.

"Peter?" I waited, then raised my voice. "Peter." I waited, then shouted, "Peter!"

He shifted. "Hmmm."

"It's ten. You said to wake you at ten."

He neither moved, nor made a sound.

"Peter."

Nothing.

I couldn't help but wonder whether he always slept this soundly, or whether he was doing it to annoy me. If the latter was so, it worked. Taking the few steps necessary to reach his bedside, I shook his shoulder. "Peter! It's ten!"

I snatched my hand back. Annoyed or not, I was affected by the firmness of his shoulder and the warmth of his skin.

He shifted, inhaled a deep breath, stretched.

I thought I'd die when the covers slipped to reveal twin dimples at the top of his buttocks.

I bit down hard on my lower lip to give myself something to think about, but the pain I caused wasn't half as interesting as those dimples, or the virile plane stretching above them, or the finer, paler skin under his arm, or the sprinkling of freckles across his shoulders.

Move, I told myself, but I couldn't budge. I'd never seen anything that had as debilitating an effect on my knees as the body spread before me.

"Ten o'clock," I sang out in a high, shaky voice. "Get up, Peter. It's ten o'clock."

He turned his head on the pillow, opened an eye and did his best to focus, without much success. I was ready to put money on the fact that he didn't know who in the devil I was—and I felt more than a little peeved, even hurt by that—when he said my name. It wasn't much more than a tired moan, but it was my name.

"Jill."

"Got it in one," I said in that same, higher-than-normal voice.

He barely moved his lips. "What time is it?"

"Ten."

Moaning, he turned his head away. "I should have been up at nine."

"I woke you then, but you told me to come back at ten."

"I'm so tired."

I hadn't considered that. I'd been too preoccupied with my nervous energy to think about why Peter was having such trouble waking up, and it wasn't as though the nervous energy was gone. But it had changed. As I stood there, unable to move from his bedside, it had become something softer and sweeter, something that I wanted to call exciting.

"What were you going to do this morning?" I asked. I was feeling the beginnings of compassion for the man. He seemed so zonked.

"Walk around," he mumbled. "Check out the local police."

"What time is Cooper due here?"

"One." He stretched again, this time half turning to his side, and in the instant before he drew his top leg up, I caught a glimpse of a line of soft, dark hair on his belly. My heart reacted wildly, and my eyes shot upward, following that line as it widened in a spray of hair over his chest. I had just focused on a small, brown nipple when it disappeared beneath the covers, which Peter drew up.

A helpless little sound slipped from my throat. Horrified, I coughed to cover it up. Between that cough and the newly risen covers, the spell was broken.

"Are you getting up?" I asked as I headed back toward the door. I didn't care that I sounded cross. Enough was enough.

Apparently not. "Eleven. Wake me at eleven."

"Oh, Peter."

"I'm beat. Too many late nights."

That's your problem, bud, I was on the verge of saying when he added, "Had to clear my desk to get here."

I should have known he'd say something like that, something I couldn't berate. I sighed. "Eleven?"

"Mmmm."

This time when I closed the door, I made no attempt to cushion its click. I didn't slam it, just... closed it. And I trotted down the stairs the way I normally did, washed the mixing bowl without taking care to be particularly quiet, talked full voice on the phone to an old friend in Boston about an orthopedic specialist, even turned the radio on to the country sound that I liked. When I'd done everything I could in the kitchen, I trotted up to my studio and did some organizing of materials, which entailed the opening and closing of cabinets. Then I trotted back down to take the muffins from the oven. While I was at it, I put on a pot of beef stew to cook. My recipe was nowhere near as good as Bettina Gregorian's, hers having far more ingredients than I could cope with. But while there wasn't the subtlety to my stew that there was to hers, it was still remarkably good.

At eleven o'clock, I put on my most nonchalant front and made my way back up the stairs. I didn't bother to knock this time, or call Peter's name from the door. For expediency's sake, I went straight to the side of the bed, took a firm grasp of his upper arm and gave it a good, solid shake.

He jumped. His head shot around, eyes opening wide on mine, though they didn't seem to see a thing. After several taut seconds, he slowly closed his eyes and sank down to the bed, but on his back. He threw an arm over his eyes. "You scared the hell out of me," he said in a quiet voice.

"I'm sorry. There didn't seem to be any other way to wake you."

"Is it nine?"

I had to smile. "No. Eleven."

He lifted his arm and peered up at me. "Eleven. I was supposed to get up at nine."

"When I woke you at nine, you told me to wake you at ten."

"Then ten."

"When I woke you at ten, you told me to wake you at eleven."

That gave him a moment's pause. "I did?"

I nodded.

"Oh." He dropped his arm back to his eyes. "I was having the most incredible dream."

Adam used to say the same thing. Then he'd reach for me and expect that I'd be as aroused as he was, only it didn't always work that way. If I was sleeping, I was sleepy, and if I was awake, my mind was on other things. Adam thought about sex a lot. I didn't. In my book, there were far more important and exciting things in our relationship than that.

Without conscious intent, my gaze slipped over the covers toward Peter's groin. But he had a knee bent. I couldn't see a thing—for which I thanked my lucky stars the instant I realized what I'd gone looking for. If he'd been hard, I wasn't sure what I'd have done.

Then again, if he hadn't been hard, I'd have wondered more.

Then *again*, maybe my mind had gone suddenly wicked. Maybe his dream hadn't been sexy at all. Maybe he'd been dreaming about winning one case or another.

I wasn't about to ask. Instead, I cleared my throat. "Are you awake now?"

"I think so."

"Help yourself to the shower," I said as I took my fill of his chest. It was solid, impressively broad at the shoulders, tapering to the waist where the covers lay, and it was a devilishly masculine blend of bone, muscle and flesh. I saw the tracings of several faint scars, but like the small one high on his cheek, they only added to the allure. "There's plenty of hot water. I had a new heater put in year before last."

"Sounds good."

"Bath towels are in the cabinet under the sink." I wasn't sure if I'd told him that the night before, but, if so, the repetition didn't hurt. I tried to think of what else he'd need to know, but I was distracted by his ribs. They weren't harshly delineated—he wasn't that lean—but they provided an interesting contour to go with the swell of his pectorals and the faint concavity of his stomach.

"I made muffins," I said quickly. "I'll put eggs and bacon on when you're ready to come downstairs—unless you'd rather not have eggs. I can understand that you might not, I mean, if you're keeping tabs on your cholesterol level. Lots of men are, nowadays. And women. I can skip the eggs. It'd be no trouble. I have cottage cheese and yogurt and plenty of fruit—"

It was as if I ran out of breath, just like that. One minute I was talking, the next minute I wasn't. Everything seemed caught up in my throat, because while I'd been babbling, Peter had slid his arm back on his forehead. Thus uncovered, his pale green eyes were focusing on me, holding my gaze captive, seeming to control the rest of me, as well. I couldn't move. Nor could I think of anything but the intimate message being conveyed, not only by those eyes but by his pose. With his arm up high like that, the entire upper half of his body was lifted, extended, made to look larger and more imposing than ever.

I sucked in a sharp breath when his hand—the one that had been lying innocuously on the quilt—closed around my wrist. He tugged. I resisted.

"Sit," he commanded quietly. His eyes continued to hold mine.

I shook my head. "Not a good idea."

"Why not?"

I couldn't think straight—at least, that was what I told myself when I didn't offer an answer. I wasn't about to say that his body excited mine too much for me to sit. I wasn't about to say that I was frightened not of him, but of myself.

He tugged harder, and I found myself perched on the side of the bed smack by his hip. Wisely, from his point of view, he didn't release my wrist; if he had, I'd surely have bolted, because my pulse was already running a frantic race and threatened to drag the rest of me with it. Rather, he anchored my cuffed hand to his chest. I curled my fingers into a fist, which was the least I could do to protect myself from the lure of his flesh.

"I shouldn't be here," I whispered.

"Why not?"

"I have things to do downstairs."

"Like?"

I tried to think, but it was difficult, being so close to him. All my energy seemed sidetracked in the effort to keep my breathing steady. I swallowed. "Like…see to the stew."

"Stew takes care of itself."

I knew that, but I'd hoped he wouldn't. "Do you cook?"

"I used to. It was a matter of survival."

The story he'd told at Swansy's about his crude beginnings came back to me in a rush. It was hard to remember he'd been mortal once. "You must eat out a lot."

"Enough. Sometimes it's just grabbing take-out on the run. I'd do more cooking if I had the time. I like cooking."

I couldn't believe the conversation. Peter had just bolted out of a dead-deep sleep, it was eleven in the morning, he was lying in bed half naked—all naked, if the truth were told—smelling faintly but deliciously of sleep-warmed man, and we were talking about cooking?

I wished he'd lower his arm. There was something exquisitely intimate about a man's armpit. Maybe it was that not many people saw it. Maybe it was simply that it was different; I shaved mine. The hair under his was soft and smooth, as was that sweet skin beneath it.

Funny, but I'd never paid particular heed to Adam's armpits. Or maybe I had, but I'd forgotten. Six years was a long time. A long time.

"Are you disappointed in me?" came the deep voice that was not Adam's but Peter's.

My eyes flew to his. "For what?"

He shrugged with one shoulder. "I don't know." But his eyes told me otherwise. In their probing green way, they said that I'd been looking entranced with his body one minute, then not so entranced the next. "Oversleeping, maybe," he improvised when I said nothing. "You hired me to work, not to sleep the weekend away."

How could I be angry when he'd obviously needed the sleep? "You were tired." I tried to casually lift my hand away from his chest, but he wasn't letting go.

"Leave it there. It feels good on my skin."

"It shouldn't be there. I shouldn't be here. You're right. I hired you to work, and now I'm distracting you."

"You're the boss. You can do what you want."

But I couldn't. I seemed to have lost control of my senses. That was the only explanation I had for not jerking my hand free and fleeing the room. Peter wasn't holding me *that* hard.

But I stayed. I stayed because I was in the thrall of the soft, sweet, exciting feelings that were surging through my insides. They were new and pleasant. I wasn't ready to oust them just yet.

"Why were you so tired?" I asked. "Were you really up late all week clearing things up so you could come here, or did you just say that to make me feel guilty?"

He frowned. "Did I say that?"

"Yes. When I tried to wake you at ten. Is it true?"

"Yes and no. There was a lot of stuff that needed to be taken care of so I'd be free, but I also had a crisis situation with one of my clients." My raised brows invited him to elaborate. He took them up on it. "I defended the man on charges of embezzlement. He was convicted on lesser counts than he'd originally been charged with, but he was still sentenced to a brief prison term. Last Monday there was a brawl in the prison yard. He's been accused of stabbing one of the other inmates."

"Oh dear."

"Oh dear is right. He would have been out on parole in another two months. Now he's facing disciplinary action that could add another six to his sentence."

"Is he guilty of the stabbing?"

"He did it, but he claims it was self-defense."

"Were there any witnesses?"

"Yeah. A prison yard full, all of whom hate my man because he isn't one of them. He's really a straight guy who made a single big mistake in life. Now that's been compounded. And the worst of it is that he has a wife and two kids. The pressure was so bad in their neighborhood that they moved, but they've been waiting for his parole to start putting the pieces together again."

"What could you do for him? Were you able to help?"

"I was up there every night this week trying to keep him cool. At the same time I was talking with every official I could get my hands on, trying to stop what's happening.

We're talking white-collar crime, here. My client doesn't know from physical violence. But if this thing escalates, he's gonna learn real quick, and that's gonna make it twice as hard for him to fit back into the mainstream of life when he gets out. I mean, if we're talking justice, let's have justice."

I could feel his tension beneath my palm.

My gaze fell. Sure enough, my fist had relaxed into a hand that was open on his chest, shaping itself to the gentle swell of muscle there. I stared at it, stared at the comparative slimness of my fingers and the way soft wisps of dark hair fringed their tips. I didn't dare move—not my hand or my arm or my body or anything that might dislodge my fingers from the heavenly groove they'd found.

"Jill?"

My gaze flew to his face.

"What are you thinking?" he asked in a voice that was deeper and more throaty than it had been moments before.

Thinking of that tone of voice, knowing the meaning of deeper and more throaty, I snatched back my hand—successfully this time—and said in a rush of words, "I shouldn't be with you here. It isn't right. You've come to defend Cooper. That's all I hired you for. It's all I want."

He lowered his arm. "Is it?"

I gave a convulsive nod. "I don't care what Samantha or Helaine or Swansy or anyone else says, I'm not available."

"You're a widow. You're not married. You say there isn't anything going on between Cooper and you—"

"There isn't."

"Then with another man? One of those stunning men you say are up here?"

It looked as if I wasn't going to live down that overheard conversation. For a minute, I wondered if I wanted to.

I should lie, I mused. I should tell Peter that there was another man. He'd never know the difference.

But he would. He'd make it his business to know, and, given that he was going to be in touch with most of the townspeople over the next days and weeks, he had the means at his fingertips.

Closing my eyes, I let out a breath. "No, there is no other man." I opened my eyes and looked into his. "But I have no intention of getting involved with anyone in the kind of way you're thinking. I had a wonderful marriage. I feel a deep loyalty to my husband. He left me a house, a boat, a way of life and a wealth of memories. They're more than enough for me."

"Are they?"

"Yes."

"Is that why your body reacts to mine the way it does?"

I swallowed. "I don't know what you're talking about."

"Sure, you do. Every time we look at each other something hot and sexy passes between us."

"No," I said and shook my head, only to become aware that Peter's hand was curled around my neck. His thumb traced the outer shell of my ear.

"It's there, Jill, and it's mutual. We don't have to be touching, but it's there. And the closer we get, the stronger it is." He took my hand, the one I'd snatched back and was holding in a fist against my stomach, and returned it to his chest. Unfurling my fingers, he dragged them up until my palm lay flat on his heart.

"Feel it?" he asked.

I couldn't have missed it. It was like broken thunder. *Ka-thunk. Ka-thunk. Ka-thunk.*

"Yours is like that, too."

"No."

"Yes." Locking my eyes with his, he slid his hand from

my neck down the column of my throat, over my sweater to my breast. Fingers splayed, he covered my heart.

Move, I told myself, but I couldn't budge. The whole of me seemed trapped beneath that large hand. Everything that I'd been and done and wanted for the first thirty-one years of my life seemed suddenly suspended. Only my heart moved. *Ka-thunk. Ka-thunk. Ka-thunk.*

In the gentlest of motions, he contracted his hand until it lightly kneaded my breast. I felt a corresponding contraction deep in my belly and sucked in a lungful of air, which served to offer that much more of me to his touch. My body swelled and tingled. I couldn't think of anything but how nice that felt, how deep, how rich.

Suddenly the heat left my breast, and he closed his hands around my upper arms and drew me forward and down.

"No," I whispered.

"Just a kiss," he whispered back. He continued to draw me down, now with his hands on either side of my head, but it was his eyes that drew me most strongly. I could see darker shards among the light green there, and though those shards were mossy, they smoldered.

I felt the smoldering to the tips of my toes, a heat that poured through my veins like a flash of white-hot light, sending sparks radiating outward all along the route. I'd never, never felt anything like it before, neither with Adam nor with any other man who'd chanced to look at me with desire. But I wasn't so naive that I didn't know what it was. I was in the midst of a passion attack so intense it scared me to death.

"No, please—"

His mouth touched mine. The sensation was so light, so new, so pleasurable that I gasped. He took advantage of that small parting of lips to deepen the kiss. But he wasn't a marauder. As though he knew how frightened I was,

he caressed my mouth with slow, gentle, moist strokes.
He nibbled here and sucked there. And he kept on doing
it, kept on doing it until all I could think about was how
lovely it felt. I didn't have to give; I simply received. Even
when he broke the contact to try a different angle, he was
the one to turn my head to the angle he sought.

I was stunned, because the pleasure increased with each
second that passed, and with each one of those seconds,
the fear seemed to fall away, well into the periphery of that
kiss. I was caught up in it, caught up in the texture and
heat and scent of it.

I'd never been a particularly sexual being, had
never given much thought to the individual aspects of
lovemaking. A kiss was a kiss, pleasurable, yes, but still
only a kiss. I'd never dreamed that a kiss could make my
mind whirl, but that was just what it was doing, which was
why, when he whispered, "Open your mouth for me," I did.

That was the extent of the demand he made. Once more
he was the doer, the taker. He explored the insides of my
lips, drew the lower one into his mouth and sucked on it,
sought out and stroked my tongue in a way that offered
such delight that I opened for more.

It seemed to go on forever, which was just what I
wanted. I wasn't in a rush to go anywhere. I had nothing to
do that was more pressing than exploring the outer reaches
of the pleasure Peter's mouth offered. So I gave myself up
to his ministrations without a peep.

At length, and reluctantly if the last, lingering touches
were any indication, he separated our mouths. I had had my
eyes closed, but when I realized that my lips were alone,
I opened my eyes. Though his were heavy-lidded, he was
watching me closely.

"Don't," he warned just as I was about to stiffen. "Don't
make something wrong about what was very right, and

don't—" he caught me opening my mouth "—say it wasn't right, because it was. I've been around a lot, and I know the difference between right and wrong. I'm not saying that there has to be anything more. We may have just hit the apex of our relationship. Maybe that's as good as it gets with us. But it was good. Don't tarnish it by getting your back up. It was just a kiss. Just a kiss. There is no grand commitment in a kiss."

I wasn't so sure. Something had definitely changed in the course of that kiss. A barrier was down. I no longer felt quite so strange sitting on the edge of the bed with Peter in it. I felt as though I had a right to be there.

Which was rationalization enough not to move, though I did pull my hands back from his chest and tuck them in my lap.

Peter settled back on the pillow. He left one hand on my arm, as though ready to catch me if I decided to flee. It was the mildest of restraints, but welcome. If I wouldn't be able to escape, I reasoned, there was no point in trying.

"Tell me about you, Jill. Tell me what makes you tick."

I stared at him for a minute, then tossed a wide-eyed look at the ceiling. "That's an impossible order," particularly when I was still feeling warm and light-headed from his kiss. "I wouldn't know where to begin." I was looking for direction from one who was more experienced in coping with the post-passion-attack muzzies.

Peter was just the one. "Why are you here? I know you said that you came here to pot, but we both know you could have done that back home. What made you leave?"

"I grew up. I got married." When he waited expectantly, I added, "I couldn't very well set up house with my husband in my childhood bedroom."

"I'll bet it was a beautiful bedroom in a beautiful house," Peter teased so gently that I couldn't take offense.

"Yes to both."

"Big brick thing? Ivy on the walls? Lush grounds?"

"You've seen it."

"No. But I know the area. I've represented people from that neighborhood."

I thought of the Humphreys. They weren't the kinds of family acquaintances I was proud of. It was one thing for Peter to represent them, that was his job, but it was something else for my father to pal around with a man who'd done what William Humphrey had. My mother kept a discreet distance, still I was amazed that the friendship hadn't hurt her career.

"Then you know just what it's like," I said.

"I know that I'd have given my right arm to grow up in something like it. So it's hard for me to understand why you left."

"It shouldn't be so hard. There are some distinct similarities between being born at the top and being born at the bottom."

"Oh yeah?" he drawled. "I'm listening."

"You're slotted. Whether at the top or the bottom, there are certain expectations you're supposed to meet. At the bottom, you're supposed to be rough, down-trodden, angry. At the top, you're supposed to be self-assured, socially adept and glamorous. In either case, there's a mold to fit into. I didn't fit into mine."

He moved his hand on my arm in a light, gently soothing motion. "I can't believe that."

"It's true."

"But you're all those things you mentioned."

"I'm none of those things—or I didn't used to be. I've come to be pretty self-assured in the past few years, and I guess I can pass in the socially adept department when I have to. But glamorous? I've never been that." I hurried on, lest he think I was fishing for compliments. "Oh, I'm pretty enough. But glamorous is more than just looks. Glamorous is an aura. It's high gloss and sophistication. It's knowing the right people and frequenting the right places. It's seeing and being seen. That all makes me very uncomfortable."

Just thinking about it, I felt shadows of the old nervousness that used to haunt me day after day. My hands involuntarily tightened in my lap. "My parents are comfortable with that kind of public life. So are Ian and Samantha. I guess I was cut from a different mold. That life never fit me quite right, and it wasn't as if I didn't try. I tried for nearly twenty years. I figured that if I tried long enough and hard enough, at some point things had to click, but they never did." I looked him in the eye. "So to answer your question, I left because I'd had it with trying to play the part of a Madigan. I was tired. I wanted to be myself."

Peter's hand lay still on my arm. He seemed totally engrossed in what I was saying. "Maybe you're right," he conceded. "Maybe there is a mold. But you have to fight, really fight to break out of the one at the bottom. From the top you just...drop out."

I had to make him understand that it wasn't as simple as that. "It's still a fight, Peter. In my case, there were endless confrontations in the library at home. Yelling and screaming may seem petty compared to what you went through, but to me it was a nightmare. I've always been a pacifist. That's one of the reasons I never fit in well at home. They're always fighting. Always. And about *really* petty things." I shuddered. "Believe me, I had to fight to break free."

At my shudder, Peter's hand began moving again. "Do you see them often?"

"Once or twice a year."

"In Phillie?"

I nodded. "They won't come here. It's just as well. Given the opportunity, they'd pick my life to pieces. So I go down there."

"On holidays."

"Not if I can help it. Holidays are happier up here. I usually just pick an odd weekend to visit."

"They must be pleased to see you."

"For the first five minutes."

"Then what?"

"Then we start fighting. I have my own ideas about things. In recent years, I've been more inclined to voice them. That's what I mean, I guess, about my being more self-assured than I used to be. My life up here is like an anchor. I feel secure here."

"Maybe that's because of the friends you've made. Maybe if you had friends like that in the other world, you'd feel more secure there."

"I have lots of friends back home."

"Friends from the old life. The Madigan life. Not ones you really like or trust, or you'd be back to visit more often."

I couldn't argue with him there. He'd effectively summed up the situation. It actually surprised me that he had, since he'd started the discussion from the other side of the fence. Big city, big name, big bucks—still he was different from the people back home. Maybe it was his background. Maybe it was just him. He didn't only listen; he heard. I had to respect that.

"Don't you ever miss the city?" he asked. The hand that had been on my arm fell down to capture one of my hands. He linked his fingers with mine. I didn't fight him. His touch was pleasurable.

"No," I answered lightly, much as I had every time I'd been asked that question during the past nine years. Then I paused. I looked down at our hands. There was something so natural, so honest about the way they were linked that I found myself confessing in a small voice, "Some things. Sometimes." My eyes quickly sought his. "But they're small things. Like visiting museums. Going to favorite restaurants. I could do them if I wanted when I go back to visit, but I usually don't bother, which means that I don't miss them all that much."

"Would you have done them with Adam?"

"Sure. Adam and I always had a great time when we did things together."

"Would you do them with me?"

I took in a deep breath to say, "Sure," nearly as automatically as I'd said it before, only the sound didn't come. Certain thoughts intruded, thoughts about opening myself up to grief. After all, Peter wasn't Adam.

Very softly, I said, "You wouldn't want to be a stand-in for another man. That's not your style."

"Damned right it's not. I wouldn't be a stand-in for Adam, any more than you'd have me for one, and we both know it." His voice lowered to a dangerously seductive level. "And you won't scare me off with that line, Jill Moncrieff. I've touched you. I've kissed you. And you weren't thinking of Adam when I did."

He was only part right. Thoughts of Adam had flickered through my mind, but by way of comparison, and Peter had come out ahead each time. That bothered me.

"Would you do it?" he asked softly.

"Do what?" I asked, feeling cross.

"Spend time in the city with me? When you come in for your show, I could take you to—"

"I don't know if I'll be going in for the show. I told you that."

"You could if you wanted to. It's your decision. We could have a nice time, Jill."

I could just picture his idea of a nice time. "Oh yeah, in a suite at the Plaza?"

"Why would I want a suite at the Plaza—"

"For the seduction you obviously have in mind. You're transparent, Peter Hathaway. I have you pegged."

"I was thinking of taking in the Metropolitan Museum and the Museum of Modern Art, going to a few shows, your taking me to your favorite restaurant and my taking you to mine. And there'd be no reason at all for a suite at the Plaza, when I have a perfectly good place on Central Park South—"

"See? I'm *right*! You have *one* thing on your mind."

"I do *not*!" He held both of my hands, now tightly. "I have a two-bedroom place, just like you do here, and I meant what I said about doing those other things. I'd enjoy them."

"You probably do them all the time."

"I don't. I've been to the Metropolitan Museum six times, and each time it was for a charity benefit. I've never been there to see the art. Same for MOMA." He was the one who seemed cross now. "And if you think I'm proud to be saying that, you're nuts. But the fact is that I haven't wanted to do those things alone, but I've never found someone I wanted to do them with."

His crossness added credence to his words, as did the fact that he looked embarrassed by what he'd said.

"You don't have to sit there looking so smug," he muttered. "I don't have the cultural background you do. You were probably eight years old when they took you to a museum for the first time. I never, ever went. I've come a long way. I've taught myself lots of things over the years.

I can hold my own in most any situation, but there are still some where I feel uncomfortable."

"Art museums?"

"Yes."

"And I wasn't looking smug. I'm surprised. That's all. And touched." Small snatches of vulnerability in a man so strong were very appealing. I was beginning to feel the force of that appeal building newly inside me.

Apparently Peter was beginning to feel something, too, because in the next instant, he came right up off the pillow and captured my mouth with his. I had no chance at all to protest; one minute he was lying flat on the bed looking vulnerable enough to kiss, the next he was doing it.

Not that I would have protested. I'd enjoyed his last kiss too much, and the instant his lips covered mine, I felt an explosion of the same intense pleasure. Actually the pleasure was even greater this time. I wasn't sure how that could be, but this new kiss seemed to have an army of feelers that were spreading joy through my body, finding and scratching niches I hadn't known I possessed.

Peter was right about one thing; something felt very right about this kiss, which was why I let it go on, let it go on just a little longer. It was a big mistake for two reasons. The first was that the longer he kissed me, the more hungry he grew, and the more hungry he grew, the more of himself he put into the kiss and the more excited I became. The second was that somewhere between a tongue thrust and a lip suck, a loud cough came from the door.

As one, and in alarm, Peter and I followed the direction of that sound to find Cooper's tall, dark frame filling the doorway.

CHAPTER FIVE

THE ONLY COMPARABLE experience I had to being found by Cooper in a compromising position with Peter was being caught with Jason Abercrombie in the Abercrombie's Newport boathouse showing him "mine" in exchange for a look at "his." We were five at the time, and I handled it well. I giggled.

I didn't know what in the hell to do now. Giggling sure wouldn't do it. Nor would jumping up and straightening an imaginary frock like a mortified maiden. I couldn't begin to think of the ramifications of Cooper's having caught us this way.

Bewildered, I looked at Peter, and in that instant several things struck me. The first was that, even sitting, he was taller than I; my eyes just reached his nose. The second was that, somewhere in the mindless course of his kiss, my hands had slipped around him; my fingers were clutching him dangerously low on his hard, bare hips. The third was that that kiss had stirred up a storm in my belly that was in no way diminished by Cooper's arrival.

Given my choice, I'd have sent Cooper away and gone back into Peter's arms.

Of course, I could think that precisely because Cooper *was* there. He was my safety net. If he hadn't appeared, I'd be terrified by the train of my thoughts. As it was, all I had to worry about was Cooper's respect for me, Cooper's respect for Peter, Cooper's willingness to work with Peter after what he'd just seen—just seen? *Continued* to see.

With slow, measured movements, I withdrew my hands from Peter's skin, but my eyes didn't leave his. Silently they told him of my inner fear and begged him to say something, do something to salvage the situation.

For a minute there, I could have sworn Peter was as bewildered as I was. It was very subtle, but I'd spent so much time looking into his eyes that I could recognize something different when I saw it. I knew that he was thinking about the very same things I was.

To my relief, he took in an uneven breath, straightened his shoulders and cleared his throat, but it was to me he spoke, and in a quiet, intimate tone that suggested a new bond between us. "I could use some of that breakfast you mentioned before—eggs, bacon and whatever muffins smell so good. Why don't you go on downstairs? I want to talk with Cooper for a minute, then I'll shower and be down."

His voice wasn't so low that Cooper couldn't hear what he said, and since there was no immediate objection coming from the door, I guessed that Cooper was in favor of the talk. I swallowed, took a breath of my own and slipped from the bed. Though Cooper moved aside to let me pass, I stopped when I reached him and looked up into his face. I wanted to apologize, or explain, but to do either would be an insult to Peter.

So, mustering a shred of humor, I said, "Watch what you say to him. He's got nothing on. A man can get very defensive when he's naked." Without allowing him time for a rejoinder, I left the room and went directly downstairs.

Several minutes later, I was working off my worry beating eggs when I heard the shower go on upstairs. Within a handful of seconds, Cooper entered the kitchen.

Determined to be nonchalant, I said, "Will you have breakfast? I made fresh muffins."

"It's a little late for breakfast."

The stove clock read noon. "Brunch, then." I frowned. "You're early. You weren't due until one."

"I was sitting home, wondering what he was doing to earn the hefty fee you're paying him." He paused and added dryly, "Interesting what I found."

I would have felt awful had not I caught sight of the faint twitch at the corner of his mouth. "You think this is funny," I accused.

Cooper gave a tiny move of his head that I knew for a shrug. "What I think," he specified, "is that I'll never forget the look on your face when you turned around and saw me there."

I was embarrassed. "You should have called from downstairs."

"I did."

"Oh." Again I caught that twitch, and while I didn't begrudge Cooper a moment of lightness what with all else he was going through, I wished it weren't at my expense. "What did he say to you?"

"That his intentions are honorable."

I snorted. "Sounds like he thinks you're my father."

"Not exactly. He asked if I minded the competition."

"What did you say?"

"I said that I wasn't competition for him, but that if he ever did the slightest thing to hurt you, I'd tear him apart."

It was the kind of Cooper statement, offered without the slightest show of emotion, that made me love the man. Unable to resist, I threw my arms around his neck and gave him a tight hug. I stepped back before he could protest. He wasn't one for grand demonstrations of affection. I never liked to push the issue.

"I'm glad you're here," I said, then quietly went back to making breakfast.

"Are you sure you want me to stay?"

The question was loaded. I looked him in the eye. "Yes. I want you to stay."

"You wouldn't rather be alone with him?"

I'd come to my senses. The passion attack was over. I could think clearly again. "No. Stay, Cooper." I looked down at the bacon I was trying to separate. "I don't want to become involved with Peter, but it's like there's a force that pulls us together. At the height of the pull, I'm someone else. All the rest of the time, I'm me. It's…disturbing."

Cooper was silent for a minute. "Then take it slow."

"Fine for you to say. Ever tried to stop a wave from breaking?" I eyed him beseechfully. "How do I do it, Cooper? How do I stop it?"

"Do you really want to?"

"Yes."

"Why?"

"Because it's pointless. It has nowhere to go. I don't have room for a man like that in my life."

"Come on, Jill."

"I don't!"

"You have room. You could make room."

He was serious. I couldn't help but be reminded of the comment he'd made the afternoon before about my buying a condo in the city with the money I was willing to spend on legal fees. "It's time," he'd said, and he was serious then, too. He'd never said anything like that to me before. I wondered whether the change had something to do with the smuggling business, and, if so, what.

"If I didn't know better," I said, "I'd think that you were encouraging me."

"I think you should follow your instincts."

"But what about Adam?"

"What about him?"

"I loved him."

"I know you did. But he's dead. You won't be breaking any rules by enjoying Peter."

"You *are* encouraging me."

He repeated that small semi-shrug. "You could do with a good tumble."

"Cooper—"

"I'll stay for breakfast, Jill. And I'll stick around after that if you want me to. But I can't stay forever. If it isn't Peter, it'll be another guy someday. You weren't meant to be a widow forever. You're a beautiful person. You deserve more than that."

As I studied Cooper in the aftermath of his words, I wondered—and not for the first time—why he and I had never become more deeply involved. I supposed that Adam would always come between us, but there was more to it than that. Something was missing. The spark wasn't there. Thank heavens it was mutual, or our friendship would never have worked. I cherished that friendship.

"Just stick around," I whispered through a tight throat and went at the bacon again. Beside me, Cooper put a fresh pot of coffee on to brew. We worked in a companionable silence for a time until Peter joined us. Then preparation for Cooper's case began in earnest.

The rest of the weekend was dominated by that case. I wasn't sure whether Peter was compensating for having been caught fooling around, or whether he was that dedicated to the law. I didn't think it was that he'd lost interest in me, because though he didn't try to kiss me again, the awareness remained. It was there each time his eyes lit on mine, whether he was reviewing facts with Cooper in my kitchen, or talking with the townsfolk in their homes, in the back room of the grocery store or in Sam's Saloon.

Still, he didn't try to kiss me again.

Saturday night he stayed downstairs reading long after I'd gone up to bed. Sunday morning he slept late again, but when I knocked on his door at the appointed hour of eleven, he awakened quickly. Not long after that he came downstairs for breakfast newly showered and looking ruggedly handsome in his limb-loving jeans and sweatshirt. I was surprised that he hadn't brought down his bag. I had expected him to leave that day to drive back to New York, but it seemed that he planned to spend the entire first half of the week with us.

I wasn't sure whether I was pleased or not.

"It makes sense to do all the groundwork now," he explained. "The more I know at this point, the more effectively I can decide what has to be done to put together a good case."

The problem was that we weren't coming up with anything new. Granted, the townspeople were nearly as close-mouthed as I'd feared, still they talked. We spent time with nearly two dozen different people, and neither Peter's gentle questioning nor my supporting presence succeeded in prying out information that would be a help to Cooper. We learned that he was well liked and respected, which I, for one, already knew. But no one could prove a plausible motive for diamond smuggling—for either Cooper or any of his crew. With the exception of Benjie, we spoke with each member of that crew, and though they were nearly as wary as their neighbors, we couldn't find anything in what they told us to merit a second look.

By the end of Monday, we'd scoured most of the town. Sitting down with Cooper and me over dinner that night, Peter talked frankly about his plans.

"Barring a major attempt on our part to pin the blame on someone else, our best hope does lie with establishing reasonable doubt. We have plenty of character witnesses, including your police chief. I'll go over my notes and decide which of the people I've met will be the strongest witnesses. I'm driving down to Portland tomorrow morning to meet with Hummel. Since he's the U.S. Attorney who'll prosecute the case, he has certain information I want—at least, he should have it. His is the burden of proof. One of the things he'll try to suggest—" Peter eyed Cooper "—is that you've been involved in things like this before. That means he'll be back-checking your bank records to try to find evidence of past large, unexplained deposits."

"There are none," Cooper said. He swiveled Peter's ever-present pad his way, took up a pencil and wrote down the names of the three banks at which he had accounts, plus the rough profit he made each week. "Deposits are always in this amount. Interest speaks for itself."

Peter nodded. "Okay. When Hummel sees this, he'll go looking farther. He'll put an investigator on the computer looking for other accounts. Are there any?"

"No."

"What about investments—stocks, bonds, real estate deals. Anything I should know about?"

"No."

"No plane reservations for a trip to South America?"

Cooper's look told him what he thought of that idea.

"So," Peter concluded, "his case will consist solely of the discovery of those diamonds in your cabin in a laundry bag with your name stenciled on it. We've definitely got a set-up here."

"By whom?" I asked. I'd wondered about that a lot. "Who would have put the diamonds there? Is there a ring of gem thieves that the authorities have been watching?

Who were the diamonds originally stolen from? And who tipped off the Customs people to check out Cooper's boat?"

Peter gave me one of those looks that was at the same time professional yet oddly intimate. "Those are just a few of the questions I intend to put to Hummel tomorrow."

So Tuesday morning he drove to Portland. I offered to go with him, but when he told me it wasn't necessary, I didn't push. Clearly he felt there were some things he could do better without me, which was just fine by me. I was actually relieved. I needed a break from those devil eyes of his. And I needed to work.

I spent the day at it, and a productive one it was. The tall vase that I threw had a particularly interesting twist to its lines; the pieces I glazed and fired were similarly inspired. Moreover there was a normalcy to working in my attic studio. It was reassuringly familiar and right in ways that Peter wasn't. I was pleased to be alone with my work and my thoughts.

Not that my heart didn't do its little catch thing when the time approached for Peter's return, or that the little catch thing didn't magnify into a wallop when I heard him come in. But that was all physical, I told myself, and physical I could overcome.

It helped that we spent the evening with Cooper, though I doubt Cooper saw things that way. He was having a difficult time with Benjie, who had returned from New York and didn't want any part of Peter, or me, or Cooper, for that matter. He said hello, then goodbye and headed for the back door. He wanted to be in Bangor visiting with his latest girl.

Cooper had other ideas for him. "It can wait," he said finally. "I want you to have dinner with us."

Peter and I were in the living room, Cooper and Benjie

in the kitchen. The house was small enough so that we could hear every word.

"Come on, Coop," Benjie complained. His voice was that of a man, though his whine was nowhere near. "She's waited six days. If I ask her to wait any more, she's goin' to bolt."

"You should've thought of that when you stayed longer in New York. I want you here, Benj. You can do what you want tomorrow, but I want you here tonight."

"I don't have anythin' to say to that guy."

"Then you can sit and listen to us talk."

"Give me two hours. Two hours, and I'll be back."

"You're staying here."

"One hour."

"You can see her tomorrow."

"You can't do this to me, Cooper. I'm old enough—"

"Damned right, you're old enough, and that means you have certain responsibilities…"

His voice grew more distant, until we could no longer hear the words. I assumed he and Benjie had moved into the back hall, and I felt immeasurably relieved.

"Nothing like being forced into eavesdropping," I whispered to Peter, who looked as though he knew what I meant.

"Do they always fight?"

"Usually. I don't understand Benjie. Cooper's been so good to him over the years without asking a thing in return. You'd think Benjie would *want* to do something. You'd think he'd be concerned about what's going on. But he couldn't care less."

Peter's voice stayed as low as mine. "Maybe he doesn't know what's at stake."

"He knows. He was here with us right after the arraignment. He knows Cooper could end up in jail."

"Does he think Cooper's guilty?"

"He says Cooper was framed, but the way he says it is incredible. Pure fact. He knows the answer—a frame—that's all there is to it. And when he's done saying that, it's like he has nothing more to say. The discussion's over. He washes his hands of the whole thing." I gave a low grunt. "Much as I love Cooper, Benjie isn't one of my favorite people."

"I get the impression you're not alone," Peter said. "To a man, the people we've spoken with have had good things to say about Cooper, but what about Benjie? No one ever grouped them together. No one ever volunteered information about Benjie. When you stop to think of it, they were very happy to skip over him as though he didn't exist."

"That was generous of them," I decided. "Benjie's been in and out of trouble for years. More than one of those people have been at the butt of his pranks. Forget pranks—he's been known to shoplift. Can you believe that? In a town this size, where everyone knows everyone else, he shoplifts."

"Maybe that's why he does it, because he knows his victims. He knows they like Cooper. He counts on Cooper getting him off the hook."

"Which is exactly what Cooper does. The two of them disagree on most everything, but Cooper's nearly always the one to give in."

"I'm surprised they work together."

"Cooper insists on it."

"I'd think Benjie would object."

"Are you kidding? He may be just this side of juvenile delinquency, but he's not dumb. He knows a good thing when he sees it."

"Does he work?"

"In his fashion. I'd say he's with the boat on maybe seven out of ten trips, and even then I doubt he works as hard as the rest of the crew. What other job could he have where he's paid well and can do most anything without risk of being fired?"

"Cooper has his hands full."

"I'll say. Benjie is gorgeous, and he knows it. He can also be a charmer when he sets his mind to it. It's a dangerous combination." As always when I thought about Benjie, my heart went out to Cooper. I was angry on his behalf, angry at Benjie.

Being able to sound off like this was a luxury. "He has a mean side, Benjie does." I sent Peter a reproachful look. "He's the type to feed firecrackers to a duck. He's the type to take joy in eating bacon from a pet pig. If he were a little older, a little smarter, a little more traveled, I'd be looking closely at *his* bank account. He'd be just the type to stash diamonds in his brother's cabin and then keep his mouth shut when the trouble started. In any case, you can bet he's not sorry the *Free Reign* is impounded. That means Cooper can't make him work."

"If he doesn't work, he doesn't make money. So how does he support trips to New York and cute little numbers from Bangor—or shouldn't I ask?"

"You shouldn't ask."

Peter looked mildly dismayed. "Cooper seems like such a down-to-earth, straight-thinking sort. Doesn't he know that he's not doing the kid any favors by covering for him that way?"

"I'm not sure whether he does or doesn't. You have to understand Cooper. When he feels strongly about something—one way or another—he feels *strongly* about it. He doesn't do things in half measures. His loyalty to me is a prime example. So's his indulgence of Benjie. The kid is his little brother. He adores him. He can be firm, but only to a point. When push comes to shove, he gives in."

"It didn't sound like Cooper was giving in just now."

"Just wait. He'll be back without Benjie."

Sure enough, several minutes later, Cooper returned alone. "He's gone to Bangor," he said tightly. He ran a hand through his hair, and for a minute I thought he was going to say more on the subject of Benjie. But he simply dropped his hand, turned toward the door and said, "Let's go."

We drove several towns over to a restaurant that was owned and run by friends of mine, a pair of displaced Baltimorians who offered the closest thing to nouvelle cuisine to be found in these parts. Cooper hated the menu, I could tell. He was a meat-and-potatoes man, and though I was usually partial to similar simplicity, I found the variety of offerings welcome.

So did Peter, which surprised me. I would have guessed he had nouvelle cuisine coming out of his ears, but he claimed that the regional specialties made this menu different. We had fun running through the choices, had fun teasing Cooper when he couldn't make up his mind.

The food was wonderful, as I'd known it would be, which was why I'd chosen this particular restaurant. I wanted to impress Peter. I wanted him to know that we Mainers had our own pockets of sophistication—though Cooper, bless him, seemed bent on denying it. He had dry comments about the table setting, the food when it finally arrived, even the other diners, and though I doubt he intended it that way, he was really quite funny.

I felt surprisingly good, and the two glasses of wine I'd had—a Puligny-Montrachet that Peter ordered—had little to do with it. I was pleased to be out with these two men—Peter, who excited me, and Cooper, who made the excitement safe.

For the first time in months I'd dressed up, which wasn't saying much by city standards, but it was a switch for me. It was also something that the Friday before I wouldn't have thought I'd enjoy doing, but enjoy it I did. On a whim, I'd worn a wool suit that I'd bought in Phillie the year before. Though it wasn't much more than a slim, knee-length wool skirt, a silk blouse and a hip-length blazer, more businesslike than dressy, with the double strand of pearls that my parents had quite hopefully given me when I'd turned eighteen, I felt feminine.

No doubt some of that feeling came from my legs being exposed. I didn't miss the way Peter stared at them when he first saw me, then kept stealing little looks from time to time. Nor did I miss the way he looked at my hair, which I'd washed and blown into a gentle pageboy that pooled on my shoulders. He'd never seen it down like that. Either he had a thing for long hair or for blond hair, because he seemed intrigued. And that made me feel good.

In fact, I was feeling *so* good that it was a lucky thing Cooper came back to the house with us, or I'm not sure what I'd have done. But he came inside and sat down with Peter to ask where the case went from there.

For the next hour or so, Peter told of all he hadn't learned from Hummel, then launched into a discussion of petitions, motions and writs. I tried to follow what he was saying, but I kept getting distracted by one thing or another. First it was his mouth, lean and hard and masculine as he talked. Then it was the contrast between his crisp white shirt and his rich brown hair, then the fine hairs on the back of his wrist, just barely visible beyond the sleeves of his dark blue blazer, then the way his gray slacks flexed with his thigh as he threw one knee across the other. Then it was back to his mouth, which held me for a fancifully long stretch.

Then my eyes grew heavy, and the next thing I knew,

Cooper was shaking me awake. "Better me than him," he said with a pointed glance at Peter. I had the distinct impression they'd discussed who would do the shaking, even had a laugh or two over it. Though I wasn't wild at the thought of that, I had to be pleased that, despite their differences, they were getting along. Then again, those differences weren't as great as I'd originally thought. Peter was not to the manor born, as I'd been.

Not that I cared. In fact, at that moment I didn't care about much of anything but going to bed. It had been a long time since I'd had wine, *plus* an after-dinner drink. I was feeling it.

Not so Peter. I didn't know how long he stayed in the living room talking with Cooper, but when I awoke the next morning—granted it was nine and absurdly late for me— he'd already put the coffee on to drip and was in the process of making something that smelled incredibly tempting. Using Bisquik, some apples and the confectioner's sugar he'd found on the shelf he'd created the lightest apple pancakes I'd ever tasted. He said he'd added a secret ingredient, but when I figured out that there were already five ingredients that I could count, I didn't bother to ask him what it was. I wouldn't make a recipe that had six ingredients. Better to let Peter make them for me again.

Better to let Peter make them for me again.

As soon as I thought it, then did a double take on it, I rejected the idea as unwise. Still, after we'd spent the morning talking with the harbormaster, who was also the town manager and the resident historian, after Peter had stowed his bag in the Saab for the return trip to New York and turned to me, I couldn't resist asking, "When will we see you again?"

"Is that the royal 'we'?" he teased.

I shrugged inside my coat, feeling shy in a way I hadn't felt before.

His eyes held mine. Like a beacon in the fog, their luminescence spread through every bone in my body, making my awareness of him crystal clear.

"You are like a royal," he said, and his voice was no longer teasing, but low and a little rough. "You're different from the people here. You may not want to believe it, but you are. And they know it. I've seen it in the way they approach you. They give you the kind of deference saved for someone of special stature. It even happened at the restaurant last night. You're a princess. The Madigan heiress."

"But they don't know about my background. I don't talk about where I come from."

"That's part of the mystique." His eyes didn't leave mine as he mulled over the word. "It is a mystique. On the surface, you're what you chose to be, a woman who has given up the city in favor of the simple life of an artist on the coast. But you're more complex than that, and the things that you are, the things you were born to be, refuse to be totally buried. They come out in your manner, in your approach to problem solving, in your tastes—" He paused and said even more softly, "But that didn't answer your question, did it?"

I was a little stunned that he'd given such thought to my character. It was even more flattering than the attention he'd paid my legs the night before. "No," I murmured.

"That's because I don't know the answer. There's a lot of work to be done from my office. Most of it's legal work, technical stuff, but there's research, too. I'll call Cooper when I have questions for him. And you."

Did that mean he'd call Cooper when he had questions for me? Or call *me* when he had questions for me? Or call me sometime, questions or no? He was telling me *nothing*, which made me wonder all the more. But I didn't want to sound unduly interested, so I didn't press. And then the opportunity was gone when Peter took me by the arm and walked me back to my door.

I looked up at him. The wind was playing havoc with his hair, styling it just the way I liked it. "Will you be driving all the way through?"

"I'm not sure." He seemed distracted. "I'll play it by ear. See how I feel."

"You ought to stop for coffee, at least. It's a long way."

He said nothing to that. When we reached the front door, he guided me over the threshold, then turned to face me. I looked up at him and swallowed hard. He seemed so serious.

And so dear—that thought caused my heart-catch this time. Contrary to what I'd expected, contrary to what one part of me wanted, I *liked* Peter Hathaway.

"Thanks for everything, Jill," he said in a low, deep, slow voice.

His sincerity embarrassed me. "I promised a hotel. It was a little unconventional, I suppose, and you had to make your own breakfast this morning, but it was shelter against the wind."

"That it was," he murmured, and in the pause that followed I could have sworn I saw a wistful look. "I'm going to miss you."

My heart caught several more times in quick succession, then sped on. Frightened to think of where that would—or wouldn't—lead, I fought it with a grand show of bravado. "You are not," I scoffed. "You're going back to the city, to your busy practice and your associates and your exciting friends and the Beautiful People who throw interesting parties several days a week. You're going back to that two-bedroom condo on Central Park South, which will probably look like heaven compared to what you've seen in this town."

"Not heaven. Just New York."

Wistful—sad—I couldn't quite figure it out and then understand it. Big name, big city, big bucks couldn't really be sorry to be leaving, could he?

"Come here," he growled. Taking me by the elbows, he drew me to him, and, in the same fluid motion, lowered his head and commandeered my mouth. His lips were like a fire out of the cool ocean air. His kiss was a scorcher.

It was what I'd wanted, what I'd feared. It set the fires inside me burning with an intensity not to be believed. It was, I supposed, the culmination of several days of exchanged looks, remembered heat and good, old-fashioned, lusty imagination—and I had to confess that I was as guilty as he was. But that didn't excuse it by a long shot.

Was it right? It sure felt it, but that was probably what Eve had thought when she neatly cupped that apple in her hand and took a big bite. The difference between Eve and me was that I couldn't just stand there and chew, debating the pros and cons. I was weak-kneed, for one thing, and had to slide my arms around Peter's waist for support. For another thing, the hunger in his kiss was stirring my blood and making me dizzy, meaning I couldn't think straight.

It seemed to be a recurrent malady when I was around Peter, but it was at its worst when he kissed me. His mouth was wet and hot, eating at mine as though he hadn't had a meal in days, which indeed he hadn't, if the time were counted from our last kiss. He was making up for the lapse, using not only his lips, but his teeth and tongue to stoke the fires that crackled within me.

And it wasn't only his kiss that was doing me in. It was

his body. The way he'd drawn me to him had brought us together in a way we hadn't been before. Our coats were open; our bodies touched, more than touched, pressed, strained. His arms were around me inside my coat. One splayed hand was exploring my upper back, the other was open on the seat of my jeans, holding me close. I could feel the hard muscles of his chest, the hard muscles of his arms, the hard muscles of his thighs. City man though he was, he was ruggedly male. That maleness made me buzz.

I'd never been as turned on by a man's body before. Through a haze of light-headedness, I was aware of the length of his legs, which gave him the height to make me feel delicate, and the breadth of his chest, which made me feel feminine. I was aware of the leanness of his waist beneath my hands, then the ropey muscles of his back when I slid them higher. I was aware of the angle of his chin and the firmness of his lips and the fact I was tipping up my head to better grasp his kiss.

Along with all of these things, I was aware of a growing need, a rising expectancy in my body that cried for assuagement. Peter was giving me a taste of heaven, but a taste was no longer enough. So I went looking for more. For the first time, I took part in the kiss. I nipped at his mouth as he'd done to mine, stroked his tongue, sucked his lips. I discovered that being an active player in the lovemaking was heady, but it didn't give me the relief I sought. When the tingling in my breasts became uncomfortable, I rubbed against him to ease the ache, and when he backed me to the doorjamb and leaned into me, I made room for his leg between mine. There was an ache there, too. He ministered to it with the insistent pressure of his thigh, while he brought his hands forward and covered my breasts.

I cried aloud at the explosion of sensation and was

panting when his mouth left mine. His own breathing was rough against my cheek as he held me still for a long, painful moment. The last thing I felt before he levered himself away was the lustiness of his desire.

He stood before me with his hands by his sides, his weight on one hip and his head bowed. It was a minute before I returned to earth enough to realize how far gone I'd been. Looking up at that bowed head, knowing that if he'd backed me into the living room and lowered me to the sofa, I'd probably have been the one to reach for his belt, I didn't know what to say.

After all I'd said about loving Adam and not wanting to be involved with another man, I'd put on quite a show. He'd have been right to call me a fraud.

He wasn't calling me anything, though, but continued to silently stand there with his head hung low, while the pace of his breathing gradually slowed. Only then did he lift his gaze to mine.

"I have to leave," he said. The lingering thread of hoarseness in his voice was the only remnant of passion. Though his eyes were as compelling as ever, the sexual drive that had darkened their spokes was gone. "See ya."

With neither a smile nor a touch nor a single other word, he left me at the door, walked straight to his car, climbed in, backed around and drove off.

I watched in disbelief, waiting for him to step on the brake, roll down his window and call out something sweet like, "I'll phone you tonight," or, "Take care of yourself until I get back," or, "Wow, what a kiss!" But he didn't stop. The Saab continued on down my drive, rounded a curve and disappeared. By that time, I'd run to the side of the house and had my eyes glued to that curve. I held my breath and waited. I blinked. My mouth dropped open.

"See ya?" I murmured dazedly, then, "See ya!" After

a second, I put my hands on my hips and cried, "*See ya!* Is that all you have to say after what just happened? You kiss me to oblivion, put your hands all over me, and all you have to say is, *See ya?*" I whirled around and stormed back to the house. "You are a first class *jerk*, Peter Hathaway. No wonder you've never been married. No woman will *have* you. Women don't want a man who takes what he can get and then pulls on his boots and says—" I dropped my voice to imitate Peter's "—See ya." My voice shot up again. "Goodbye and good *riddance*," I yelled to the wind. Stalking inside, I gave the old oak door a mighty shove.

"Who does he think he is?" I muttered. I paced in a small circle, gesturing with my hand as I ranted, "Who does he think *I* am? A princess—hah! The Madigan heiress—*hah!* Does he think I'm made of stone? Does he think I turn myself on and off like a faucet? Doesn't he know I'm human? Doesn't he know what he's done to me?" Feeling suddenly deflated, I stopped pacing and stood in the middle of the floor. I saw nothing but shades of bleakness. In a weak voice I said, "Doesn't he know what I've done to myself?"

My legs wobbled. I sank to the floor, pulling my knees to my chest and cinching them in with my arms. Then I buried my face and cried.

CHAPTER SIX

I RECOVERED, OF course. It wasn't often that I resorted to tears, but when I did, they were marvelously cathartic. By the time I wiped my eyes and rose from the floor, I'd decided that the life I'd shaped for myself over the years was too strong to be shadowed for long by something as ephemeral as desire, particularly when other shadows loomed darker.

With Peter's departure, the pall of Cooper's dilemma settled over me again. On the one hand, I felt better having hired Peter; for whatever else I might begrudge the man, his competence had never been an issue. Knowing that he was back in New York working on Cooper's behalf was a comfort. On the other hand, I was frustrated. I wanted to do more. I wanted to take an active part in Cooper's defense. I wanted to find out who had set him up.

The problem was how to do it. I thought about it a lot over the next few days, and when I wasn't thinking about it, I was swept up in my work. Between the two, my mind was constantly busy. I didn't leave myself time to think about Peter Hathaway or his kiss or his "See ya."

The potting went well. By the first of the week, I had completed three new pieces that I felt Moni would love. As always before a show, I'd been worried. But with those pieces done, my worries eased. The ball was rolling. I felt reasonably confident that I'd be able to produce more than enough to make the show different.

In keeping with my determination to stay on Cooper's case, I spent Tuesday morning with Benjie Drake. He was the one member of the crew whom Peter hadn't had much of a crack at, and though I knew Benjie hadn't had anything to do with the smuggling itself, I wasn't putting it past him to have seen or heard something that he took upon himself to judge insignificant.

He wasn't thrilled that I'd stopped by. "Cooper's not here," he said. He spared me only a cursory glance as I walked into the kitchen, where he was in the process of fixing some sort of drink that looked suspiciously like a hangover remedy, which made sense, seeing as he looked suspiciously hung over.

"That's okay. I thought you and I could talk."

"About what?"

"Cooper. The boat. The crew."

He was silent for a good, long time, during which he stood at the counter with his back to me and one hand on his hip, and forced down the concoction he'd made. Studying him from the rear, I had to admit that he was well built. Only an inch or two shy of Cooper's height, he had the same wedge-shaped body, the same hard lines. I could see why girls panted after him, though, personally, I preferred more maturity in a frame. Cooper's body had that maturity, a fullness that spoke of time and life and love. Peter's had it even more, along with a sexiness the other two lacked. But then, like beauty, sexiness was in the eye of the beholder.

I was a beholder when it came to Peter.

Miffed at the thought, I settled into a chair at the table, scowled at Benjie's back and waited. My scowl faded. Eventually, he turned.

He looked like hell. Forget the wrinkled jeans and shirt that he'd clearly slept in. Forget the stubble on his face and

the redness in his eyes. His expression was a world-weary
one, far too old for his years.

"What about them?" he asked in a disgruntled tone.

"He's in trouble, Benjie." We both knew I was talking
of Cooper. "He's in trouble, and if we don't come up with
something, he could go to prison."

"He won't. That New York dude'll keep him out."

"Peter isn't a miracle worker. The fact is that those stolen
diamonds were found in Cooper's possession." I wanted to
impress that on him; I wasn't sure if he understood its
significance. "That's like getting caught with your hand in
the till. It's hard to say you're innocent when they catch you
that way." I paused. Either Benjie was unaffected by what I
was saying, or his mind was on hold. His face looked blank.

"Maybe I should come back another time." I started
to get up.

"Don't. Say what you have to."

What he was thinking, I knew, was *Get it over with,
then get out and leave me alone.* What *I* was thinking was
that Benjie didn't deserve Cooper, but then, it wasn't the
first time I'd thought it. On the one hand, I wanted to like
Benjie. I wanted to be compassionate. The kid had lost his
parents in a tragic way, and even before that his life had
been hard. It was sad that he acted out, sad that he thought
getting drunk was macho, sad that he wasn't in therapy.

But damn it, it was sad only to a point. Past that point,
it was hard finding compassion for a boy—man—who
seemed without a drop of it for anyone else, least of all
his own brother.

I contemplated leaving, simply to be free of Benjie, who
set me on edge each time I was with him. Then I thought
of Cooper's predicament and settled back in the chair.

"I was saying," I repeated, quite willing to drill it into

Benjie's head, "that the diamonds were found in Cooper's cabin. Someone obviously put them there."

"You already know what I think," Benjie said and turned around to drag an opened bag of potato chips from the shelf.

"He was framed. But by whom? And why? You work on the boat, Benjie. Do you think it was one of the others?"

"How should I know?" he mumbled through a mouthful of chips.

"You should know because you work with them."

"So does Cooper. Does he know?"

"He says he'll vouch for each of them."

Benjie's mouth twisted dryly. "Smart Cooper," he muttered under his breath.

"What's that supposed to mean?"

He shrugged. "That he knows. If he says they're innocent, they're innocent."

I decided to overlook his sarcasm. "Maybe not. Maybe there are some things he doesn't see. Maybe there are some things you can see that Cooper, being captain of the boat, can't see."

"I doubt it." He shoved more chips into his mouth.

"Think, Benjie. Think."

"You think I haven't?" He chewed fast, then swallowed. I could see that he was angry, but if his anger produced even the slightest clue, it was worth it. "What do you want me to do—pull something out of thin air just to give you someone to blame? You love Cooper. In your eyes, he's perfect. You'd probably be happy to pin this on *anyone* else just to clear him."

"I want the guilty party found. That's all."

"And then what? You'll drum it into Cooper's head that you've saved his life, so he'll be forever beholden to you? He won't marry you, y'know. He won't ever marry you."

I was taken aback by the venom in his tone. It sounded as though he hated me, but I couldn't imagine why. Okay, so we'd never been the best of friends, and that had created some tension because Cooper and I *were* the best of friends. But Benjie and I had never come to blows. I closely guarded the feelings I had about him, so that no one but Swansy— and now Peter—knew them. I'd never shared them with Cooper. I would never bad-mouth Benjie to him.

Rather than take the defensive and argue that Benjie's reasoning was all wrong, I said, "Of course, Cooper won't marry me—any more than I'd marry him."

"Bullshit. You'd marry him if he asked, but he won't ask."

"You sound like you two have discussed it."

"We don't have to. I have eyes. I see what Cooper's feeling and what he isn't. I'm not *that* dense, Jill."

"I never thought you were dense. All I thought was that maybe something happened on the boat, something that seemed perfectly normal at the time but that in hindsight could be looked at a different way." I held up a hand. I didn't want to fight, not with Benjie, who was just then more boy than man. "Okay. For the sake of discussion, we'll assume that the crew of the *Free Reign* is innocent. We know that the diamonds had to have been stowed in Cooper's cabin while the boat was docked at Grand Bank, since that was the only stop she made. Who could have done it?"

He looked at me as though I were the dense one. "Any one of a hundred people who were walkin' around the docks."

"Did you notice anyone paying an unusual amount of attention to the *Free Reign*?"

"Sure. There was a waitress at a lunch place right there. We went out the first night. She couldn't take her eyes off the boat after that. Couldn't get enough of catching looks at me. I know, 'cause I watched her, too." He cupped his hands in front of his chest and grinned. "Great pair of jugs."

I made a face. "That's disgusting."

He looked at my breasts. "Yours aren't bad, either." The grin vanished when his eyes rose. "But it doesn't mean a thing to Cooper. He wouldn't give a damn what kind of boobs you got. He's not interested."

Unable to help myself, I cried, "Benjie, what's *with* you? Why are you so hung up on my relationship with Cooper? I *know* he's not interested in me, either for marrying or for sex, and I'm not interested in him those ways, either. If you think I'm going to barge in and steal some of his attention away from you, you can relax. I won't do that. I'm no threat to you." It seemed absurd that he'd think I was. If he'd been ten, or twelve or fifteen, I might have bought it. But at twenty?

Tossing the bag of chips to the counter, he tugged open the refrigerator, took out a half-gallon bottle of milk, put it to his mouth and drank. My first thought was that it was going to spill all over him. My second thought, when it didn't, was that he was obviously practiced in drinking that way. My third thought was that it was a pretty unsanitary thing to do. My fourth thought was that it wasn't my job to tell him.

Wearing a ridiculous white mustache over his dark stubble, he looked at me and said, "I never thought you were a threat. More like a pest. You butted in where you didn't belong. Cooper was doin' just fine with McHenry."

"Wrong. McHenry is a local lawyer who does just fine when the charge is disturbing the peace or driving to endanger. Smuggling of stolen goods is a little over his head." I paused. "But I thought you had confidence in Peter. You said before that he'd get him off."

"Sure, he will. So would McHenry if you'd left him alone." None too gently, he returned the milk to the fridge. "Cooper isn't as helpless as you think. And he isn't alone. He has people b'side you to take care of him."

"I'm glad to hear it," I said and pushed myself to my feet. Benjie wasn't going to tell me anything new, and I'd had enough of him for one day. "Thanks for the warning, Benj." I headed for the door. "I'll make sure that I don't set myself up for a fall where Cooper's concerned."

I was halfway out the door when Benjie's voice followed. "You don't have to be sarcastic—"

Gently but firmly, I closed the door.

That run-in with Benjie—and it could only be called that—bothered me. I didn't mention it to Swansy at first, because I thought maybe I was making something out of nothing. Benjie had always been contrary. He wasn't really behaving out of character—except for those references to Cooper and me. He'd never made them before. I wondered why he did now.

Obviously it had to do with the case, but I wasn't sure which part. Was it the case itself, or Peter's involvement in it, or something as simple as my presence in his kitchen when he wanted to be alone? Fragments of his thoughts kept echoing in my mind, unsettling me enough so that by the time Friday rolled around, I was ready to talk.

"It's infuriating," I told Swansy soon after I arrived. "Cooper shouldn't be going through this, and given the fact that he is, Benjie shouldn't be adding to his grief. What's the matter with that boy?"

"He's a victim of circumstance."

"I know that, and I try to be gentle, but it's hard. He doesn't like me."

"You're smarter 'n he is, so you make him nervous."

I shook my head. "He thinks I'm going to come between Cooper and him. I told him I'd never do that."

Swansy was silent. She gave me that gentle smile of hers that urged me on. I fell easy prey to it.

"He thinks I have designs on Cooper. Serious designs—like marriage. Isn't that a hoot? Cooper and me and marriage? Forget the me part. Cooper and marriage? Somehow I don't associate the two."

She remained silent.

"Why is that?" I asked. "There've never been starbursts between Cooper and me, but why not with someone else? He's a special guy. He doesn't say much. He takes a little getting to know, but once you do he has so much to offer."

"He doesn't think so."

"That's crazy."

"Sometimes people have reasons for bein' crazy."

"What are Cooper's?"

She was quiet for such a long time that I was about to speak myself, when she said, "He had a sweetheart once. Maybe he still loves her."

My eyes went wide. I sat forward. "Who?" But Swansy wasn't about to tell, and I knew it. She wasn't a gossip. She dropped hints of secrets here and there only when she felt there was a need for it. In this case, the need had to do with my understanding Cooper better. The identity of the woman wasn't important, simply that there'd been one once upon a time.

"Cooper and a sweetheart," I murmured. "Interesting." Many times I'd pictured Cooper's women, the ones he went to for sex. I'd never pictured a sweetheart, though, one he went to for love. "Does Benjie know about her?" It would explain his utter conviction that Cooper would never marry me.

"It was a long time ago."

"Where is she now?" I asked. Swansy didn't answer. "Did she marry someone else?" Still no answer. "She must have. Otherwise she'd have been with Cooper."

"If she loved him."

Oh dear. Cooper had loved her, but she hadn't loved him back. The hurt I felt for him quickly turned to anger. "She was a fool, then, a fool. Men like Cooper don't come along every day."

"T'hear you talk, you'd think you were in love with him yourself, girl."

"I do love him, but not in that way. I respect him. I admire him. It's not that he has great ambitions, or that he's some kind of superstar, but in his everyday existence, he's an eminently capable man."

Swansy gave a slow, thoughtful nod but didn't say a word.

"Adam wasn't." I remembered our lives together. "Poor Adam. He was a dreamer far more than a doer. We were both so excited about leaving home. I'd had it with my family, and he'd had it with his."

"Real different, your families."

"But just as stressful. In my case it was social pressure as in materialism, jealousy and spite. In his case, it was an obsession with upward mobility. His family was where mine was two generations ago. They kept pushing Adam, pushing him to do better in school, to earn more money each summer, to befriend this executive's son or that politician's daughter. When he told them he was going to be a fisherman, they went nuts."

Swansy sat very still.

I hung my head. "Maybe they were right." Dark thoughts filled my mind. "Adam wasn't an athlete. He wasn't physically coordinated. Aside from his height and weight, he was the most improbable of fishermen. Without

Cooper, he'd never have made it as long as he did." The darkness deepened. My voice came from a tortured spot deep inside. "I kept telling him he could do it, that he could do anything he wanted. I thought I was doing the right thing." The memory tormented me. "If I hadn't pushed, he'd have given up. And if he'd done that, he'd be alive today."

"Stop that, girl! It's not your fault he's dead. He went on the boat of his own free will, and an accident happened. They do sometimes, y'know."

"But fishing?" My eyes flew to her face. "He shouldn't have been fishing in the first place. It was a misplaced dream, a romantic notion that just didn't fit him. He hated fishing. In the end, he really hated it."

"So why didn't he stop?"

"Because I kept encouraging him to go on."

"And he wasn't man enough to stand up to you?"

The suggestion hit me like a slap in the face. I opened my mouth to deny it, then closed it again and swallowed hard.

Swansy started rocking. The gently creaking rhythm of the runners on the floor soothed my ruffled thoughts.

I took a deep, uneven breath. "I loved him."

Swansy patted my knee. "Yes, you did, girl. You loved him a whole lot. He was lucky. Had more love in three years than some men have in a lifetime."

That thought stuck with me for a long time after I left her house. Cooper was certainly one of those men who'd missed out, but as the weekend came and went, I found myself wondering where Peter stood on that score.

Then I wondered why I cared. He hadn't called—at least, he hadn't called me. He'd called Cooper several times to ask questions and update him on what was going on, but as far as I knew, he hadn't bothered to ask how I was.

It was infuriating.

I vented that fury on my work, which meant that the pieces I produced as the days passed were darker and more dramatic than the rest of the collection. That didn't worry me. They were still good. Actually they were better than good, I decided. The more I looked at them the better they seemed. And I spent hours doing that. They intrigued me.

Without doubt, they were more sensual than anything I'd done before. Sensual, sexual, erotic. Absurd as it seemed to refer to pottery in those terms, they were the ones that consistently came to mind. The joining of a handle to a pitcher, the curve of the neck of a decanter, the undulation of the sides of a decorative bowl—I stared long and hard. And much of the time I wondered whether I was seeing something in them that no one else would see.

It wasn't only in my work that I was seeing things sensual, sexual and erotic. My nights were filled with them. I'd never had an X-rated dream in my life, yet suddenly they were coming in a steady procession. At least once, sometimes twice a night I awoke flushed and damp, with a tingling in my breasts and belly and a throbbing between my legs.

Once, the experience would have been embarrassing. Over and over, it was mortifying. I could only thank my lucky stars that there was no one in my bed to witness the folly.

Then again, I supposed that the folly wouldn't be at all, if there was someone in my bed.

I was hungry, and *he*'d done it. *His* face was the one atop the body that loomed over mine each night. *His* mouth was the one that muffled my fevered cries. *His* hands were the ones that brought me to sanity's edge.

Still he didn't call.

So I called my mother. It was on a Wednesday night, three weeks to the day since Peter had gone.

"Hi, Mom," I breezed, as though my call were a regular thing. "How's everything?"

"Jillian? Jillian? Is that you calling me, Jillian?"

There had never been, nor would there ever be anything wrong with my mother's hearing. Nor was there anything wrong with mine. I could clearly hear the facetious tongue in her cheek. I let out a breath. "Yes, Mom. It's me."

"What's wrong?"

"Nothing's wrong."

"Are you well?"

"Very well."

"Are you sure?"

"Yes."

"Then you must be calling about Peter."

My mother had always been unusually perceptive. Growing up with her, I'd appreciated it at times—when I first got my period and was too embarrassed to tell her, for example, or several years later, when I refused to visit family friends whose oldest son had all but raped me the last time we'd visited.

Her perceptiveness had a down side, though. She could see through me easily, so early on, I'd stopped trying to hide my feelings.

But that wasn't to say that I never tried again.

"No, Mom, I'm not calling about Peter. There's nothing much to say about him."

"Are you pleased with his work?"

"He seems to be on top of things," I told her with what I thought was just the right amount of indifference. "The trial is set to start in three months. He has a lot of work to do between now and then."

"If his reputation stands, he'll do it."

"I hope so." In truth, I had no doubt about it, but feigning doubt helped my cause. "I worry a little that Cooper may be a small fish in a big pond. We may be in trouble if Peter has something else going on."

"Of course he has other things going on. No lawyer can support himself on one case."

"I know, but what if a *spectacular* case came along. It would overshadow everything else."

"Do you have reason to think that's happened?"

I hesitated. "No."

"But you're wondering if I've heard anything. No, Jillian, to my knowledge he hasn't fallen across anything *spectacular* since he agreed to represent your friend."

That meant he had no spectacular reason for not having called me. I sighed. "That's a relief. I was worried."

"Frankly," my mother said—unnecessarily, because she was always frank—"I'm surprised you to have to ask me. That's the kind of question you have every right to ask him yourself, since you're paying him so much money. You should have asked it at the time you retained him."

"It didn't seem necessary then. He spent five full days here. He wouldn't have been able to do that if he'd had anything of a spectacular nature going on back home. I was just wondering if anything's come up since, and the reason I haven't asked is that Cooper is the one who talks with him most."

"Cooper?"

"Yes, Mom. Cooper. You know, my friend Cooper, who is accused of—"

"But why is Cooper doing the talking?"

"Because that's the way it should be. Cooper's the defendant."

"I want *you* to talk with Peter. I want *you* to get to know him."

"Why is that, Mom?"

"Oh, *please*, Jillian. Must I spell it out?"

She didn't have to. I knew just what she was going to say, but I wanted to hear her say it anyway. "Yes."

She gave a sigh that seemed to convey the years of frustration I'd single-handedly caused her. "What am I going to do with you, Jillian? There are times when I wonder where your mind is—but I do know where it is. It's up there in that godforsaken old house you have on that godforsaken cliff. I felt a glimmer of hope when you called for the name of a lawyer for your friend. It was clearly the right thing to do. I thought that maybe your mind was beginning to work again. But it isn't. It's atrophying up there. If you can't even see that Peter Hathaway is husband material, you're a lost cause."

"Husband material for whom?" I asked, all innocence.

"*You!* Who else would I be concerned about!"

"But he must have dozens of women in the city," I remarked, then held my breath and prayed that Mom was just riled up enough to lack her usual perception.

My luck held up. She sounded indignant. "If he had dozens of women in the city, I'd never be pushing him on you. No daughter of mine needs used goods, *particularly* in this day and age. There's so much going around! That's *all* we need."

"It only takes one contact with the wrong woman to do the damage."

"The man is very careful, Jillian. I checked that out before I ever called you with his name."

"What do you mean, you checked it out? How can you check out something like that?"

"I know people. I know people who know people, and one of those people knows an old flame of Peter's. It seems he's a one-woman man. He doesn't run with the crowd the way some of them still do, AIDS or no AIDS. He had a long-term relationship with this particular woman, and before that there was a long-term relationship with another woman."

"And before that another one? How about after? What's he been doing with himself since that old flame friend of your friend?"

"He dates casually. Nothing more."

"Does he use condoms?" I asked, thinking how far I'd come from the day I couldn't tell my mother I'd gotten my period.

"Good Lord, Jillian, how would I know something like that?"

"You know everything else."

"Not everything. I don't know for sure why none of those relationships ever ended in marriage." She grew pensive. "I do wonder about that. It's surprising that, successful as he is, he doesn't want a family."

"He's in his prime. He has time."

"Still, it's better to have children when you're younger. Look at your father and me. We were just out of school. Our children are grown now, but we're still young enough to lead active, exciting lives."

I wanted to remind her that they'd led active, exciting lives even when we'd been kids. Money could buy whatever child care was needed. That didn't mean the children always benefitted from the arrangement, but it did permit their parents to lead active, exciting lives.

I fantasized differently about Peter. "Maybe he wants to wait to have children until he's at a stage in his career when he can afford to be an active father. Men are doing that nowadays."

"Do you think he'd make a good father?"

I'd thought about that. "I don't know. Several times when

he was up here, there were kids around. He didn't go ga-ga over them. But he wasn't bothered by them. If anything, he seemed a little shy. I suppose it's understandable. He had an older brother who left home early on, but there were no younger siblings. He's had no experience with kids."

"Does that bother you?"

"Why would it? I'm no more experienced than he is."

"If you were to have children, one of you should know what you're doing."

"We'd learn pretty quick." Only after the words were out did I realize what I'd said. I'd stepped right into it. Once a shrewd defense attorney, my mother hadn't lost her touch. "Hypothetically, of course. Neither of us is planning on having children, least of all together."

"You've discussed it?"

"Of course not!" I couldn't believe how quickly I'd lost my advantage in the discussion. Taking a slow breath, I went on more calmly. "My relationship with Peter is professional. Much as I hate to disappoint you, we didn't fall in love at first sight."

"Maybe you will on second sight, or third."

"Not likely. I'm not interested in falling in love again."

Mom gave one of those wise laughs that I hated. They usually preceded a truism. This time was no exception. "I'm sorry to be the one to tell you this, Jillian, because you don't usually believe what I say, but love happens sometimes whether we want it or not."

"Not to me," I insisted. "I'm very much in control of what is and is not going on in my life."

"Then why did you call, if not to pump me on what I knew about Peter Hathaway's social life?"

"I called," I told her, sounding remarkably mature and unruffled, given that she had me pegged, "to tell you I've decided to go to the show in New York. You're on the mailing list, so you'll be getting a notice with the details, but it's on for the second week in November. The opening is on Sunday afternoon, but there's going to be a pre-opening thing the Friday evening before. You're all invited to that, if you want to come," I knew they wouldn't, "or if you want to stop by during the regular times. I was thinking maybe you'd take the train up and we'd meet for lunch one day."

"Do you have to be at the show the whole time?"

"I should be, since I've decided to go."

"But do you have to?"

"Not necessarily."

"Then why not come home for one of those nights? I'll invite everyone over. We can have a nice family dinner together." She paused, and I could just see one elegant brow arching. "Unless you were planning to be home for Thanksgiving anyway."

I wasn't, and she knew it. I had hoped that one or more members of my family coming into New York, which they did often enough, would eliminate my need to go to Philadelphia. But my shows didn't appeal to the Madigans, and I could see why. If my work was being shown at the Guggenheim, they'd have been there in a minute. The Fletcher-Dunn Gallery was something else. *I* found it exciting, because the patrons of the gallery appreciated the kind of work I was doing, though it wouldn't bother me if I never had a show, and I certainly didn't aspire to the Guggenheim.

One part of me thought it was too bad that my family couldn't recognize my career by putting in an appearance at my show. The other part was just as happy to keep them separate from my work. So if I had to go to Philadelphia, I supposed I could.

"How does Monday night sound?" I asked.

"Off the top of my head, it sounds fine," Mom answered.

"I'll check with everyone here. If there's a problem, I'll let you know."

"If I don't hear from you, then, I'll give you a call when I get to New York. I'll be making reservations at the Park Lane."

"The Park Lane? Why the Park Lane, when your father can get you a suite at the Parker Meridien for next to nothing?"

"The Park Lane is fine for what I want," I told her. I didn't like taking favors from my father's friends, because the favors almost always involved a catch, and I didn't want to owe anyone a thing. Besides, I liked the Park Lane. It was on Central Park South. "Take care, Mom. I'll talk with you soon."

I pressed the button on my phone, then released it and punched out Moni's number in New York. I wanted to tell her that I'd decided to attend the show. I also wanted her to make the hotel reservations for me, and to see that an invitation to the pre-opening reception was sent to Peter.

After all, he was my best friend's lawyer, on retainer to me. And he lived in New York. If nothing else, he could fill me in on the latest developments in Cooper's case.

CHAPTER SEVEN

COOPER'S CASE WAS the last thing on my mind as November progressed and the show drew near. The first thing on my mind was work. I was determined to give Moni everything she'd asked for and more, which meant that I spent most of my waking hours in the studio.

Of course, I still made time for Swansy and Cooper and the others who were so dear to me. Seeing them each day, being part of their lives was as important to me as my work. They needed me, and being needed was a vital part of my makeup. It was one of the main things that had been missing in my old life, where people's needs for each other were selfish, usually material and almost always fickle. Adam had come along with an emotional need that I'd filled to a tee. We'd moved here, and I'd found that in my own small way I could fill the needs of even more people. Even after Adam died, the sense of fulfillment remained.

In fact given that satisfaction, I wasn't quite sure why I was working so hard for this show. I hadn't done it for either of the other two shows I'd had. Shows didn't impress me, certainly not with my own skill as a potter. I potted for the creative outlet it gave me. Yes, I enjoyed seeing my finished product and improving on it next time, but I'd have been just as happy to sell in the small crafts shops that dotted New England as to sell in New York. There were times when I rued the day Moni had seen my work in that Kennebunkport shop.

The thing was, I didn't want my career to run away with itself so that I lost the simple pleasure of potting. So I was very careful, very careful as I spent hours in that attic in preparation for this show, and I would have stopped at the first feeling of drudgery.

It never came. I had all the energy in the world, along with a drive that surprised me. I wanted this show to be the best I'd had so far, and I was willing to invest the time and energy to make it so.

The drive lasted until three days before I was to leave for New York. I'd finished everything I'd be showing. Cooper had helped me crate the pieces. He and Norman Gudeau, the local boy I hired, had loaded the crates on a U-Haul, and Norman had set off for New York.

There wasn't much left for me to do but pack, and there wasn't much of that to do because I'd decided to fly down a day early to shop. I was free to do nothing but think about the trip.

That was when I was forced to admit to the source of my energy. With no other outlet, I thought about Peter, and when I thought about him, I thought about sex. The excitement I'd felt when I'd been working with clay remained with me, only now I knew it to be anticipation. My heart caught more times each day than I cared to count, and the tingles that began with those catches, then spread through my limbs before retracing their routes and gatherings in a low coil of need in the pit of my stomach, could only be called arousal.

I was a fool, I told myself. Peter wasn't interested in me. If he were, he would have called, but he hadn't done that once. He called Cooper regularly, but I hadn't heard his voice since that last, despicable, "See ya." And I had no cause to expect that I'd see him in New York. Just because Moni dropped him an invitation to my show didn't mean he would put in an appearance. I intended to call him while I was there, purely on a professional basis, of course, but a phone call wasn't a face-to-face visit.

And I craved a face-to-face visit as I'd never craved anything before.

I fantasized. I fantasized about what he'd look like wearing city gear, then what he'd look like wearing nothing. I fantasized about lying naked on his bed, watching him approach with that tight-hipped walk of his, only I'd see his hips in the flesh, I'd see his flat belly and his thighs and the dark thatch of hair from which would jut the promise of my relief.

At times the strength of my fantasies appalled me. In an attempt to dispel them, I wandered through the house trying to remember things that Adam and I had done in each of the rooms. But the memories had faded. They were sweet, cherished in corners of my mind and heart like roses that had been pressed in a scrapbook years before. Like those roses, their smell was gone, as was the soft, velvety feel of their petals and the richness of their color. They couldn't begin to compete with the heat and vibrancy of my fantasies.

With orgasmic pacing, those fantasies came and went in waves. When they ebbed, I could function as I'd done for so long before Peter entered my life. When they began their surge, though, I was without the control I'd always prided myself on. Nothing seemed to help, least of all remembering Adam. Something stronger had taken me over. I was in its grip, as surely as Adam had been taken by the sea.

It was worse at night, early in the morning, late in the afternoon. More than one dusk found me walking out on the bluff, then sitting atop a boulder and hugging my legs tightly together. The cool November wind whipped through my hair, slapped my heated cheeks, buffeted my huddled form, but the relief I sought wasn't there. The sea was Adam, yet it wasn't Adam's ghost that swayed with the tide, taunting me by coming and going, coming and going.

You could do with a good tumble, Cooper had said, and he was right. The screaming need in me was a physical one. A man's possession would do the trick. Once. Just once. Then I could get on with my life.

WHEN I HIT New York on Thursday afternoon, it was every bit as bad as I'd always found it. The crowds bothered me. The traffic bothered me. The steady drone of mechanical noise, so different from the steady rhythm of the sea, bothered me.

What bothered me most, of course, was that Peter was out there, thinking about heaven only knew what, but not me. In typically female fashion—though I'd have screeched if someone had used those words to me—I took my frustration out in the stores. The salespeople didn't mind it a bit, but then, who would mind a bonanza in commissions?

I went from one to another of the small boutiques that over the years I'd come to know. By the time I was done with my spree, a bevy of shopping bags hung from my shoulders and elbows, and my wardrobe was richer by two suits, two dresses, a silk slacks-and-blouse outfit, shoes, stocking and handbags to match the finery, a pair of jeans, a hand-knit sweater and some of the sexiest underwear that I'd ever seen, much less bought. My final purchase was a huge canvas pouch to carry all the others home to Maine.

Every step of the way back to the hotel, I called myself ten kinds of fools. But I didn't stop and turn around. Nor did I consider returning what I'd bought.

Thursday evening, wearing one of those new dresses,

I had dinner with Moni, and with Bill Fletcher and Celia Dunn, the owners of the gallery, who assured me, as Norman already had, that my pieces had arrived safely and were in the process of being put on display. I was pleased to hear that, but in a distracted sort of way. My thoughts were elsewhere.

I was back in my room by eleven, feeling the same insidious restlessness that had plagued me at home. Strangely, it was heightened by everything about the city. The life I'd chosen for myself was so different from this, and the crowds, the traffic, the noise made me feel removed from so much of what I'd been.

That was, I supposed, why I felt no guilt at the thought of the purchases I'd made that afternoon. It was also, I supposed, why first thing the next morning I phoned Samantha's hairdresser—Samantha *always* went into Manhattan to have her hair done—and took the space opened up by a ten o'clock cancellation. I didn't want my hair cut, just shaped and styled, and while I was at it, I had a facial, then a manicure and pedicure. One thing seemed to lead to the next. It had been a long time since I'd sat in a chair and let myself be pampered. I wasn't about to say that I'd have the patience to do it more than once in a great while. Still, it was nice. It made me feel feminine, and when I walked out of the place, I felt unusually attractive—all of which coordinated well with the feelings of sensuality that were a stirring brew in my belly.

Friday night's reception was scheduled for six-thirty, to catch all the budding young executives, male and female, before they headed out for the weekend. I was to be there by six, and for that I started dressing at four. I wanted to look just right. After all, if I'd gone to such an effort with clothes and hair and nails, I didn't want to blow the effect by putting myself together wrong.

I did just fine with my bath, which was lightly laced with jasmine-scented bath oils, courtesy of the Park Lane. I did just fine with a heavily laced silky white teddy, with a garter belt and sheer navy stockings. But when I began on my makeup, I ran into trouble, and it had nothing to do with a lack of practice.

My hands shook. They were obviously echoing the tremors that rippled continuously through my insides, but that knowledge didn't help when it came to drawing the finest of navy lines under and over my lashes. The process took forever and involved several wipe offs and redos, which involved my lavender eye shadow as well. Then I had to repair the damage I did when I accidentally brushed mascara across the bridge of my nose. By the time I'd finished with faint strokes of blusher and focused on my lips, I settled for a simple peachy gloss, rather than something darker and more dramatic but harder to apply.

To this day, I'm not sure whether it would have been better or worse if I'd known Peter was coming. Not knowing for sure, I was frightened he wouldn't come. If I'd known he *was* coming, I'd have been all the more frightened by the possibilities. I needed him. My body needed his. The mere thought of it sent my temperature up a degree or two, and I wasn't thinking about much else so I was in a constant state of warmth.

In heat, so to speak.

When a last-minute case of the jitters struck, it was all I could do not to tear off silk, lace and makeup, throw on my jeans and take off for a hike through the park. But a woman didn't do that in New York. And I knew it wouldn't solve my problem. I'd tried fresh air and hiking back home, and it had done little to curb the desire that had taken root and was flourishing, like an exotic mushroom, in the dark, moist, feminine recesses of my body.

Gathering what composure I could, I finished dressing. My hair took little more than the flick of a brush to restore it to the condition in which Samantha's hairdresser had left it. The only jewelry I wore was a pair of large white enamel discs that were simple enough to complement rather than compete with my suit, the new one I'd bought for the occasion. It was of navy silk, with a petal skirt that hit the knee, a white blouse whose gently ruffled collar dipped low, and a jacket that was nipped in at the waist before flaring down six inches into the semblance of a bustle. With those sheer navy stockings, navy shoes and bag, I felt quite chic.

But shaky, damn it, shaky.

By the time I reached the gallery, I was thanking my lucky stars I'd been born a Madigan. If I looked cool and calm and together, it was only thanks to years of training under the most demanding of masters.

Stand straight, Jillian. Shoulders back. Chin level.

Look at the person you're talking with, Jillian. Let him think he's the most interesting one in the world.

Don't touch your hair. Don't touch your clothes. And whatever you do, Jillian, don't touch your face.

Smile gently, Jillian. We didn't spend thousands on orthodontia work to see you grimace.

Mother would have been proud if she'd been there. *I* was proud. As the invited guests—mostly people from the gallery's A-list, plus those who'd bought my pieces before—began to arrive, I moved around the room with Bill Fletcher, who knew them all. He introduced me to small groups at a time. Smiling my gentlest smile, I nodded my way around the faces, shook hands where hands were offered, answered questions about my work and about living in Maine. My life-style seemed to fascinate New Yorkers and was as good a conversational gambit as any.

When wine was passed, I accepted a glass from Bill and managed to hold it remarkably steady. From time to time I sipped, but I wasn't any more eager to imbibe than I was to sample the hors d'oeuvres that were making the rounds.

The gallery meandered through three rooms, each at slightly different levels. Bill guided me along, passing me at one point to his partner, Celia Dunn, who took up the circulating where he'd left off. Though I would have liked to have stayed in the front room to monitor the new arrivals, that wasn't always possible. I was alert, though. Between gentle smiles and small talk, sometimes under the guise of considering a question that had been posed, I unobtusively scanned the heads in sight. Though my pulse raced in anticipation each time, there were never even any close calls. I knew what Peter looked like. No other man, regardless of how closely his height and coloring resembled Peter's, held himself quite the same way.

He arrived at seven-thirty. Incredibly, I felt his presence before I saw him, though whether it was wishful thinking that made my heart beat faster or extrasensory perception, I'll never know. We were in the innermost of the three rooms at the time. I had just finished telling a middle-aged couple from Westchester what it was like to work overlooking the ocean when I looked toward the door to the second room, and there he was.

His eyes met mine. I will never forget that first moment of visual contact for as long as I live. My heart caught and held. The faces that separated us seemed to fade out, along with the sound and everything else about the room. We were alone with each other, and the fire in his eyes told of his desire.

"…artistry is intricately entwined with the tides, don't you think?" the female half of the couple was asking.

The sound of her voice shattered the walls of our private

tunnel. I tore my eyes from Peter's and returned them to her, sucking in a surreptitious breath to put my lungs back to work. Since I couldn't begin to speak yet, I nodded and prayed she'd continue talking, which she did. That bought me a minute's recovery time.

It took far more than a minute. One didn't drop from heart-stopping heaven back down to earth with a snap of the fingers, or, in this case, a shift of the eyes. Peter's appearance had burned its way into me, raising my pulse, my heat, my awareness of myself as a woman. Since I couldn't make any of that go away now that he was in the room, I could only hope to control it until I was free to give it its head.

"...he worked in stone. Quite interesting work. Have you seen his things?"

"Uh, no. I'm hoping to, though," I said a bit breathlessly and darted a glance at Peter, who was winding his way around clusters of guests, coming closer, ever closer.

Celia, bless her soul, must have sensed my distraction, because she graciously took up the slack. "Mrs. Moncrieff works exclusively in clay. The approach is quite different from what it would be if she were working with stone, as is the practicality of the finished pieces. Her work has a unique feel to it."

"I can see that," the woman said and turned, with her husband and Celia, to the display stand on her right.

Peter approached on her left, but he wasn't any more interested in my pottery than I was. His eyes were riveted to mine. After pausing for a second on the outskirts of our group, he closed the small distance between us, slid an arm around my waist and brought me into a close hug.

Unable to help myself, I gave a tiny moan of relief. I was right back up there in heaven, sent there by the feel of his large, hard body against mine, the pressure of the arm that held me to him, the clean scent of soap and man, and the heat, oh, the heat. It was as sexual as heat got and radiated from him the way I supposed it was radiating from me. But what sent me to an even higher plane was the knowledge that he'd come.

He bent his dark head and pressed a warm kiss on my cheek, then eased me back and said in a low, rough rumble, "Good to see you, Jill."

In the eyes of the world, we were simply old friends, good friends. Though his hand lingered on my waist a bit longer than was necessary, it dropped to his side when Celia returned to us. He stayed close enough, though, so that by dropping my own hand, I could link my fingers with his in the shadow of my skirt.

I introduced him to Celia. She immediately recognized his name and was genuinely delighted that he'd stopped by, but before she could say much, Bill approached with a new group for a new round of introductions. With an effort I maintained my outward composure, smiling sweetly, talking rationally. All the while my stomach fluttered in response to the large man by my side.

Not about to let him run off with a stupid "See ya," I held tightly to his hand, but even in spite of that, he showed no sign of wanting to leave. He stood close, his shoulder backing mine, and he remained very much in the wings as though to profess that this was my night.

I began to wish that it wasn't. What I wanted to do was to go somewhere private with Peter, but the reception was slated to last until nine, and being the guest of honor, I couldn't very well disappear. At one point, under the guise of using the ladies' room, I excused myself and led Peter into Bill's office. The door had barely clicked behind us, blotting out the noise of the gallery, when he pressed me against it and captured my mouth.

There was nothing gentle about his kiss. It contained a fierce hunger that wasn't about to be contained. While his lips ground into mine, twisting and turning them to his will, his tongue ravished the inside of my mouth with deep, rhythmic thrusts.

Neither the kiss, nor its fierce hunger was one-sided. The fever in me had been building, craving just this outlet. Anchoring my hands in his hair to hold him close, I fought for my own satisfaction. My mouth was never still. At times it worked in counterpoint to his, at times in direct opposition, and though there was near violence in what we did, neither of us was close to being sated when a discreet knock came at the door.

"Oh Lord," Peter whispered. Pressing his forehead to mine, he dragged in a harsh breath.

My own breath was coming in short, sharp gasps that had as much to do with my arousal as with my frustration at having been interrupted. I didn't let go of his hair.

The knock came again.

Peter let out another, "Oh Lord." Pressing a light, moist kiss on my lips, he dragged my hands from the back of his head down his shoulders and over his shirt. He flattened them on his middle. "Later," he whispered, and his luminescent green eyes held the fire that promised more, far more of what we'd just shared.

I was thankful to be leaning against the door, because that look did nothing to still my quivering thighs. If anything, the fire inside burned hotter than it had before that kiss. My own look must have told Peter as much, because he swore softly, squeezed his eyes shut and bowed his head. After several seconds of utter silence, he straightened, bodily removed me from the door and opened it.

"Is Jill all right?" Moni asked. "I saw her head this way."

"She's fine. Just needed a break." He turned to me and asked in a low, gritty voice, "All set?"

With a nod I let him return me to the party, but I didn't let him move far from my side. He'd made me a promise behind the closed door of that office, and I intended to make him keep it. That knowledge was the only thing that made the burning inside me bearable.

Nine o'clock was forever in coming. I should have enjoyed those moments of glory, and if the circumstances had been different, I might have. People complimented me on my work, on my suit, on my choice of gallery, on Moni, and while I hadn't become a potter with an ego trip in mind, I wasn't immune to flattery.

Nevertheless, I couldn't appreciate it or anything else in that gallery except the tall, lean, hard-muscled man who stood by my side. So the minutes crept. I couldn't eat; I couldn't drink. I nodded and smiled and carried on chit-chat, but all the while my mind raced ahead to the satisfaction that waited. There were times when my cheeks grew crimson with my thoughts, and times when the cause for my smiles would have shocked those who received them if they'd known the truth. Every so often I was so distracted that I missed a question. Peter helped me out then, providing the answer requested while he warned me awake with a touch to my arm, my waist, my hand. Of course, those touches were counter-productive; they only sent me off again. But the effort was sweet.

He apparently had greater self-control than I did, though I suppose that was imperative. The male of the species had it harder—no pun intended. If he was aroused, it showed.

Conversely, I could be—and was—in a state of sexual readiness with no one the wiser. No one could see that my insides were hot and achy, or that the sensitive flesh at the apex of my thighs was moist and swollen. Peter knew, of course, and that turned me on all the more. The minutes dragged until we could be alone.

Nine o'clock found us talking with a trio of latecomers. I was ready to swear they'd shown up purely for the sake of the wine and hors d'oeuvres; they didn't seem particularly interested in my work. But then, I wasn't particularly interested in my work, either.

Peter looked at his watch.

I smiled at the trio. "Will you excuse us?"

They did, of course. I led Peter through those others of the guests who lingered. When I found Moni, I leaned close and without pretense asked, "When can we leave?"

She shot a glance at Peter, then eyed me smugly. "I'd be in a rush, too, if I had him."

I bit my lip. I didn't want to be rude, but the hunger within me had reached a fever pitch. Having struggled to cope for the better part of the evening, I'd just about run out of smiles.

Mercifully, Moni seemed to realize that. But her smugness gave way to the concern of a friend. "Will you be okay?" she whispered. She didn't look at Peter again, but I knew she was thinking that she'd been the one to urge me to come to New York for the show, and in that sense I was her responsibility.

I didn't want to be anyone's responsibility but Peter's. "I'll be fine," I whispered back. I squeezed her hand and turned to leave, but her hand did a turnaround on mine to stay me.

"Are you sure?"

"Very sure. Very sure, Moni. I'll call you later tomorrow." This time she didn't hold me up. Peter went for my coat, while I said goodbye to Bill and Celia as graciously as I could in as little time as possible.

Moments later, Peter and I were half-walking, half-running toward Park Avenue, where we caught a cab.

"Your place or mine?" he asked in a thick voice.

I leaned toward the cabbie. "The Park Lane, please." As I sat back, Peter's hands framed my face—not so much to hold me still, I felt, but to anchor himself—and his mouth covered mine. A single touch was all it took. Like an explosion waiting to happen, a myriad of sensations rocked my body. I gasped into his mouth, then choked out a tiny cry when he filled mine with his tongue.

Needing an anchor of my own, I pushed my hands inside his coat, inside his suit jacket and, palms flat, over the firmly muscled planes of his pinpoint-cotton-covered chest. I ended up clasping his sides for the support that I needed. The world seemed to be spinning out of control around me.

We kissed with the desperation of lovers who needed to be naked and in bed, not fully dressed in the back seat of a cab. I wanted Peter to touch me, to touch me all over, but not once did his hands fall farther than my neck. It occurred to me that he did it deliberately, knowing that he'd lose control if he allowed himself greater liberty. But that reasoning was small solace for the parts of me that ached.

Freeing one of his shirt buttons from its hole, I slipped my fingers inside and rubbed their backs against the soft hair of his chest. Then I freed a second button and slid my whole hand inside. This time, I moved my palm over his nipple. When I felt its sharp rise, I substituted the pad of my thumb for my palm.

He bit my lower lip sharply, then soothed the bruise by sucking it into his mouth, but if he'd meant the injury as a warning, I ignored it. In fact, the tiny pain heightened my pleasure. I wasn't sure if that made me perverted, and I didn't care. The only thing I cared about was pushing the

pleasure as far as it would go so that I could reach the pot
at the end of the rainbow.

I wasn't going to reach it with a kiss. I knew it, Peter
knew it, and the cabbie knew it.

"Almost there, folks," he called back with a trace of
dry humor.

I gave a soft, choked cry of frustration and sat back
against the seat. Not about to stand for that, Peter drew
me to his side and held me tightly. I could feel the tremors
that shook his large frame, could see the way he shifted
against the bulge in his pants, but the fact that he was as
uncomfortable as I was didn't ease my ache. I tried tipping
my head and opening my mouth on his neck, but the male
tang of his skin and its faint roughness under my tongue
only tightened the knot in my belly. I tried shifting position,
sliding one of my legs between Peter's, but he wouldn't
help me enough to give me the right leverage.

This time he closed his teeth on my ear, but instead of
sucking to soothe, he whispered, "Hold on, babe. We'll
be there soon."

"I'm on fire," I whispered back.

"Me, too. Soon. Soon."

"I can't wait," I cried softly. That was when I felt him
slip a hand between my legs. It climbed the length of my
stockings and spread over the warm, soft skin of my thigh
before fitting itself to the hot delta that craved it.

A tiny animal sound slipped from my throat, followed
by a long, broken breath that grew even more ragged when
he began to stroke me. His fingers were on silk; his thumb
slipped beneath. Then he seemed to lose patience, because
with a single sharp pull he released all four of the small
snaps at my crotch.

His fingers found me, touched me. I heard him moan
against my temple, and in the wake of the moan came

sweet, low, sexy words of praise. I wanted to tell him that I needed more, but I'd momentarily lost the capacity for speech. All I could do was to shift my thighs to offer more of myself to him.

That was when the cab came to a jarring halt at the hotel.

"You owe me four-eighty," the cabbie called.

I nearly screamed in frustration. I would have paid him ten times that amount to keep on driving, but that would have been short-sighted of me. We'd reached a haven. Privacy awaited. While Peter paid the cabbie, I dug my room card from my purse. Peter took it from me as he helped me from the cab, and, hand in hand, we all but ran into the lobby.

The elevator took forever to arrive. Impatiently we waited with our teeth clenched, our hands tightly locked and our heads tipped back to monitor the car's progress. Years before, I'd waited nearly as impatiently for an elevator, only that time my father had been the man with me, and I'd been dancing from foot to foot.

I had no intention of entering the bathroom this time, unless Peter wanted to make love in the tub. I was game for that. I was game for most anything, so desperate was I to feel him inside me.

The elevator arrived. We stepped inside and pressed the proper button, but just as we were turning to each other, two young boys skidded breathlessly into the car. I told myself that that was just fine, that a public elevator was no place for hanky panky, that I'd just stand quietly strangling Peter's fingers with mine until we reached my floor.

But I'd have happily zapped both boys with a real version of the space guns they held, and when I was through doing that, I'd have happily zapped their parents.

The boys raced off at the fourteenth floor and were instantly forgotten. Peter wove a handful of fingers into

my hair, leaving his thumb to caress my mouth. My lips
parted under their gentle pressure, but only to allow that
caress to spread inside. He didn't kiss me, and I didn't
miss it, because his eyes, holding mine in their thrall, were
silently telling me of all the things he intended to do once
we were alone and undressed.

A frisson of excitement shook my limbs, adding to the
quivering inside that I couldn't control. It didn't help that
beneath my very lovely navy silk suit, my very lovely white
teddy was wide open. That was but one of the things Peter
was saying with his electric green eyes.

We nearly missed my floor. The elevator opened,
waited, then began to slide shut before Peter bolted forward
and put a shoulder to the door. He drew me out with his
other hand and didn't let go as we hurried down the hall.

It took him a minute to fit the entry card into the slot.
I could hear the frustration in his impatient growl. The
door finally opened. We went inside. It closed. We were
alone at last.

The silence in the room was broken only by the muted
sounds of the city far below and the beat of our thunderous
hearts. We didn't waste time listening to the message in
the beat. We already knew it. There was no time to lose.

Our coats were no sooner gone when we came together,
Peter pulling me so hard and high against him that my feet
left the floor. Our mouths fused in a wet, tongue-tangling
kiss. I began to push at his suit jacket, then went at it more
efficiently when he returned me to the floor. Breathing
hard, he ignored my jacket and went straight for my blouse.
But his fingers caught on the small pearl buttons, and,
while I tugged at his tie, he rasped, "You do it, Jill. I'll
tear it." He abandoned my blouse and displaced my hands
from his tie, which he proceeded to tear at irreverently.

Hastily I dispensed with my jacket. Taking shallow little

breaths, I kicked my shoes aside, unzipped my skirt and pushed it down my legs, then hopped from one foot to the other until I was free. Heedless of the fine fabric, I tossed it blindly aside. My fingers raced to my blouse, but there I paused, because that was what Peter had done. His tie and shirt were gone, his belt unfastened and his trousers unzipped, but he was staring at me, at that part of me between my waist and my knees that was so erotically displayed.

I didn't give a damn about erotic displays, at least not about mine. I wanted to see Peter. I wanted to touch him, taste him, satisfy the awful craving that was eating me alive. So I covered the small distance between us, opened my mouth on his chest and I slid my hands, palms flat, into his trousers.

He was hot and heavy, fully-aroused and throbbing with desire. My fingers closed around him. I strained upward in an attempt to align our body parts.

Peter wasn't having that just yet. Capturing my mouth in a suctioning swoop, he forced his hands between us, fiddled with the buttons of my blouse for another impatient second, then tugged. The pearls didn't make a sound as they fell to the carpet, not that we'd have heard if they had. We were too busy trying to kiss, trying to breathe, trying to get me out of my blouse and Peter out of his pants.

Buck naked, he was a strong and beautiful animal. I only had a second to register that fact when he slipped one arm around my back and the other under my bottom and lifted me against him. His mouth met mine. I coiled both arms around his neck, overlapping them tightly. My legs wound around his waist.

In a single fluid movement, he turned, lowered me to the turned-back bed and thrust deep into me. The shock of it brought a sharp cry from my throat.

He went very still. "Jill?"

I panted softly and tightened my arms around his neck. "I've hurt you."

"Oh, no." My body had already begun to adjust to his size, and even at that very first moment of possession, my reaction was more one of surprise than pain. As we lay coupled so tightly, I could feel tendrils of pleasure blotting out surprise, and at the tips of those tendrils were tiny pinpoints of heat.

A fine sheen of sweat broke out over my skin. I closed my eyes. The thought that Peter was embedded inside me was nearly as electric as his eyes.

In a gentle move, as though he were gauging my ability to take him, he carefully undulated his hips. But if he'd intended it as an exploratory measure, it was his undoing. "I can't stop," he breathed hoarsely, then more frantically, "I can't stop, Jill." His broad shoulders trembled under the force of restraint as, devoid of gentleness, he reared up over me.

He drew back, then slammed forward. I cried out again, this time at the fire his thrust stoked, and when he drew back again, I matched his motion.

There was no stopping either of us, then. His body grew slick with sweat. His hair fell in swaying spikes on his forehead as he drove into me again and again. I met each thrust head-on, raised my legs on his back to deepen his penetration. I couldn't seem to get enough of him, nor could he of me. Sliding a hand under me, he lifted my bottom and drove even higher. I think he'd have possessed my entire body if he'd been able—not that what he was doing was much different. The point of his possession seemed to control everything else about me, from the way my fingernails raked his damp back, to the way my head thrashed from side to side, to the short, sharp bits of breath I labored to take.

In a soul-shattering moment, I sucked in a lungful of air and arched into a powerful climax. The spasms went on and on. They were enhanced by Peter's explosive movements, then his final grunting plunge. As his big body shook, I felt the surge of liquid heat deep inside.

For what seemed an eternity, he lay over me, but I didn't mind the weight. It was warm, male, delicious, as was the scent that hovered around us. Eyes closed, I savored that, like an after-dinner drink taken on the tails of a fine red wine.

When he started to move, I clenched my legs tight around him. "Don't go," I whispered, suddenly afraid that he'd up and leave. I might have climaxed, but I was far from sated.

Taking me with him, he rolled to his side. I looked up into his face to find his green eyes heavily lidded and warm. "I'm not going anywhere," he said hoarsely. Levering himself up on an elbow, he closed his hand around my leg, which was under him, and gently pulled it forward. "I don't want to crush it." He eased it down next to the other. His expression was almost reverent as he watched his own fingers skim the silk-clad length.

I looked down then to see what he had, but I saw nothing reverent in a pair of legs sheathed in sheer navy, a pure white garter belt and a white teddy whose lacy hem was bunched up under my breasts.

Peter was looking there, too. He ran his fingertips under my breasts. "You are beautiful," he whispered.

"I think wanton is the word," I whispered back. Though there was no one to hear us, it was an intimate moment.

He fanned his hand over my stomach. "Wanton matched the way I felt. I don't know how I made it through your show." He grunted. "I don't know how I made it through the past few weeks."

I sank a hand into his hair and tugged. "You didn't call me."

"You didn't call me."

"You're the man. You're supposed to do it."

"These are the eighties. You're an independent woman."

"Not that independent."

"How was I to know? You women have us so confused sometimes we don't know whether we're coming or going."

His reference to women in the plural was a generic one, which was the way I took it. I wasn't about to consider the other women he'd known personally, not at a moment when he was all mine.

But he felt it important. Sobering, he shaped his hand to my jaw and said, "I may have been pretty wild as a kid, but lately there haven't been a whole lot of different women in my life." His thumb coasted over my skin. "I'm clean. You won't catch anything from me, but I haven't guarded you against pregnancy. You're not using anything, are you?"

I shook my head. "I bought condoms." My cheeks went red. "They're in my purse."

"That's good. I wouldn't want a pregnant purse on my hands." His thumb moved higher to explore my flushed skin. "Are you embarrassed because you left them in your purse, or because you bought them in the first place?"

"Both. I've never done anything like this before."

"What kind of risk did we take?"

"Not a big one. It's the wrong time of the month. Besides, I don't get pregnant easily." His eyes requested an elaboration that I felt it only fair to give. "I didn't use anything for three years, and nothing happened."

"You wanted children then?"

I nodded, but I refused to dwell on what might have

been. I refused to dwell on anything that might take away from the moment and Peter. Knowing the perfect diversion, I dropped my gaze to his toes and slowly drew my eyes north. I'd seen his upper half before, but the lower half was new and exciting. His legs were long, lean and scarred, but beautiful nonetheless and spattered with the same dark hair that painted patterns over his chest. His thighs were tightly muscled. His sex, at rest now, lay in a thick nest of hair.

Suddenly he shifted, rising to his knees.

"Where are you going?" I asked in alarm.

"Nowhere." He took one of my legs, put my foot flat against his belly and ran his hands up the slender length of dark blue silk. When he reached my garter belt, he unfastened its hook, released the stocking from its hold and slowly rolled it down.

I was fascinated. When I'd bought the lingerie, it had been with the wearing in mind. I'd been feeling sexy and wanted to feel even sexier. On some level, I must have wanted Peter to see it and think it as sexy as I did, but through all my fantasies I never pictured him removing it.

Maybe that was why I found it so exciting. Watching him so intent on his task, though his skin barely touched mine, I felt my heart begin to pound.

When he finished with the first stocking and dropped it to the floor, he gently shifted that leg aside and took up the other one. He repeated the unsheathing process, revealing more and more pale skin. Again, when my leg was bare, he dropped the stocking to the floor. This time, keeping my foot flat against his middle, he bent my knee out and ran his hand all along the inside of my leg.

With one leg on the other side of him and my knee as he'd bent it, I was completely exposed to his gaze. I found that, too, exciting. He made me proud of my body, proud to be a woman. When, of their own accord, my breasts began to swell with that pride, Peter looked their way. His gaze rose higher to my face, fell back to my breasts, then lowered to the most private of my feminine parts.

His thumb touched me, then his fingers. He opened me, stroked me, teased my secret flesh until it was hot and moist. By this time I'd turned my head against the intensity of the pleasure. When he suddenly slid his hands under me and up my back, then lifted me to face him, I opened my eyes.

"Hold on," he instructed in a whisper as he draped my arms around his neck.

For a minute we sat there, locked eye to eye. I knew the story my face told. My eyes were bright, my cheeks pink, my lips moist, parted and inviting.

Peter's face held tell-tale signs of its own. His skin was damp, his eyes intense. Small brackets on either side of his nose told of the self-control he was exerting. And his mouth was open to allow the free passage of what was very close to heavy breathing.

Looping my arms loosely around his neck, I held on. I watched him, watched him closely.

Reaching behind me, he unhooked my garter belt. It fell aside to leave me totally bare from the waist down. Peter looked at my stomach, looked at his hands on my stomach, looked at the gentle movement of my flesh when he began to lightly knead it. His fingers slipped lower, seeming irrevocably drawn to the pale nest between my legs. But at the first small gasp I gave when he drew me open, he moved his hands higher again. They didn't stop this time until they cupped my breasts.

With a care that was in sharp contrast to the frenzied way we'd made love earlier, he took hold of the bunched hem of the teddy and drew it over my head. I had to release his neck to free my arms, and before I could grab onto him again, he threaded his fingers through mine and held my hands off to the sides.

For the first time, I felt shy. I wasn't sure whether it was my total nudity, or the shameless way I was sitting, or the intentness with which Peter studied my body, but at that moment I would have given anything for a sheet to draw up.

"Don't look away," Peter whispered just as I realized that I had. "You are—" he paused, as though seeking the words "—the realization of a fantasy. I've been thinking about just this, imagining it since the first time I saw you." Placing my hands at the back of his waist, he drew me onto his lap. As my body came into full contact with his, I forgot my shyness. For one thing, he was magnificently aroused and made no attempt to hide it. For another, the sense of homecoming was stunning.

We fit perfectly. My head found its niche on his shoulder, my breasts nestled gently against his chest, my thighs framed his hips. I felt comfortable and content. I felt protected. I felt whole.

Which wasn't to say that I complained when Peter tipped his head to nibble on my neck. Or that I fretted when he began to play with my breasts. Or that I raised a fuss when the magic of his fingers stirred up new yearnings between my legs.

This time there was tenderness. We explored each other more slowly, savoring all the little things we'd missed in the savagery of our first joining. But where I'd thought nothing could match the explosiveness of that first time, I was wrong. The slow rise, the gentle savoring, the feint and parry, the holding back—all led to a wildness that was every bit as combustive as savagery.

This time when we lay in the aftermath of orgasm, our limp bodies slick with sweat, our hearts pounding against each other, I couldn't deny the fact that Peter did to me what no man had ever done. I'd thought it earlier, now I thought it again. He made me feel whole.

Peter took it one step further. When he'd recovered enough to speak, he raised himself on an elbow above me, pressed a gentle kiss to my lips and said, "I love you."

I hadn't expected that. I didn't want it. The words were too strong, too soon. They suggested and demanded. They evoked thoughts of things I wasn't ready to face.

He must have seen the panic in my eyes, because he ran his tongue over my chin, ending in a feather-light kiss, and said, "I'm not asking you to love me back. Not yet. All I want is time together to see if it's real. There's been something between us from the start. Part of it's physical, and that physical thing builds when we're apart, so we come together and think of nothing but sex."

Cupping my throat, he looked me straight in the eye. "But there's more, Jill. There's a whole lot more. I know you don't want it to be there, but it is—just like when we first met, you didn't want there to be anything physical, but you reached a point where you couldn't deny it. You'll reach that point about the rest. I know you will. But we need time together for that."

I didn't want to think about love. I *couldn't* think about love. Neither, though, could I think about walking away from Peter. I'd come to New York to see him. I wanted to be with him. If he wanted to think about deeper things, that was fine, as long as I could just enjoy him in the here-and-now.

"Time, Jill," he repeated, pinning me with a pale green stare. "Can you give me that?"

"On one condition," I whispered. "You'll have to feed me. I'm starved."

CHAPTER EIGHT

SWANSY WAS IN an uproar when I reached her house early Wednesday morning. She was watching the talk show that she watched every morning at that time, and the topic was rape. "Have you ever heard anythin' so stupid?" she warbled, then snorted. "Men bein' raped by women—it can't happen unless the man wants it, and then it ain't no rape. But those men yammer on, tryin' to drum up sympathy for the pain they've suffered. I don't buy it. Don't buy it for a minute."

I studied the three men alternately captured on the television screen. "They seem sincere enough," I said. "Apparently they buy their story, even if you don't."

"It's hogwash. Men are bigger 'n stronger 'n we are. They have the advantage every time, so we have to be on our toes up here—" she tapped her head "—if we don't want 'em to run roughshod over us."

I looked at Swansy, so petite, yet so strong, and though I wasn't making any judgments about the possibility of a man being raped, I couldn't argue the merit of a woman's being on her toes. I'd gone flat-footed through the past four days, taking everything Peter had given. Now I needed to get back on the ball.

Rebecca nudged her cold nose under my hand. I was stroking her muzzle when Swansy said, "Well?"

"Well, what?" I wasn't really in the frame of mind to discuss men who'd been raped.

She came through for me as she had so many times before. Pressing the remote control, she turned off the TV. "Sit down and tell me, girl. Tell me everything."

I sat. Rebecca put her head on my thigh. "Where should I begin?"

Swansy's smile was sweet and knowing. "How was the flight?"

"Smooth."

"The hotel?"

"Lovely."

"The show?"

"Wonderful."

"Did they love you?"

I shrugged and gave a sheepish smile. Though she couldn't see it, I like to think it came out in my voice. "I guess so. We sold lots."

"And your man?"

"My man?"

She didn't speak, just sat there directing that sweet, expectant smile my way.

"Peter," I said. I dragged in a deep breath, held it for a minute, then let it slip back out through my teeth. "Peter was incredible."

Swansy's smile didn't widen. She wasn't about to let me know whether my comment pleased her or not. For a blind person, she played poker like a pro.

And like a sap, I fell for her bluff and began to talk. But then, that was what I'd come for. Swansy was my sounding board. My thoughts desperately needed an airing.

"He came to the reception on Friday night, and except for a meeting he had with a client on Sunday morning and Monday night when I went home, we were together every minute. He is a…remarkable man."

I wasn't sure how else to describe him. An extraordinary

lover? A great lay? A sexual wizard? I didn't really want to tell Swansy that Peter and I had spent the better part of our time together in bed, because I was afraid she'd get the wrong idea.

Then again, it wasn't the wrong idea. It was exactly what we'd done. But what Peter had taught me about lust would burn Swansy's ears.

Then again, maybe not.

But where a man and a woman were concerned, some things were sacred.

So I focused on what we'd done *out* of bed. "We spent a lot of time at the gallery. I felt I owed it to Moni, and to Bill and Celia. And when Peter had to work, I sat in a corner of his office pretending to be a law student observing. But otherwise we were free. He took me to his favorite French restaurant. We ferried out to the Statue of Liberty. We went to the Museum of Modern Art. We saw a movie at midnight, then ate huge corned beef sandwiches at an all-night deli. And we walked up and down the avenues, just talking."

"Sounds nice," Swansy said.

"It was. I've always hated New York, but I think that's because I've let it use me, rather than the other way around. Peter and I used it for the things it had to offer. But there are times, like when we were talking over coffee, when we could have been anywhere. The city took a back seat then."

Swansy nodded.

I sank deeper into the chair, my thoughts distant as I absently scratched Rebecca's head. "We talked about everything. That surprised me."

"How come?"

"Because we're so different. We come at life from very different angles. I originally came from money. He didn't. He's living with it now. I'm not. We have contrasting views on some things, but still we were able to talk. I can see why he's a success as a lawyer. He's bright and quick and so logical that it's sometimes hard to disagree with him."

"But you did."

"Sure, I did. He liked that. It makes me wonder about the other women he's known. I can't believe he's been attracted to 'yes' ladies all these years."

"He never married any of 'em. Maybe that's why. Maybe what he had with 'em was sex."

That's what he has with me, I almost said, but Peter swore it wasn't so. More than once over the three days we spent together, he told me he loved me, and never did he do it in the throes of passion. He pointed that out quite bluntly. It was early on Tuesday afternoon, when I was getting my things together to check out of the hotel. Peter took me standing up, with my back to the fire escape instructions tacked on the door. We were both fully clothed—and as hot as ever.

"I'll miss you," he murmured when it was over.

"Don't kid me, bud," I teased. "It's my body you'll miss. It's been a slave to yours since Friday night."

He didn't crack a smile. "No. I'll miss you. All of you. That's what I love." He planted a wet kiss on the pulse point on my neck. "If I only loved your body, I'd tell your body I loved it, but do I? Have I ever said those words when we were making love?"

I hadn't thought about it before, but when I did, I had to admit that he hadn't. I shook my head.

"That's because my love for you isn't rooted in my balls. It's here—" he touched his heart "—and here—" he touched his head. "If love is worth beans, it's rational. It involves things like respect and trust. Very rational."

I'd felt threatened by the words when he'd said them, and I still did. Maybe it had something to do with what

Swansy had said about a woman having to use her brains to fight a man's brawn. What was a woman to do when a man used both brains *and* brawn?

"Well," I sighed, returning to Swansy and the present, "whatever it was with his other woman, it isn't now. He's not seeing anyone special."

"'Cept you." Her voice held a very subtle note of inquiry.

I was quiet for a time before acknowledging it. "Except me. He's flying up this weekend."

After a pregnant pause, she said, "You don't sound real happy about that."

"I'm not sure if I am."

With the nudge of her foot, she began to rock back and forth, but she didn't say a word.

So I went ahead and voiced the worries that had been nagging at me since I'd left New York the day before. "I was happy at the time. We'd had such a fun time together, Peter and I, that I didn't want to leave him. When he suggested he come up this weekend, I jumped at the idea." I looked at my hands, straightened my fingers, stacked one set on the other. "Then I headed back here, and the closer I got, the more confused I felt." I looked at Swansy. "I don't know what to make of our relationship. I don't know what I want it to be."

"What does Peter want?"

"Everything."

"Everything?"

"Everything—well, maybe that's not true. Or I don't know if it's true. We haven't talked about the future. I don't know what he wants down the road, but he says he loves me. He says it's the real thing, and that it's going to grow. He says that I'm everything he's dreamed about for years."

Swansy sighed voluminously. "Ah. So pretty. He'd sure make a better scriptwriter than the loony who writes—"

"I'm serious, Swansy!" I cried. "Peter can be straightforward and tough and demanding, but he's a romantic. He says beautiful things to me, and they're all from the heart. How can I deal with that?"

"Do you love him?"

"Of course not. I loved Adam. I won't love another man. And besides, I haven't known Peter long enough. He hasn't known *me* long enough. Two extended weekends—that's all we've had. How can he say he loves me after just that?"

Swansy rocked, and smiled.

"How can he, Swansy? Isn't this whole thing a little fanciful?"

"If it's fanciful, that's because you need it to be. He'd be good for you, Jillie."

"Good? He'd be awful! Look at him. He's a hot-shot lawyer. He buzzes in and out of courtrooms all over the Northeast, and when he's not traveling on business, he's doing bizarre things like exploring uninhabited islands in the South Seas."

"Sounds exciting."

"Maybe to you, but I like my life here. I like the quiet and the routine. I like the sameness of it."

"You feel comfortable here."

"Yes!"

"Secure."

"Yes!"

"You feel completely satisfied, a total woman."

I took a breath and opened my mouth, then shut it without saying a thing. I should have known Swansy would cut right to the heart of the matter.

"What am I going to do?" I wailed softly.

"What do you want to do?"

"Turn back the clock and make things the way they were before."

"Would you feel like a total woman then?"

"I was happy then."

"You didn't know what you were missing."

"I knew what I was missing. I just didn't want it."

But she was shaking her head. "You didn't know. You hadn't met him then. Sorry, girl. Even if you could turn back the clock, you're a different woman now. Nothin's ever goin' to be the same."

I stared at her hard, hoping she could feel it. "What kind of friend are you? I came here for comfort."

Back and forth she rocked. "You came here for me to tell you that what you did with that man in New York was all right, and I'm sayin' it was."

"That's just *it*. It *was* all right in New York. I was a different person there. But now he's coming here, and I'm not sure I'll be able to handle it."

"You will."

"I won't. This is Adam's turf."

"Hogwash!" Swansy muttered, suddenly impatient. She stopped rocking, and without the creak of the runners on the floor, the room seemed starkly quiet, a perfect foil for her high, wavering voice. "It was always more your turf than Adam's. Face it, girl. Right from the start, you were the one who fit in here, not Adam."

"But this was where he lived. This was where *we* lived. This town, that little house on the bluff are all part of my life with Adam."

Swansy sighed. "Know somethin', girl?"

"No. What?"

"If Adam hadn't died, you'd never have stayed together."

"Swansy!"

"It's true. So you can set this place up in your mind as a shrine, but if he was alive, he'd have left."

"But...but he loved me," I argued in a small voice.

"I'm sure he did, but he wasn't as strong as you. He'd've stuck with the fishin' as long as he could, then he'd've made you choose between this place and him. I'm guessin' you'd've chosen this place, so don't talk about it being Adam's turf."

I was feeling a little defeated. "You know what I mean."

"No, I don't. I see that y've lived here alone for double the time you lived here with Adam. I see that y're on the other side of thirty and still sleepin' in an empty bed. And I see that if you keep on the way y're, y'll find yourself an old lady like me with no one to leave her house to when she dies."

I glared at her, then grumbled, "You see an awful lot, for a blind lady."

"When the Good Lord took my sight, He gave me something in its stead."

"Yeah. A sharp tongue."

"Better a sharp tongue than a deaf ear. I ain't got no deaf ear. I hear what you're saying, and what you're not saying, and if you're coming to me for advice, then that's what I'm givin' you."

"I don't like it."

"So what're you going to do?"

"Change the subject."

"Fine," she bit out, then went quiet. After a full minute she resumed her rocking. Her expression, which had been as cross as her voice moments before, slowly gentled to the one I knew and loved.

Nothing had been settled. I felt as confused as I'd been when I arrived. Somewhere deep inside, I knew that Swansy wasn't all wrong, but I couldn't quite separate the right part from the wrong part, and the whole thing was getting me down. I needed a diversion.

"Swansy, about this business with Cooper," I began,

testing the waters to see if she'd go along with the change. I took her silence as a positive sign. "I've been thinking."

"Don't know when you've had time to do that," she murmured to herself—wholly for my benefit. I figured she couldn't quite let me get away scot-free, but it could have been worse.

"I've been thinking," I repeated, gaining courage as I turned my mind in the direction of those thoughts. "Something isn't quite right."

"Course not. Cooper's in trouble."

"I know that, and I know that Peter is doing everything he can possibly do on the legal end. Still, something isn't quite right."

Swansy rocked.

"On this end," I added.

Swansy rocked.

"I've been thinking. Someone has to know something he's not telling us. I can't believe that a total stranger waltzed onto the *Free Reign*, went straight to Cooper's cabin, straight to the laundry bag with his name on it and stashed stolen diamonds there, then waltzed back off the boat without anyone knowing a thing about it. Cooper never leaves the boat unattended. Someone was there the whole time. All along, we've contended that the person on guard was asleep when whoever it was stashed the diamonds. I keep wondering about that."

Swansy continued rocking, encouraging me on with a soft, "Um-hmm."

"The guard is assigned on a rotating basis, so theoretically any one of the crew members could have been on duty when the diamonds were stashed. Peter and I talked with each of them. Except for Benjie."

I watched her closely, but she gave nothing away. So I went a step further. "Those men are all hard-working guys.

When they finally agree to talk, they're blunt, heart-on-their-sleeve fellows. Neither Peter nor I had cause to doubt any of them. But we weren't able to talk with Benjie."

The creak of the rocker came and went, came and went.

"Benjie is the only member of that crew who has the slightest blemish on his record." I threw an arm to the top of my head and looked toward the ceiling. "I mean, I know it's absurd even to be thinking this, because he's only twenty, and he's strictly a two-bit troublemaker, and I can't imagine how he'd possibly have connected with anyone big enough to be involved in smuggling diamonds into the country—" Grabbing a breath, I looked back at Swansy. "But, damn it, Benjie is so *hostile*. I think he knows something."

My words hung in the air for a good long time before breaking apart like so many pieces of dried mud. I waited for Swansy to pick up the gauntlet in Benjie's defense. After all, she'd known him far longer than I. She remembered when he'd been born.

But she didn't pick up the gauntlet. Instead, she said, "Could be."

I grew instantly alert. "Could be?" I repeated expectantly.

She rocked silently.

"Lord, Swansy, don't stop there. You know something, don't you?" When she didn't answer, I said, "This is Cooper's future we're talking about. The trial won't be happening for a good three months, and in the meanwhile he's going through hell. We both know that he's innocent, but if you know something else—"

"I don't *know* something. But there are certain possibilities."

"Like Benjie being involved in the smuggling. Why would he have done it? Who would he have done it for?

And how could he stand around here and keep his mouth shut when his own brother is taking the flak?"

As Swansy rocked, she pursed her lips. I schooled myself to remain silent. After all, if she could pull a Swansy on me, I could pull one right back on her.

It worked. After a time, she said, "Nothin' was ever simple when it came to Benjie. There's a whole lot goin' on in his mind. Maybe he has a right to it. I don't know. An' maybe he has a right to take it out on Cooper. I don't know that, either. But I wouldn't be surprised if he knows more than he's lettin' on."

"I'm going to talk with him," I said and started to rise from the chair.

"Stay put," Swansy ordered. She waited until she heard the rustle of the cushions before sitting forward in her rocker and reaching for my hand. "Think first, Jillie. Don't do anythin' rash. I may be all wrong, and if that's so, you're only gonna stir up hard feelings."

She had a point. But I couldn't sit and do nothing. Besides, I was a fast thinker. "Okay," I said. "I've thought. And what I'm going to do, very calmly, is to talk with Cooper. He's protective of Benjie, so I won't make any accusations, but a few subtle questions might do it. I want to know whether Cooper has any suspicions of his own."

Giving my hand a squeeze, Swansy sat back in her chair and resumed rocking.

No ONE WAS home at Cooper's house. I busied myself visiting people in town until noon, when he returned. He wanted to know first thing about my trip, so I gave him a rundown on the show. Then he asked about the night I'd spent with my family.

"They're the same," I said lightly. "They always will be. Dad and Ian are like two peas in a pod. They see life in terms of dollar signs. Samantha is the social climber. My mother is the political power broker. Dinners at the Madigan house are high-pressure affairs."

Cooper watched me closely with those dark eyes of his. "You seem pretty calm. It didn't throw you so much this time?"

"No. Maybe I'm finally getting stronger."

"Maybe you had other things on your mind."

"Maybe." I wasn't sure how much of that I wanted to broach with Cooper.

I was trying to decide, when he said, "Peter called before I left this morning. He mentioned that he'd spent time with you."

"He did?"

Cooper nodded slowly.

I moved to fill what promised to be an awkward silence. "I watched him work. He has associates running here and there doing research and preparing motions while he focuses on the creative end. It's very impressive. I wish you could have been there."

"No, you don't."

The look on his face told me I wasn't going to get away with much. "You're right. It would have been embarrassing, what with us making love on top of the desk." I took a quick breath, then raced on. "Cooper, we have to talk about Benjie."

Cooper's mouth twitched at the corners. "Did you really do it on a desk?"

I made a face. "Of course not." Then, serious again, I repeated, "*Benjie*, Cooper. Is anything special going on with him?"

"But you did make it together?"

I sighed. "Do I ask what you do with your women?"

"No. But this is different. Peter is the first man I've met in a long time who's strong enough for you."

I looked him straight in those opaque eyes of his. "I want to talk about Benjie."

He eyed me right back. "I don't."

"Why not?"

"Because there's no need. Benjie is my concern. No one else's."

I'd already blown my chances for subtlety, so I went right to the heart of the matter. "I think he's hiding something. I think he knows more about those diamonds then he's letting on."

Cooper's eyes narrowed slightly. "What makes you think that?"

"He's been so surly lately. He resents my presence, and Peter's presence. I think he's afraid we'll uncover something he doesn't want uncovered."

"Like what?"

"Like...*I* don't know. Like maybe he saw someone board the boat and stash the diamonds. Like maybe he knew the person. Like maybe he was doing someone else's bidding and stashed them there himself." I tossed a hand in the air. "It's bizarre to be thinking that a twenty-year-old could have done that, especially when he's your brother, but something's strange about this whole thing, Cooper."

I paused. Cooper's feelings were totally shuttered behind his dark eyes, but the darkness itself made me uneasy. It was thicker than usual.

I sighed. "Do you know anything? Has Benjie said anything to you? I know that you've always tried to protect him, but if he's somehow involved in this and you don't speak up, you'll be the one to take the fall."

Cooper stretched his long legs in front of him, but there

was nothing easygoing in his lines. "I want Benjie left out of this."

"You do know something."

"Benjie is innocent."

"But he's somehow involved. Tell me, Cooper. Please. I don't want you going to prison for something you didn't do."

"You hired Peter so that wouldn't happen."

"But he can only do so much."

Cooper stared off at the wall. His expression was tighter than ever when he looked back at me. "You're spending a lot of money on this, Jill, even though you know I didn't want it. Well, I've agreed to be represented by your man, but that doesn't mean that I've sold him my soul. You're right; he can only do so much. I'm not asking that he prove me innocent, or that he prove anyone else guilty. All I'm asking is that he establish reasonable doubt in the minds of those jurors."

"But if Benjie has information that can prove your innocence...."

"Leave Benjie alone."

"He's an adult. At some point he has to take responsibility for his actions."

"Do you think I don't know that?" Cooper barked.

I backed off a bit, but only to the extent of moderating my voice to a more gentle tone. "Then tell me what you know. Tell *Peter* what you know. If Benjie saw something, he'll be protected. If he was actually involved, he could get immunity by testifying for the state."

"Leave it, Jill." His voice was as darkly ominous and unyielding as his eyes.

I felt pushed to a crossroads, where I had to choose between respecting Cooper's wishes for the sake of our friendship or risking that friendship for the sake of his future. It was a no-win situation.

"I don't like this," I whispered, my voice breaking.

"Don't you dare cry."

"I don't like it at all."

Leaning forward, he reached for my hand. When I offered it, he closed his fingers tightly around it. "Everything's going to be okay, Jill. Trust me. Trust Peter. I'll be fine."

How many times I said those words in the course of the next few days I didn't know, but at some point they ceased referring to Cooper and began referring to me. That point came when I realized I missed Peter.

I didn't know why I missed him. On top of my worry about Cooper, I had plenty to do to catch up on what I'd missed while I'd been gone. But still there were those times—odd times, quiet times—when I felt lonely in ways I hadn't felt since right after Adam had died.

It was bad enough that I still craved him. I'd have thought that after the sexually active four days we'd spent together, my body would be sated. The problem was that sexually active wasn't necessarily sexually exhausted. All I had to do was to recall any one of the things we'd done together and my temperature rose.

Worse, though, the craving wasn't only physical. I kept thinking about the time we'd spent together in New York and how much I'd enjoyed it. I remembered the satisfaction I felt when we talked, even when we disagreed. I remembered the meals we'd eaten together. I remembered showering while he shaved. I remembered the silences we'd shared, when we'd each been lost in our own thoughts with only the link of our arms or our hands to connect us. I remembered the pleasure in that, and I missed it.

I'll be fine, I told myself. It was the novelty of Peter that had gotten to me. I'd calm down. I'd get used to being alone again. I'd fall back into the old groove. That's what I wanted.

Still, I looked forward to his arrival with growing enthusiasm, and by the time Saturday finally arrived, I felt as though I'd been waiting four weeks, rather than four days to see him.

I drove into Bangor to meet his plane, and the feeling was much like the one I'd had the week before, when I'd first caught sight of him at the show. At the moment he passed through the terminal door, I felt everything else in the room fall into a hazy background. This time, there was nothing to shatter the moment. I went toward him, first at a properly sedate walk, then a bit faster, finally at a light run. Peter had set his carryon down by the time I reached him, and when I flew into his arms, he caught me tight, whipped me off my feet and whirled me around.

We kissed long and well.

"Let's get out of here," he growled at last. With his bag over his shoulder and his coat over his arm to hide his arousal from the world, he ushered me to the parking lot.

We talked the entire time during the drive to my house—about his work, about Cooper and Benjie, about little nothings from the weekend before. As soon as Peter stopped for a breath, I picked up, and the instant I stopped, Peter started again. Listening to us, one would have thought that we either had to squeeze a whole lot in a very little time, or that we were totally starved for conversation.

I'm not sure it was conversation that we were starved for. As soon as we parked the car and went inside, Peter dropped his things and picked me up in his arms.

"Where'll it be?" he asked in a hoarse whisper.

But the light in his eyes asked another question, one I'd

been asking myself since I'd returned. It was one thing for Peter and I to make love in the neutral territory of a hotel in New York, another for us to make love in my house. I'd never doubted that we would make love if he came. But where? In my room or his? Which bed would we share during the night—the one he'd slept in before, or the one I'd shared with Adam?

When I'd first returned from New York, I'd have said his room. Just as I'd chosen the Park Lane over his Central Park South apartment. Both involved less of a commitment. But in the course of the past three days, I'd done a turnaround. I couldn't tell Peter I loved him, but I could tell him how much he'd come to mean to me.

"My room," I whispered, and he took me straight there. Laying me down on the bed, he came down on top of me. After kissing me senseless, he rolled away long enough to tug off my jeans and release himself from his pants. Then he slid into me with all the ease and excitement of a cherished lover.

He drove everything else from my mind. Not once did I think of Adam, of the fact that this had been our bed or that I'd sworn I'd never share it with another man. There was a certain rightness in what Peter and I were doing. Between that rightness and the mind-blowing rapture that burst upon and between us, there was no room for doubt.

Nor did I doubt myself when, much later, having properly undressed and made love a second, more leisurely time, we lay quietly in each other's arms. Peter's presence had settled into my bedroom, taking it over, leaving no room for anyone else. I was feeling too content for second thoughts.

I had second thoughts about Cooper, though. I discussed them in greater detail with Peter, and when we stopped in to see Swansy later that afternoon, we raised them with her.

"Cooper wants Benjie left alone," I said, "and he's rigid enough about it that I know something's up. What is it, Swansy? Do you know?"

Swansy shook her head.

Peter tried his hand. "I've spent a lot of time on this case. Things are looking pretty good, since the government can't offer either a motive or a connection between Cooper and any known smugglers—or crooks of any kind, for that matter. Customs officials were tipped off by an anonymous phone call, but they have no idea who made it and who, if not Cooper, it was aimed to catch. So the only evidence against Cooper is the diamonds themselves. With the right approach, I can probably sway the jury. Probably. Not definitely. And if things go against us, Cooper winds up in jail. Anything, Swansy, anything you know would be a help."

"I don't know anythin' about diamond smugglers," Swansy protested, almost as though we'd accused her of being one.

"Then about Cooper and Benjie," I prompted. "Why is Benjie so difficult? And why is Cooper so determined to shield him?"

"B'cause Cooper Drake is a loyal man. You know that, girl."

"I sure do. But blind loyalty's no good."

"Tell that to a man in love."

Peter murmured in my ear, "She has a point. I can personally vouch for that." When I shot him a don't-confuse-the-issues look, he added a quick, "That's why spouses can't be called to testify against each other in court."

I rubbed my head against his cheek. "But Cooper's not in love, and he doesn't have a spouse. He loved a girl a long time ago—"

"Still loves," Swansy corrected. "Name's Cyrill."

"Cyrill? Was she from here?"

"Nope. Worked here, though. She was a waitress at Sam's when it was run by Sam's daddy."

"And Cooper loved her."

"Dearly."

Over my shoulder, Peter seemed deep in thought. So I turned back to Swansy. "Blind loyalty? Between Cooper and Cyrill, or Cooper and Benjie?"

Swansy shrugged.

I had the distinct feeling that there was a message in something she'd said, but I wasn't quite sure what it was. "So Cooper's protecting Benjie the way he would have protected Cyrill if she'd still been around?"

Swansy shrugged.

Peter was more on the ball than I. "Cooper's protecting Cyrill now?"

Swansy began to rock in her chair.

I turned to Peter. "Cooper's never mentioned her. Neither has anyone else in town. I had no idea she existed."

"Like Cooper, the people in this town protect their own."

"But Cyrill isn't one of their own."

"Cooper is. So's Benjie."

"But what does any of this have to do with the charges against Cooper?" I cried, looking up at Peter. He looked down at me. Then we both looked over at the little old lady in the chair. "Swansy?"

She rocked, shook her head, closed her eyes.

"Come on, Swansy," Peter coaxed. "We'll find out anyway. You'll save us time by telling us what you know."

Very softly and in a warble that sounded uncharacteristically vulnerable, she said, "I'm one of the townsfolk, and Cooper's one of mine. Don't make me betray him more 'n I already have."

Her plea hit home. Much as I wanted to help Cooper, I knew that I couldn't ask Swansy another thing. She'd done her share. She'd pointed us in a new direction, and in so doing, she felt she'd betrayed a friend. No, I couldn't ask her for more.

That didn't mean I couldn't ask anyone else. When I looked up at Peter, I saw him thinking the very same thing. I also saw him thinking about the reticence of the townspeople and the risk we took of alienating Cooper.

We had our work cut out for us.

CHAPTER NINE

PETER AND I spent most of Sunday visiting with people we'd discussed the case with the month before. Our excuse was a need to double-check certain statements they'd made, and we threw in mention of Cyrill as casually as possible, but we didn't fool anyone. The standard reaction to the mention of her name was a clamming up. Clearly everyone knew who she was, but no one was talking. That left us to do some detective work on our own.

Her full name was Cyrill Stockland. We got that much after spending Sunday night poring through the cartons of records that sat in the basement of Sam's Saloon. She'd waitressed there for seven months, twenty-two years before. The forwarding address was a diner in a small town in New Hampshire, and though we didn't expect that she'd still be there, we drove over Monday morning just in case.

Peter had already decided to stay with me until Tuesday. I wish I could say that I approached the search for Cyrill with utter gravity, given Cooper's predicament, but the fact was I felt a distinct sense of adventure. Spending time with Peter, traveling through the back roads of New England with him, was a treat.

As far as the New Hampshire diner was concerned, Cyrill Stockland didn't exist. The cook, though, sent us to see the owner of a rooming house where most of the town's transient help stayed at one point or another. The owner remembered Cyrill.

"That one was a beauty," he told us, though only after he'd moved out of earshot of his wife, who, like him, looked to be in her late sixties. "My Mary didn't like her. Stuck up, she said. Had fancy notions, she said." He shrugged his stooped shoulders. "Me, I just thought she was pretty. Had a nice beau, too. Tall fellow. Dark."

I wondered if that was Cooper, but if the man had known more at one time, he'd long since forgotten. He was able, though, to give us the name and address of a country inn in the northwest corner of Massachusetts.

"Used to be run by some friends of mine," he explained. "When she said she wanted to move on, I sent her there." He scratched his sparsely haired head. "Don't know if she ever made it, or if the new owners ever heard of her, but it's worth a try."

We had nothing to lose. Since we'd already driven so far south, it made sense for Peter to rent a car early Tuesday morning and continue on into the city while I drove back home. A country inn sounded like a perfect place to spend Monday night.

The inn in question turned out to be a gem. Owned by two men who were probably gay but definitely friendly and gourmet cooks at that, it was nestled in a wooded glen along the Appalachian Trail. Though neither of the men had heard of Cyrill Stockland, one of them promptly picked up the phone, called the previous owners and, after a phone call back several hours later, presented us with the name of a private club in Westport, Connecticut, where Cyrill had gone to work when she left the inn.

Tucking that information under our belts, we set about enjoying ourselves for the few remaining hours we had together. We ate dinner by candlelight, sat for a time by the fire in the living room, then retired to our room. It was furnished with authentic antiques, but the only one that truly interested us was the bed. This we utilized for far more active endeavors than sleeping, before finally, reluctantly, succumbing to exhaustion.

In the morning Peter headed for New York while I returned to Maine. As far as friends like Swansy and Cooper were concerned, I had simply been off having a good time with Peter—which was the truth, but not the whole truth. I figured the whole truth was better withheld until I really had it.

I celebrated Thanksgiving as I had for the past six years, with a group of twenty-some-odd friends who congregated at Sam's Saloon. We all chipped in with the cooking, my contribution being two large blueberry jello molds. They were surprisingly delicious given that, in addition to water, there were only three ingredients required.

I was home by dusk. Peter was spending the day with the family of a colleague of his and had promised to call. We had arrangements to make for the weekend, when we were planning to resume our search for the mysterious Cyrill, so I didn't want to miss his call.

At least that was the reason I gave myself for waiting eagerly by the phone. After the call came through, though, after we'd talked and arranged and talked some more, then hung up, I acknowledged that the fullness I felt inside had little to do with Cyrill Stockland.

I didn't question myself further when I left the next morning at the crack of dawn to drive south. Peter and I had agreed that I'd fly to New York and spend Friday night with him at his place, then we'd set out together on Saturday to tackle Westport. But I was too impatient to wait until mid-afternoon for a flight, and since Westport was right on the way, I decided to make a stop.

The manager at the country club had a fascinating story to tell. It seemed that Cyrill Stockland had indeed worked for him and had been quite a hit among his other employees. In fact, when she'd become pregnant, two of them had actually come to blows over which of them had fathered the child. Needless to say, she'd been asked to leave the club. The manager thought he remembered something about her continuing on into New York, but under the circumstances, she'd been given severance pay in cash and hurried out the door. He had no forwarding address. He did, though, still have in his employ one of those men who had fought over her. He had since married another woman and had five children, and the manager wasn't sure whether he'd welcome inquiries about Cyrill Stockland. I managed to persuade him to introduce me nonetheless.

The man in question had moved up in the ranks to become the head groundskeeper of the club. Along with his position must have come a certain amount of self-confidence, because he had no problem thinking back to the days when he'd fought another man for the privilege of claiming the paternity of Cyrill Stockland's child.

"Hoot of it is," he told me, a crooked smile dancing on his round face, "we never even made it together. But I was young and full of myself. And I was damned if the other guy was gonna take the credit. Me and him argued about nearly every woman who stepped foot in the club." He winked at me.

The wink left me cold. As far as I was concerned, there was nothing remotely sexually attractive about the man. He was nowhere near as tall, as well-built, as bright or amusing or compelling as Peter. The sooner I finished with him and went on to New York, the better.

"Did you keep in touch with Cyrill after she left?"

"Nah. Like I say, I had no real stake in it. And she wasn't the kind of girl you kept in touch with. She was ambitious.

She was moving on and up, she said, and she had that look about her like she'd really make it one day."

"Do you know where she went?"

"The city."

"New York?"

"That's the one."

"Do you know where in New York?"

He shook his head. "It's a big place. She wanted to get lost while she had the kid, then she figured she'd climb out of her hole and make her fortune."

Cyrill Stockland knew the score. New York was precisely the place to make a fortune, and the place to get lost, which didn't help my search a whole lot. Mildly discouraged, I thanked him for his time. I turned to leave, paused, then turned back. "When did all this happen? If you were to pin down the birth of her child to a particular time, when would it be?"

"I can tell you exactly when it was," the man said without hesitation. "I was here just a year when I got in that fight over her. I know 'cause I nearly blew that first raise I'd been counting on. It was twenty-one years last June when I started here, so she musta had her baby just about twenty years ago."

I hadn't been keeping a particularly close watch on the dates, other than to note that Cyrill hadn't stayed in any one place for long. Now, hearing that she'd given birth to her baby twenty years before, something clicked.

Excited, I thanked the groundskeeper a second time, left and drove into New York. Peter was in conference across town when I arrived at his office; he hadn't expected me until later. I waited patiently at first, then less patiently, until finally he returned.

The look of high pleasure that lit his face when he saw me sitting there was ample compensation for the wait.

Kicking his office door closed, he strode across the oriental carpet, put his hands on either arm of my chair, leaned low and captured my mouth. Without touching any other part of me, he made me feel like a million.

He didn't touch any other part of me because he didn't trust himself that far—but he only told me that later, when we were in his apartment with no need for restraint. And we showed none there. Not only were we celebrating our reunion, but with a few phone calls and a little string-pulling on Peter's part, we'd made a major discovery.

"Who'd have thought it?" Peter murmured against my neck. His hands were under my sweater busily working on the buttons of my blouse. "Who'd have guessed Cyril was Benjie's mom."

I tugged off his tie and dropped it where we stood. "But that's the least of it," I argued as I pulled the tails of his shirt from his trousers. "Cooper's Benjie's dad! Not his half brother. His *dad*!" I slid buttons through holes as quickly as I could. "It was right there on the birth certificate. Clear as day. So why didn't we know? Why didn't anyone say anything?" Pushing the shirt off his shoulders, I had just enough time to press my lips to the hair on his chest when he pulled my sweater over my head.

"Like the people in town?" He tossed the sweater aside and dispensed as quickly with my blouse. "Maybe they didn't know."

"They had to know Cooper's mother wasn't pregnant— help me with this, Peter." I couldn't get his belt undone.

He quickly took care of it. "Not necessarily. If a woman's a little overweight to start with, she could go away for a month and come back with a baby, and the people around her might, just might believe it was hers." He'd released the front closing of my bra as quickly as he had his belt.

Peeling the lacy cups from my breasts, he tossed the bra aside.

We were both taking short, shallow breaths, as though we'd just come in from a sprint. Our hands tangled from time to time. That slowed us down and increased the impatience.

"I think they knew," I decided as I gingerly worked his zipper over his arousal. "I think they all knew, just kept it to themselves." I slipped my hands inside. "Maybe that's why they were so tolerant—ahhhh, Peter..." He'd taken half of my breast into his mouth and was drawing on it so strongly that I felt the pull all the way to my womb. Momentarily abandoning the treasure in his briefs, I dug my fingers onto his hair and held on.

"Peter—ahhhhhh—it always comes down to this." I gasped when he did something powerful to my nipple with his teeth, then felt instantly bereft when he raised his head.

"Shall I stop?"

"Lord, no!" I met his mouth in a hungry kiss and slipped my hands back into his briefs. He was hot and hard. The feel of him against my palms sent tiny currents of excitement through my fingers, up my arms and into the rest of my body. I stroked his distended length, taking pride when he grew even more rigid. It seemed that much more and he'd burst—I was feeling the same way inside.

He swore then and, setting me back, went at the rest of my clothes in earnest. "You distract me so much sometimes," he growled, bending on a knee to tug down my skirt and panty hose together, "that I can't concentrate on what I'm doing."

"You were doin' just fine," I teased in a whisper. "You felt just right to hold."

His pale green eyes, shimmering with darker shards and smoldering now, speared me with a hungry gaze.

Then he lowered his eyes, leaned forward and kissed me where no one but he had ever kissed me before. It was suitable punishment for my teasing, because I nearly lost it there and then, particularly when his kiss grew deeper, his tongue more aggressive.

"Please!" I cried.

He knew what I wanted. With several rough tugs, he freed me of the last of my clothes, then did the same for himself. For an instant when we were both naked, we just stood there looking at each other's bodies. But our inner demands were insistent. I had to touch him, had to feel the heat of his body on mine, in mine, and it was clear from the urgent way he reached for me that he felt the same.

Our bodies came together in a crush, fitting as perfectly as ever. My arms went around his neck, my legs around his hips when he lifted me, and when I felt the full force of him slide inside, I let out a small cry of pleasure.

To this day, I can't begin to describe that feeling of having Peter inside. It was so many things—fullness, heat, excitement, satisfaction, completion, security—that it boggled my mind.

"Ahhh, Peter," I cried, "what you do to me."

"Tell me," he whispered. "What do I do?"

With his large hands spread under my bottom, he moved his pelvis. I felt him withdraw nearly completely, then slowly, tauntingly return. "You make me burn," I managed to gasp against his neck. "Can't you feel it?"

He didn't answer at first, and when he did, his voice was deep and husky. "I feel it, babe. I feel it." Holding our bodies locked tightly, he carefully lowered me to the bed. Still buried deeply inside me, he held himself up on his arms and looked down into my face.

He was beautiful. His eyes, his face, his body—he was a beautiful person. Tears came to my eyes at the thought of how lucky I was to have him. He made my heart swell to twice its normal size.

His lips touched mine with a gentleness that belied the throbbing I felt inside. "It does always come to this," he said hoarsely, "because this is what I need." He raised his head. His eyes met mine. "It's only when we're together like this that I know you love me."

A knot swelled in my throat to rival the swelling of my heart, and I knew he was right. I hadn't put the word to the emotion I felt, and I didn't want to do it now, but there was no doubt it was real. Nothing else could explain the things he made me feel, even the sense of security I'd thought about moments before. I felt secure when we made love because during those times, Peter was unconditionally mine. I didn't have to share him with anyone or anything. I could touch him and kiss him and hug him and love him. I liked it that way.

With a low moan, he squeezed his eyes shut. "What was that? What did you just do?"

I hadn't realized I'd done anything until my muscles relaxed. "This?" I whispered. I clenched them again.

He made a rough sound, swallowed, nodded. His arms began to tremble. But his eyes, heavy-lidded moments before, grew suddenly large and intense. "I belong here, Jill. I belong inside you, not just when we're making love, but during all the other times, too. You have my heart. You'll always have it. I want yours."

"You have it," I whispered, framing his head with my hands.

"Now. But for always? It's no good if it's only when we're in bed."

I wasn't ready to say the words. Nor could I lie and deny them. So I slipped my hands into his hair and brought his head down to my mouth. Silently I told him how I felt.

It wasn't enough.

Peter lowered himself to his elbows. He held enough of his weight so that I wasn't crushed, but our bodies touched at every possible point. Like the soft, swirling hair on his chest, his voice was a sensual abrader. "I'm insecure about some things, Jill, and you're one." His breath was warm above my face, his eyes hot. "I think about you all the time we're apart, and it eats at me that you may not be thinking about me, too. I need to know you are. I need that commitment. I want you to take the sum of everything that's you, turn it over and endorse it to me. For deposit only. No turning back. No withdrawals. Forever."

I heard what he said, and part of me wanted just that. I didn't feel threatened; it wasn't a question of losing myself in Peter, as much as being all the richer for a merger with him. But I needed time. I had to come to terms with certain things, and I wasn't about to do that now, not with the sight and scent and feel of him surrounding me.

"Show me what you want," I whispered, and he did. He loved me with everything that was him, and then some, and it was the most glorious feeling in the world. At times he was gentle, at times fierce, making me feel alternatively like a precious jewel and an enchantress. I couldn't say whether I preferred one feeling to another because they were both part of the whole, and the whole captured my mind to such an extent that analysis was impossible.

By the time we fell back to the sheets with our limbs entwined and our skin dewy, though, I knew that there'd never be another love for me like Peter.

We dozed off, awakening after an hour to make love again. After another nap, we awoke ravenous for food of the material kind, but the shower we took first led to a rebirth of passion. It was nearly midnight when Peter opened his front door to two large, loaded pizzas.

Nothing but crumbs remained—Peter ate his own pie, plus three slices of mine—when we took our large, loaded stomachs into the den, wrapped ourselves in each other and a large afghan that Peter had picked up in the course of his travels, and began to talk.

Peter must have known that I wasn't ready to tackle the issue of love and commitment that night, because he bypassed it to talk about Cooper and Cyrill. "Tell me what you think."

I snuggled deeper within the bands of his arms. "I think that Cooper fell hard. He was eighteen, Cyrill seventeen when she came to town. It sounds like she wasn't the type to fall in love. She had plans. But she must have been taken with Cooper, enough to have an affair with him, and the affair went on long after she left Maine."

"Cooper obviously knew when she became pregnant."

"Or learned soon after. He was close enough when the baby was born to claim him and take him home."

"I wonder what kind of deal he had to make."

I tipped my head on his upper arm so that I could see his face. "What do you mean?"

"If Cyrill intended to make it big in New York, the last thing she needed was a baby. I wonder if he had to convince her to go ahead with the pregnancy."

I sucked in a breath. "You think she might have wanted an abortion?"

"Maybe. She sure didn't want the baby, if she allowed him to be taken from her and raised as someone else's child."

My heart ached for Benjie. "Poor kid. Imagine the rejection he's probably felt over the years."

"If he knows the truth."

"I'm sure he does. It would explain the time Benjie

told me in no uncertain words that Cooper would never marry me."

"All that would explain was Benjie's knowing Cooper's feelings about Cyrill."

"No. It was more. Benjie's vehemence was exactly like that of a kid being loyal to his mother—or wishing that one day his parents would get back together."

"It could have just been Benjie's natural raunchiness," Peter said.

I was wondering the same thing. Then I shook my head. "Cooper wouldn't keep something like that from him." I paused. "Would he?"

"I'm the wrong one to be asking. You've known him far longer than I have."

"But as a man, looking at Cooper, considering your impressions of him, what do you think?"

Peter seemed confused as he looked into my face. "I'd guess no, but that's all it is, a guess." He let out a soft breath. "But whether Benjie knows the truth or not, the facts of his parentage go a long way in explaining the complexity of Cooper's feelings toward him."

I returned my cheek to Peter's chest. "It's so strange— Cooper being Benjie's father. So hard to believe, after all these years." But the more I thought about it, the more I realized that it wasn't so hard to believe after all. "It gives new meaning to lots of things Cooper's said about Benjie." For a minute, I was lost in thought. Then, looking up at Peter, I went straight to the heart of the matter. "Do you think Benjie smuggled those diamonds onto the *Free Reign*?"

"I don't know."

"Do you think Cooper knows?"

Peter arched a brow and shrugged.

I thought of Cooper loving Cyrill and being hurt. I thought of his loving Benjie and being hurt. "Cooper's always been so good. He's always been there for Benjie. But the stakes have never been so high before. It breaks my heart to think of his going to prison for him."

"If he's as innocent as he claims, he's prepared to go to prison for *someone*."

He fell silent, but something in his words caught in my mind. The same something caught in his mind, too, because I felt the slight pickup of his pulse at the same time that his eyes opened wider. "I wonder."

"Is it possible?"

"Anything's possible."

"Probable, then?"

"If he loved deeply, he'd protect one nearly as staunchly as the other."

"But where is she now?"

"Good question."

"How do we go about finding an answer?" I asked, but Peter was already shifting me on the sofa and rising. Wearing nothing but a pair of sleek navy briefs, he padded around the desk, opened a drawer and removed the Manhattan phone book.

"No Cyrill Stockland," he concluded after he'd run through the list. He removed a second phone book from the drawer and checked, then a third. He wound up with five C. Stocklands, none of whom he could call at one in the morning, and by that time, I'd had enough of looking at the bunching muscles of his shoulders as he leaned over the desk. With the afghan draped shawllike around me, I went to his side and spread the shawl to cover him, too.

Turning to me, he said gently, "We'll find her, babe. Trust me. We'll find her."

HE DID, THOUGH it took four more days and a private investigator to do the trick. But the wait produced a bonus. Cyrill Stockland did, indeed, live in New York, but under the name of Cyrill Kane. Though she hadn't quite made the fortune she'd hoped for twenty years before, she was still trying. She ran with a fast and dubious circle of friends, one of whom was reputed to be a jewel thief.

Even more condemning, one of the investigator's sources had heard rumor that Cyrill and the thief had a new angle that involved Cyrill's "kid."

Peter told me all of this on the phone in the middle of the week, and I nearly went out of my mind with frustration keeping it to myself until he arrived late Friday afternoon. But I couldn't tell Swansy, who already felt guilty for having put us onto Cyrill, and we'd agreed to confront Cooper together.

It was a wise agreement. In all the years I'd known Cooper, he'd never turned as dark as he did when Peter told him about what we'd learned.

Cooper kept his voice low, but there was a palpable tension in it. "I said I didn't want an investigator."

It was a revealing first statement. "You knew?" I asked in a dismayed whisper.

He glared at Peter. "Who told you to hire an investigator?"

"As your lawyer, it was my decision to make."

"I didn't want one."

"That's not the issue," I put in. "Did you know?" Still he didn't confirm or deny what we'd learned. "Cooper?"

The force of his gaze was on Peter. He didn't look at me once. "Can you defend me the way we originally planned?"

"Without mentioning any of this?"

"That's right."

"It's crazy, man."

"Can you do it?"

"Sure, I can do it—"

"You can't!" I broke in.

Peter held up a hand to me. To Cooper, he said, "But it doesn't make any sense. It was one thing when we thought that a total stranger had stashed those diamonds on the boat. But if Benjie is in business with Cyrill, you've got a problem that isn't going away so fast. If you're acquitted, he'll keep at it until he's caught. If you're convicted, he's going to have to live with that. Think he can?"

Cooper's eyes were coal black. "Benjie is innocent."

"Perhaps in the most general sense," Peter said, "but if he was the one who put those diamonds on the *Free Reign*, then stood by and watched you go through hell, somewhere along the line he stops being so innocent."

I felt totally stymied. "Does he know that you know the truth?"

Cooper spared me a glance then. Its harshness was moderated only slightly by the feelings he had for me. As though knowing he couldn't—or didn't dare—sustain any semblance of gentleness for long, he looked back at Peter. "I don't want him touched."

Peter tried to reassure him. "Benjie would be all right. I could get him off with a suspended sentence because of his age and the circumstances—"

"I don't want his name brought into this at all."

"He'd end up with nothing more than probation. It might do him good."

"No."

"Cooper—" I began to protest, but he'd apparently had enough. Storming past us, he whipped his coat from a hook by the door and left with the slam of aged oak.

I looked at Peter. Then I grabbed my own coat from the chair on which I'd dropped it moments before. "I'm going after him."

"Maybe you should give him time to think."

"If I do that, he'll convince himself he's doing the right thing."

"He already has."

"Then my job will be harder, but I have to try."

"I'll come," Peter said.

He was reaching for his coat when I put a hand on his arm. "No. It'd be better if I see him alone." The look in Peter's eyes said that he wasn't so sure about that, but I knew what I was doing. "Cooper and I have something special." I moved my hand to his face and brushed my thumb across his lips. "It's not what you and I have, but it's still deep. I want to appeal to it, but if you're there, it'll be harder. Cooper will use you to keep me at arm's length." I paused. "I have to try, Peter."

He didn't move, didn't make any attempt to change my mind. Going up on my toes, I put my mouth where my thumb had been. *I love you,* I thought, and nearly said the words. At the last minute they caught in my throat. I didn't know whether it was the particular circumstance, or whether I just wasn't ready to say them, but by the time I returned my heels to the floor, the moment had passed. I quickly fastened my parka, pulled up my hood and turned toward the front door, only to be stopped by an unexpected sight.

Benjie was standing stiffly in the kitchen doorway.

He had clearly overheard my final conversation with Peter and, just as clearly, had seen me kiss him, but how much he'd heard of what we'd said to Cooper, I didn't know. Nor, at that moment, did I care. Cooper was my main concern. I was very happy to leave Benjie to Peter.

I sent Benjie a look that I hoped was at the same time dignified and imploring, cast a last glance at Peter, then left in search of Cooper.

Dusk was beginning to settle over the coast, bringing

with it an increase in the wind and the cold. When I didn't immediately see Cooper on the pier, I huddled more deeply into my coat and headed down Main Street. At the very end, I worked my way down a twisting path that opened onto a small cluster of rocks. Cooper was squatting on one of the larger rocks, tossing pebbles into the frothing sea.

I continued on down until I stood close behind him. Without turning, he knew I'd come. No doubt he'd been expecting me.

His voice rose above the tumult of the tides. "It won't work, Jill. You can talk until you're blue in the face, but I'm not changing my mind. I don't want Benjie involved, and that's that. The issue is closed."

I opened my mouth to launch into my arguments anyway, then closed it again and rethought what I wanted to say. Cooper glanced at me. Pressing my fists deep into my pockets, I came down on my haunches by his side so I wouldn't have to shout.

"Tell me about her, Cooper. Tell me what she was like."

He shot me another glance, this time in mild surprise. Then he tossed a few more pebbles into the sea, and just when I was beginning to wonder whether he'd answer, he began to speak quietly. "She was beautiful. Tall, blond, curvy in all the right places. The first time I saw her, I felt like I'd been hit. Knocked the air right out of me."

I certainly knew what that was like, but I'd never imagined Cooper being susceptible to lightning like that. "Love at first sight?"

He shrugged. "I was just a kid. The only girls I'd known were the ones around here, and they weren't satisfying me when I needed it." He took a breath. "She was younger than me, but more experienced. One night with her, and I was hooked."

I wanted to ask why he hadn't married her and kept her

here, but I already knew the answer. Cyril wasn't slowing down for anyone. "How long did it go on?"

"We were together the whole time she was here. I followed her a couple of other places. Then she went to New York. She was always straight about that. She told me she'd never marry me. She didn't want the boonies, and she didn't want me, but she had my baby, and I wanted him. He was a little bit of her."

He was a lot of her, I was thinking sadly. "Have you seen her since Benjie was born?"

He shook his head.

"Did you try?"

Again he shook his head. He tossed another pebble into the surf, then said in a voice so small that I nearly missed it, "I was afraid."

"That she'd turn you away?"

After a bit he shrugged. "She knows where I am. She knows I'd take her if she just said the word."

That was what was so hard for me to understand. The Cooper I'd know, respected, loved was an independent and pragmatic man. I had trouble conceiving of his being a slave to a woman, particularly one who wasn't worthy of him. "You'd do that, even after all this time?"

He pushed out his lips, thought a minute, nodded. "I still dream about her."

I could bet she was the one on his mind when he slaked his physical needs on other women. "Do you still love her?"

He took up another pebble, rubbed it against the larger rock for a minute before tossing it away. "Yes, I still love her," he admitted angrily. "And don't ask me to explain it. But there's a certain feeling. It comes every time I think of her. Call it an obsession if you want, I'm sure it's that, but I can't stop it."

He tossed his pebbles with greater passion. I wondered

whether he got relief doing that and contemplated trying it out. I was feeling very frustrated.

"Tell me what it's like, Cooper. Tell me what it's like to love someone so much that you'd sacrifice your entire future for her."

He cast me a sharp sidelong glance. "I don't have to tell you. You're the expert on the subject."

My heart skipped a beat. "What do you mean?"

"You and Adam. You're sacrificing your future for him."

"I am not."

"You are, and he's not even around to see. At least in my case I'll know that Cyrill is free because of what I've done."

"That doesn't make *sense*."

"It does to me, and that's all that counts."

"But she wouldn't do the same for you."

"Neither would Adam for you."

"Obviously not, since he's dead."

"He wouldn't have done it if he'd been alive. And if the tables had been turned, he *sure* wouldn't have done it. If you'd been the one to have an accident and die, he'd have been out of here like a shot, and he'd never have come back."

Swansy had said nearly the same thing not so long before. I hadn't wanted to hear it then, and I didn't want to hear it now. "Why are you saying this, Cooper? You and Adam were so close!"

"Yes, we were." He swiveled on the balls of his feet to face me more fully. "But I wasn't in love with him, so I could see him more clearly than you could. He had a whole lot of strong points, but none of them had to do with this kind of life. And you knew it. You knew it wasn't working, and you might have done something about it, but then he upped and died, so it was too late." He barely paused for a breath. "You've spent the last six years idealizing him,

Jill. You felt guilty about his death, so you made yourself a living memorial to him."

I stood quickly. "That's not true—"

"It is," he argued right back as he, too, straightened. His face was shadowed by the oncoming night, but I could sense the tightness of his expression. "You've refused to think anything negative about him. You've pushed your love to a place where it probably never was, and because of that, you're holding back on Peter, even though he's just right for you. So if you want to talk about sacrificing futures, *you* tell *me*."

"You're wrong."

"I don't think so. I know you, Jill. I can see how you relate to Peter, and you haven't related that way to any other person here, including Adam. You look up to Peter. He excites you. You come alive when you're with him. He challenges you. Maybe he frightens you for the same reasons, because for years now you've been with people who don't challenge you at all, and that's easy. It's comfortable. And it's everything you didn't have when you were growing up, but there has to be a middle of the road somewhere. You can't close yourself off and take the easy way out for the rest of your life."

I put my hands to my ears, shook my head and turned to leave, but Cooper caught my arm. "Think about it, Jill."

"There's nothing to think about. And how did we get off on me, anyway? We're supposed to be talking about you!"

"But you're the issue. Your life is the one that can be changed." He tightened his grip on my arm, dipped his head a bit and spoke more urgently. "Don't you see, Jill? I'm a lost cause. I'm stuck in whatever kind of bind this is, and as long as Cyrill is alive, and as long as Benjie's her son, I'll be the way I am. No other woman I've met gives me the kind of feeling she gave me, so if I settled for another woman, I'd be settling for second best. What kind of woman wants to be second best?"

He had his answer when I remained silent.

"So forget saving me," he said. "I'm too old to change."

"You're not too old. You're too bull-headed."

"And you? Are you too different?"

"Yes!"

"Doesn't look it from where I stand."

"I'm just being careful. I don't want to rush into anything."

"Well, let me tell you, sweetheart, you go on clinging to Adam and see where it gets you. It's gonna get you nowhere. *Nowhere*."

"I don't have to listen to this," I muttered. Wrenching my arm from his grasp, I ran back up the path. It was darker now. I stumbled once or twice and felt Cooper reach for me. Each time, though, I caught my balance and ran ahead. When I reached the street, I walked as quickly as I could toward the north end of town.

"Don't blow it, Jill!" Cooper yelled from somewhere behind me.

"Why not?" I yelled back. "You've done it. Why can't I do it, too?"

"Because," he said, keeping pace with me from one step back, "lonely is a lousy way to live. If another woman had come along to knock me in the gut the way Cyrill did, I'd have grabbed her fast. But no one ever came."

"What does that have to do with me?"

"You've got Peter."

I stopped dead cold and faced him with my hands on my hips. "And you think that what I have with Peter matches what I had with Adam? You've got a hell of a lot of nerve assuming that." Before he could respond, I whirled around and strode quickly down the street again.

Moments later he caught my hand and stopped me again. His voice was deep and oddly gentle as it came through the darkness and the cold. "You mean a lot to me, Jill. We've been friends since you moved here, and I've valued that. There have been times since Adam died when I thought I was crazy not to stir something up with you. Not that you'd have gone for it, but it might have been worth a try if only to keep you here as my friend forever. Only I can't do it. You deserve more—more than I can give you, more than any man around here can give you. I don't much like the idea of your leaving, but you need broader spaces—"

"I'm not going anywhere."

"You will. You love him."

"I'm not *going anywhere.*"

Rather than contradict me again, Cooper wrapped his arms around me and drew me close. I was so surprised by the gesture, coming from him, that I didn't protest. I had the feeling that he was telling me without words how much he meant all he'd said.

We didn't stand there for long—it couldn't have been more than ten seconds—before he held me back and looked down into my face. The faint glow from the Prentiss's front light post gave his eyes a liquid sheen. I knew it had to be the light; Cooper would never cry. He was too strong, too controlled. Still, the thought of it held as much meaning as his hug had.

Together we turned and walked on down the street. We hadn't gone more than five or six paces when first Cooper, and then I, stopped again. Standing a dozen yards ahead, at the point where the pier joined Main Street, stood Peter and Benjie.

Intuitively I knew they'd made a deal.

CHAPTER TEN

I WAS FEELING very much alone. Peter had left me that way in what was probably one of the shrewdest nonlegal moves he'd ever made.

He'd made his share of shrewd legal moves, too, before he returned to New York. It seemed that Benjie had overheard most everything we'd said to Cooper, and though he'd known the truth about Cyrill for years, something in Cooper's manner had touched him. That seemed miraculous to me, seeing as I'd always thought Benjie to be such a dyed-in-the-wool brat, though I supposed he had to inherit a *little* of Cooper's character.

At any rate, Benjie had decided on his own, it turned out, with the barest encouragement from Peter, that Cooper deserved more than he'd gotten. At that point Peter's expertise came into play. He made the appropriate phone calls, met with the appropriate officials and took Benjie into Portland when the wheels of justice shifted into gear. He maneuvered U.S. Attorney Hummel so deftly that Benjie was all but guaranteed a suspended sentence based on his testimony against the others.

That testimony was a sore point, since it meant pointing a finger at Cyrill. Again, Peter came through for us. Through a bit of clever arguing, before Cyrill's name was ever introduced, he managed to extract a promise from Hummel that she would be given leniency if she, in turn, agreed to testify against the mastermind of the plot.

According to Benjie, this man had used them both. We all knew that Cyrill could well blow it all by refusing to cooperate when she was apprehended, but at least the road was paved for her to have an easier time.

Though the charges against Cooper were dropped, he wasn't thrilled with the goings-on. His brain told him that what had happened was for the best. His heart wasn't as cooperative. Instead of simply fretting about himself now, he fretted about Benjie and Cyrill. He wanted to be able to do something, but there was nothing to be done. Though he had his boat back and his ability to work, he felt more upended than before.

So I couldn't go crying on Cooper's shoulder when Peter returned to New York without me. I couldn't cry on Swansy's shoulder, because she'd become less than sympathetic to my plight. Nor could I cry on the shoulders of any of my friends in town; that just wasn't my role in their eyes.

Time and again, I wondered why Peter hadn't confronted me before he'd left. He knew that there would be no legal reason for him to return to the coast before the trial, which would now be at least four or five months off. And it wasn't as if I had another show coming up soon in New York. Nor was it as if we'd had a fight or anything. We were as close as ever. We had moments of explosive passion and moments of quiet camaraderie. He continued to tell me he loved me, and he did it often.

But he didn't ask whether I loved him back. He didn't demand to hear the words. He didn't ask what I was doing with the rest of my life. He didn't even ask what I was doing with the rest of my week.

At least he hadn't left with a dumb, "See ya." And he did call, I have to stay that. He phoned me every evening at seven-thirty or eight, almost as though he was coming home to me after a long day's work. He'd ask how my day had been and what I'd done. I'd ask about his. But we didn't make plans to see each other.

He was calling my bluff. He was sitting back there in New York waiting for me to do something. I can't say that he was waiting smugly, because deep inside, Peter wasn't that kind of person. I had the feeling that he was truly nervous that I'd decide to live out the rest of my life in solitude on the coast of Maine.

Certainly the solitude he'd afforded me gave me time to think, and I did that with the brutal honesty that I'd avoided before. Given Peter's retreat and the fact that if I didn't do something I could well lose him, I knew that I couldn't keep on playing the games I had. Indeed, the time for brutal honesty had come.

I loved Peter. I'd known it for some time, but now I faced it head-on. I thought of how wonderful I felt when we were together. Cooper was right; I did come alive when I was with Peter. He excited me. He made me feel intelligent and attractive, feminine, cherished, protected. He made me feel that I could face the entire world—and then my family—with my chin held high. He even made me feel sexier than Samantha.

Mostly, though, there was that feeling of wholeness, which I'd never known before.

Adam hadn't made me feel whole. I spent a lot of time thinking about that. Adam was handsome and honest and gentle. He had a great voice and stars in his eyes, and I loved him very much at that time in my life. But it was as though he was an adjunct of me. Swansy had laid it out right; I was the stronger of the two of us. I was the one who carried the emotional weight, as well as the material, if the truth were told.

Facing my guilt was something else. I spent hours

shivering on the bluff in the freezing cold, looking out to sea, trying to communicate with Adam. I wanted him to know that whatever I'd done I'd done with the best of intentions. If I'd been blind to his needs or wants in my own drive for independence from my family, I was sorry. The last thing I'd ever wanted was for him to be hurt.

For so many hours I concentrated, looking out to sea that way. And I kept waiting to feel his forgiveness, but it never came. Adam was dead and gone. For the first time I accepted the finality of it. And with that acceptance came the realization that the forgiveness I sought had to come from myself.

In time it did come—largely with the realization that what I felt for Peter didn't detract from the memory of what I'd felt for Adam. I loved both men, Adam, then, Peter now, and I loved them in very different ways. Adam was an important part of my past. Peter was my future.

Increasingly I began to dream about the future. I dreamed about keeping my place on the shore and Peter's place in the city, and maybe even buying a country place in between. I dreamed about taking trips with Peter to the far-off and unusual places he favored. I even let myself go and dreamed about having children. Peter's children. It was a...heart-catching thought.

I think what finally did it, though, was that Monday noontime at Swansy's. I hadn't seen Peter in two weeks, and two long, lonely weeks they'd been. I'd just come off another weekend with seemingly everyone doing fun things but me, and when I arrived at Swansy's, she was listening to her soap.

I stood there with my eyes glued to the television set, watching a kaleidoscope of human drama. In the space of thirty minutes, I heard mention of birth, death, feast, famine, crime, adventure and mischief. I felt like a voyeur, like a fly on the wall of life, and it struck me that that wasn't the way I wanted to live. I wanted to do things, to experience life firsthand, well beyond the scope of my potting. And I wanted to do all that with Peter.

After two weeks alone, time was suddenly of the essence. Without a word of explanation, I gave Swansy a long, tight hug. Then I rushed home, changed clothes, packed a light bag and drove to the airport.

I was in New York by five. Knowing that Peter would still be at the office, I taxied to his place on Central Park South. The attendant didn't know me. He wouldn't let me up without Peter, but that was fine. I was here. I could wait.

That was just what I did for three hours until finally he returned from the office. I was sitting in the lobby watching the door when he came into sight. I stood quickly, then folded my hands in front of me and waited.

Our eyes met. My heart did the same catching number that I was sure it would do for Peter until the day I died. Slowly and with deliberate steps, I walked over to where he stood.

"I didn't know you were here," he said a little apologetically, a little cautiously. "Have you been waiting long?"

I nodded. "The time was good, though." I felt a tiny smile escape. "It gave me a chance to back out."

Something like hope flared in his wonderfully luminescent green eyes, and only at that instant did it hit me that I had never once doubted he'd want me. I had never feared he'd change his mind. It was a tribute to the way I trusted him, to the way I trusted his love.

When he continued to eye me with a very cautious hope, it occurred to me that he hadn't been as sure of me. He still didn't know what my verdict was. It wasn't that he trusted me any less than I trusted him, but that not once had I told him in words how I felt.

It was time. I raised a hand to his cheek, then slid it down and grasped the lapel of his topcoat. "I do love you, Peter."

The hope in his eyes became less cautious and more sure, but it was still only hope. "What is it you want?" he asked in a whisper, as though he was almost afraid to say the words at all, let alone aloud, lest he didn't like the answer. I understood. For all he knew, I could love him but not be willing to make the commitment he craved.

"I want," I said taking a deep breath, "years and years of things like afternoons at the museum and weekends at the shore, long nights of loving and breakfasts in bed. I want a very small wedding, a house in the country with a studio out back, and two or three or four kids, or as many as is necessary until we get at least one of each sex."

"One of each, eh?" he asked, grinning now and pleased enough with my proposition to slide his arms around my waist.

I nodded. "I want a little boy to carry on the best of you, and a little girl to carry on the best of me. I think we're both pretty special."

His grin widened. "Y'do?"

I nodded, but I'd had enough of cuteness. My expression sobered. "I want us to be together always, Peter. I've felt only half-whole these past two weeks. I can live with making that deposit you wanted as long as you stick around to fill the void." I paused for the beat of my heart. "Will you?"

The look on Peter's face was so rich with love that he

didn't have to answer. But he did it anyway. "Will I ever," he said with such feeling that I burst out laughing. It was a laugh of pure happiness, the first of many, many to come.

* * * * *

**Being one of the guys
isn't all it's cracked up to be....**

**A charming and humorous tale from
New York Times bestselling author**

KRISTAN HIGGINS

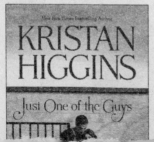

When journalist Chastity O'Neill returns to her hometown, she decides it's time to start working on some of those feminine wiles. Two tiny problems: #1—she's five feet eleven inches of rock-solid girl power, and #2—she's cursed with four alpha-male older brothers.

BESTSELLING AUTHOR COLLECTION

CLASSIC ROMANCES IN COLLECTIBLE VOLUMES

New York Times **Bestselling Author**

DIANA PALMER

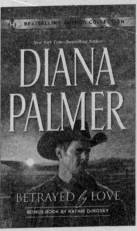

Cattle rancher Jacob Cade rarely denied himself anything—except for Kate Walker. As his younger sister's best friend, she was always off-limits...until now. Kate knows Jacob isn't offering forever. Aren't a few precious memories with the man she loves better than none at all? Even if that surrender breaks her heart....

BETRAYED BY LOVE

Available August 28 wherever books are sold!

Plus, ENJOY the bonus story *The Rough and Ready Rancher* by *USA TODAY* bestselling author Kathie DeNosky, included in this 2-in-1 volume!

www.Harlequin.com

NYTDP0912

REQUEST YOUR FREE BOOKS!

2 FREE NOVELS
FROM THE ROMANCE COLLECTION
PLUS 2 FREE GIFTS!

YES! Please send me 2 FREE novels from the Romance Collection and my 2 FREE gifts (gifts are worth about $10). After receiving them, if I don't wish to receive any more books, I can return the shipping statement marked "cancel." If I don't cancel, I will receive 4 brand-new novels every month and be billed just $5.99 per book in the U.S. or $6.49 per book in Canada. That's a saving of at least 25% off the cover price. It's quite a bargain! Shipping and handling is just 50¢ per book in the U.S. and 75¢ per book in Canada.* I understand that accepting the 2 free books and gifts places me under no obligation to buy anything. I can always return a shipment and cancel at any time. Even if I never buy another book, the two free books and gifts are mine to keep forever.

194/394 MDN FELQ

Name _____
(PLEASE PRINT)

Address _____ Apt. #

City _____ State/Prov. _____ Zip/Postal Code

Signature (if under 18, a parent or guardian must sign)

Mail to the **Reader Service:**
IN U.S.A.: P.O. Box 1867, Buffalo, NY 14240-1867
IN CANADA: P.O. Box 609, Fort Erie, Ontario L2A 5X3

Not valid for current subscribers to the Romance Collection
or the Romance/Suspense Collection.

Want to try two free books from another line?
Call 1-800-873-8635 or visit www.ReaderService.com.

* Terms and prices subject to change without notice. Prices do not include applicable taxes. Sales tax applicable in N.Y. Canadian residents will be charged applicable taxes. Offer not valid in Quebec. This offer is limited to one order per household. All orders subject to credit approval. Credit or debit balances in a customer's account(s) may be offset by any other outstanding balance owed by or to the customer. Please allow 4 to 6 weeks for delivery. Offer available while quantities last.

Your Privacy—The Reader Service is committed to protecting your privacy. Our Privacy Policy is available online at www.ReaderService.com or upon request from the Reader Service.

We make a portion of our mailing list available to reputable third parties that offer products we believe may interest you. If you prefer that we not exchange your name with third parties, or if you wish to clarify or modify your communication preferences, please visit us at www.ReaderService.com/consumerschoice or write to us at Reader Service Preference Service, P.O. Box 9062, Buffalo, NY 14269. Include your complete name and address.

Things aren't always as they seem...when it comes to mysteries of the heart.

Three timeless classics from #1 *New York Times* bestselling author

NORA ROBERTS

appearing together in one beautiful volume for the first time!

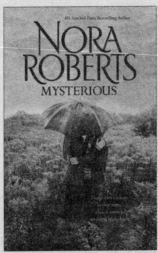

MYSTERIOUS

Available now!

BARBARA DELINSKY

77618 SANCTUARY	___ $7.99 U.S. ___ $9.99 CAN.
77494 FRIENDS & LOVERS	___ $7.99 U.S. ___ $9.99 CAN.
77425 DREAM MAN	___ $7.99 U.S. ___ $8.99 CAN.
77345 TRUST	___ $7.99 U.S. ___ $7.99 CAN.

(limited quantities available)

TOTAL AMOUNT	$ _____
POSTAGE & HANDLING	$ _____
($1.00 FOR 1 BOOK, 50¢ for each additional)	
APPLICABLE TAXES*	$ _____
TOTAL PAYABLE	$ _____

(check or money order—please do not send cash)

To order, complete this form and send it, along with a check or money order for the total above, payable to Harlequin HQN, to: **In the U.S.:** 3010 Walden Avenue, P.O. Box 9077, Buffalo, NY 14269-9077; **In Canada:** P.O. Box 636, Fort Erie, Ontario, L2A 5X3.

Name: _____
Address: _____ City: _____
State/Prov.: _____ Zip/Postal Code: _____
Account Number (if applicable): _____

075 CSAS

*New York residents remit applicable sales taxes.
*Canadian residents remit applicable GST and provincial taxes.

HARLEQUIN® HQN™
www.Harlequin.com

PHBD0912BL